LIZARD IN A ZOOT SUIT

MARCO FINNEGAN

Graphic Universe™ • Minneapolis

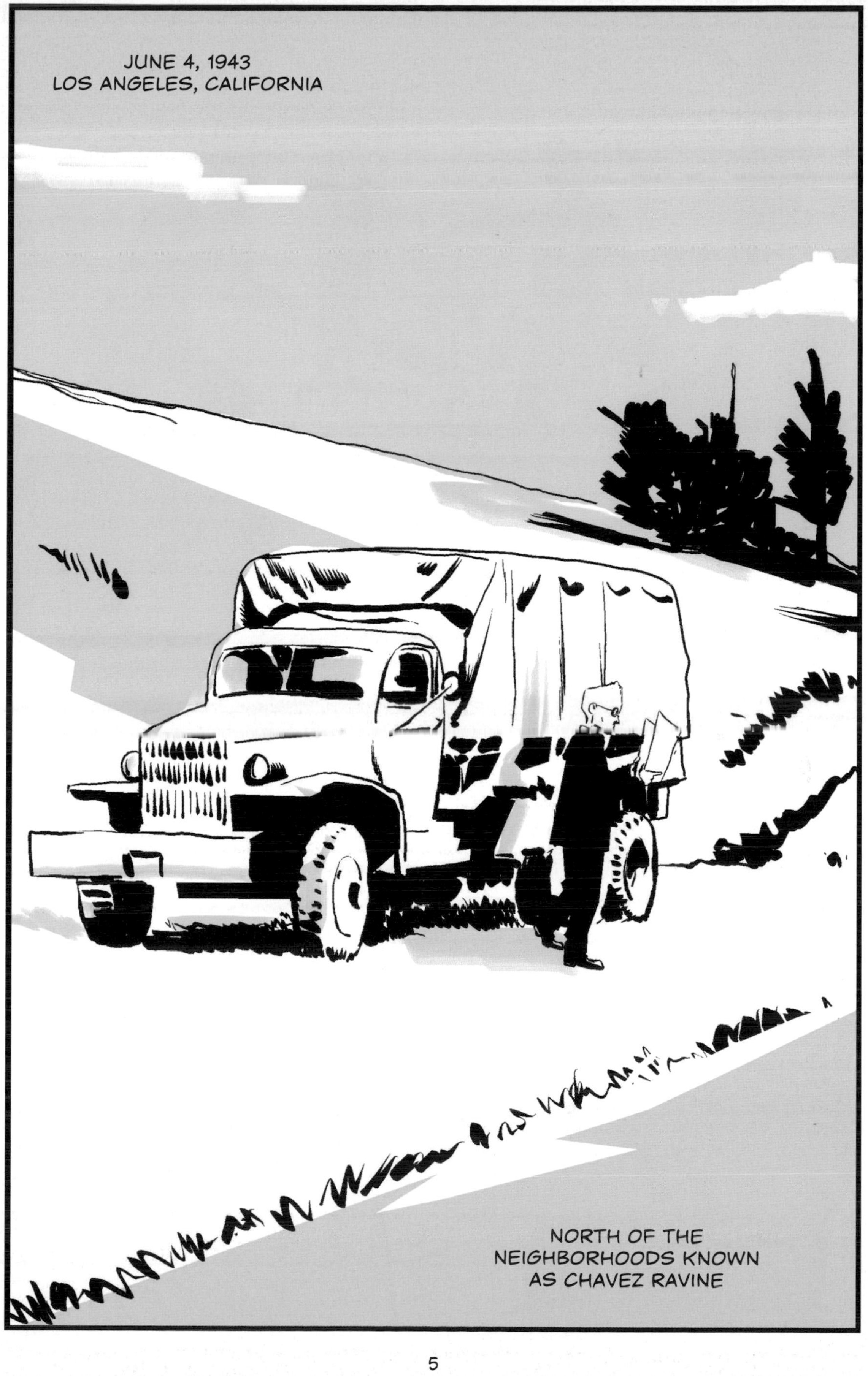
JUNE 4, 1943
LOS ANGELES, CALIFORNIA
NORTH OF THE NEIGHBORHOODS KNOWN AS CHAVEZ RAVINE

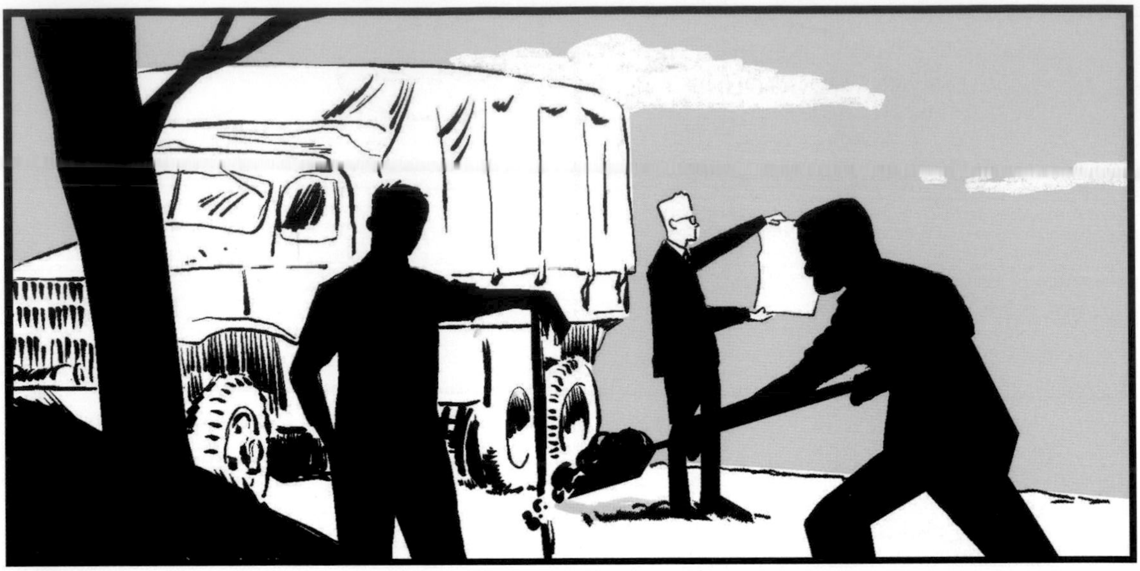

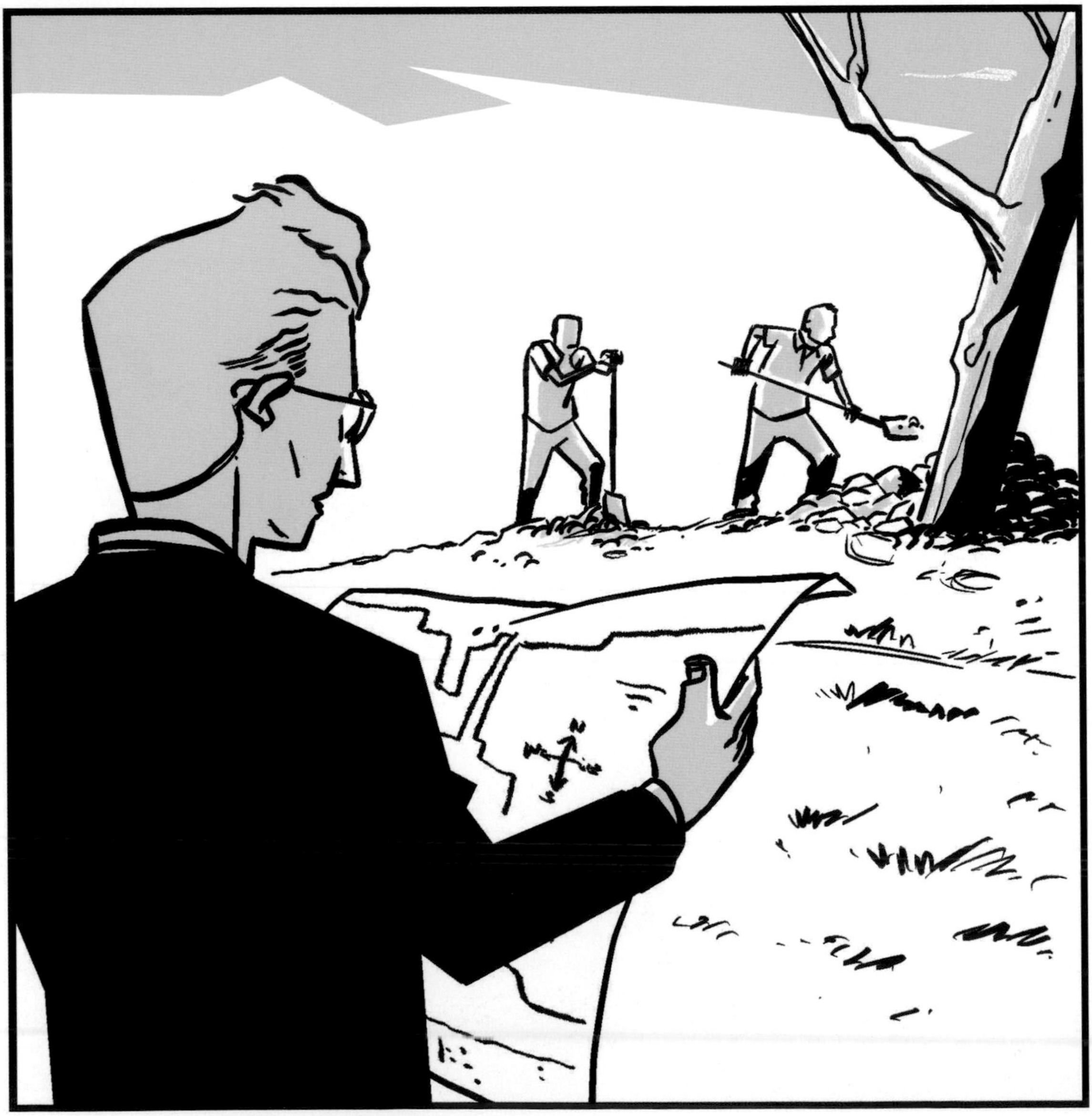

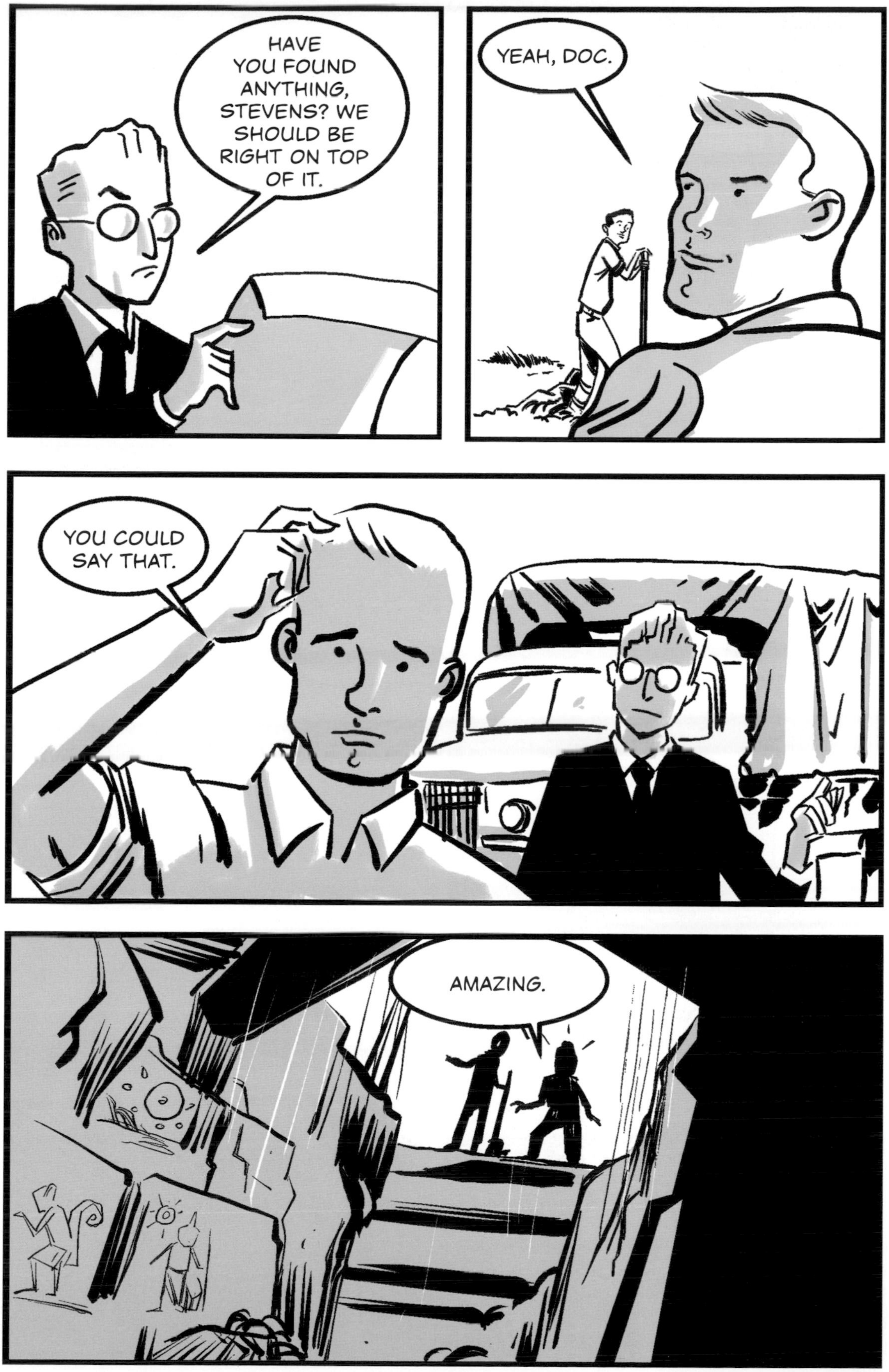
HAVE YOU FOUND ANYTHING, STEVENS? WE SHOULD BE RIGHT ON TOP OF IT.
YEAH, DOC.
YOU COULD SAY THAT.
AMAZING.

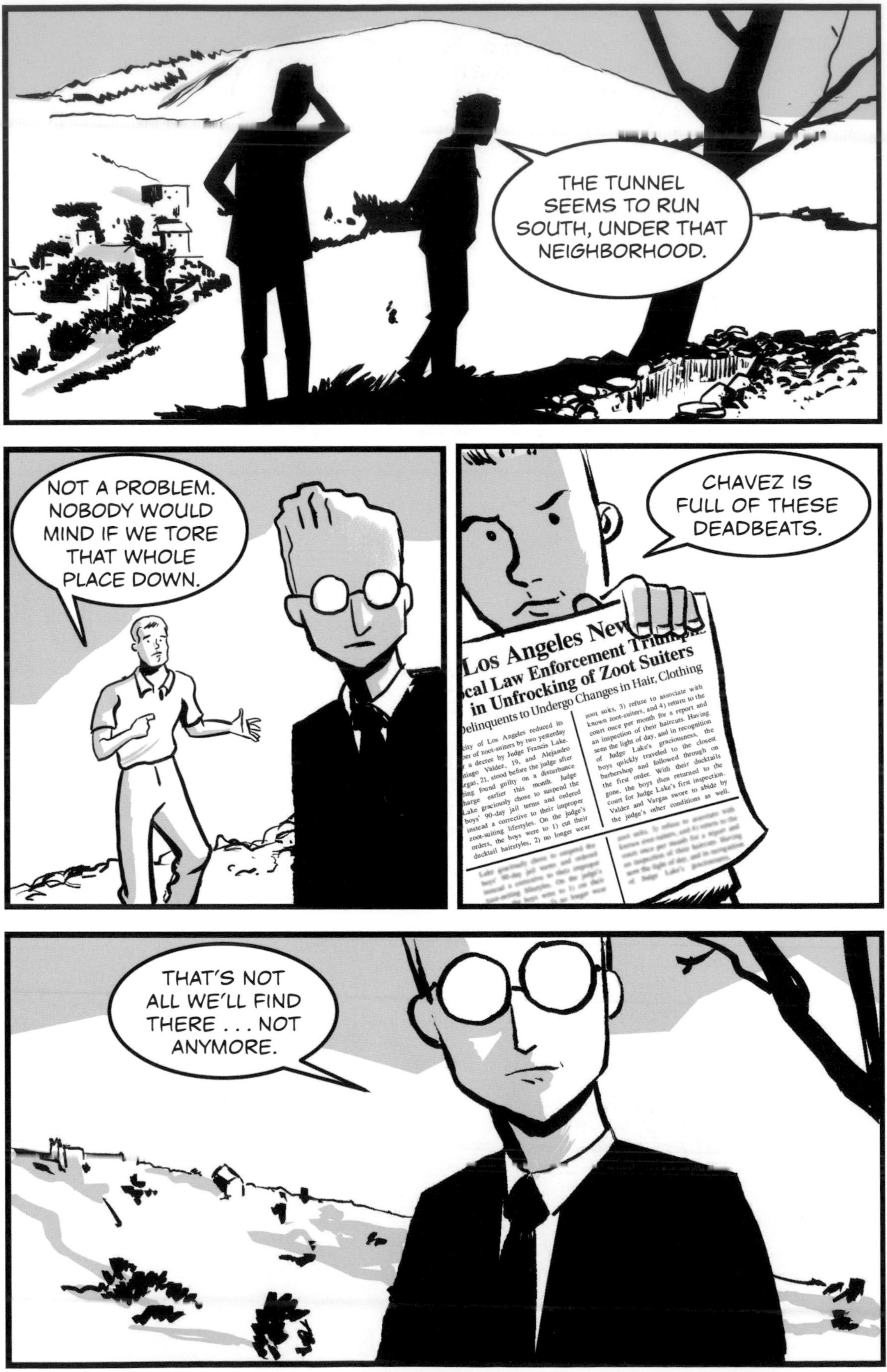
THE TUNNEL SEEMS TO RUN SOUTH, UNDER THAT NEIGHBORHOOD.
NOT A PROBLEM. NOBODY WOULD MIND IF WE TORE THAT WHOLE PLACE DOWN.
CHAVEZ IS FULL OF THESE DEADBEATS.
Los Angeles New
cal Law Enforcement Triump
in Unfrocking of Zoot Suiters
elinquents to Undergo Changes in Hair, Clothing
THAT'S NOT ALL WE'LL FIND THERE . . . NOT ANYMORE.

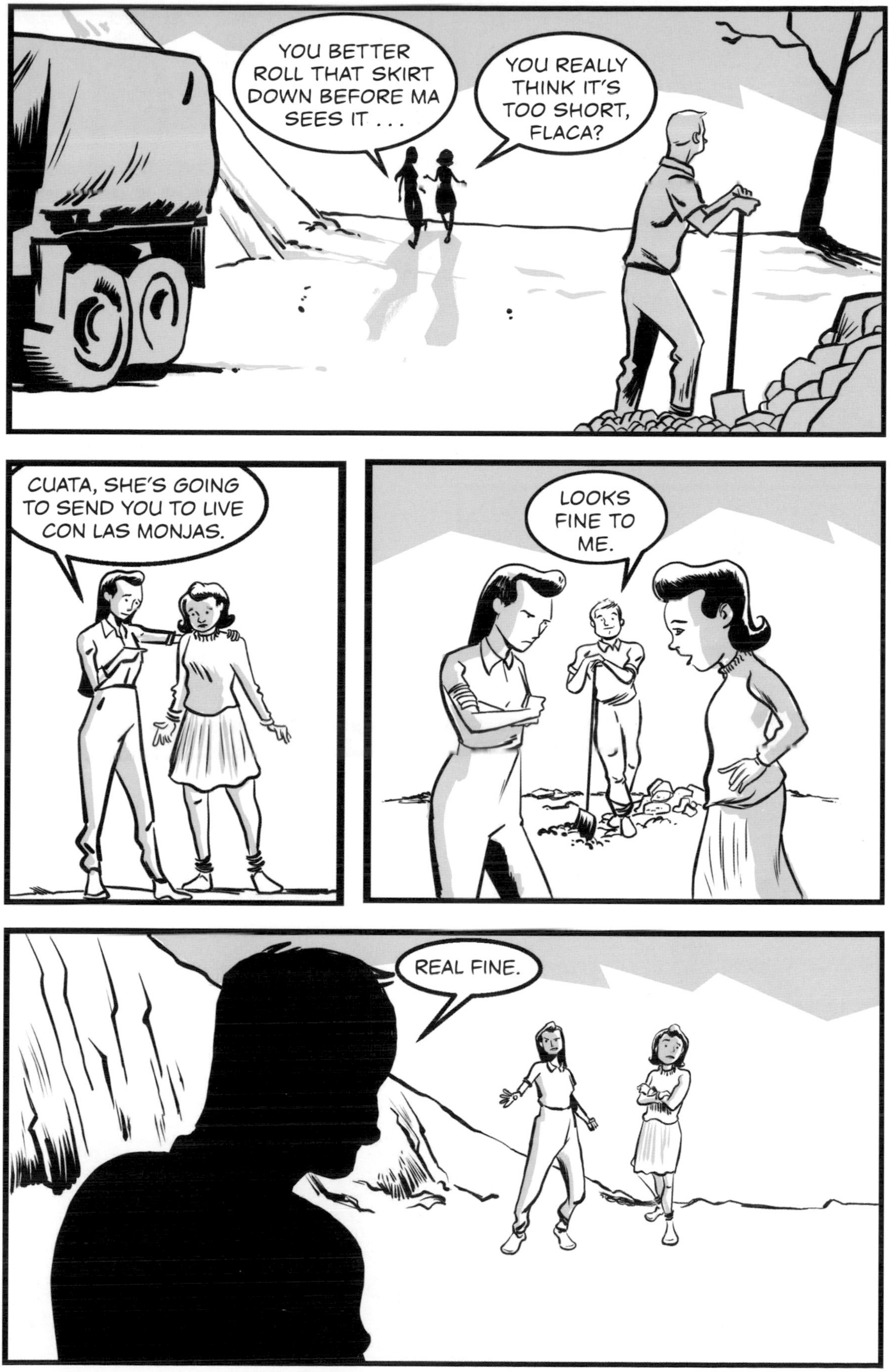
YOU BETTER ROLL THAT SKIRT DOWN BEFORE MA SEES IT . . .
YOU REALLY THINK IT'S TOO SHORT, FLACA?
CUATA, SHE'S GOING TO SEND YOU TO LIVE CON LAS MONJAS.
LOOKS FINE TO ME.
REAL FINE.

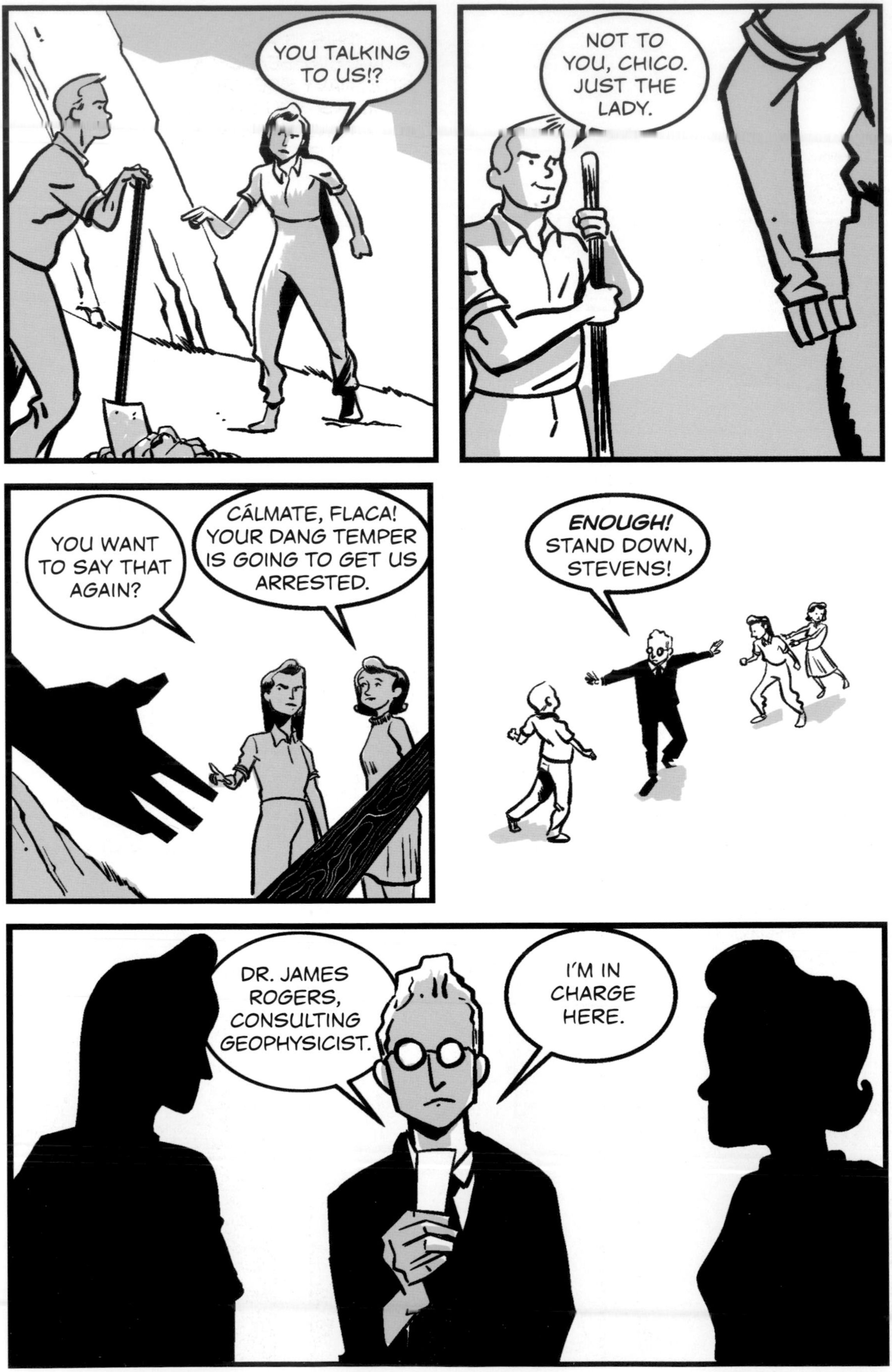
YOU TALKING TO US!?
NOT TO YOU, CHICO. JUST THE LADY.
YOU WANT TO SAY THAT AGAIN?
CÁLMATE, FLACA! YOUR DANG TEMPER IS GOING TO GET US ARRESTED.
ENOUGH! STAND DOWN, STEVENS!
DR. JAMES ROGERS, CONSULTING GEOPHYSICIST.
I'M IN CHARGE HERE.

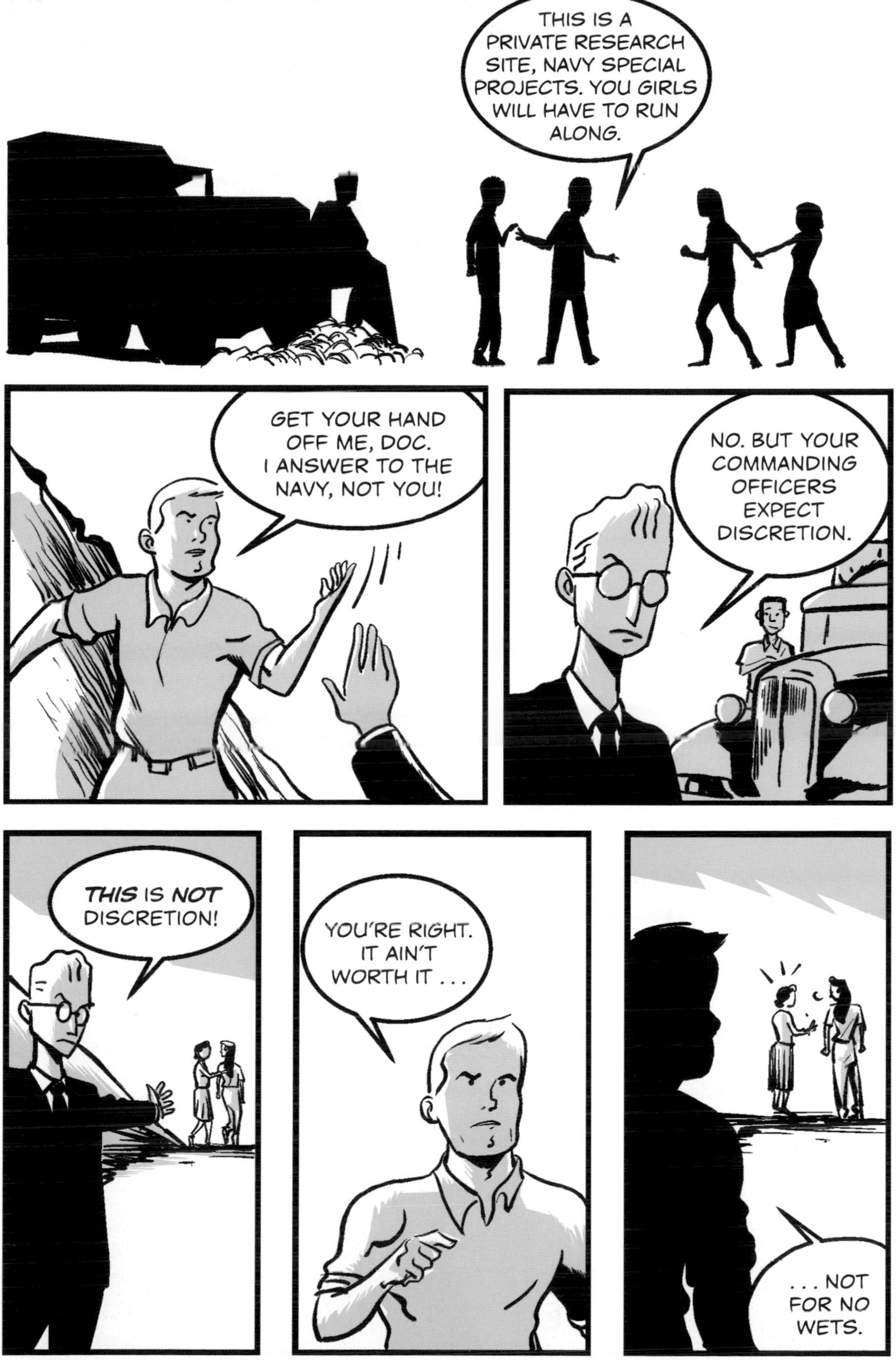
THIS IS A PRIVATE RESEARCH SITE, NAVY SPECIAL PROJECTS. YOU GIRLS WILL HAVE TO RUN ALONG.
GET YOUR HAND OFF ME, DOC. I ANSWER TO THE NAVY, NOT YOU!
NO. BUT YOUR COMMANDING OFFICERS EXPECT DISCRETION.
THIS IS ***NOT*** DISCRETION!
YOU'RE RIGHT. IT AIN'T WORTH IT . . .
. . . NOT FOR NO WETS.

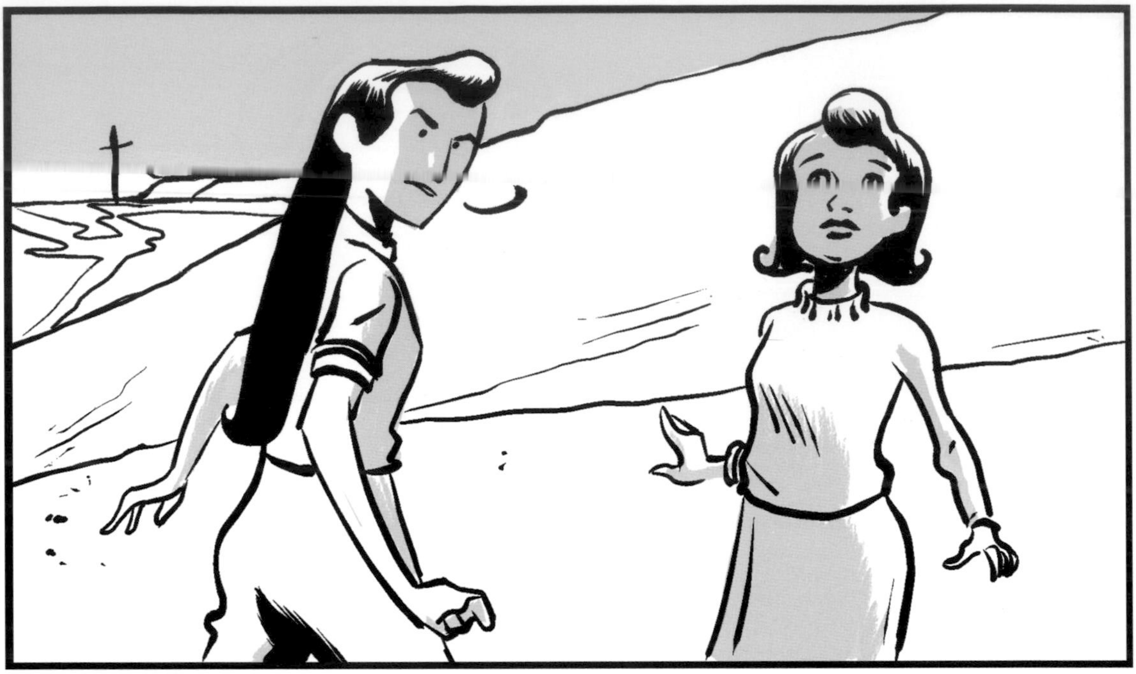

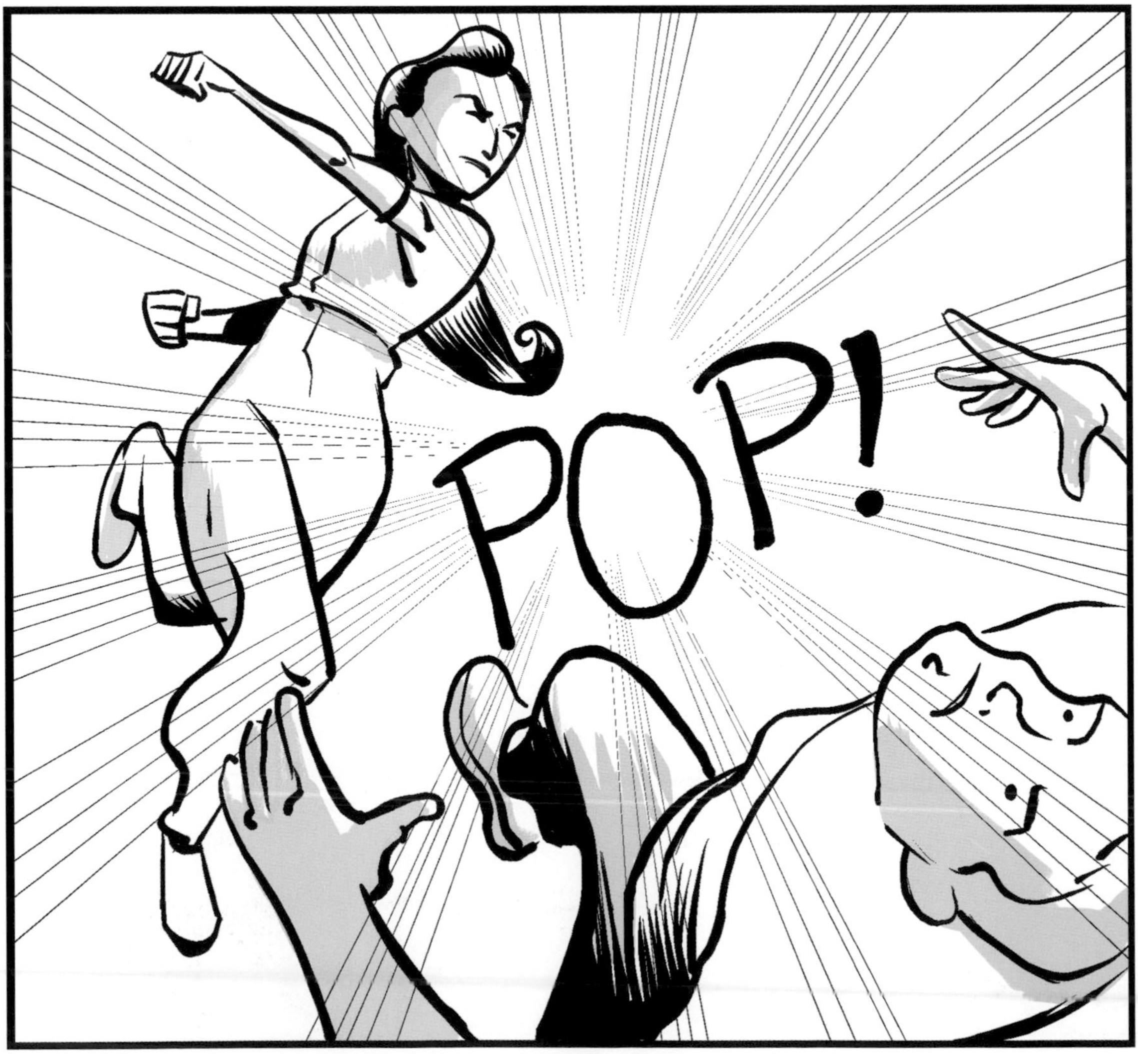
POP!

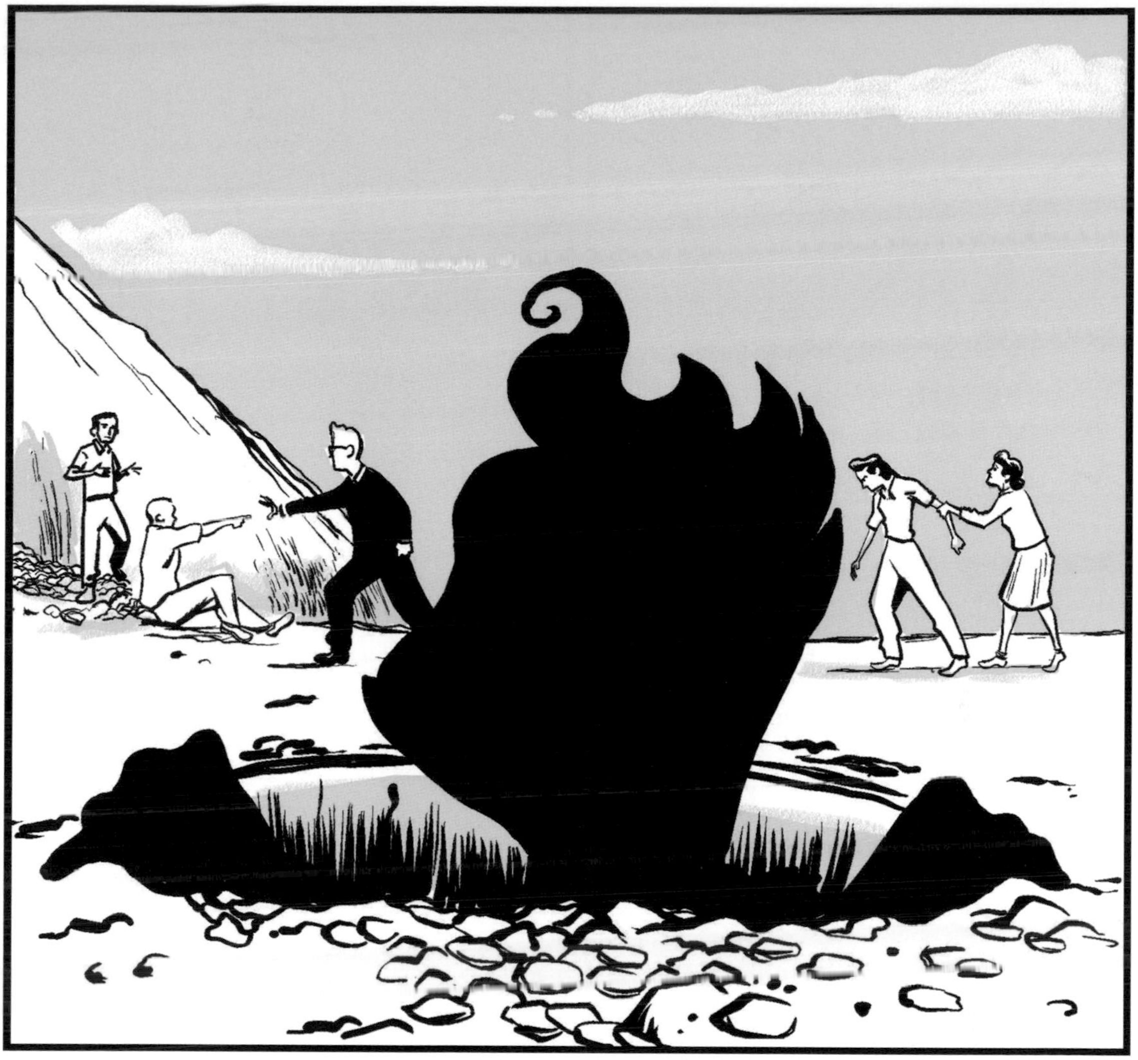

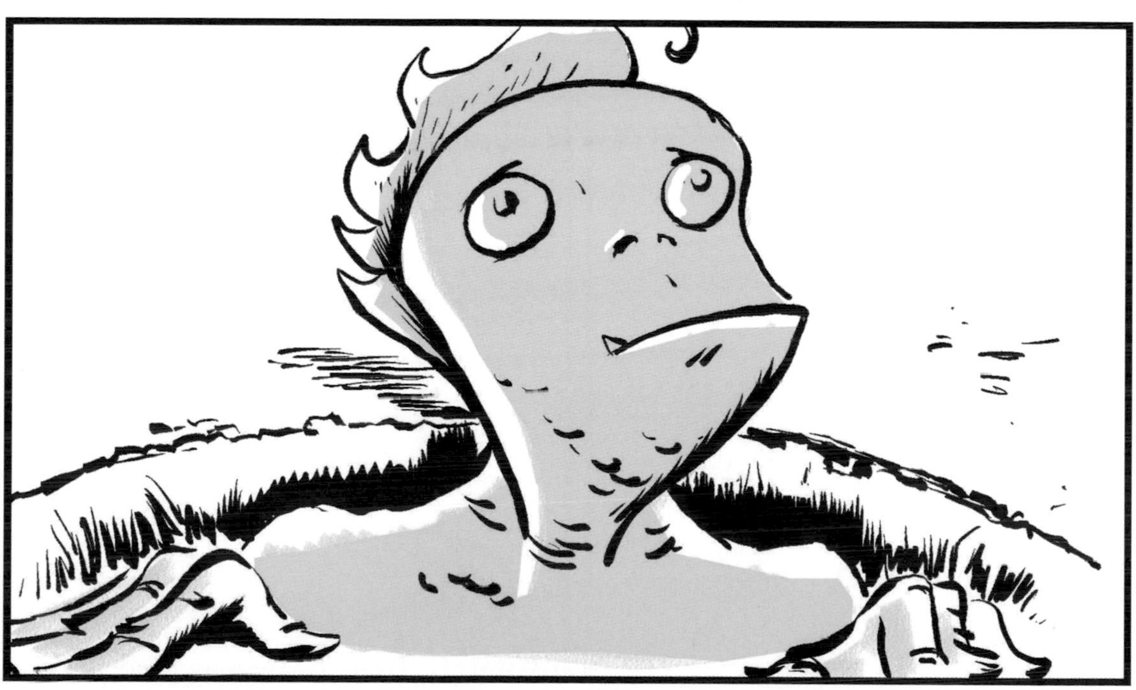

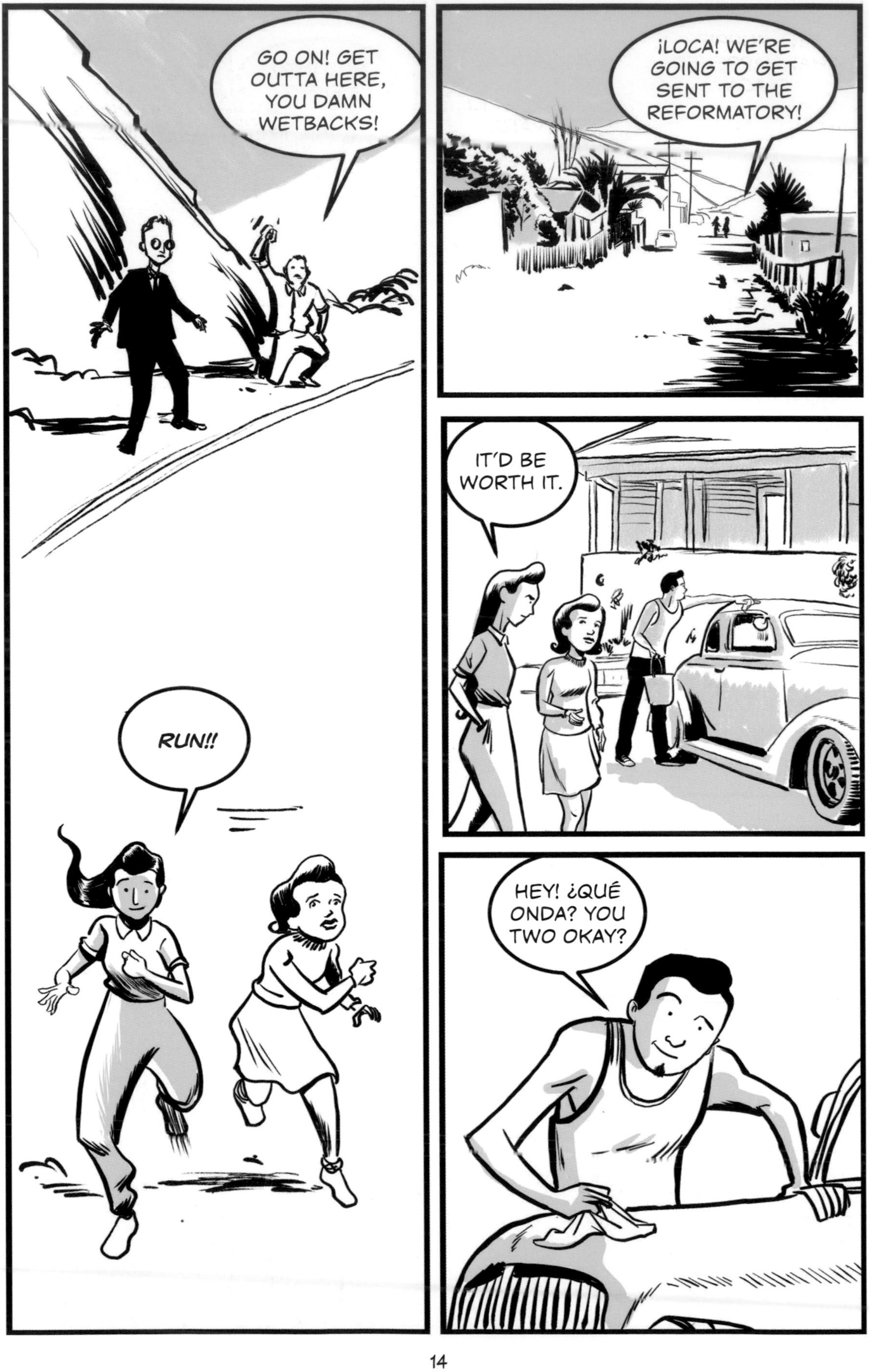
GO ON! GET OUTTA HERE, YOU DAMN WETBACKS!
RUN!!
¡LOCA! WE'RE GOING TO GET SENT TO THE REFORMATORY!
IT'D BE WORTH IT.
HEY! ¿QUÉ ONDA? YOU TWO OKAY?

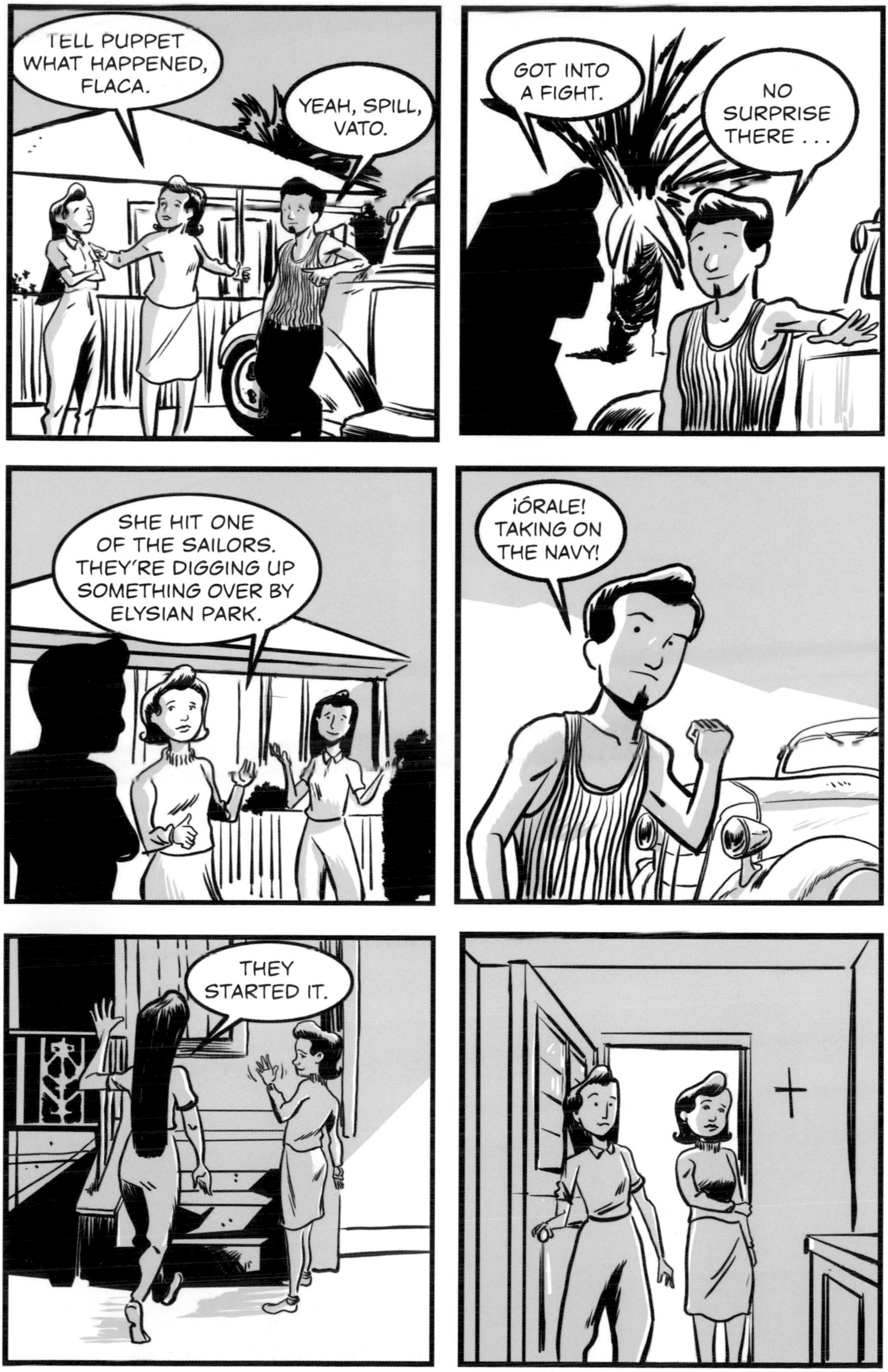
TELL PUPPET WHAT HAPPENED, FLACA.
YEAH, SPILL, VATO.
GOT INTO A FIGHT.
NO SURPRISE THERE . . .
SHE HIT ONE OF THE SAILORS. THEY'RE DIGGING UP SOMETHING OVER BY ELYSIAN PARK.
¡ÓRALE! TAKING ON THE NAVY!
THEY STARTED IT.

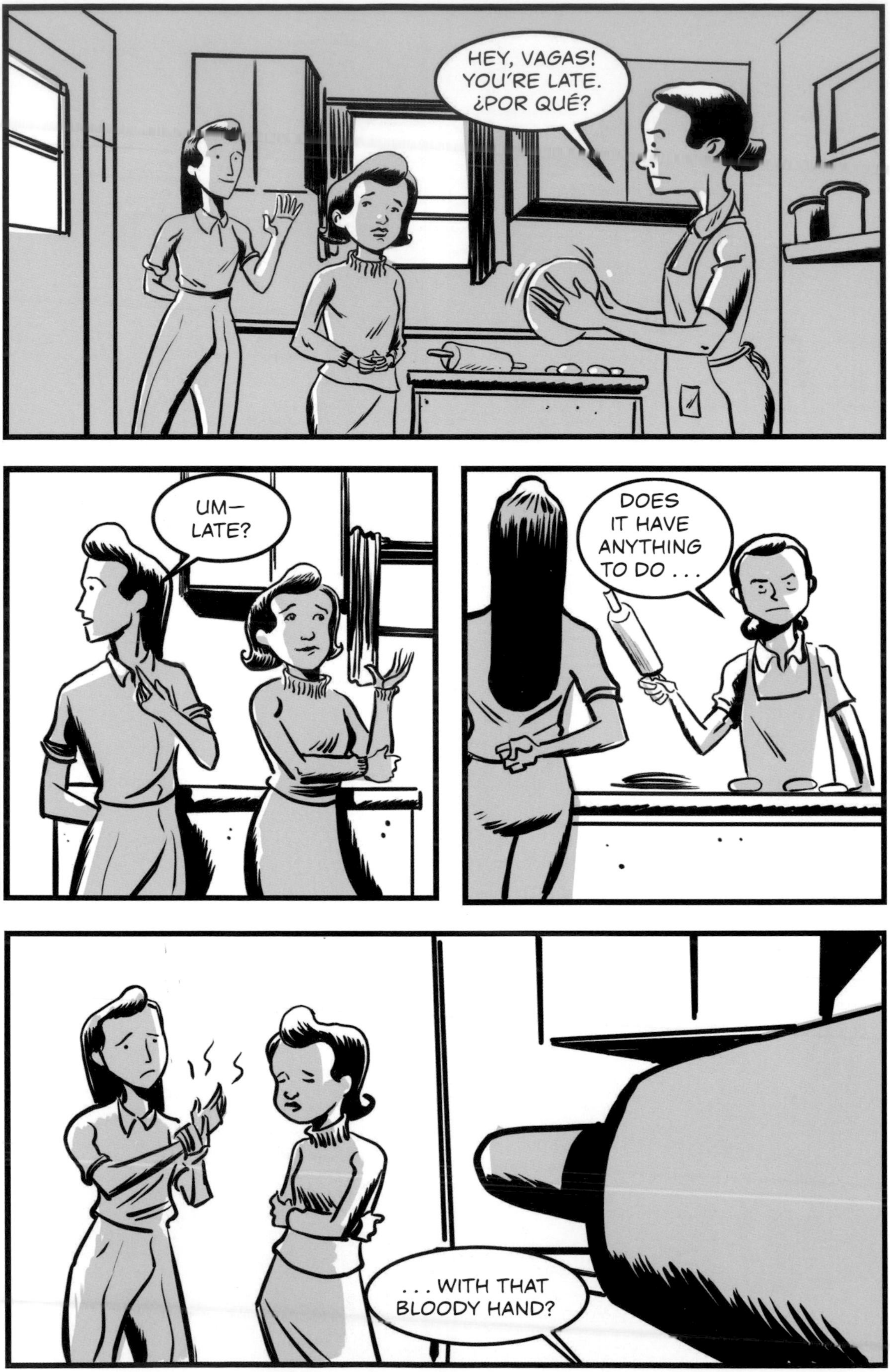
HEY, VAGAS! YOU'RE LATE. ¿POR QUÉ?
UM— LATE?
DOES IT HAVE ANYTHING TO DO . . .
. . . WITH THAT BLOODY HAND?

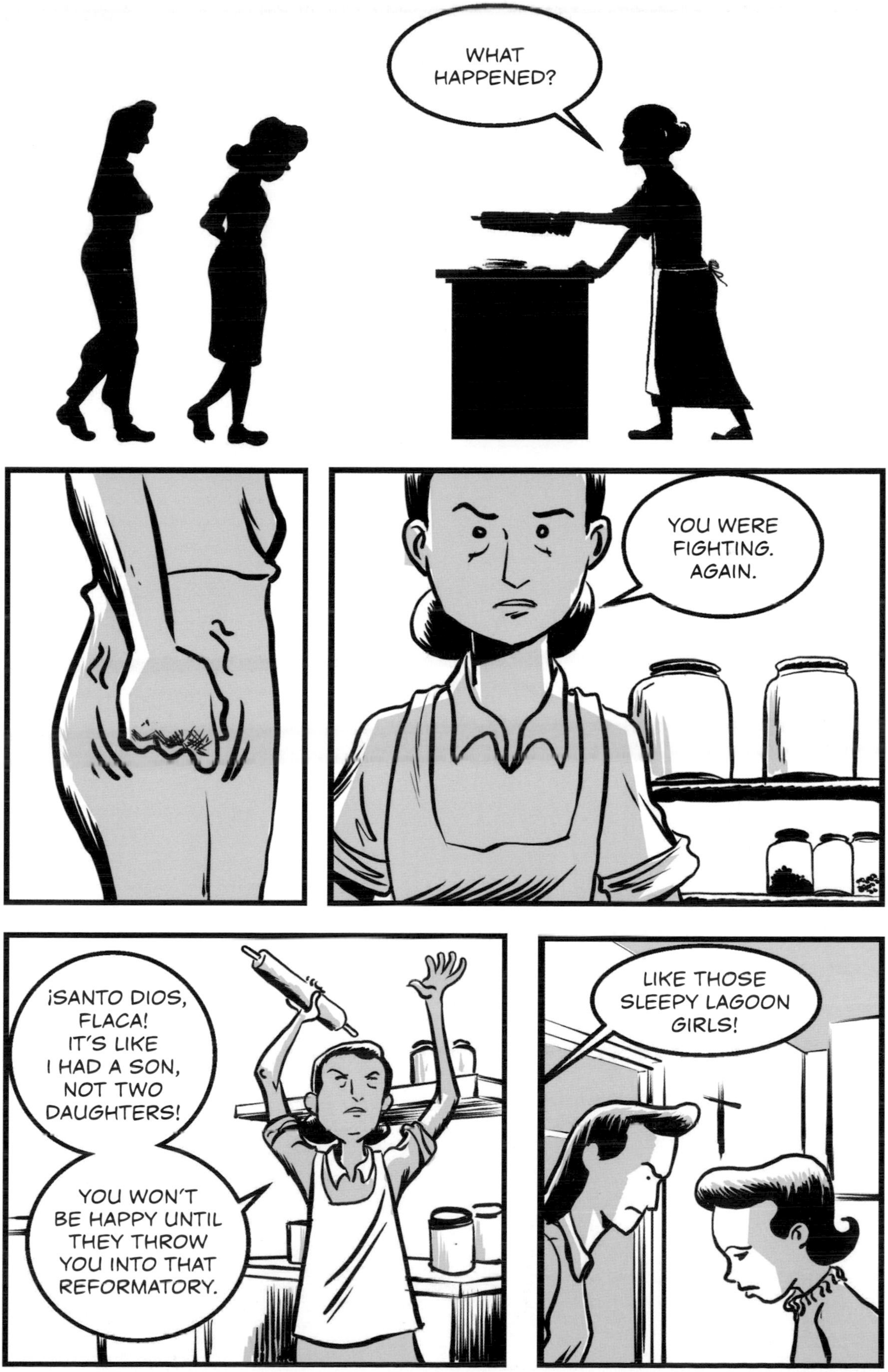
WHAT HAPPENED?
YOU WERE FIGHTING. AGAIN.
¡SANTO DIOS, FLACA! IT'S LIKE I HAD A SON, NOT TWO DAUGHTERS!
YOU WON'T BE HAPPY UNTIL THEY THROW YOU INTO THAT REFORMATORY.
LIKE THOSE SLEEPY LAGOON GIRLS!

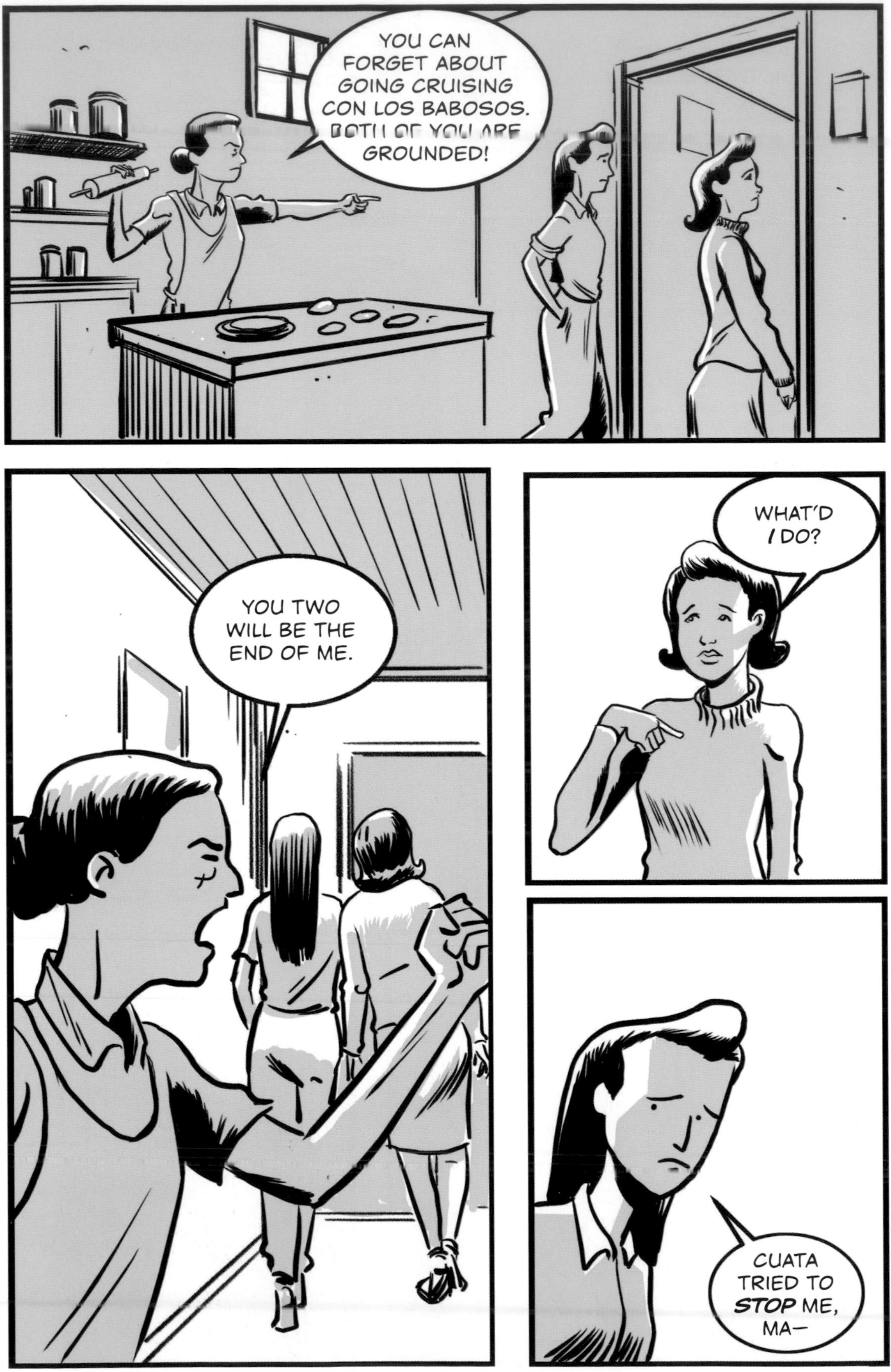
YOU CAN FORGET ABOUT GOING CRUISING CON LOS BABOSOS. BOTH OF YOU ARE GROUNDED!
YOU TWO WILL BE THE END OF ME.
WHAT'D *I* DO?
CUATA TRIED TO **STOP** ME, MA—

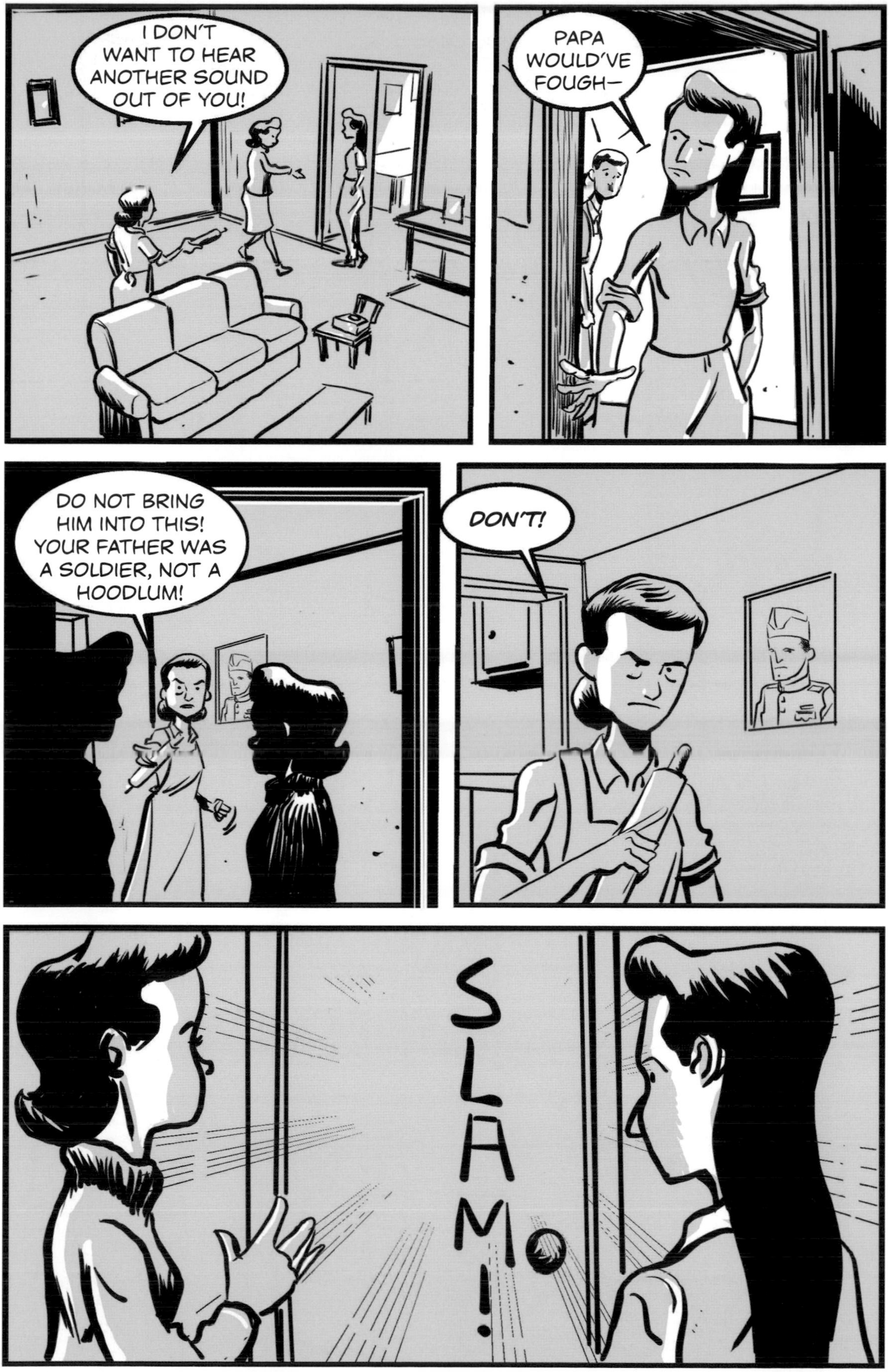
I DON'T WANT TO HEAR ANOTHER SOUND OUT OF YOU!
PAPA WOULD'VE FOUGH—
DO NOT BRING HIM INTO THIS! YOUR FATHER WAS A SOLDIER, NOT A HOODLUM!
DON'T!
SLAM!

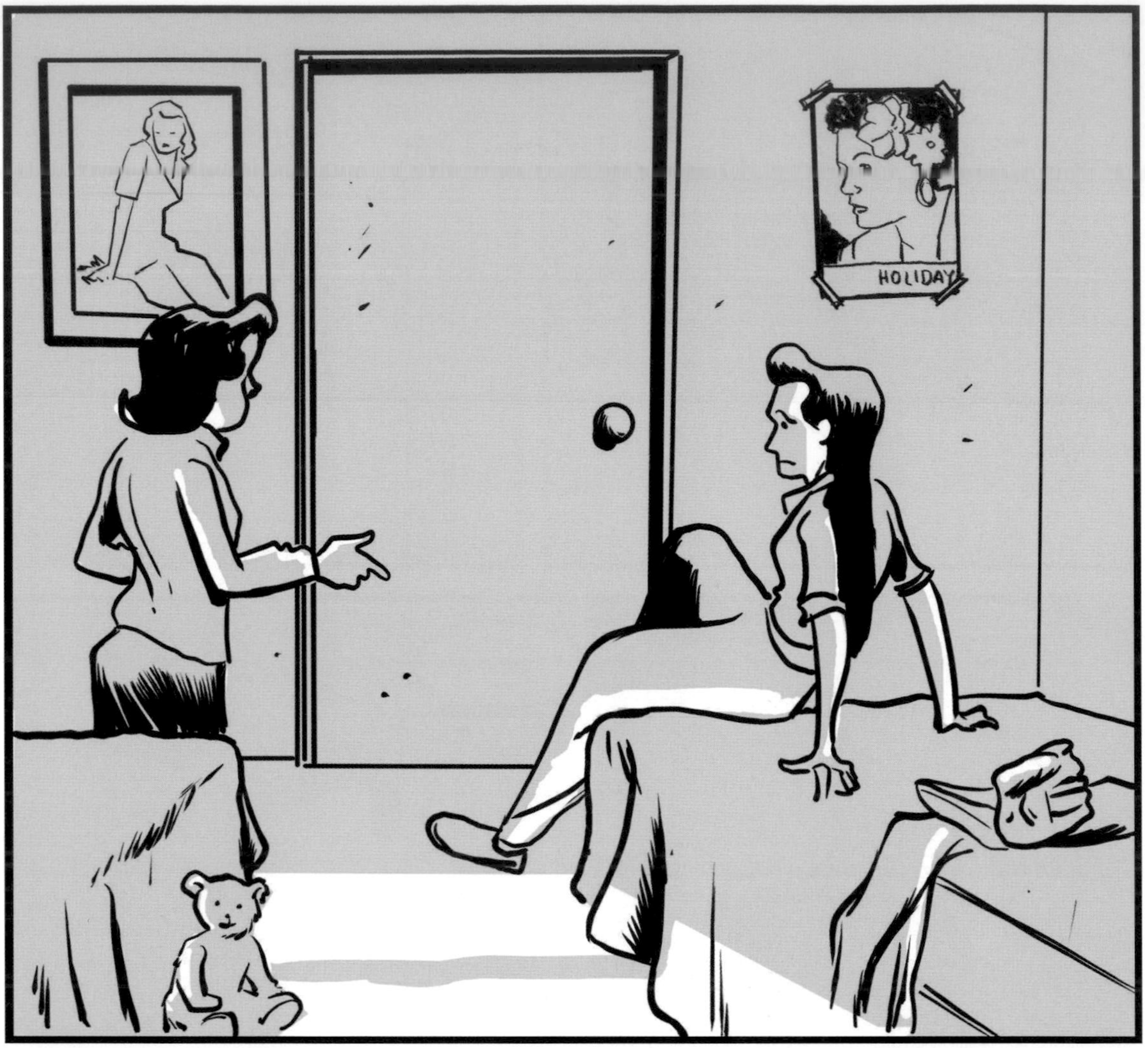
HOLIDAY

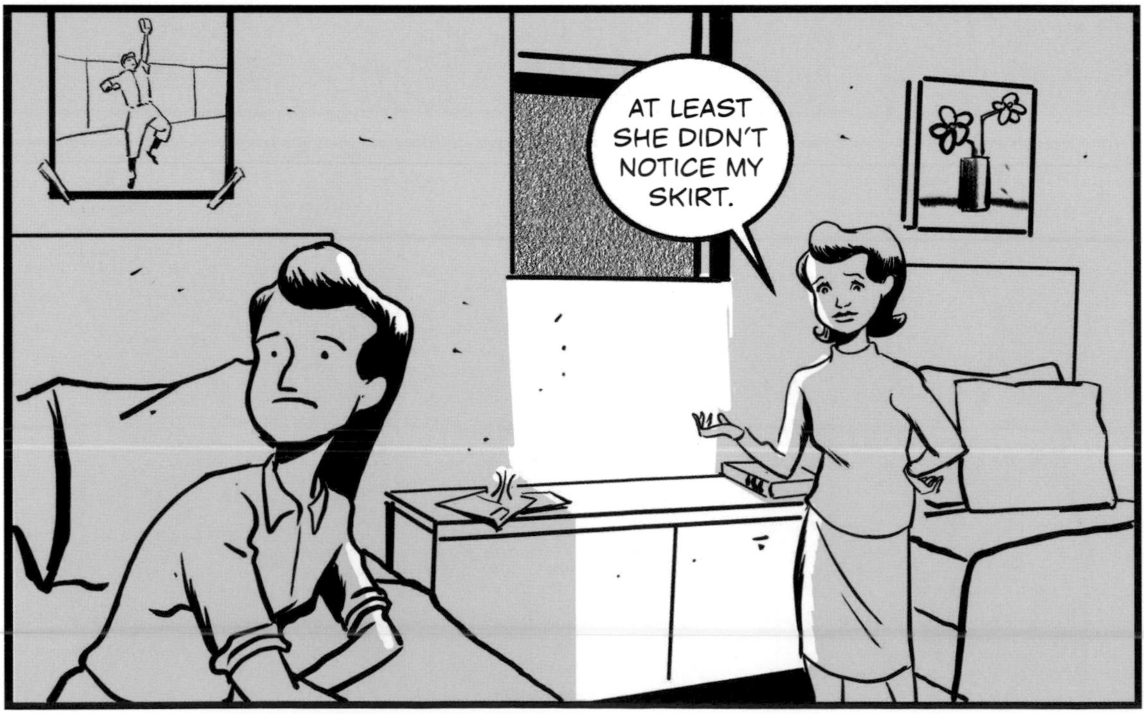
AT LEAST SHE DIDN'T NOTICE MY SKIRT.

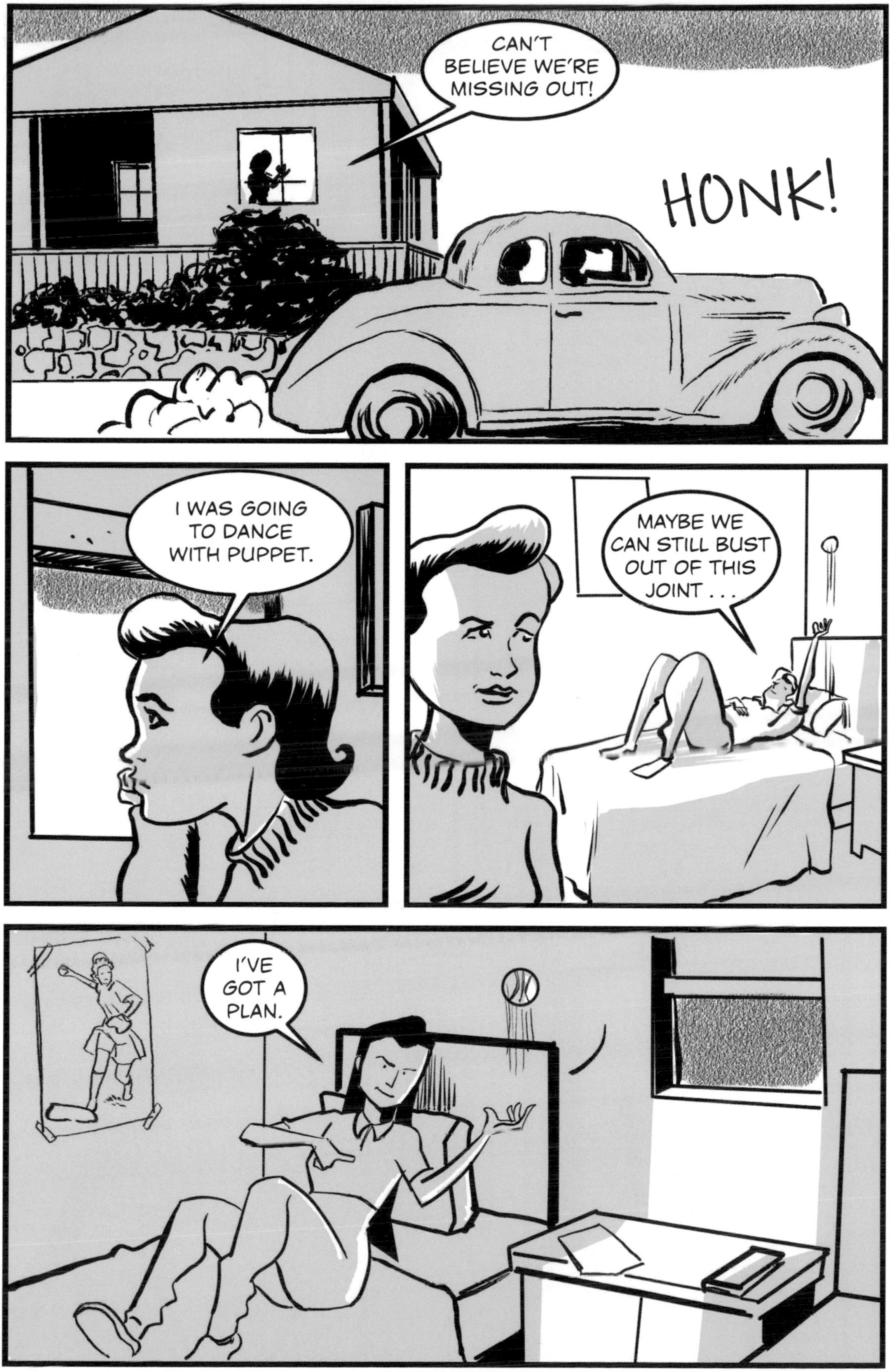
CAN'T BELIEVE WE'RE MISSING OUT!
HONK!
I WAS GOING TO DANCE WITH PUPPET.
MAYBE WE CAN STILL BUST OUT OF THIS JOINT . . .
I'VE GOT A PLAN.

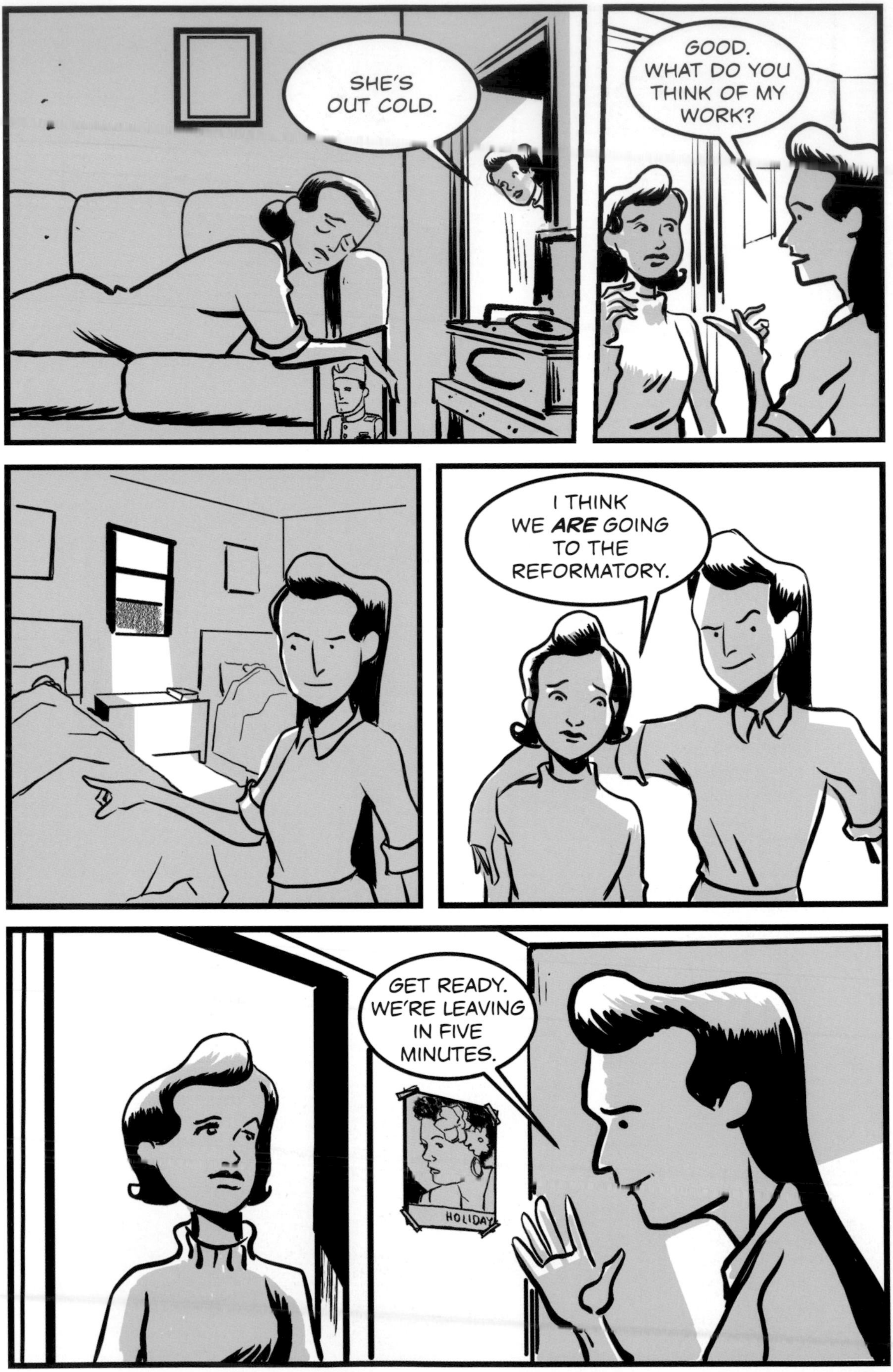
SHE'S OUT COLD.
GOOD. WHAT DO YOU THINK OF MY WORK?
I THINK WE **ARE** GOING TO THE REFORMATORY.
GET READY. WE'RE LEAVING IN FIVE MINUTES.
HOLIDAY

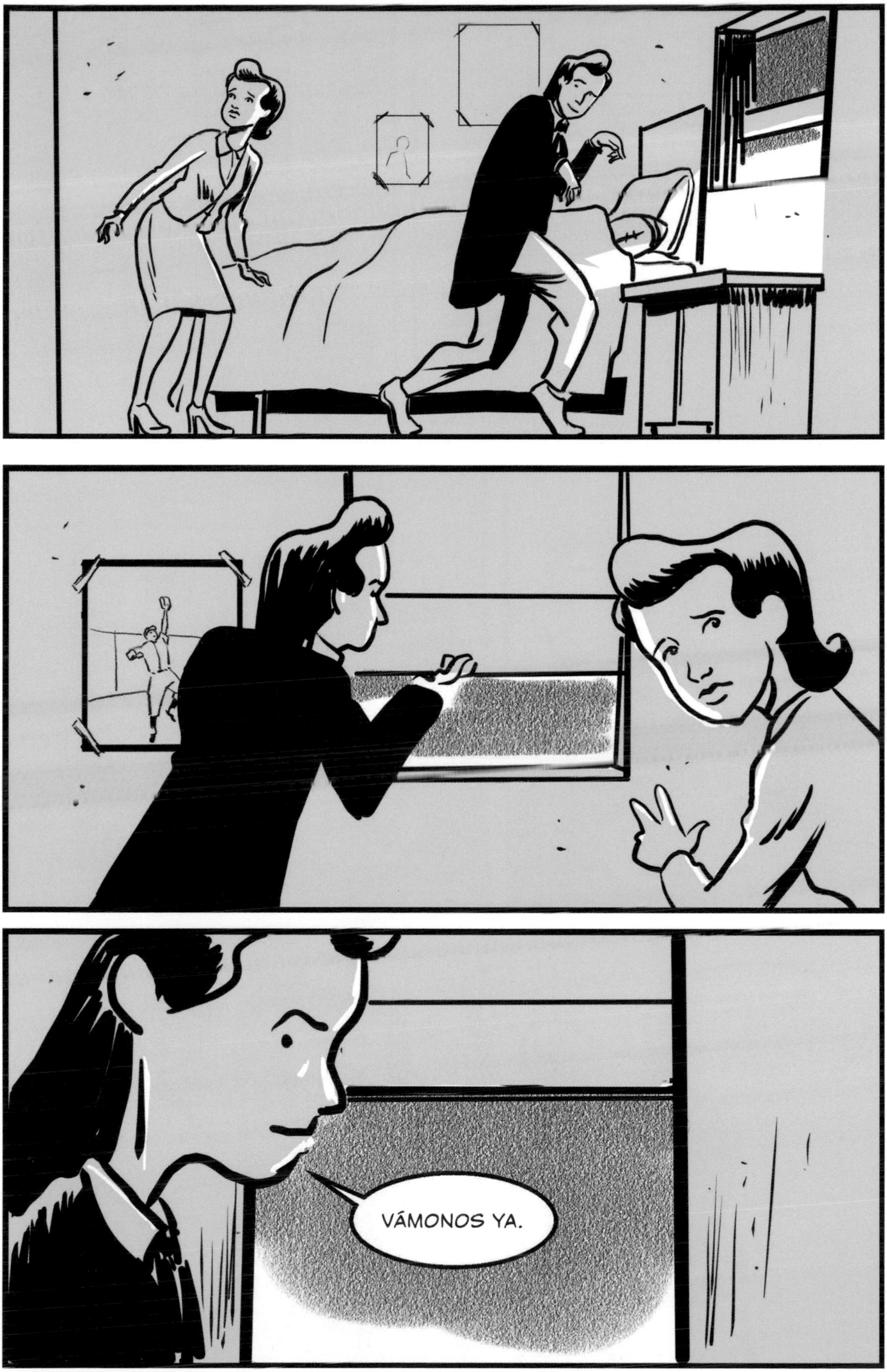
VÁMONOS YA.

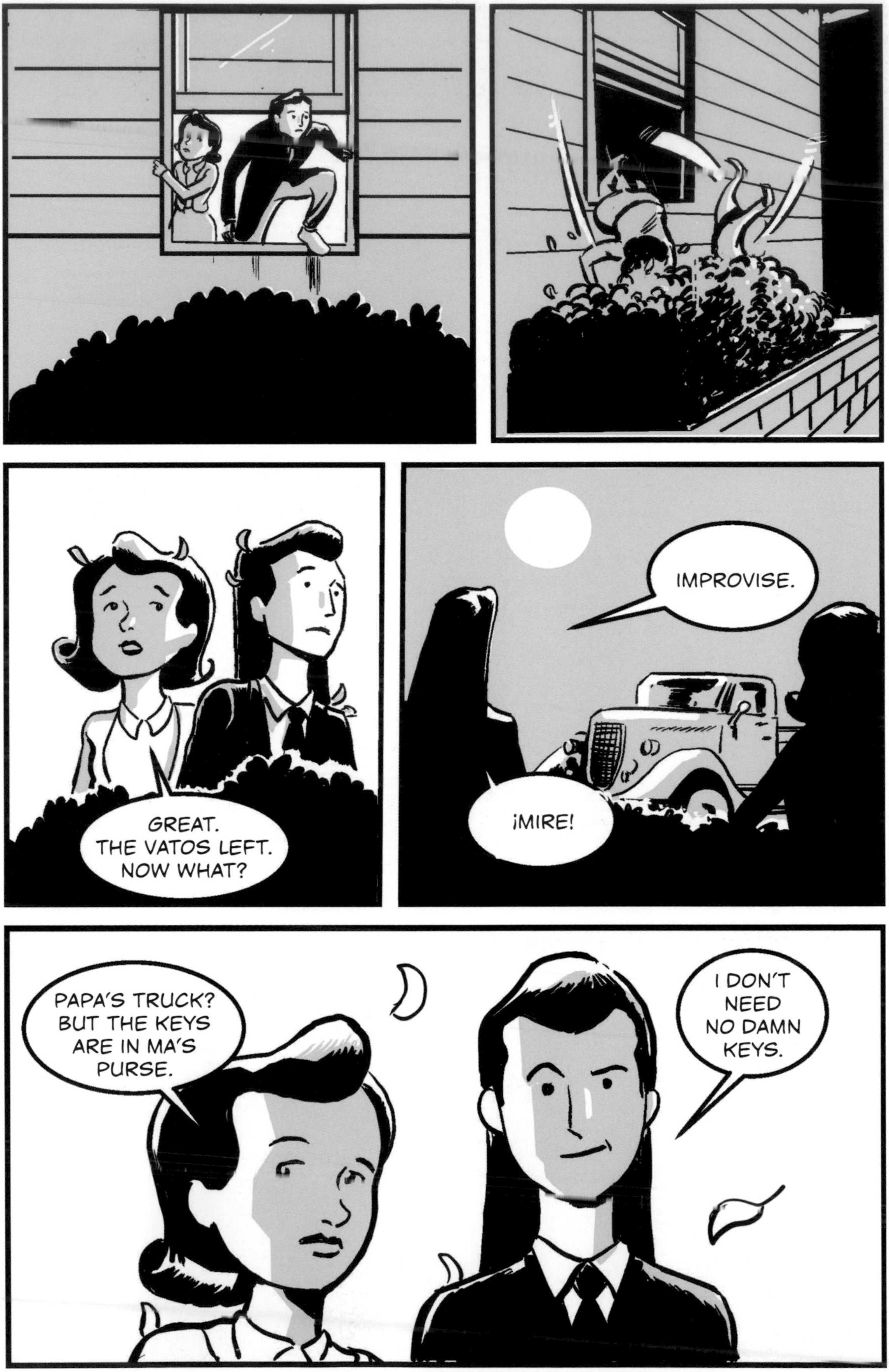
GREAT.
THE VATOS LEFT.
NOW WHAT?
IMPROVISE.
¡MIRE!
PAPA'S TRUCK?
BUT THE KEYS
ARE IN MA'S
PURSE.
I DON'T
NEED
NO DAMN
KEYS.

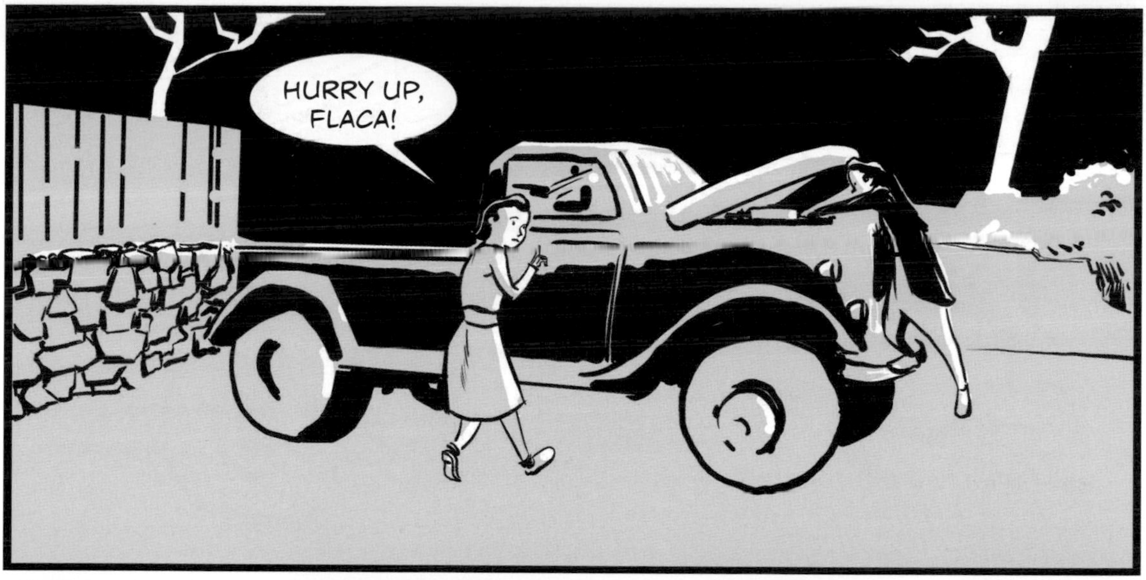
HURRY UP, FLACA!

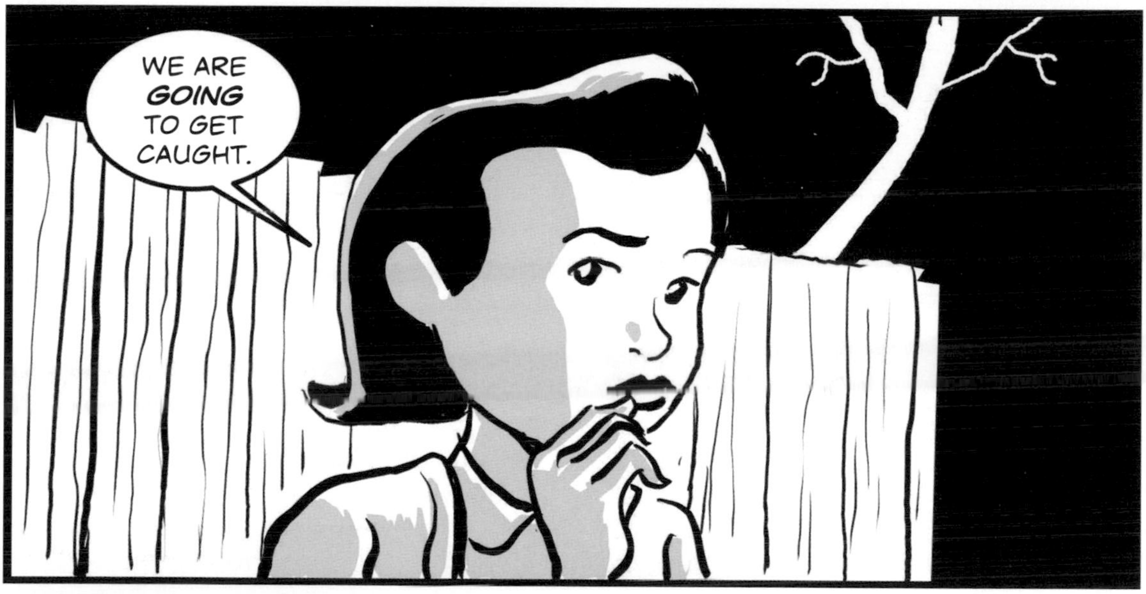
WE ARE *GOING* TO GET CAUGHT.

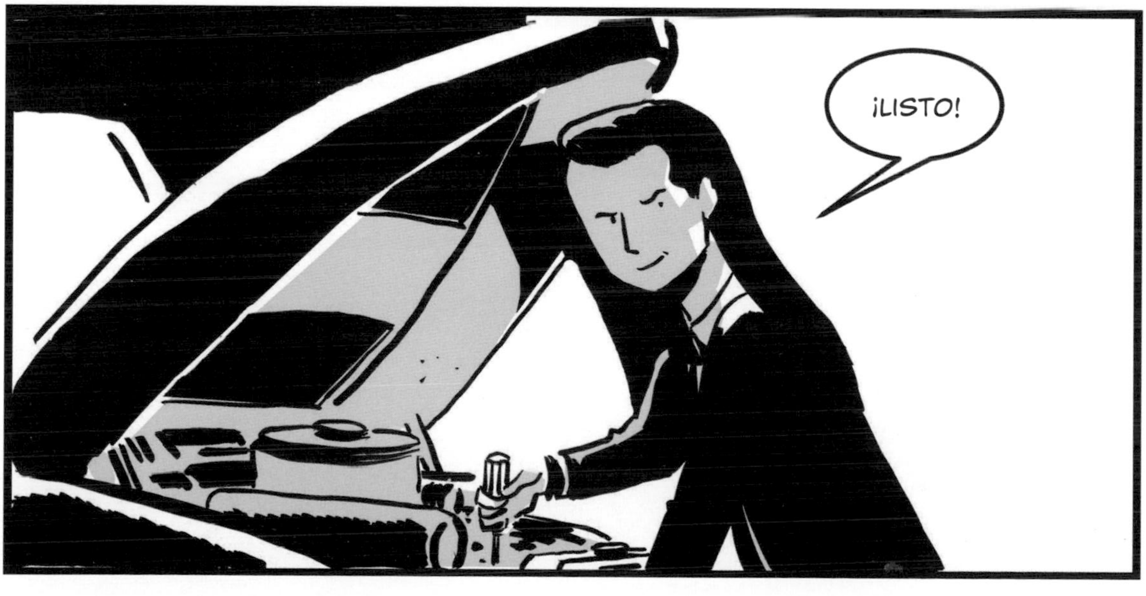
¡LISTO!

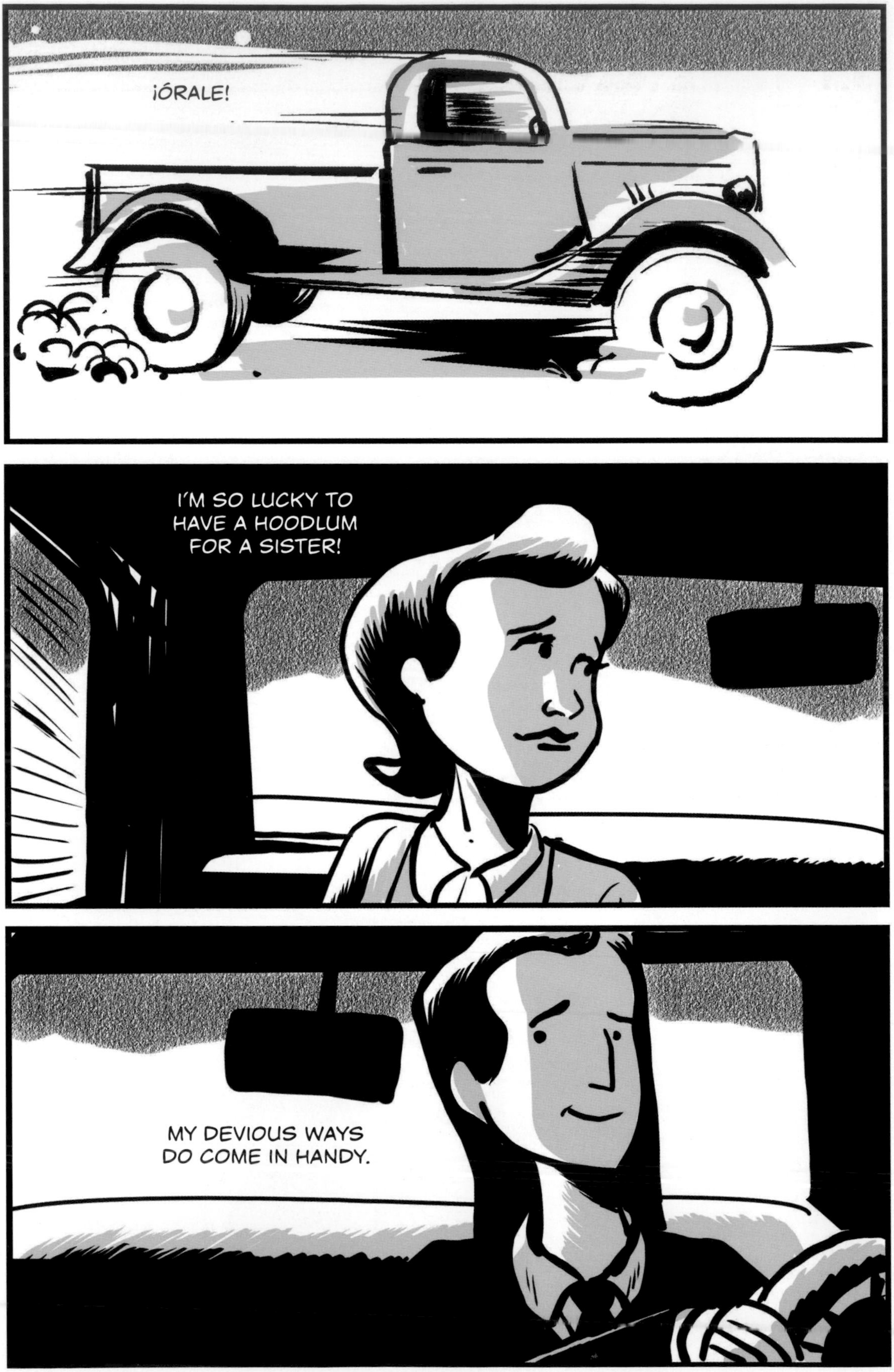
¡ÓRALE!
I'M SO LUCKY TO HAVE A HOODLUM FOR A SISTER!
MY DEVIOUS WAYS DO COME IN HANDY.

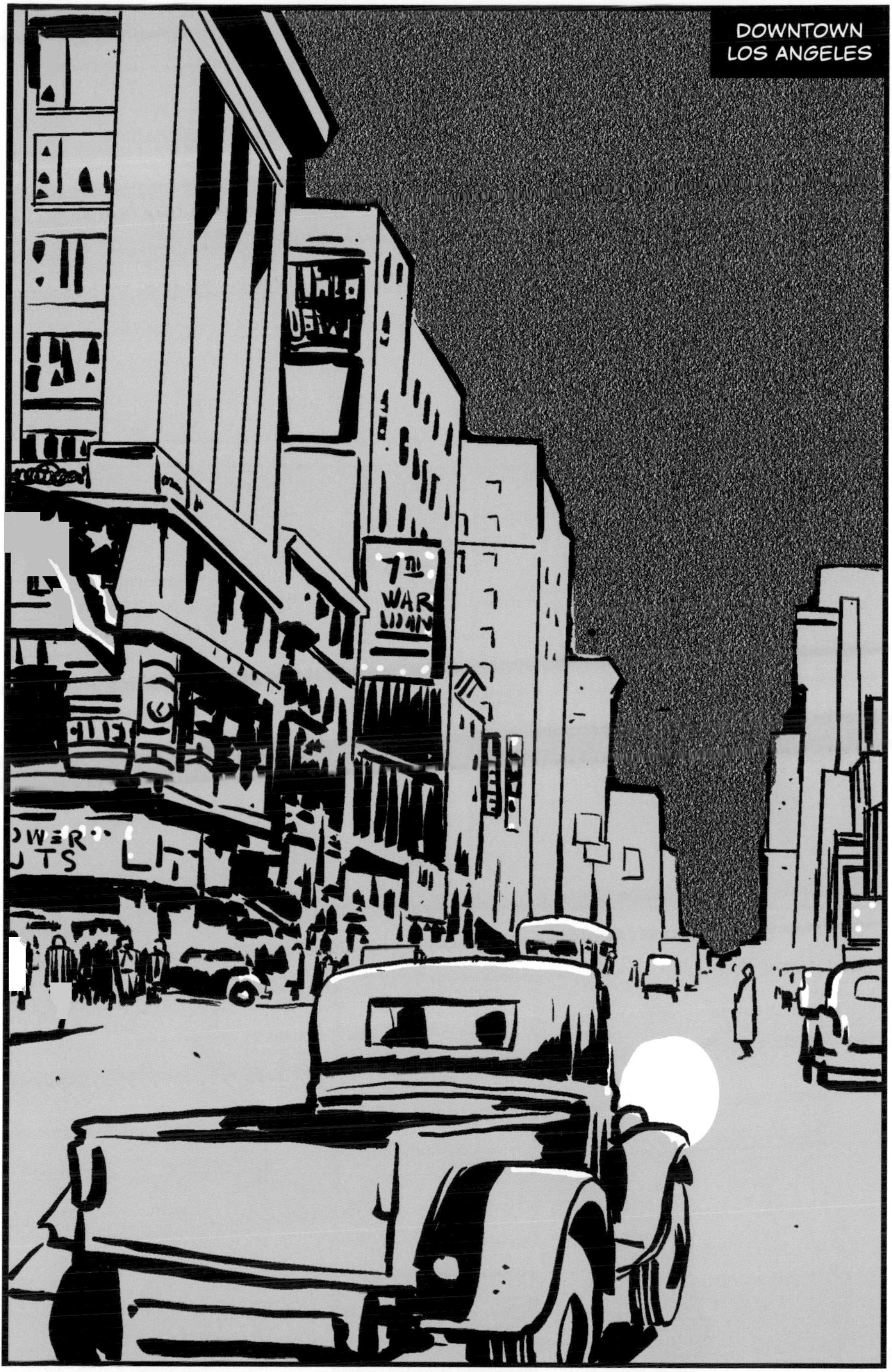
DOWNTOWN
LOS ANGELES

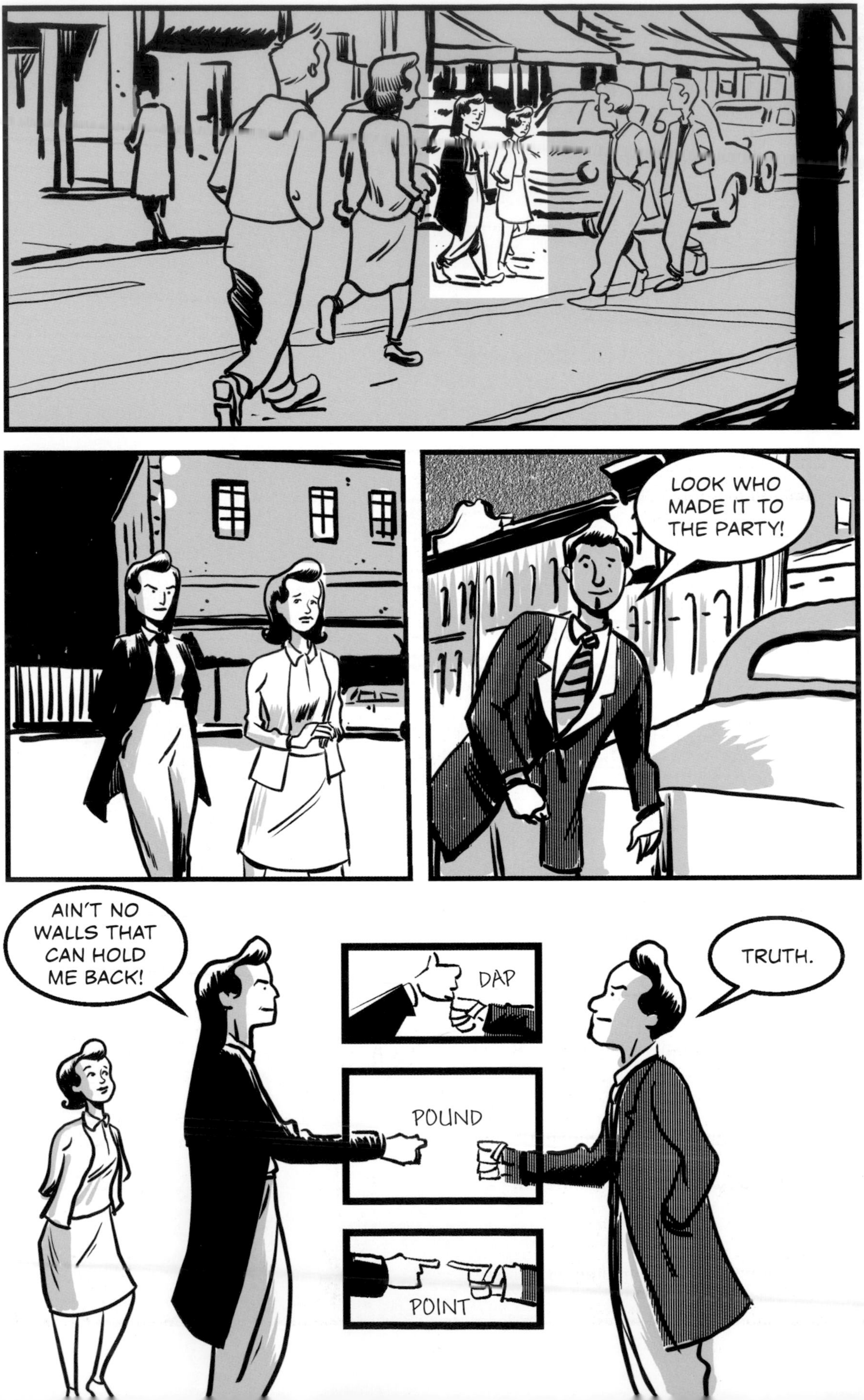
LOOK WHO MADE IT TO THE PARTY!
AIN'T NO WALLS THAT CAN HOLD ME BACK!
DAP
POUND
POINT
TRUTH.

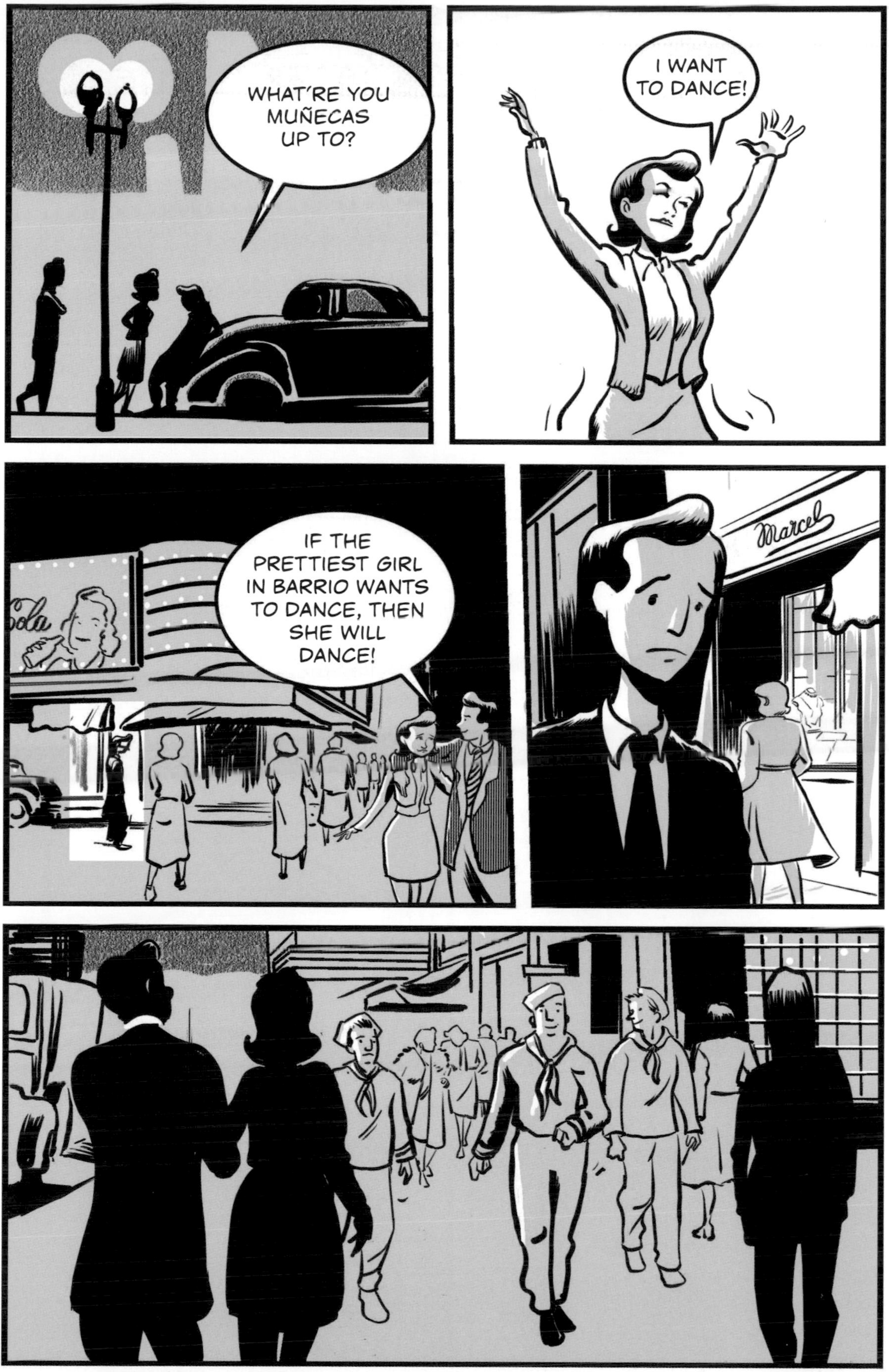
WHAT'RE YOU MUÑECAS UP TO?
I WANT TO DANCE!
IF THE PRETTIEST GIRL IN BARRIO WANTS TO DANCE, THEN SHE WILL DANCE!
Marcel

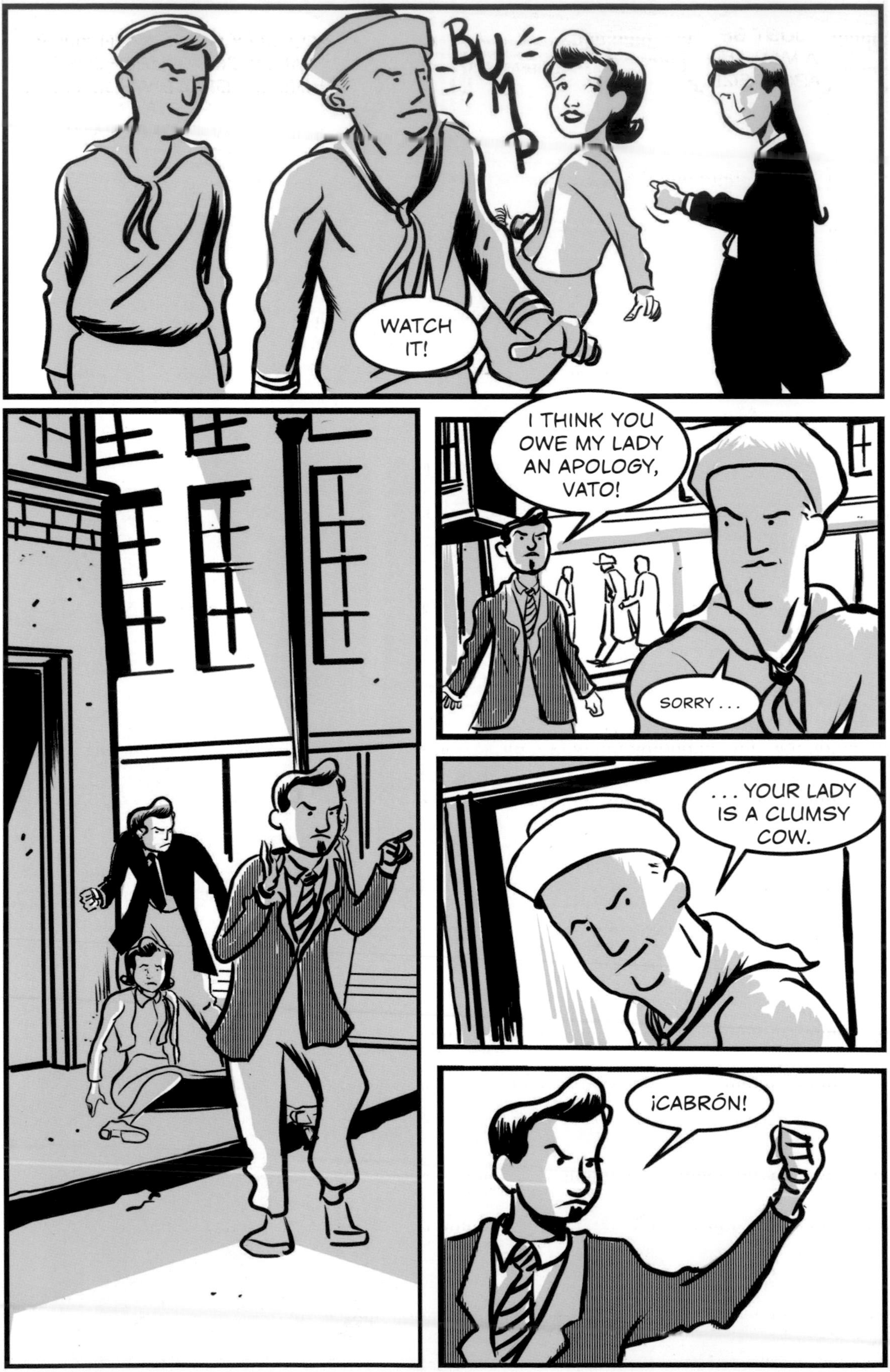
BUMP
WATCH IT!
I THINK YOU OWE MY LADY AN APOLOGY, VATO!
SORRY . . .
. . . YOUR LADY IS A CLUMSY COW.
¡CABRÓN!

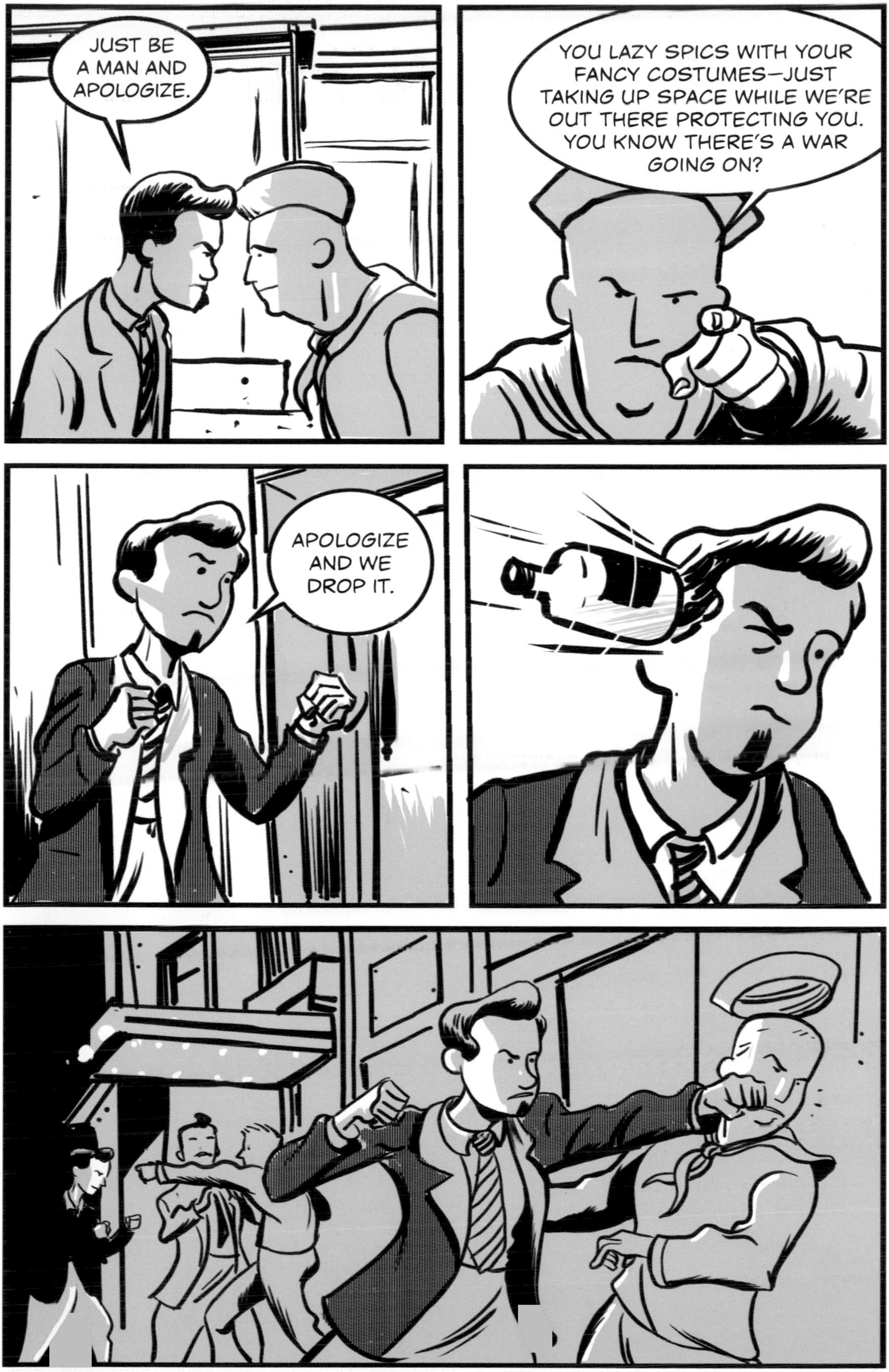
JUST BE A MAN AND APOLOGIZE.
YOU LAZY SPICS WITH YOUR FANCY COSTUMES—JUST TAKING UP SPACE WHILE WE'RE OUT THERE PROTECTING YOU. YOU KNOW THERE'S A WAR GOING ON?
APOLOGIZE AND WE DROP IT.

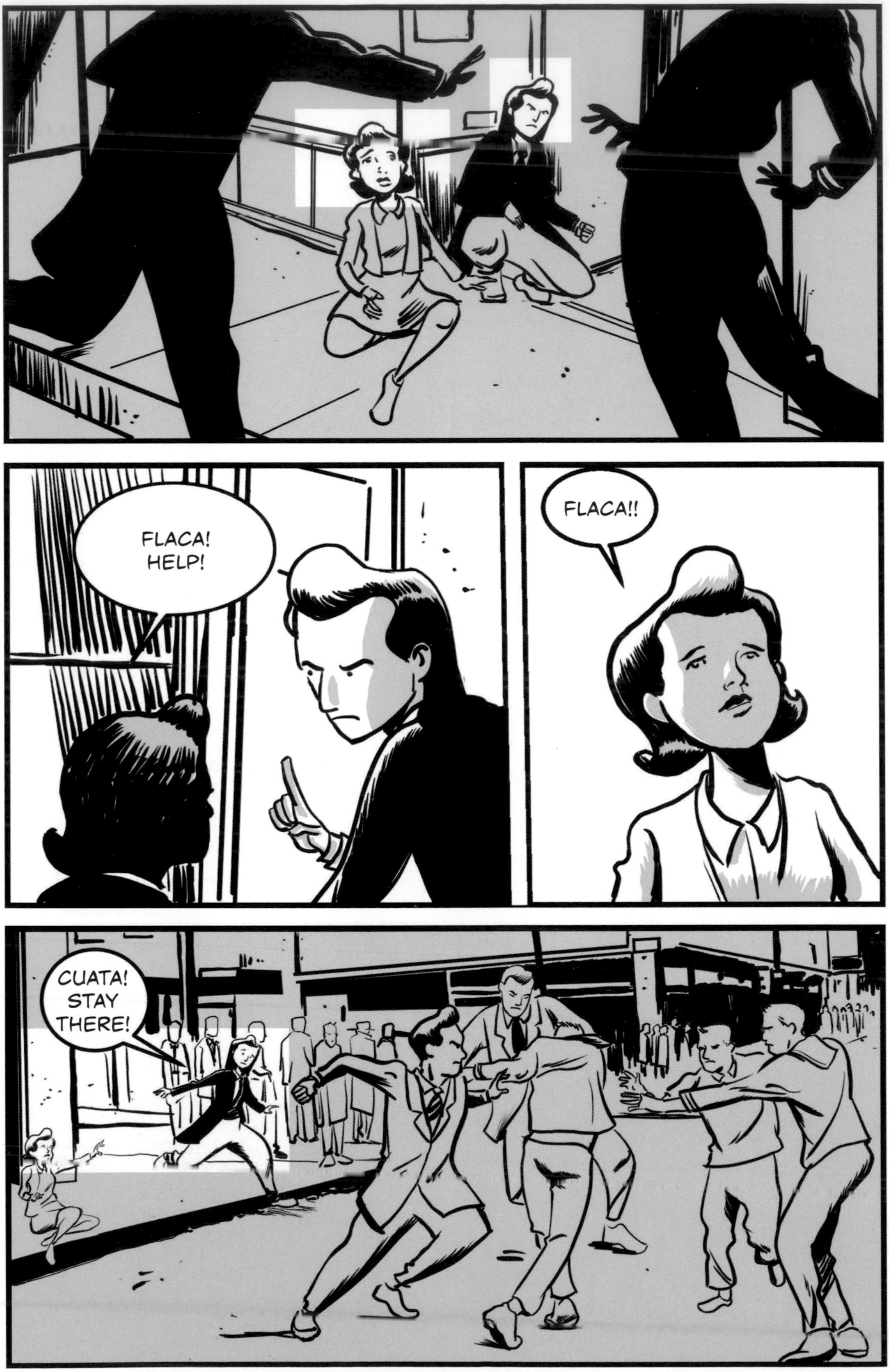
FLACA!
HELP!
FLACA!!
CUATA!
STAY
THERE!

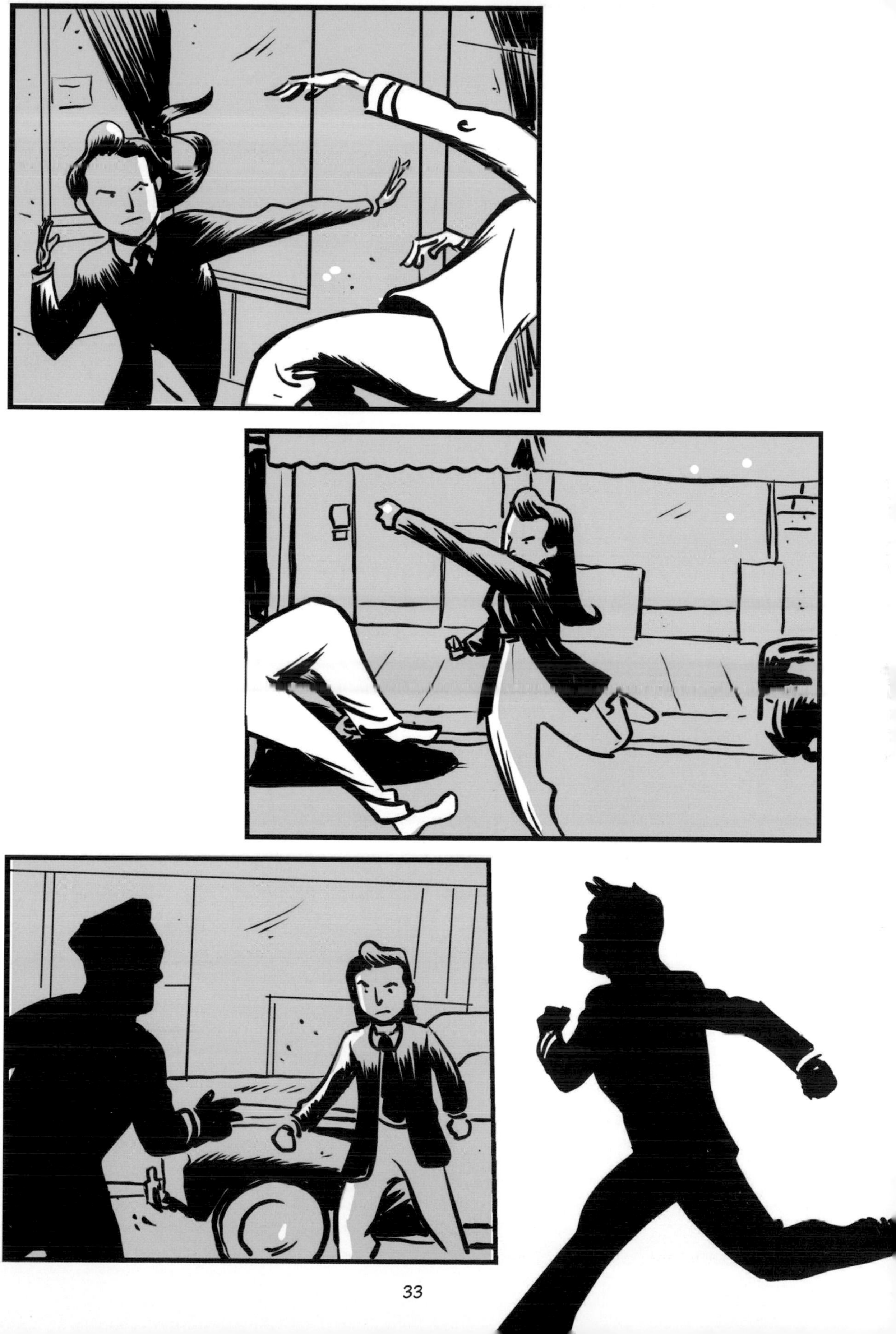

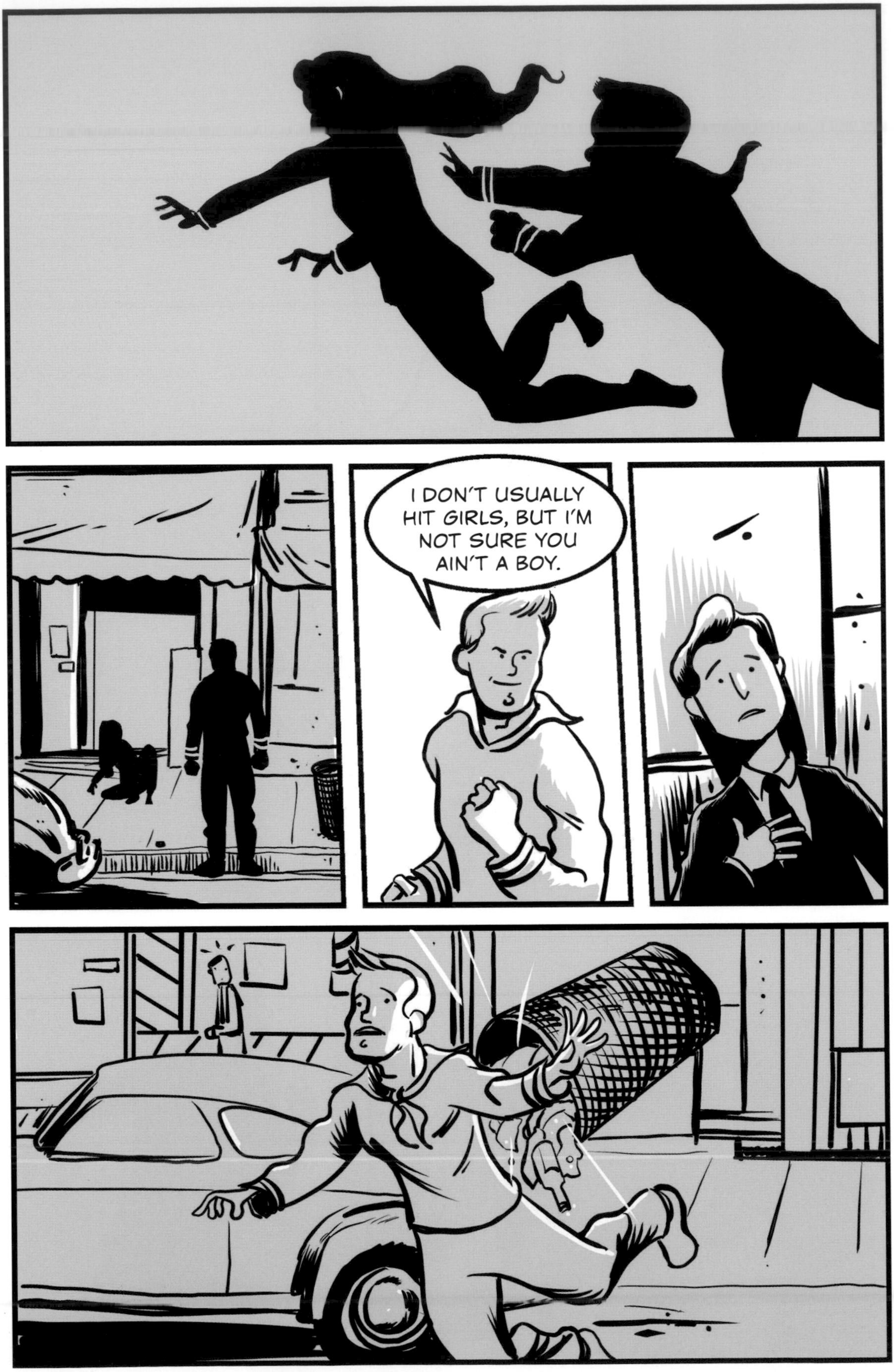
I DON'T USUALLY HIT GIRLS, BUT I'M NOT SURE YOU AIN'T A BOY.

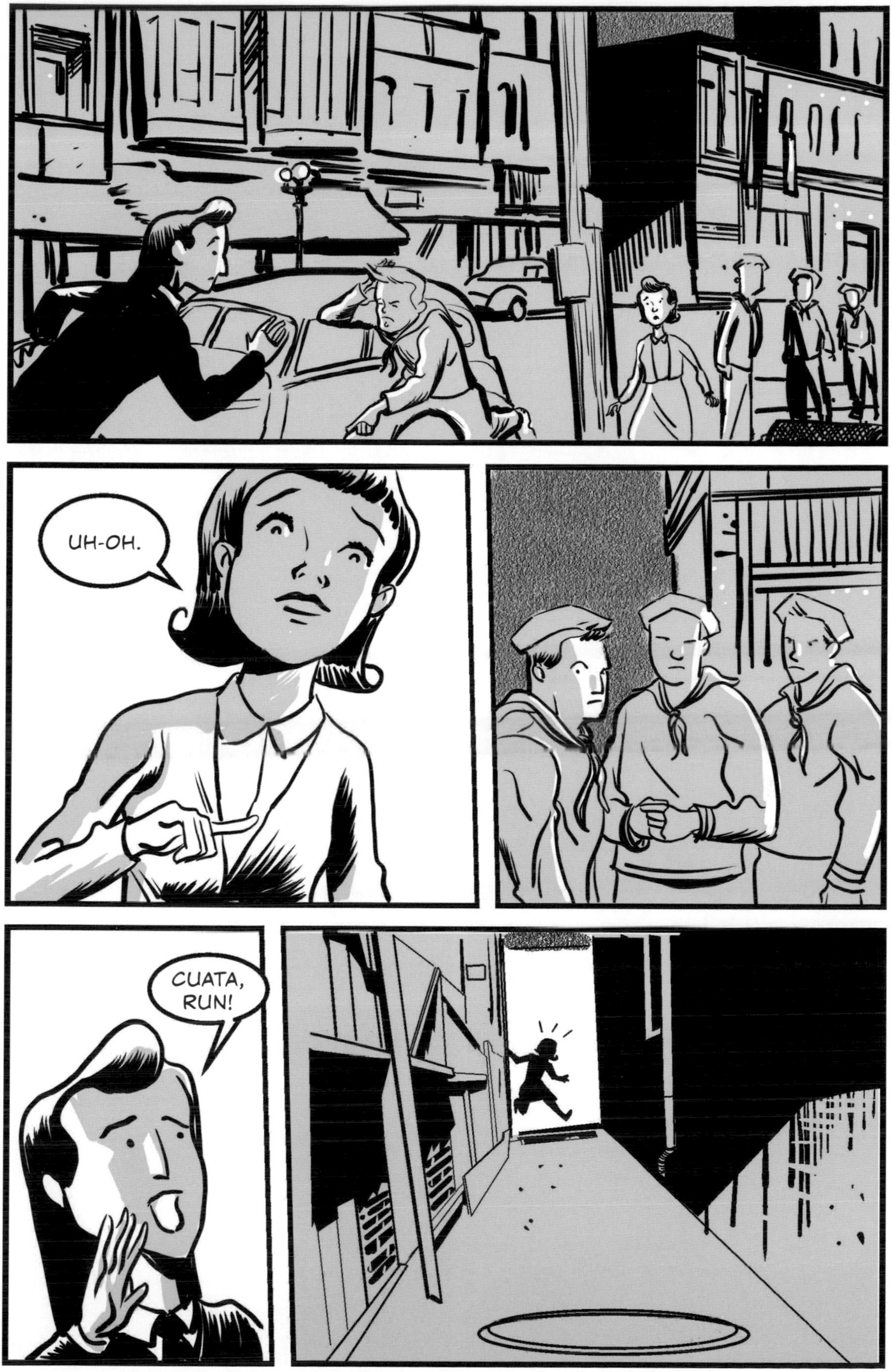
UH-OH.
CUATA, RUN!

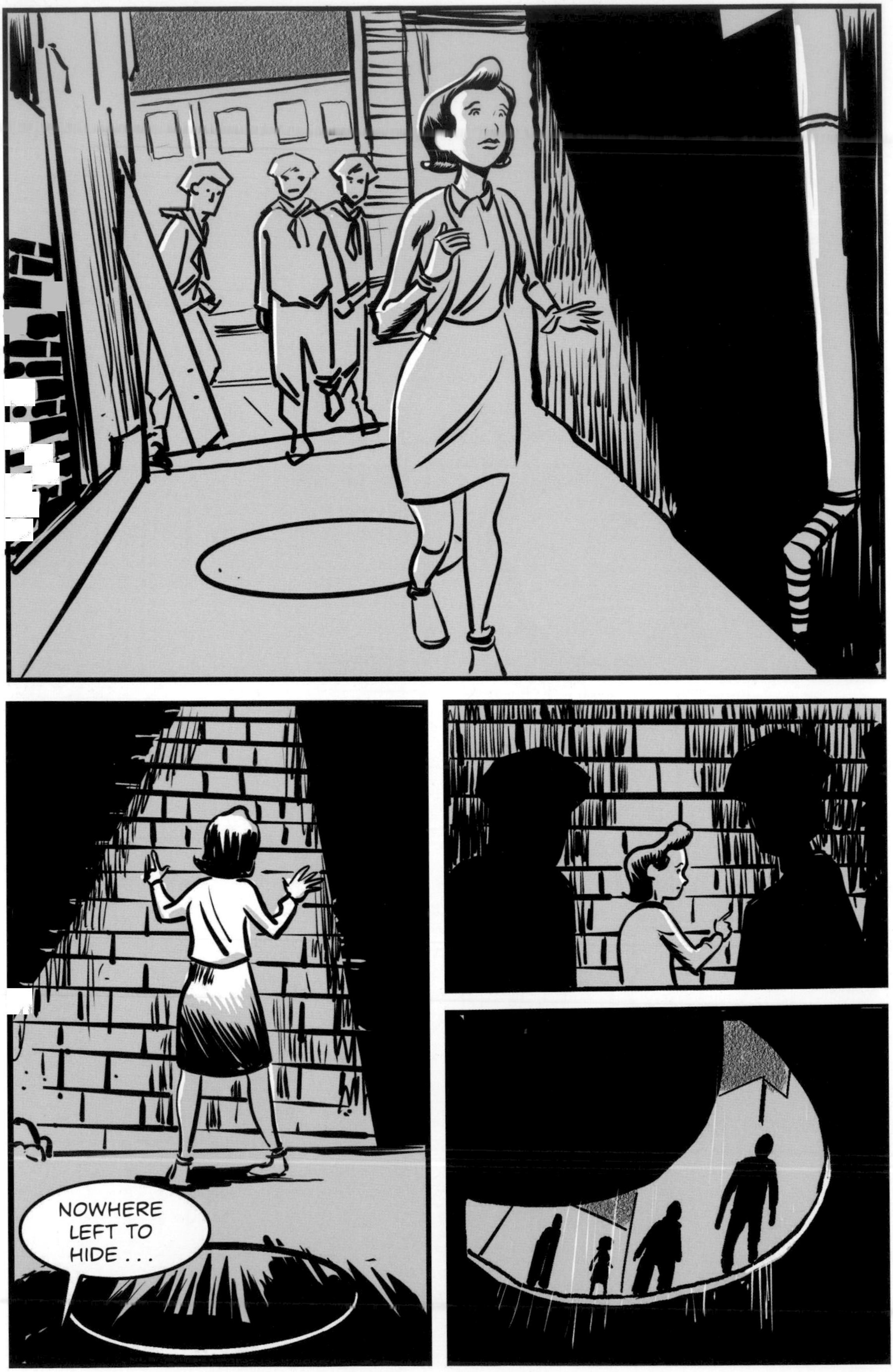
NOWHERE LEFT TO HIDE . . .

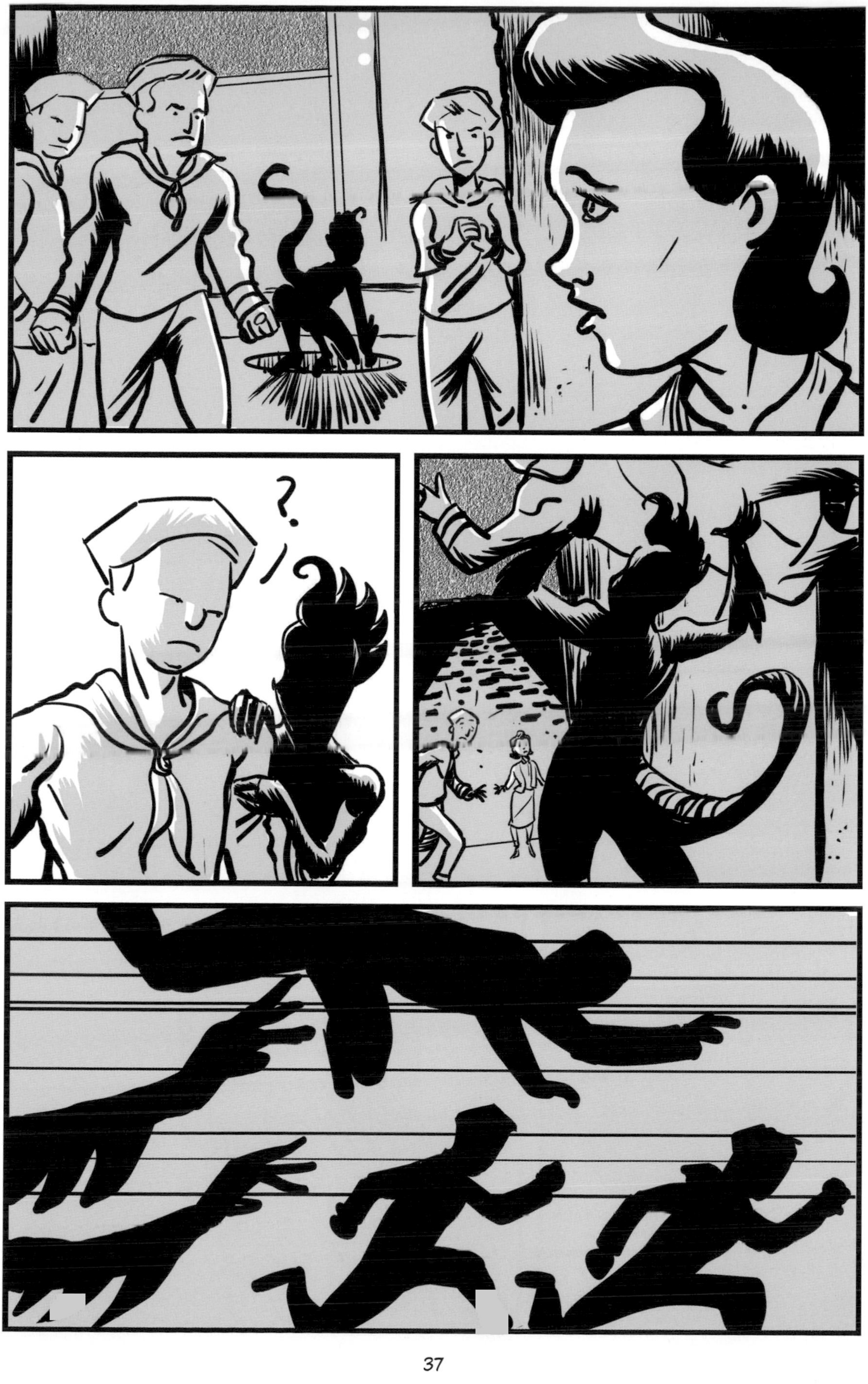
?

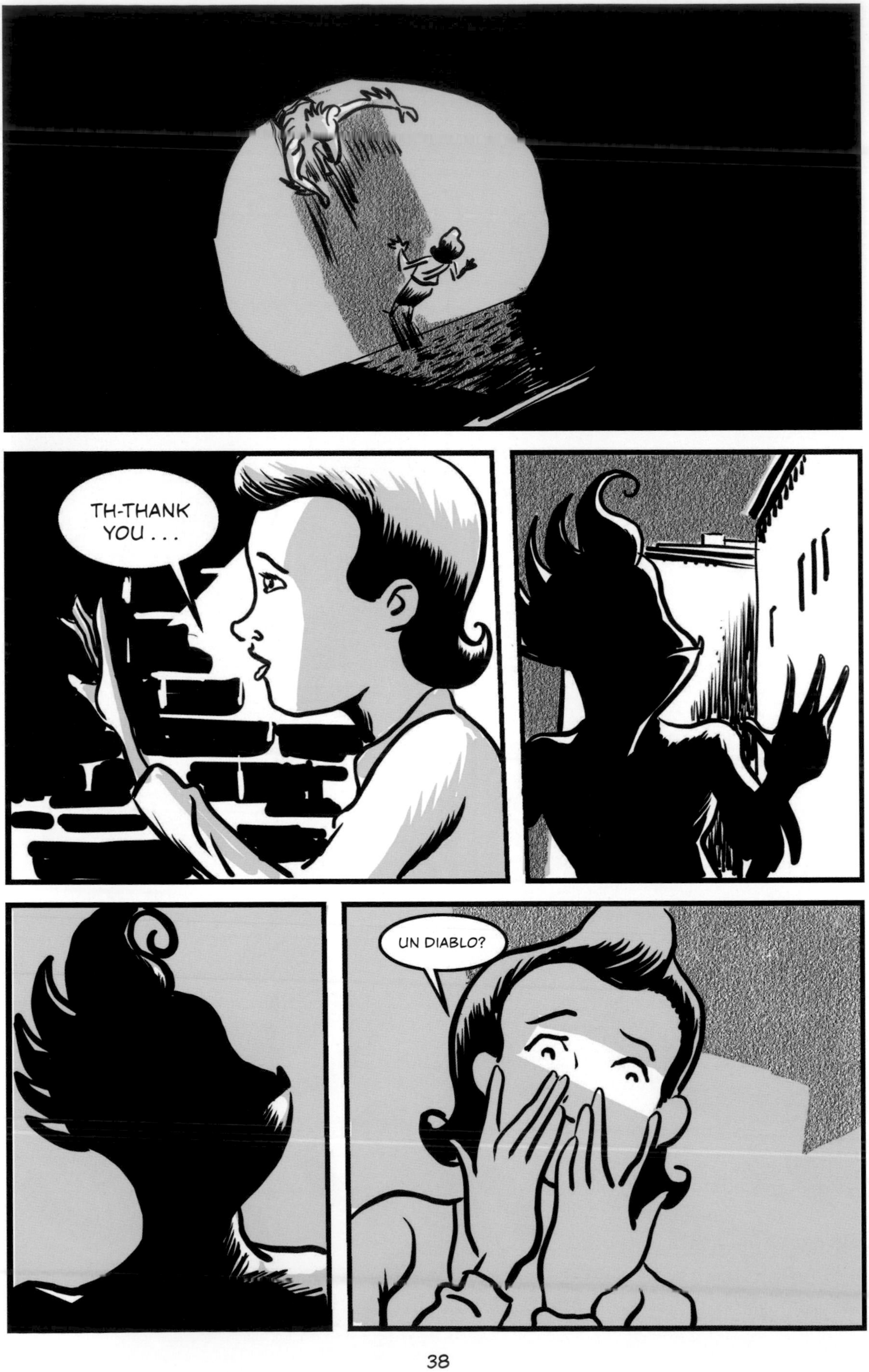
TH-THANK YOU . . .
UN DIABLO?

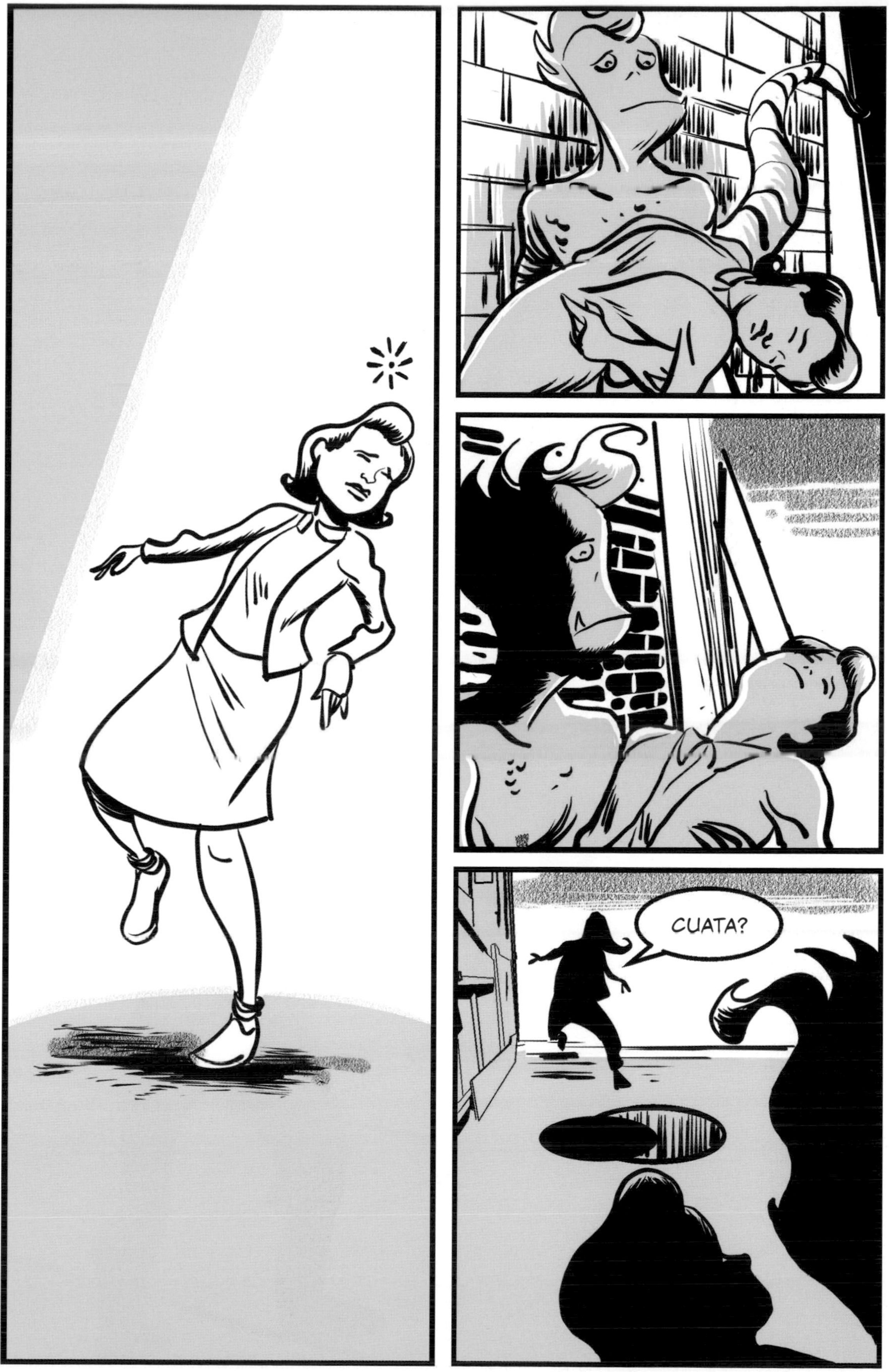
CUATA?

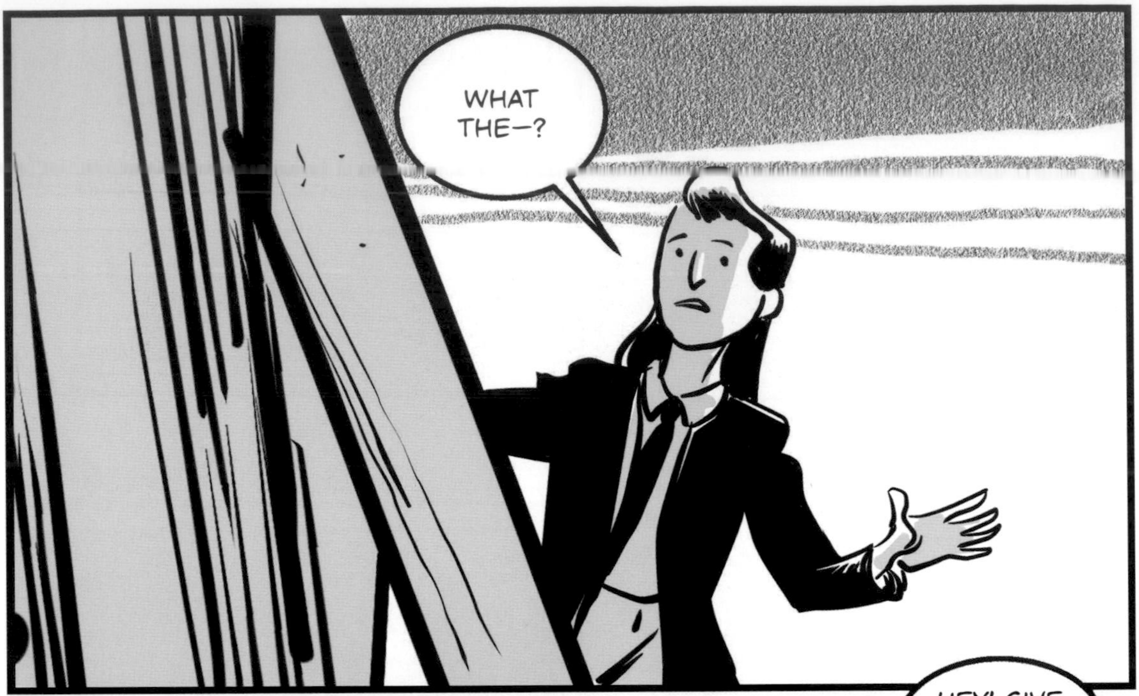
WHAT THE—?

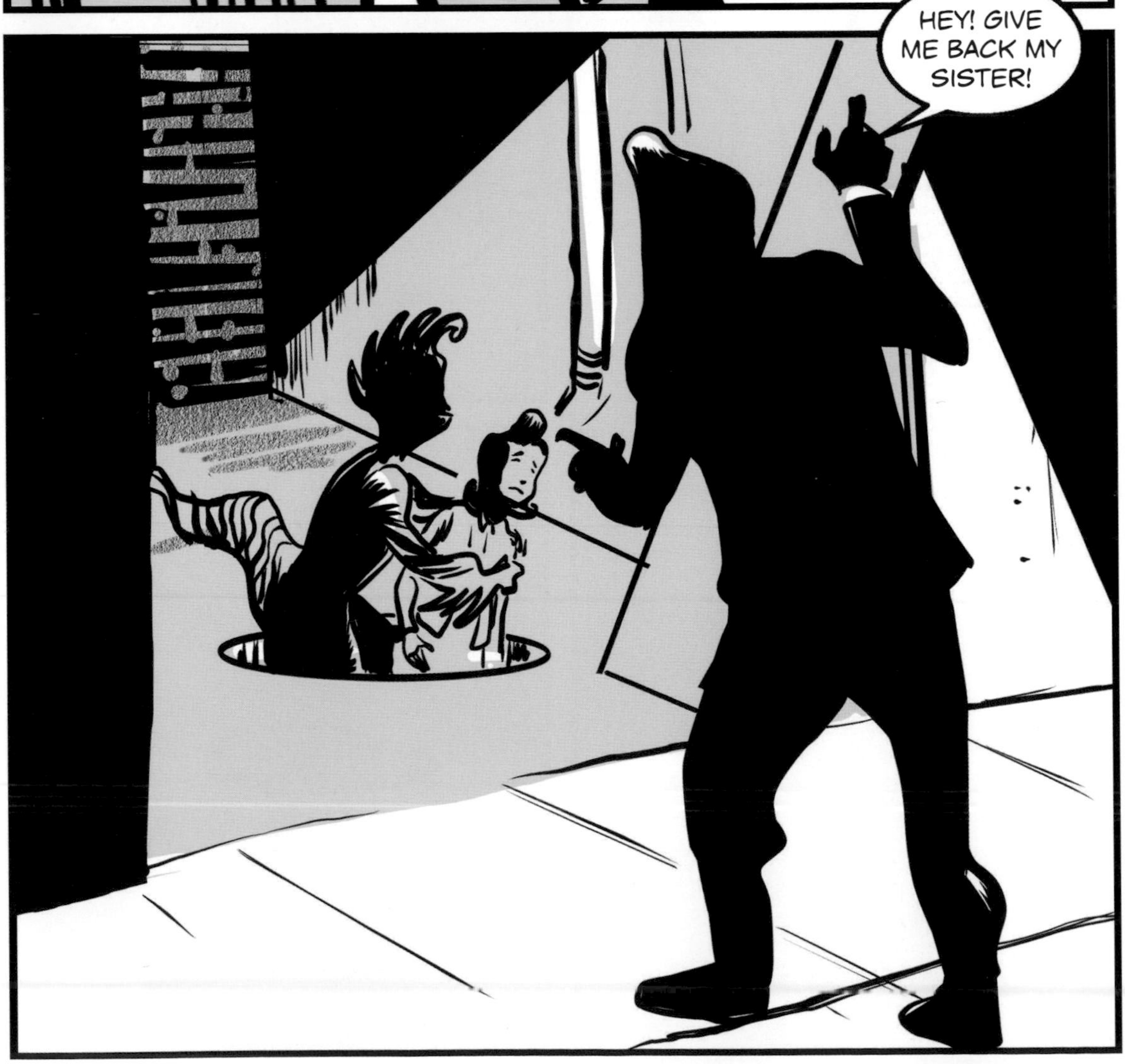
HEY! GIVE ME BACK MY SISTER!

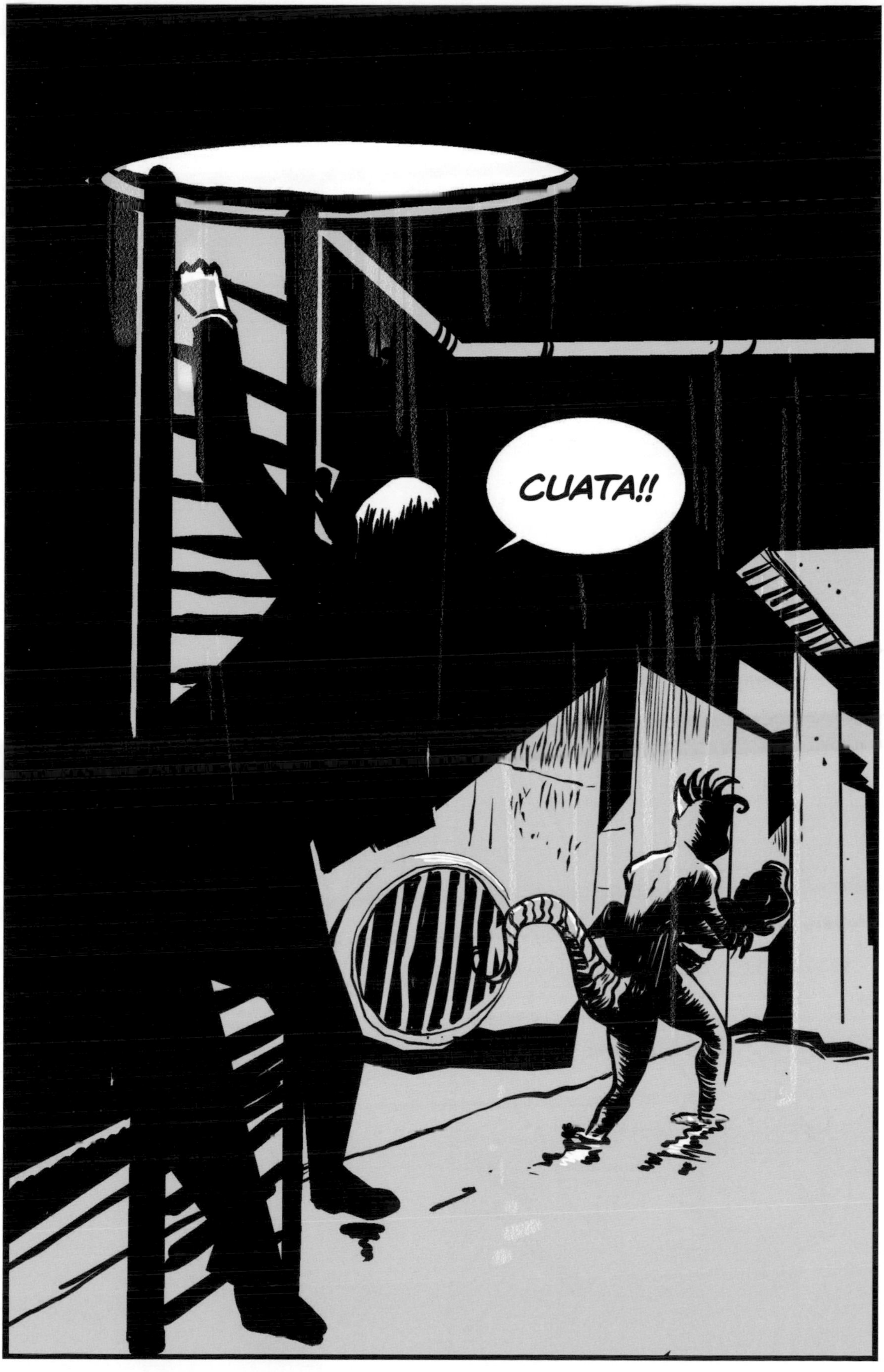
CUATA!!

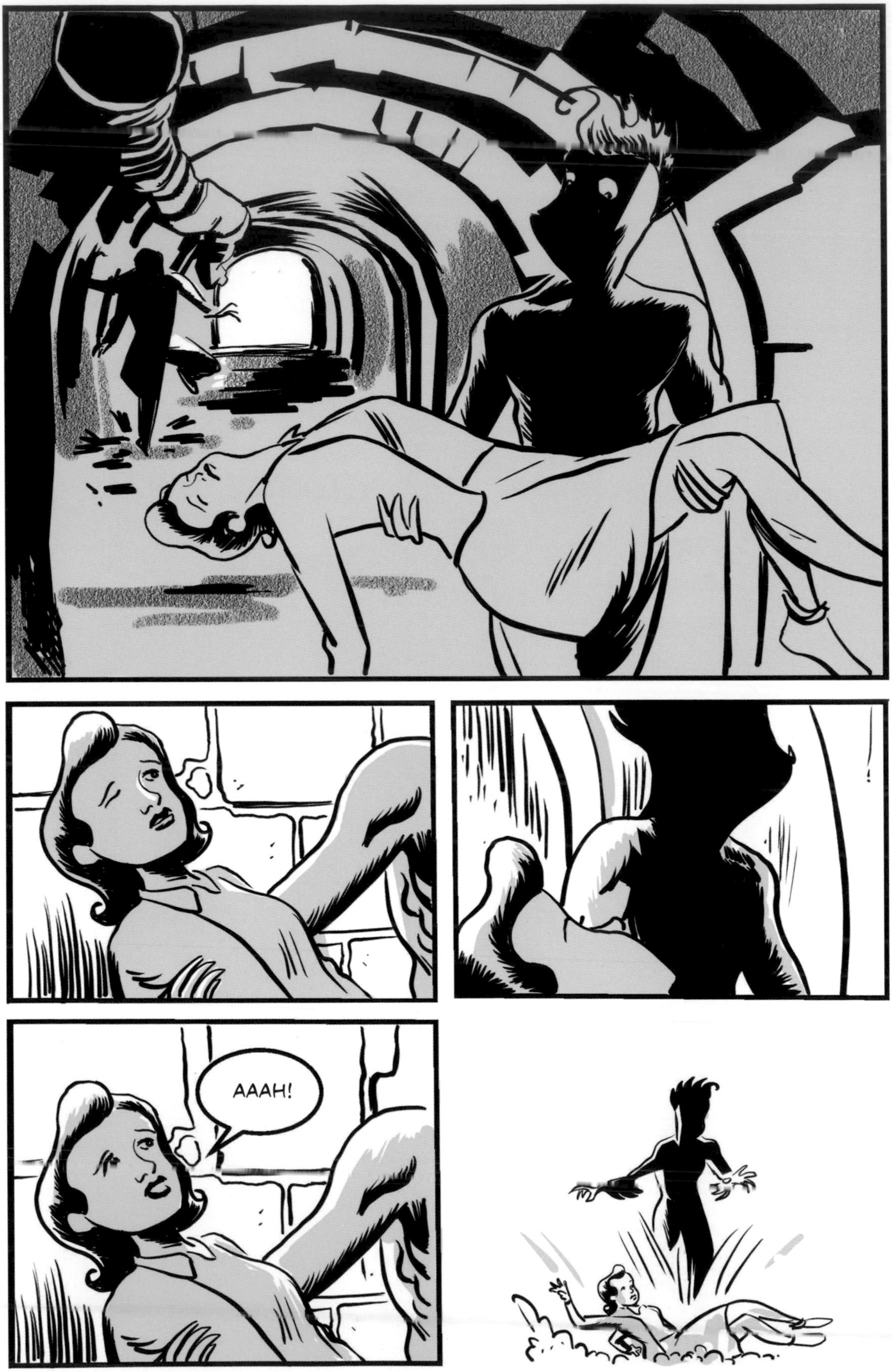
AAAH!

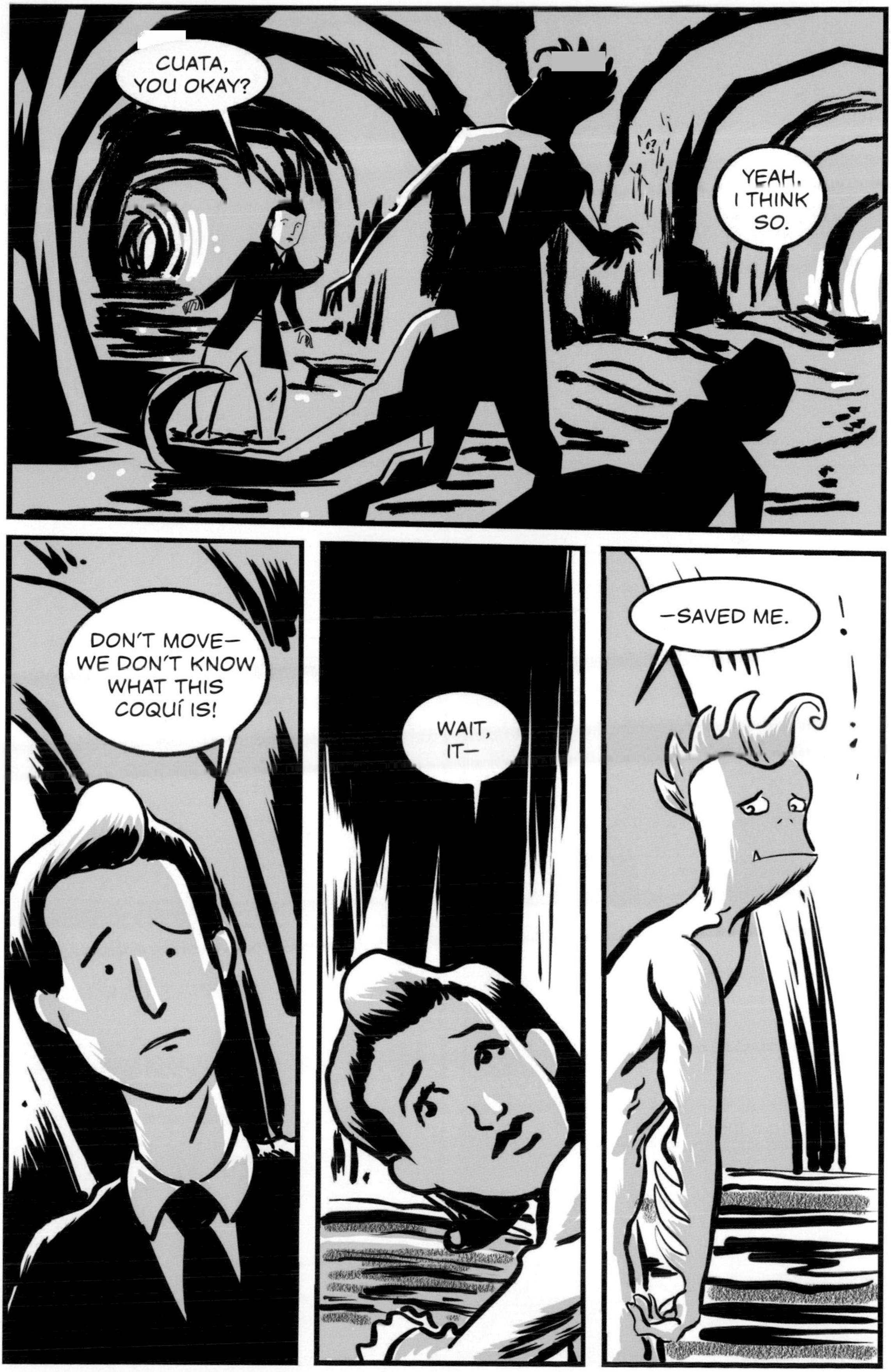
CUATA, YOU OKAY?
YEAH, I THINK SO.
DON'T MOVE— WE DON'T KNOW WHAT THIS COQUÍ IS!
WAIT, IT—
—SAVED ME.

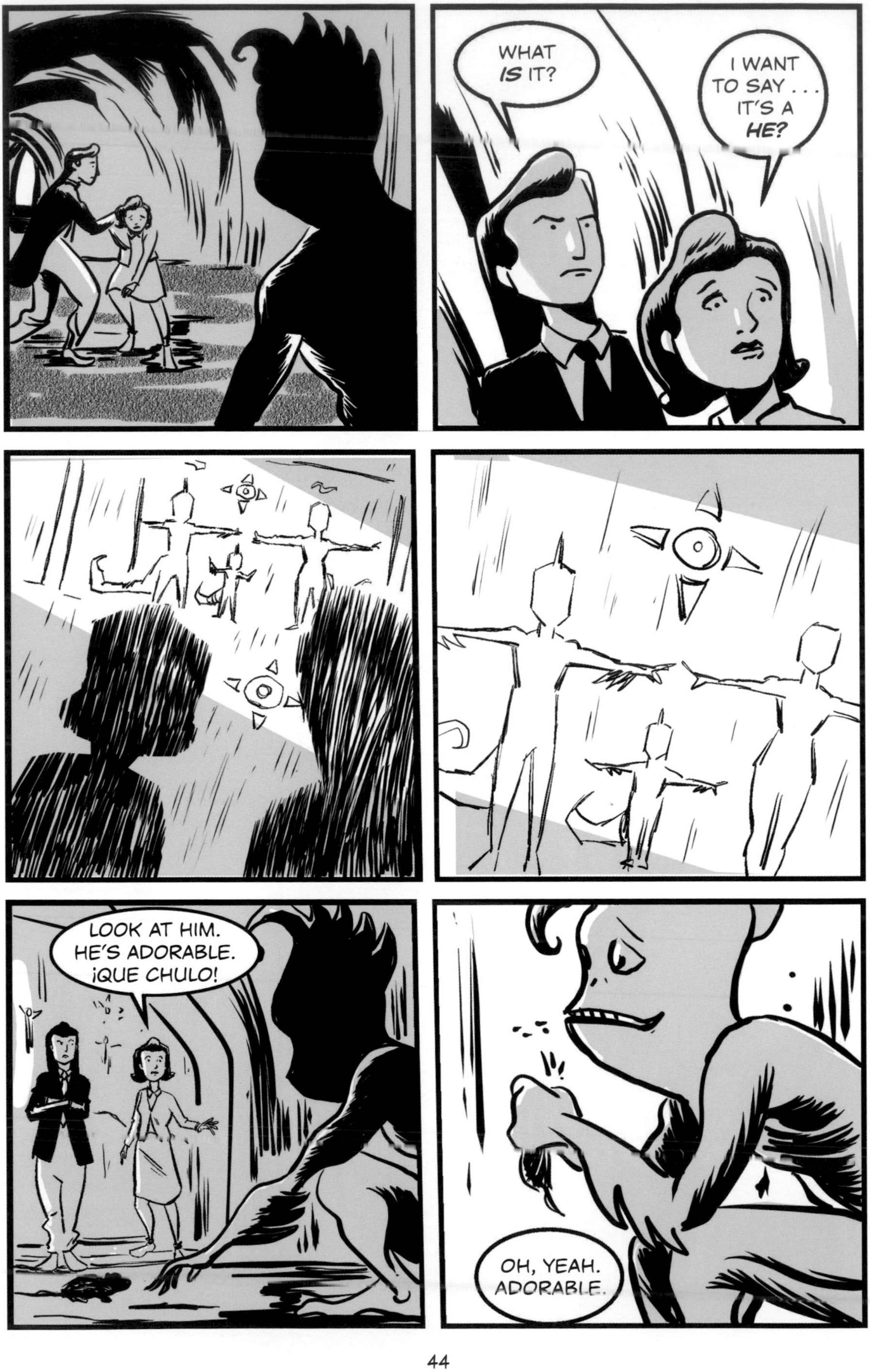
WHAT IS IT?
I WANT TO SAY . . . IT'S A HE?
LOOK AT HIM. HE'S ADORABLE. ¡QUE CHULO!
OH, YEAH. ADORABLE.

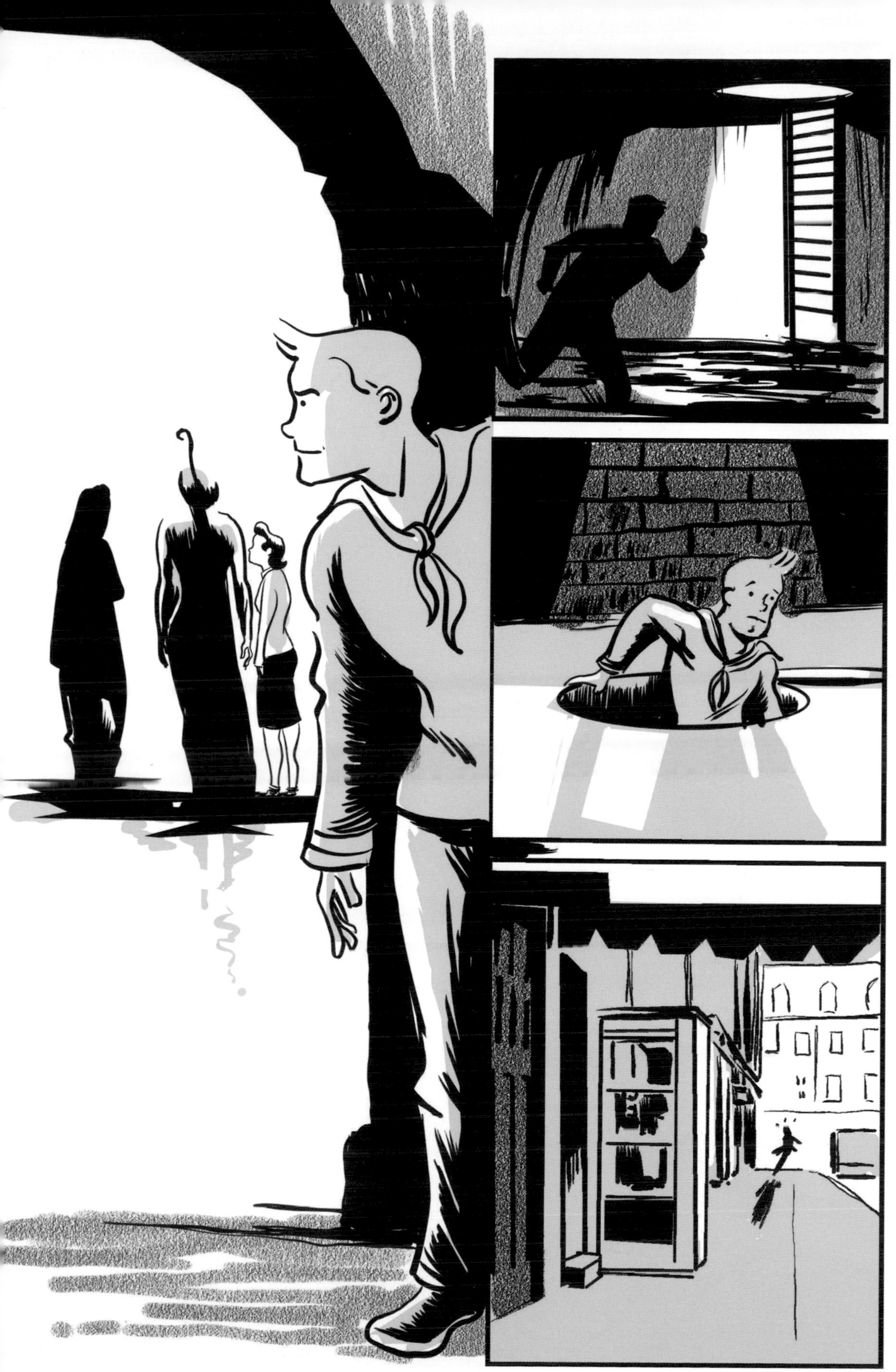

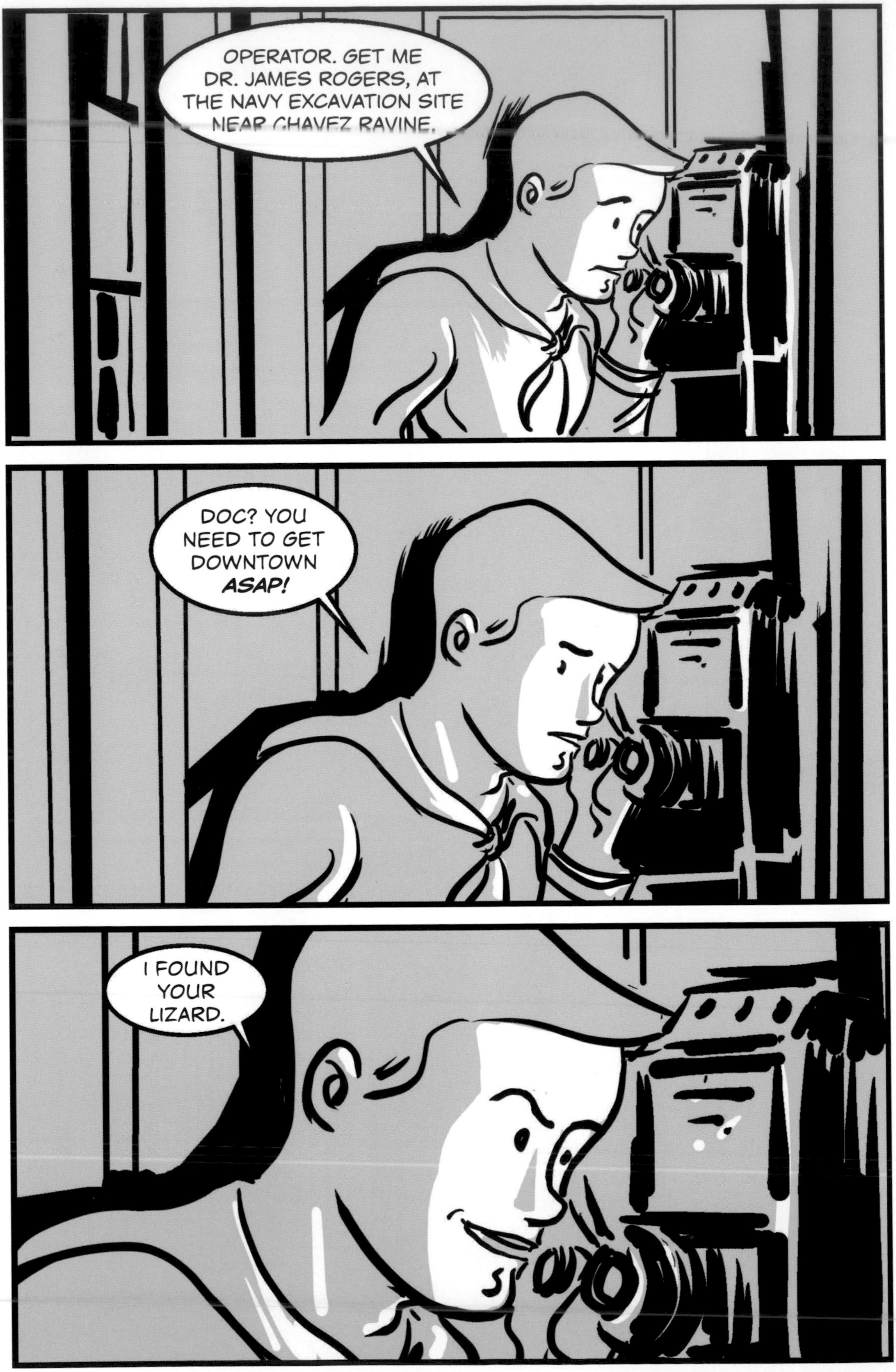
OPERATOR. GET ME DR. JAMES ROGERS, AT THE NAVY EXCAVATION SITE NEAR CHAVEZ RAVINE.
DOC? YOU NEED TO GET DOWNTOWN ASAP!
I FOUND YOUR LIZARD.

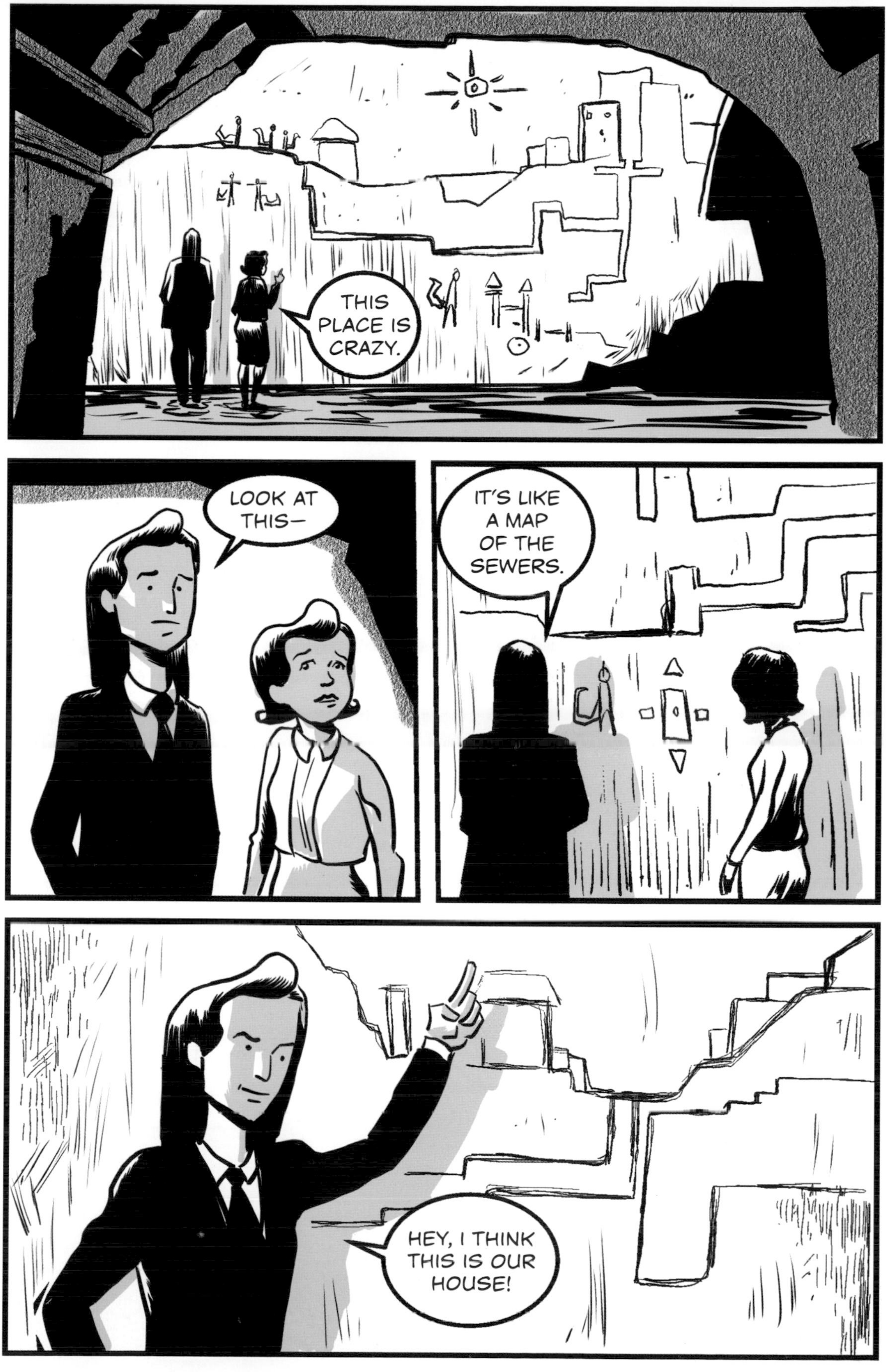
THIS PLACE IS CRAZY.
LOOK AT THIS—
IT'S LIKE A MAP OF THE SEWERS.
HEY, I THINK THIS IS OUR HOUSE!

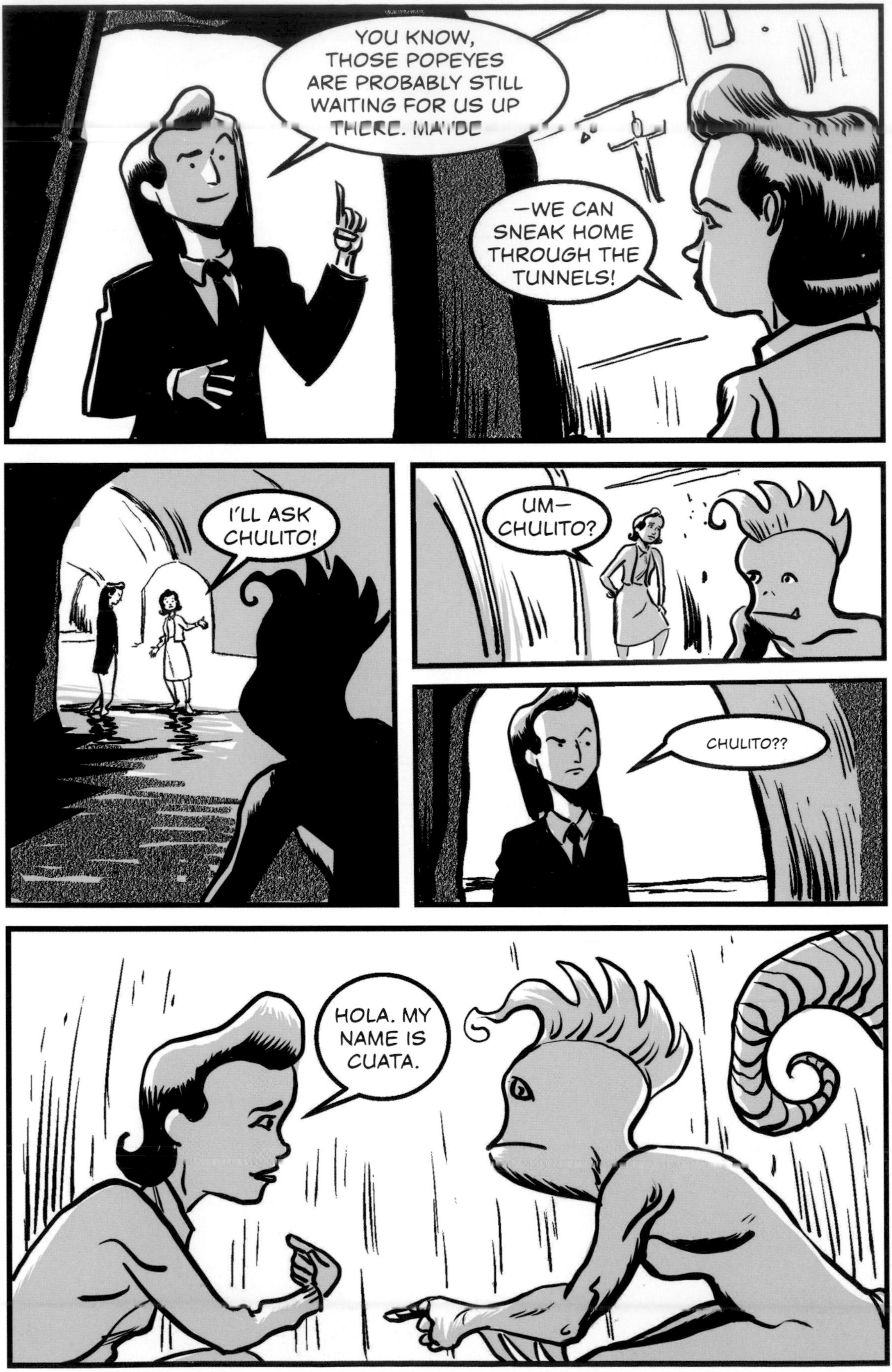
YOU KNOW, THOSE POPEYES ARE PROBABLY STILL WAITING FOR US UP THERE. MAYBE
—WE CAN SNEAK HOME THROUGH THE TUNNELS!
I'LL ASK CHULITO!
UM—CHULITO?
CHULITO??
HOLA. MY NAME IS CUATA.

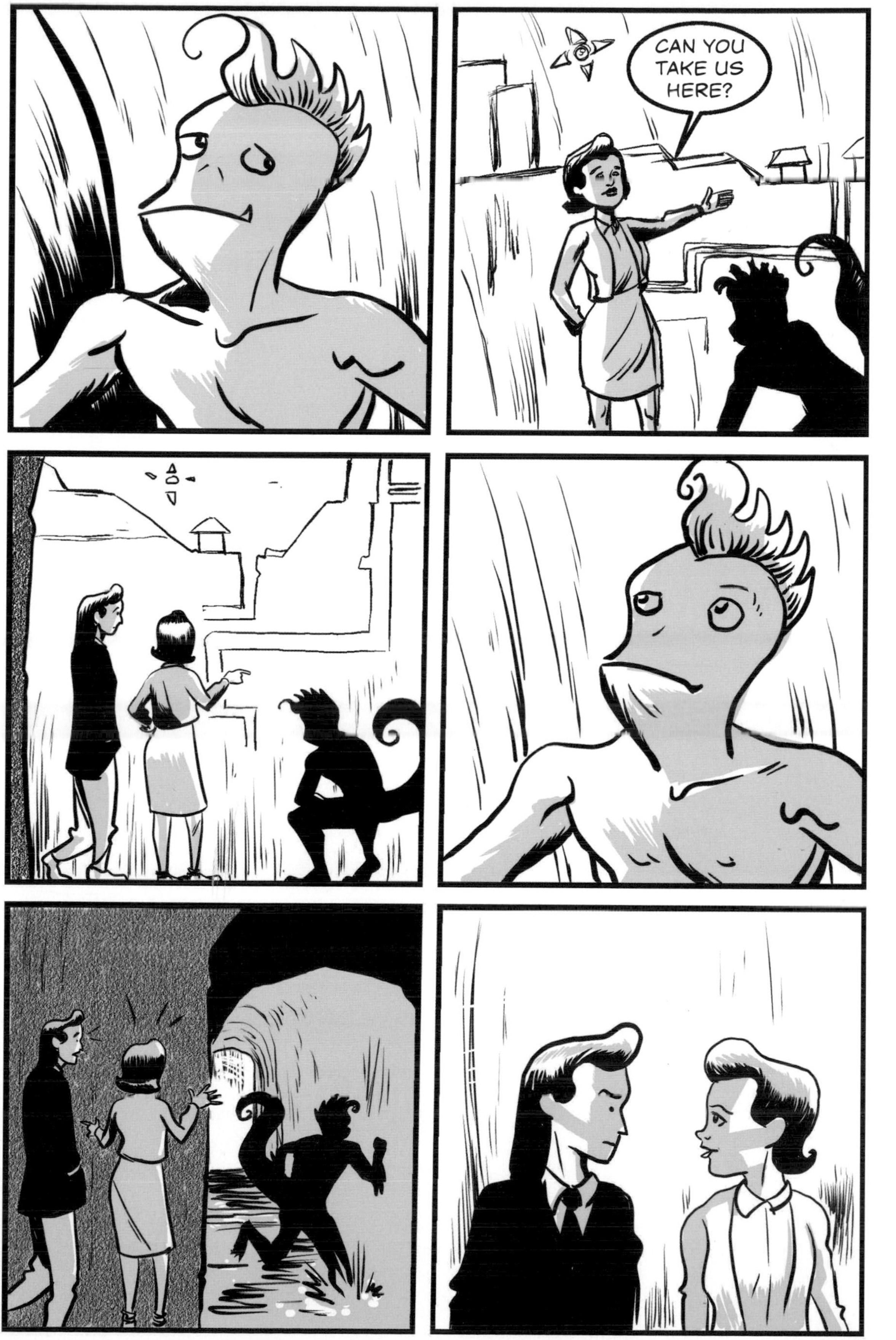
CAN YOU TAKE US HERE?

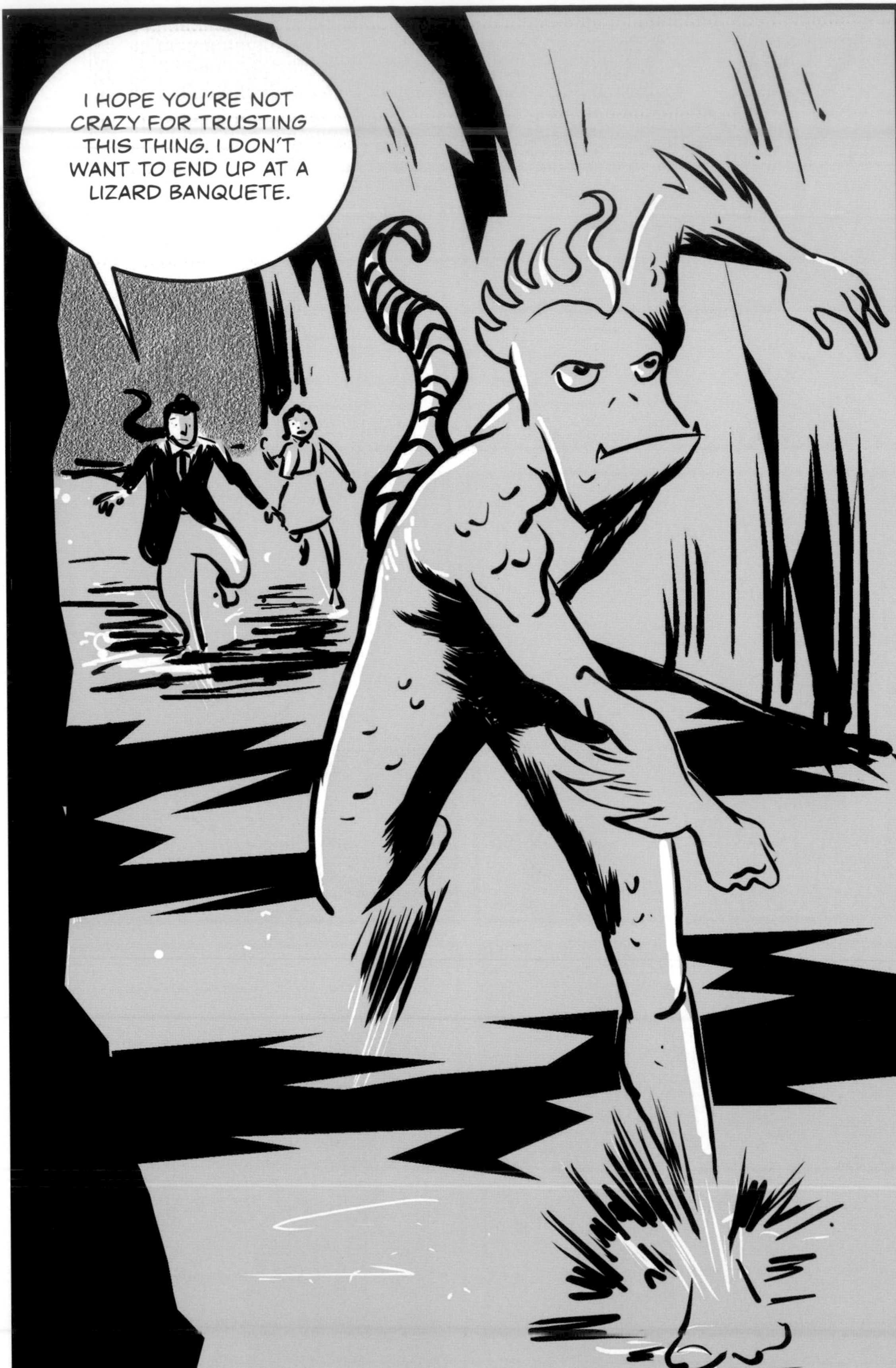
I HOPE YOU'RE NOT CRAZY FOR TRUSTING THIS THING. I DON'T WANT TO END UP AT A LIZARD BANQUETE.

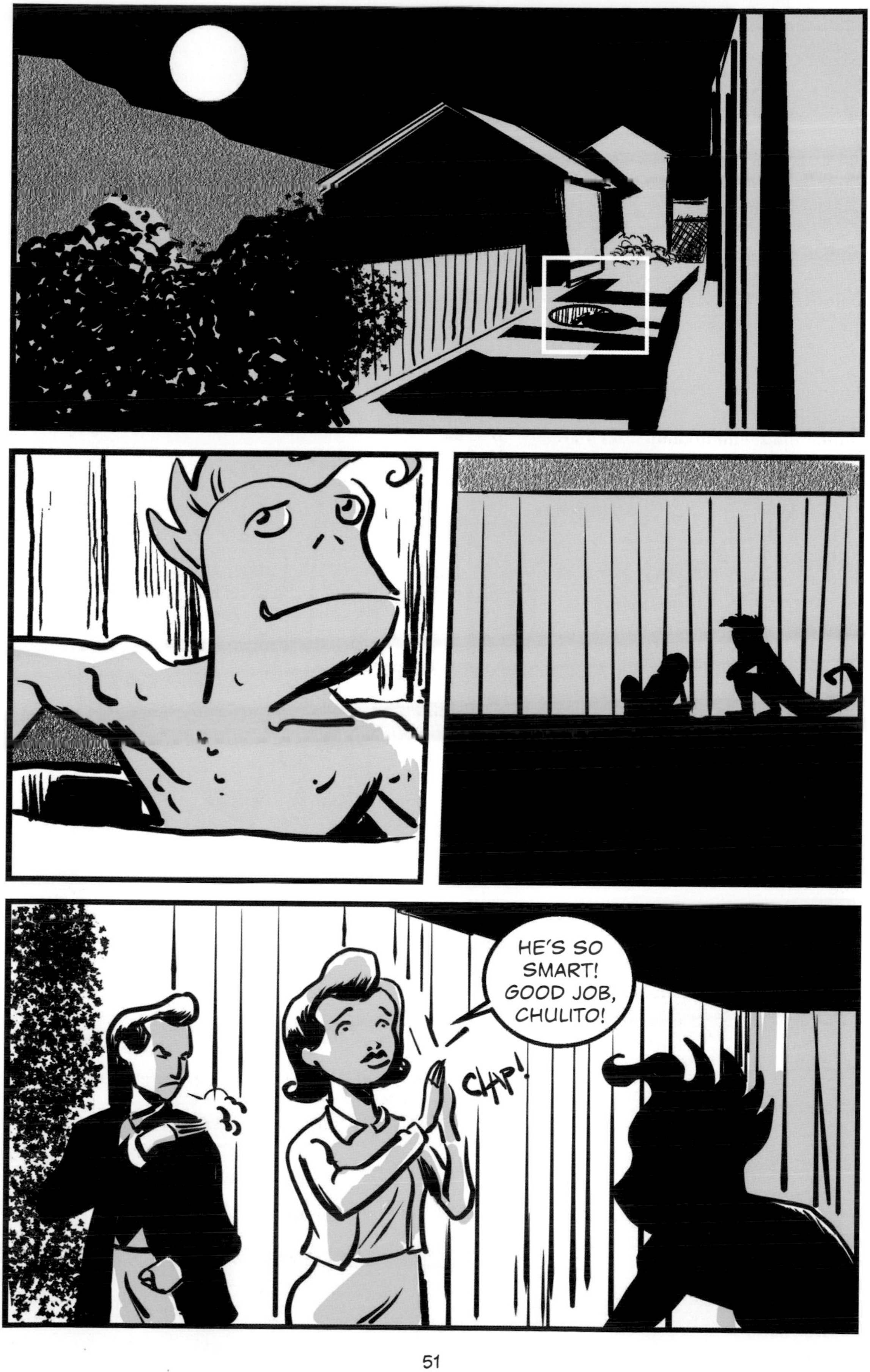
HE'S SO SMART! GOOD JOB, CHULITO!
CLAP!

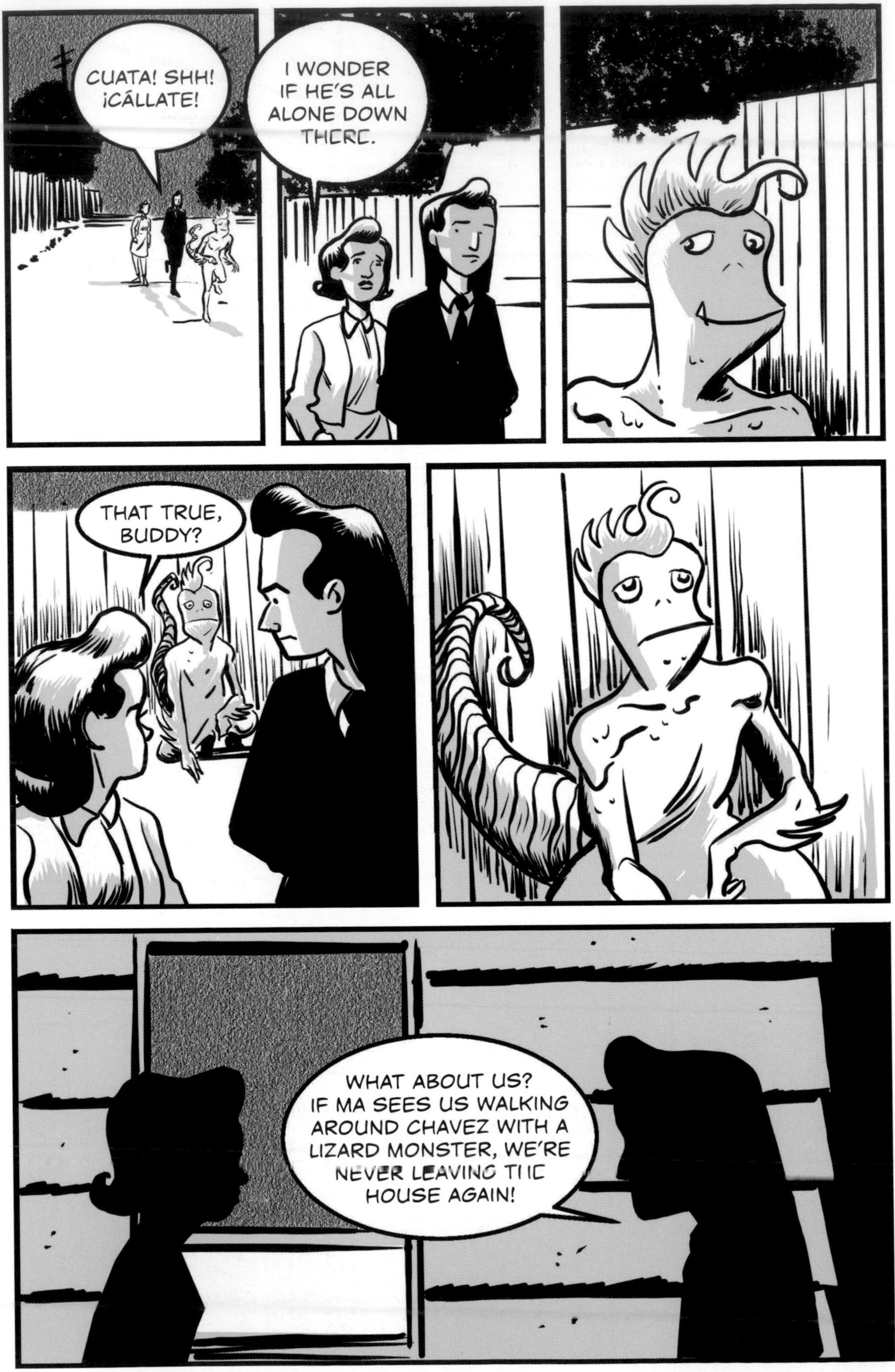

CUATA! SHH! ¡CÁLLATE!
I WONDER IF HE'S ALL ALONE DOWN THERE.
THAT TRUE, BUDDY?
WHAT ABOUT US? IF MA SEES US WALKING AROUND CHAVEZ WITH A LIZARD MONSTER, WE'RE NEVER LEAVING THE HOUSE AGAIN!

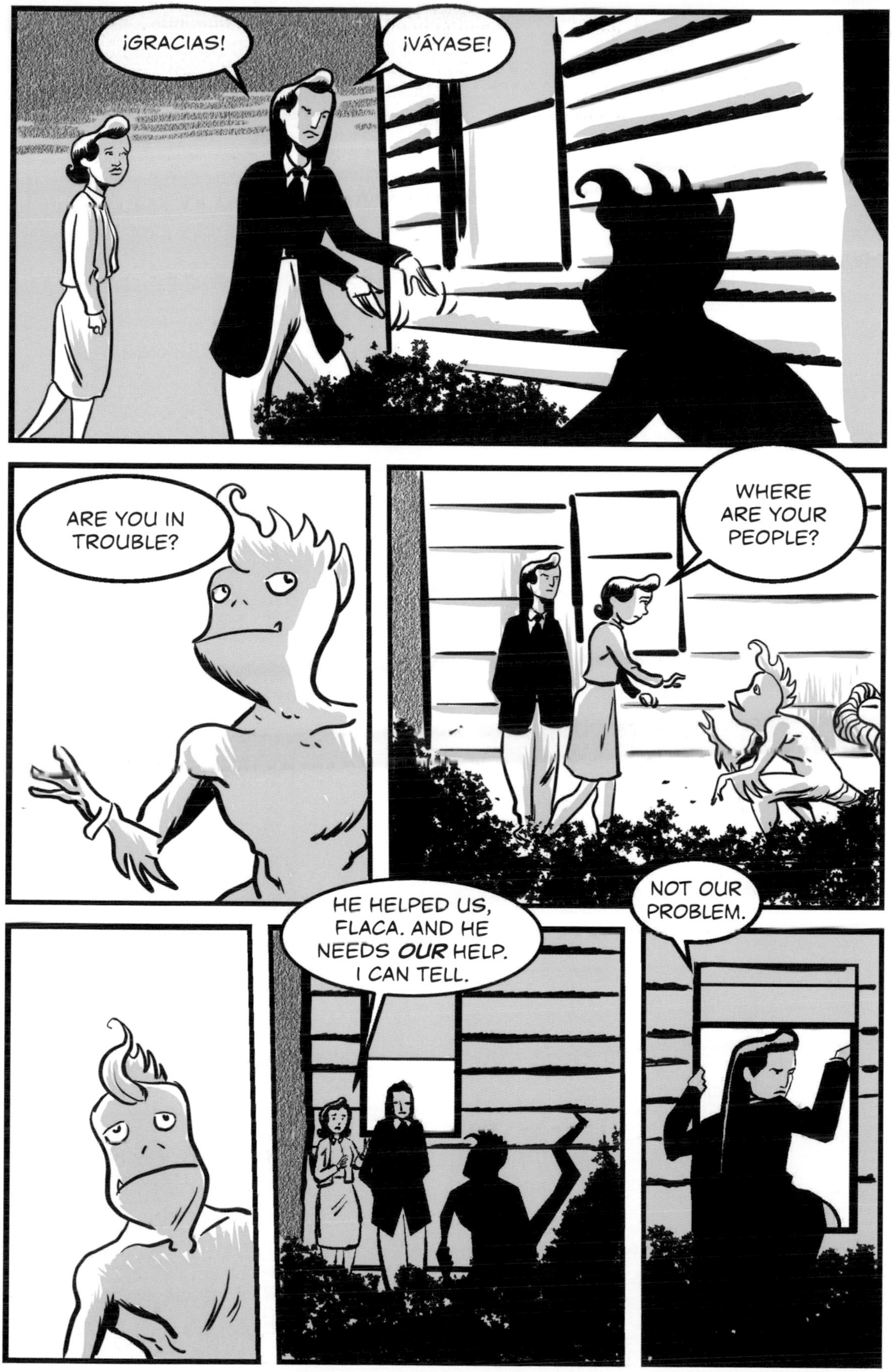
¡GRACIAS!
¡VÁYASE!
ARE YOU IN TROUBLE?
WHERE ARE YOUR PEOPLE?
HE HELPED US, FLACA. AND HE NEEDS *OUR* HELP. I CAN TELL.
NOT OUR PROBLEM.

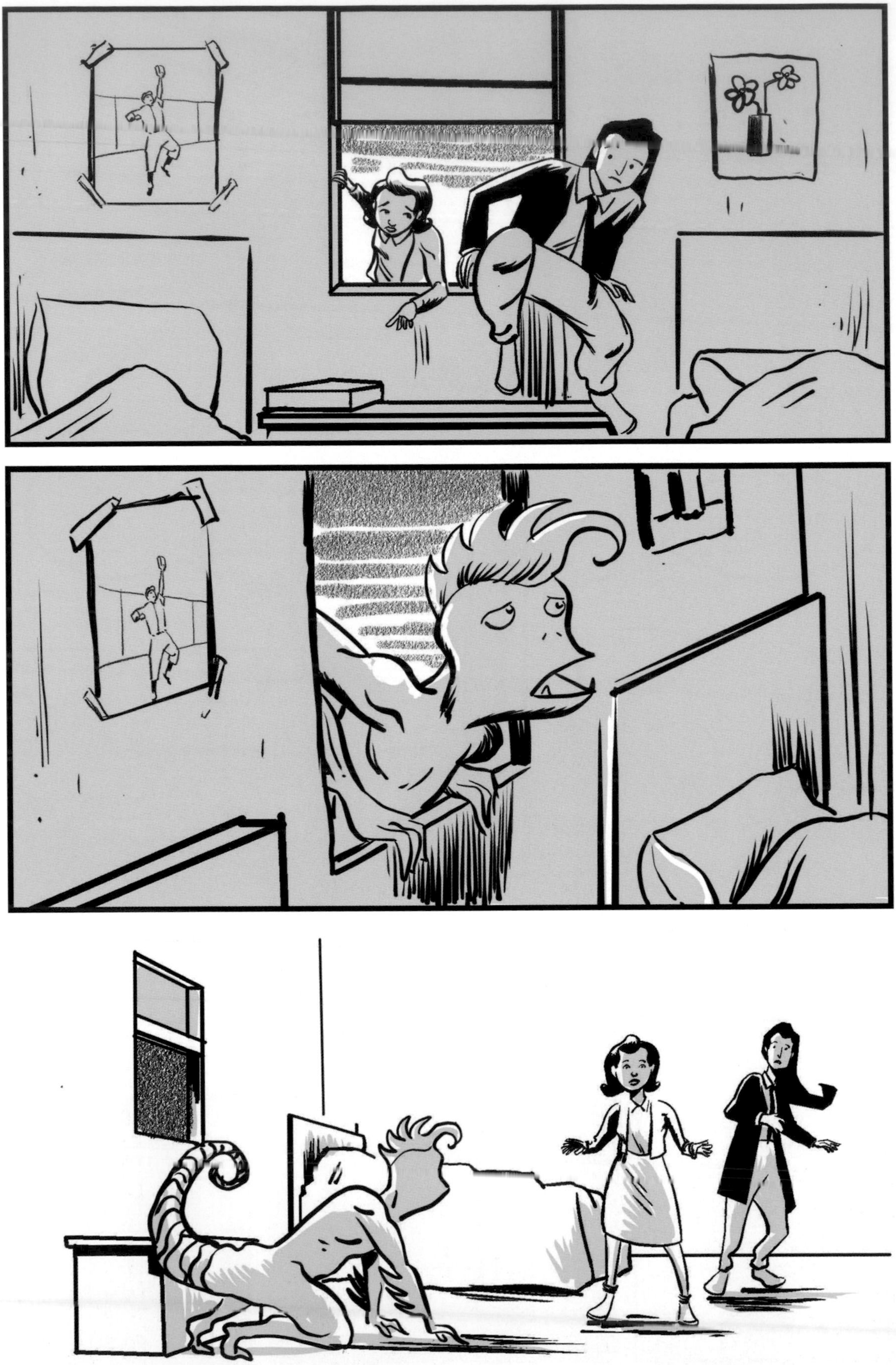

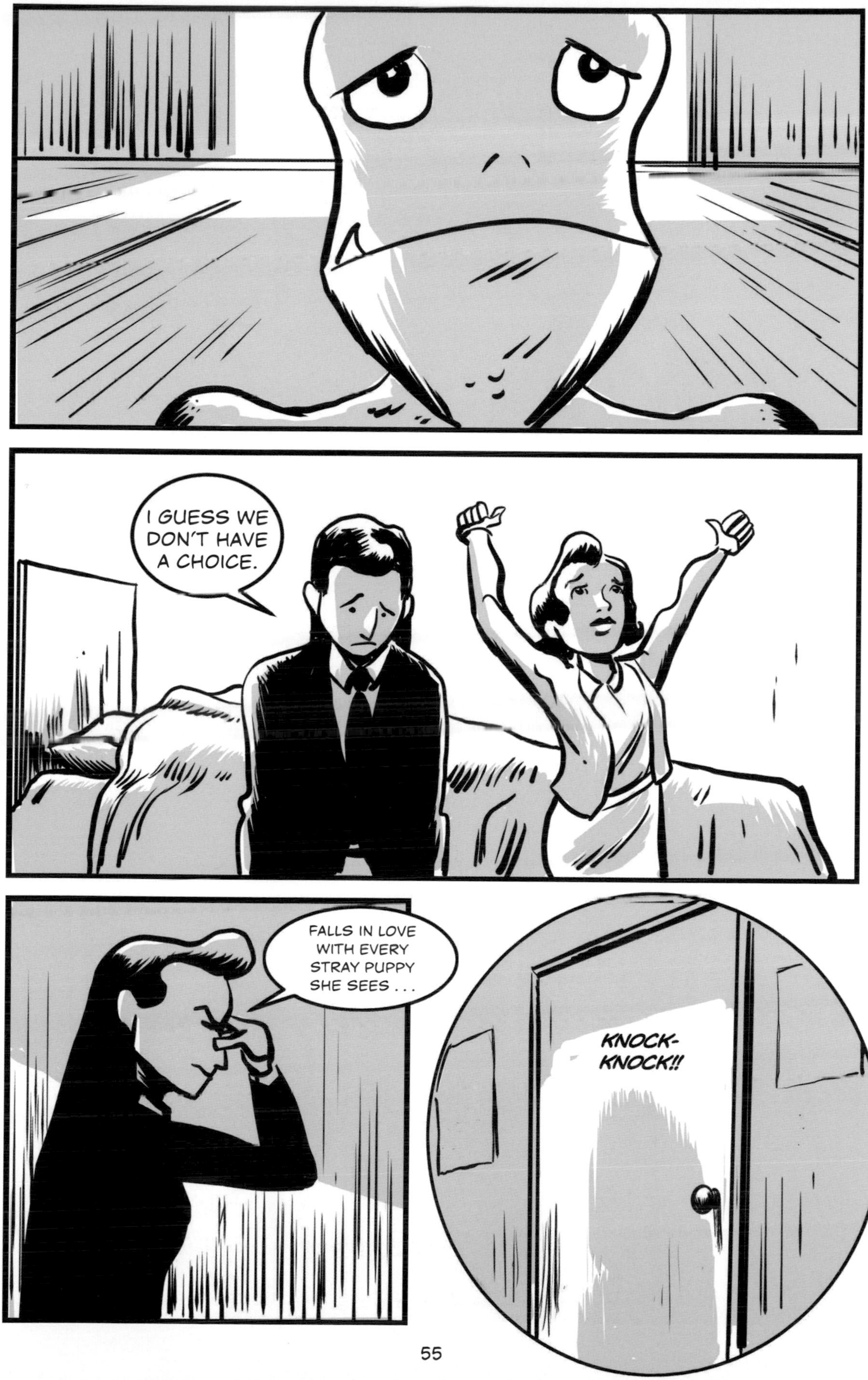
I GUESS WE DON'T HAVE A CHOICE.
FALLS IN LOVE WITH EVERY STRAY PUPPY SHE SEES . . .
KNOCK-KNOCK!!

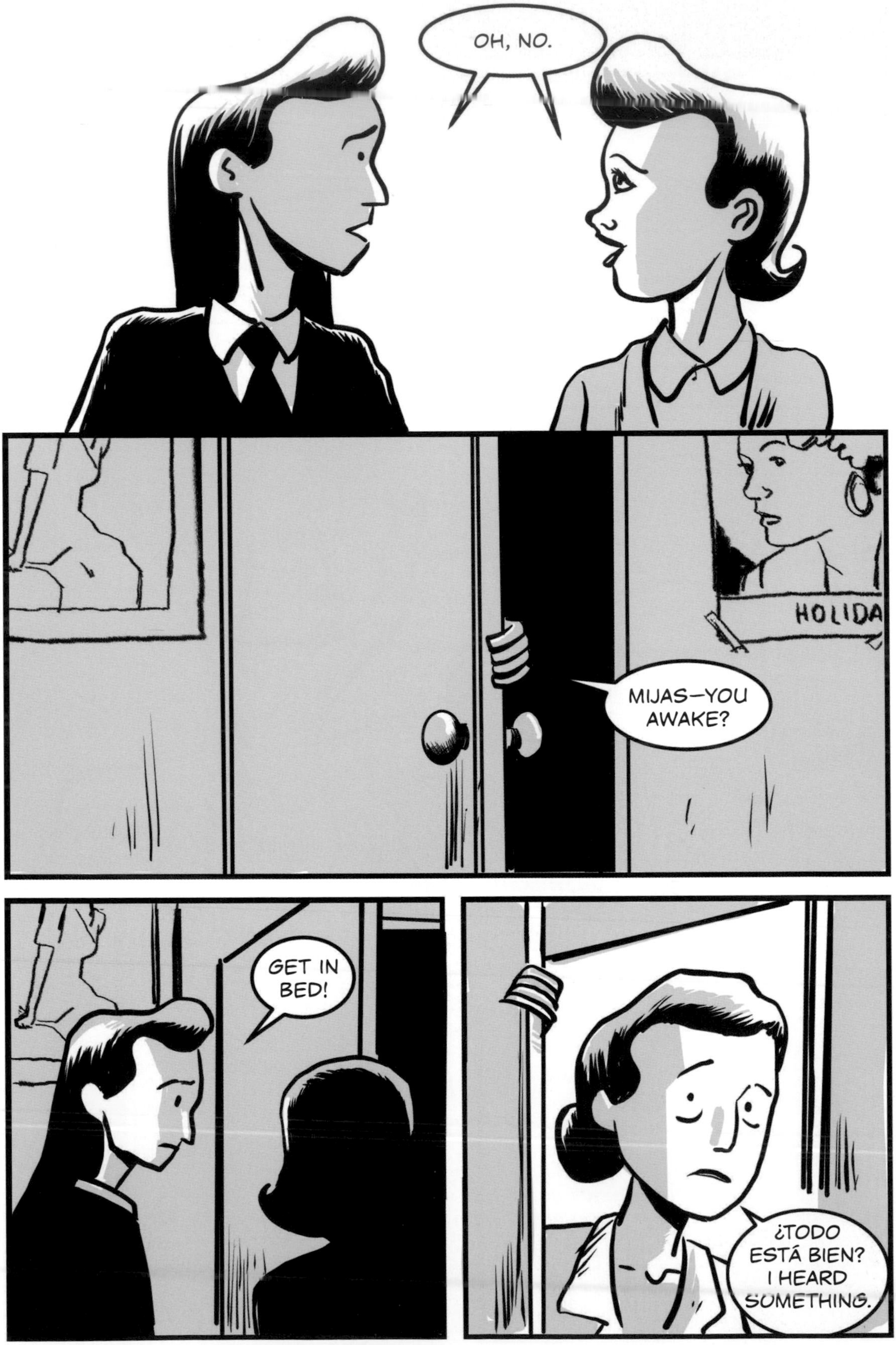
OH, NO.
HOLIDA
MIJAS—YOU AWAKE?
GET IN BED!
¿TODO ESTÁ BIEN? I HEARD SOMETHING.

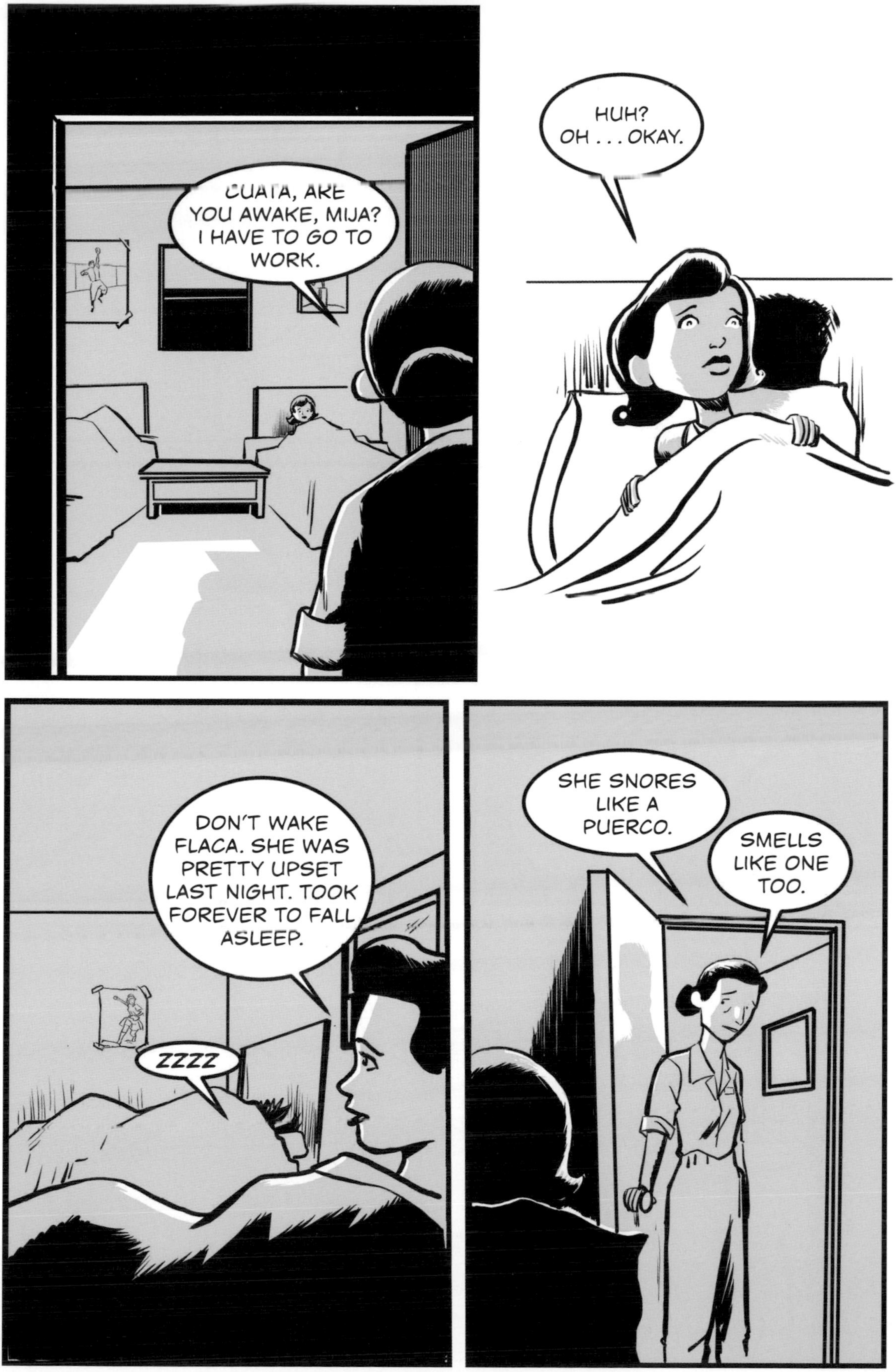
CUATA, ARE YOU AWAKE, MIJA? I HAVE TO GO TO WORK.
HUH? OH . . . OKAY.
DON'T WAKE FLACA. SHE WAS PRETTY UPSET LAST NIGHT. TOOK FOREVER TO FALL ASLEEP.
ZZZZ
SHE SNORES LIKE A PUERCO.
SMELLS LIKE ONE TOO.

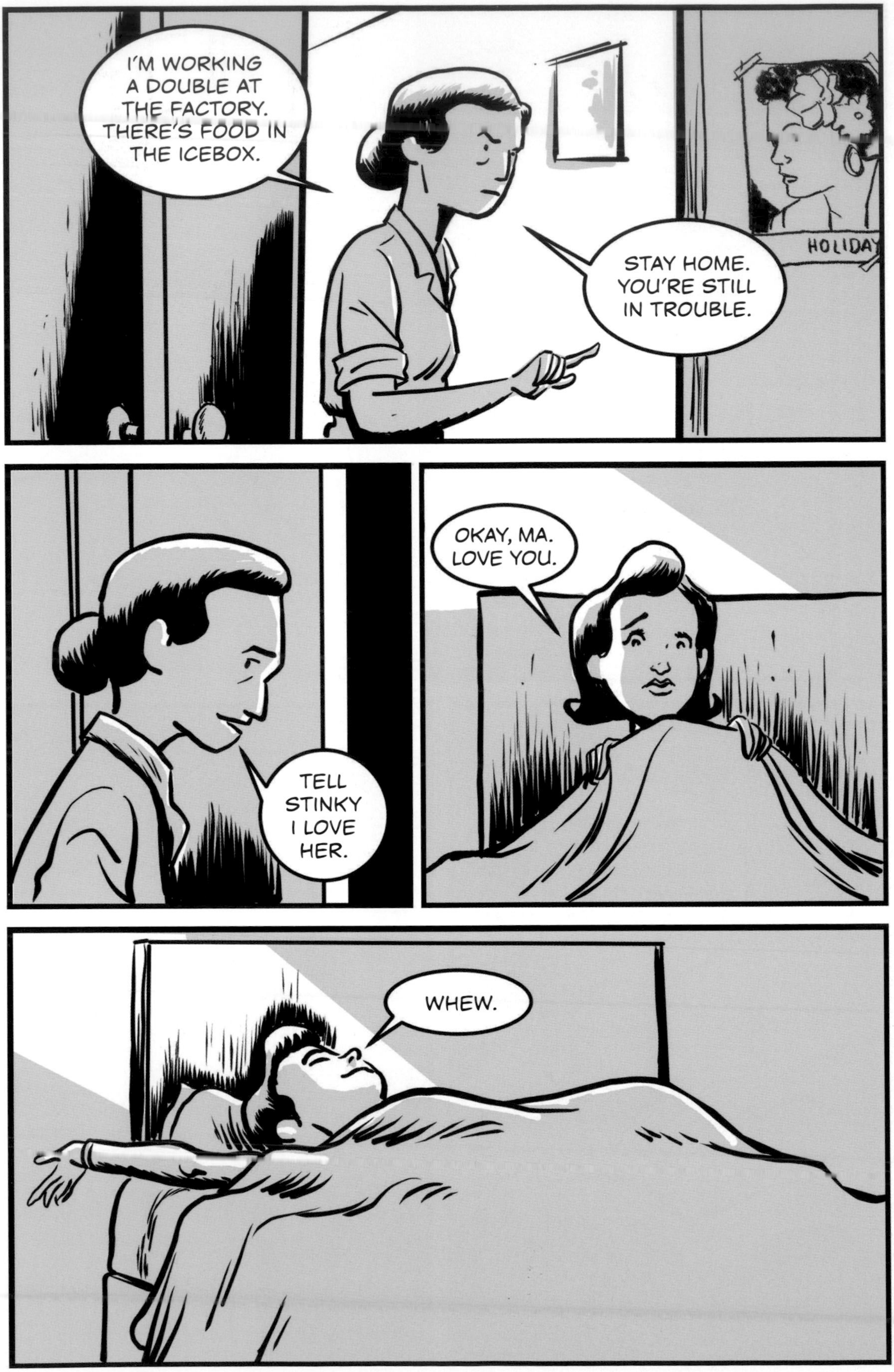
I'M WORKING A DOUBLE AT THE FACTORY. THERE'S FOOD IN THE ICEBOX.
STAY HOME. YOU'RE STILL IN TROUBLE.
HOLIDAY
TELL STINKY I LOVE HER.
OKAY, MA. LOVE YOU.
WHEW.

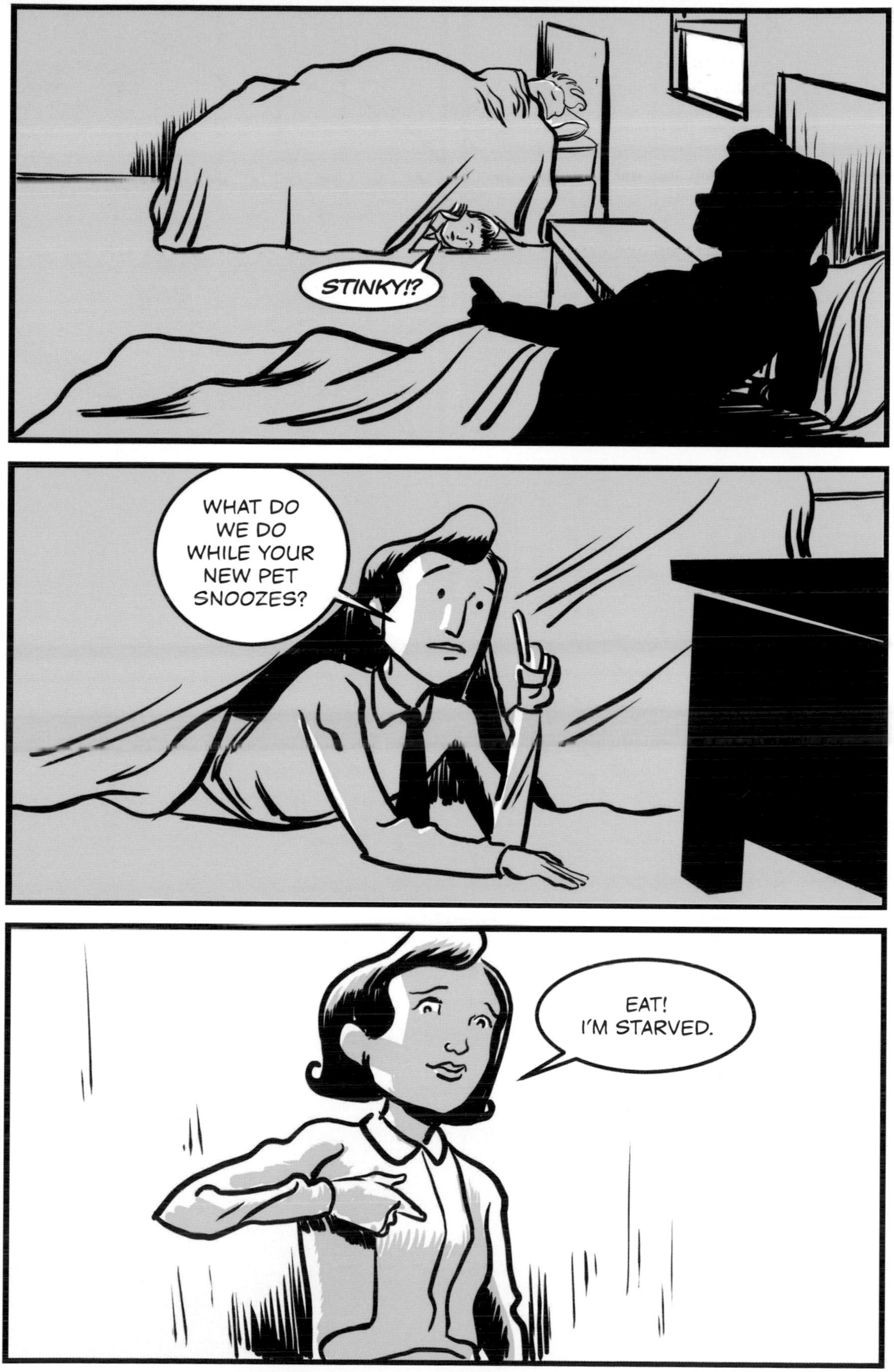
STINKY!?
WHAT DO WE DO WHILE YOUR NEW PET SNOOZES?
EAT! I'M STARVED.

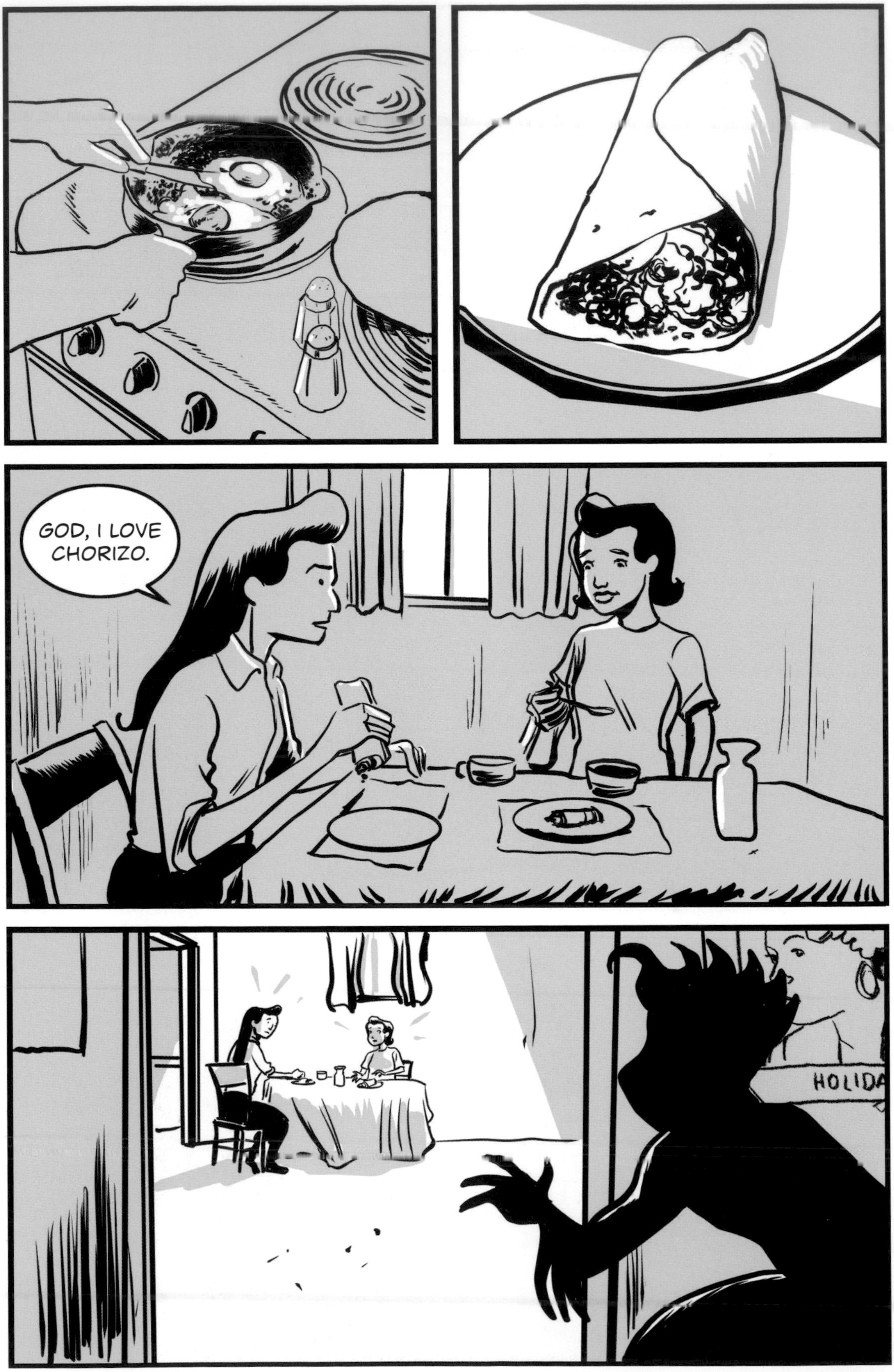
GOD, I LOVE CHORIZO.
HOLIDA

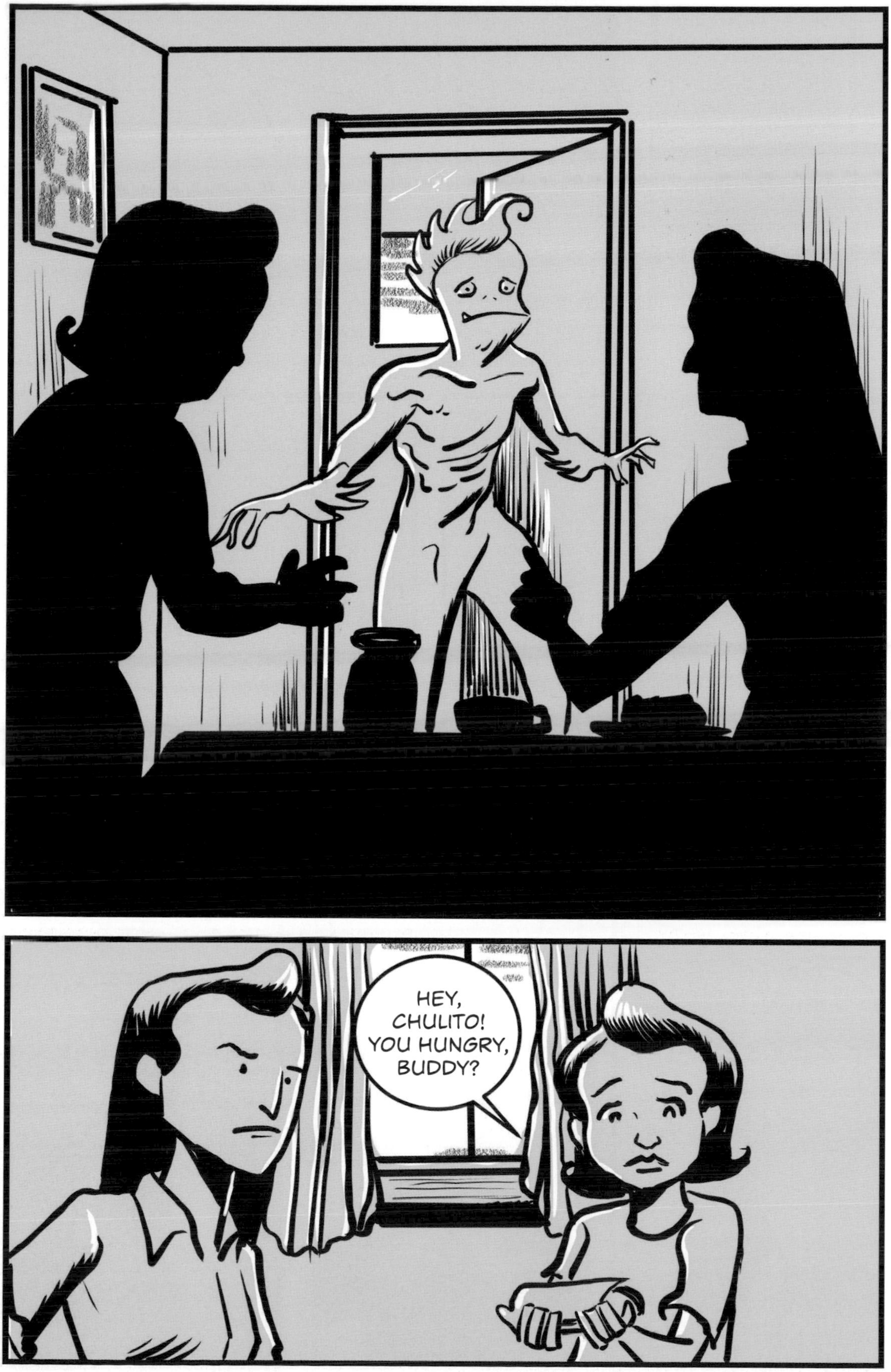
HEY, CHULITO! YOU HUNGRY, BUDDY?

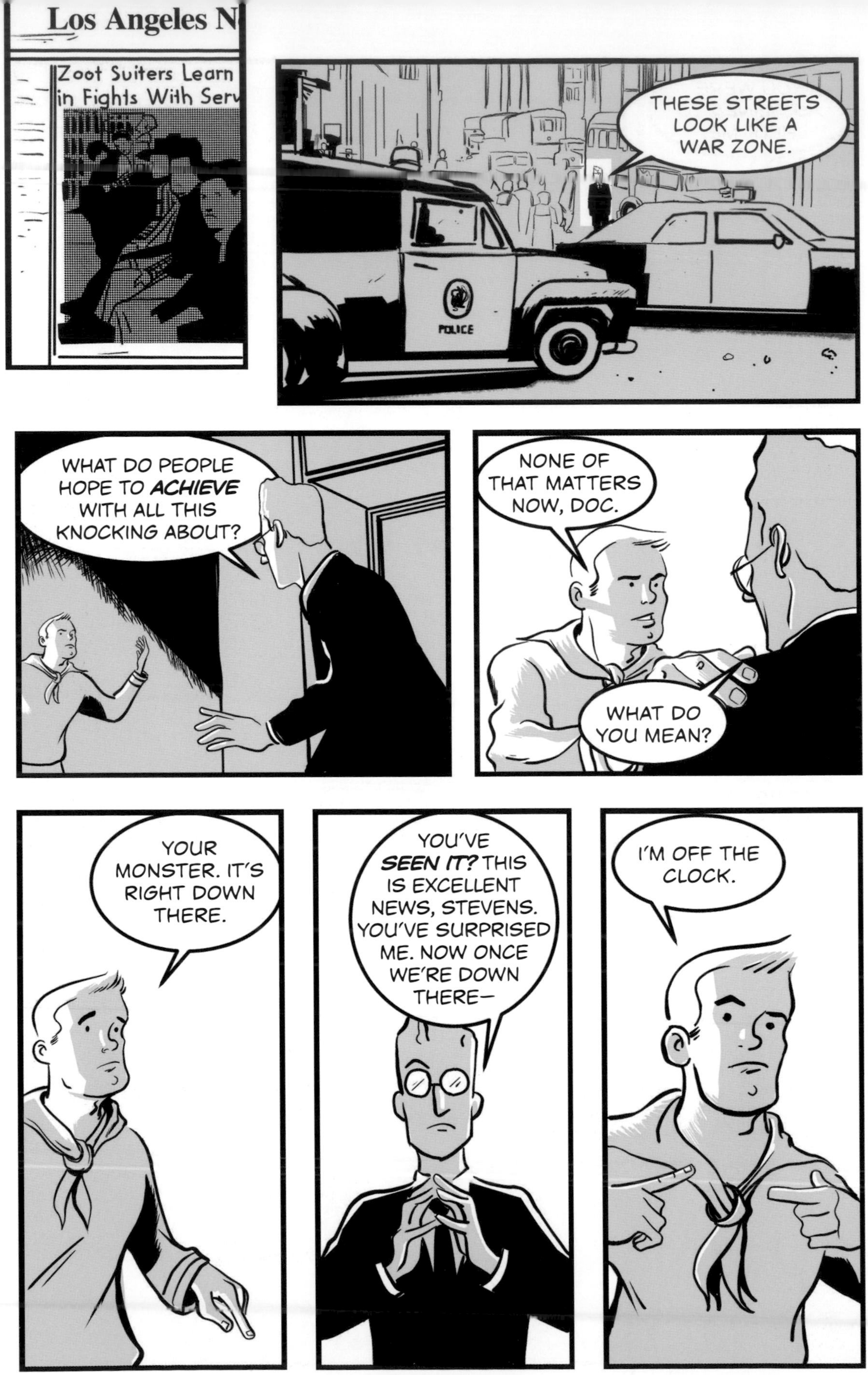
Los Angeles N
Zoot Suiters Learn
in Fights With Serv
THESE STREETS LOOK LIKE A WAR ZONE.
POLICE
WHAT DO PEOPLE HOPE TO *ACHIEVE* WITH ALL THIS KNOCKING ABOUT?
NONE OF THAT MATTERS NOW, DOC.
WHAT DO YOU MEAN?
YOUR MONSTER. IT'S RIGHT DOWN THERE.
YOU'VE *SEEN IT?* THIS IS EXCELLENT NEWS, STEVENS. YOU'VE SURPRISED ME. NOW ONCE WE'RE DOWN THERE—
I'M OFF THE CLOCK.

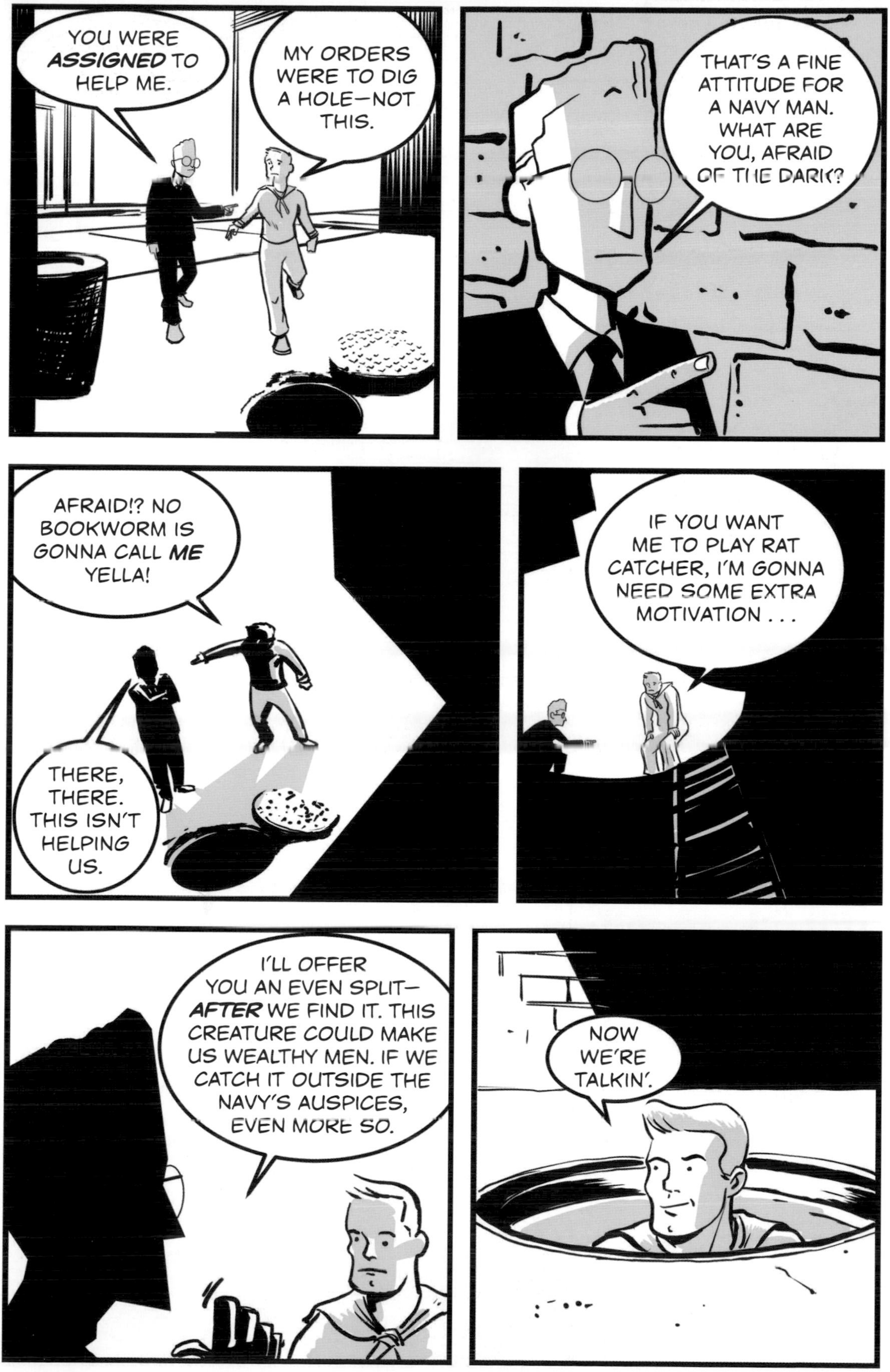
YOU WERE ASSIGNED TO HELP ME.
MY ORDERS WERE TO DIG A HOLE—NOT THIS.
THAT'S A FINE ATTITUDE FOR A NAVY MAN. WHAT ARE YOU, AFRAID OF THE DARK?
AFRAID!? NO BOOKWORM IS GONNA CALL ME YELLA!
THERE, THERE. THIS ISN'T HELPING US.
IF YOU WANT ME TO PLAY RAT CATCHER, I'M GONNA NEED SOME EXTRA MOTIVATION . . .
I'LL OFFER YOU AN EVEN SPLIT—AFTER WE FIND IT. THIS CREATURE COULD MAKE US WEALTHY MEN. IF WE CATCH IT OUTSIDE THE NAVY'S AUSPICES, EVEN MORE SO.
NOW WE'RE TALKIN'.

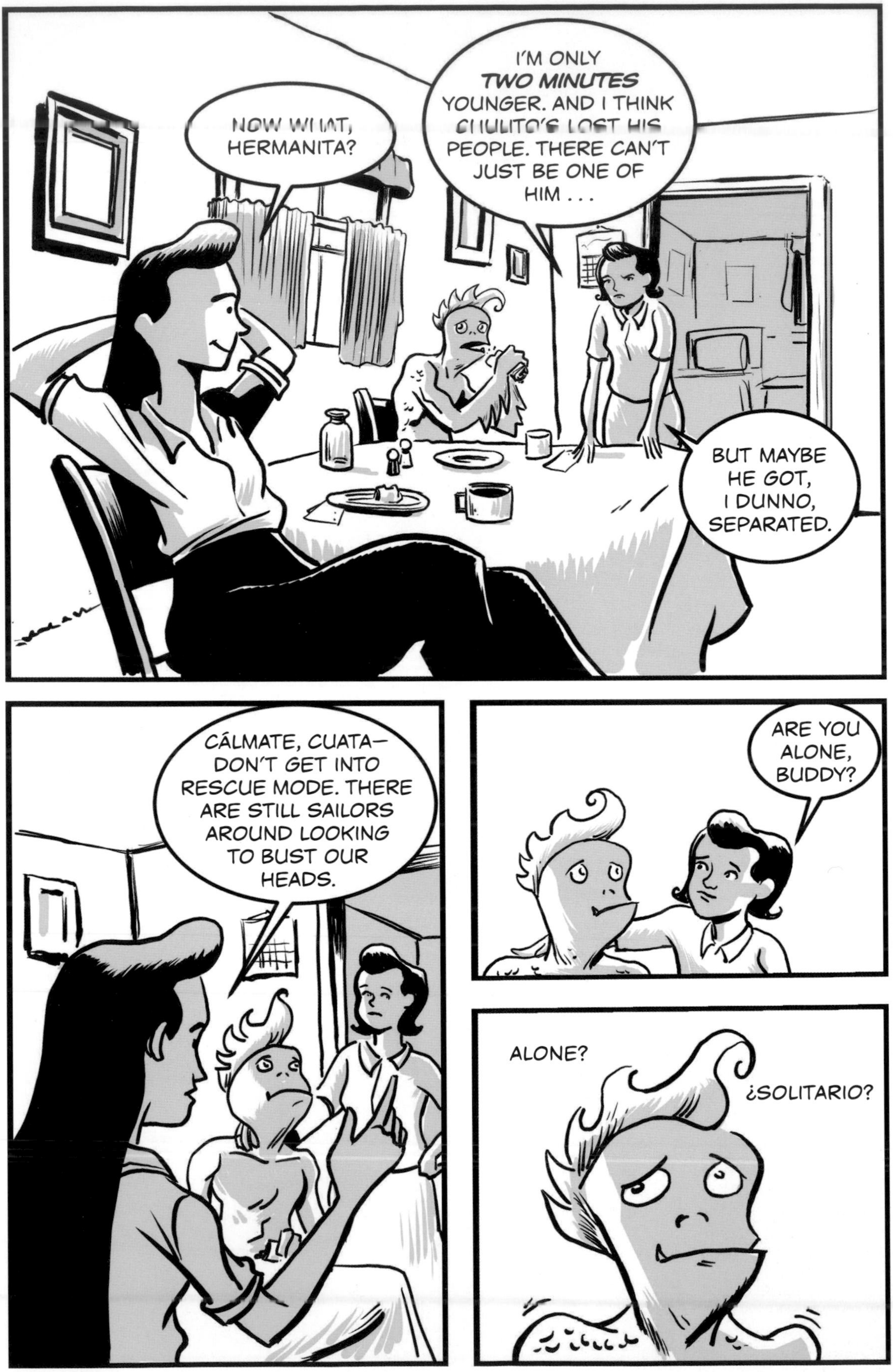
NOW WHAT, HERMANITA?
I'M ONLY *TWO MINUTES* YOUNGER. AND I THINK CHULITO'S LOST HIS PEOPLE. THERE CAN'T JUST BE ONE OF HIM . . .
BUT MAYBE HE GOT, I DUNNO, SEPARATED.
CÁLMATE, CUATA— DON'T GET INTO RESCUE MODE. THERE ARE STILL SAILORS AROUND LOOKING TO BUST OUR HEADS.
ARE YOU ALONE, BUDDY?
ALONE?
¿SOLITARIO?

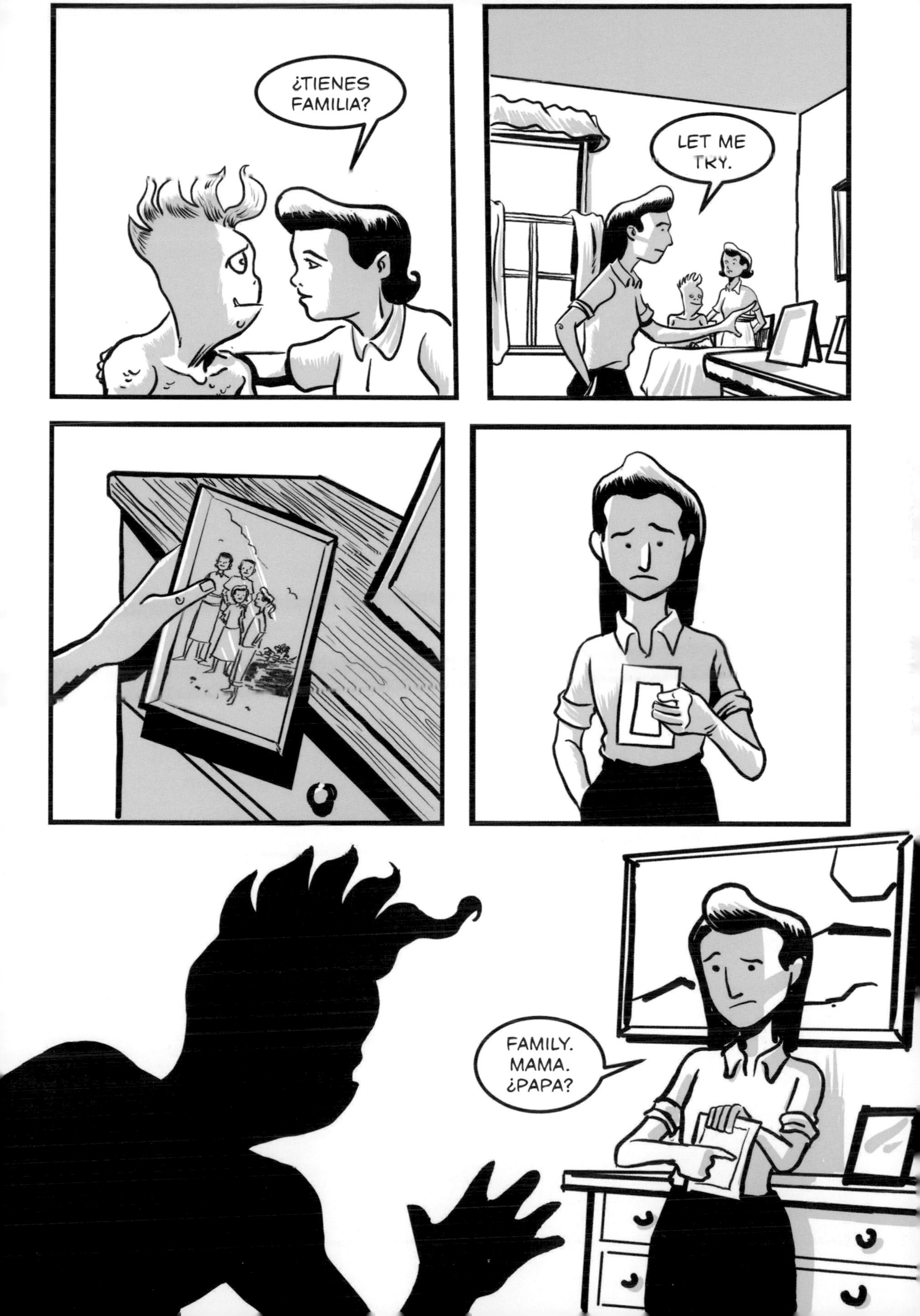
¿TIENES FAMILIA?
LET ME TRY.
FAMILY. MAMA. ¿PAPA?

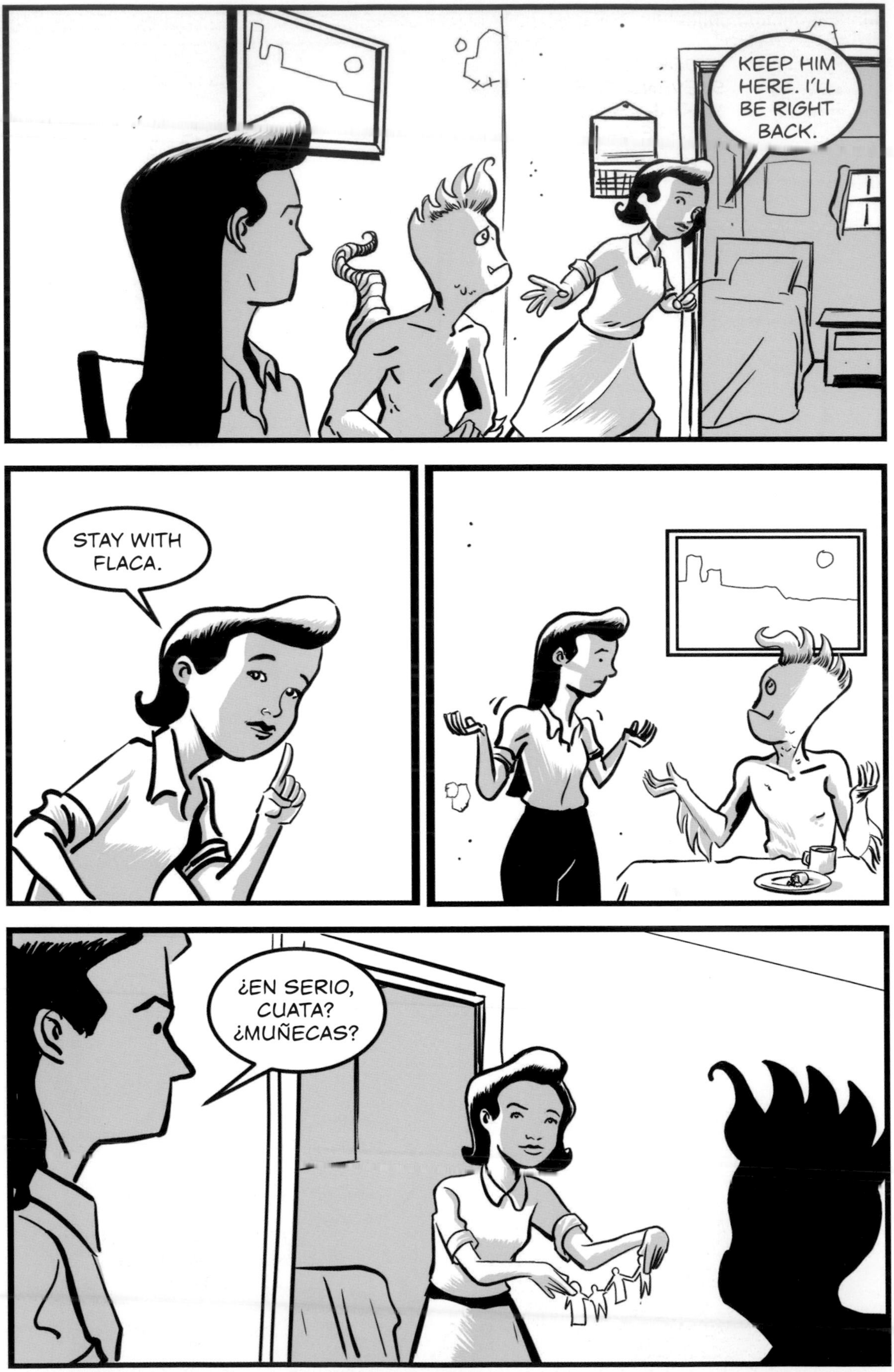
KEEP HIM HERE. I'LL BE RIGHT BACK.
STAY WITH FLACA.
¿EN SERIO, CUATA? ¿MUÑECAS?

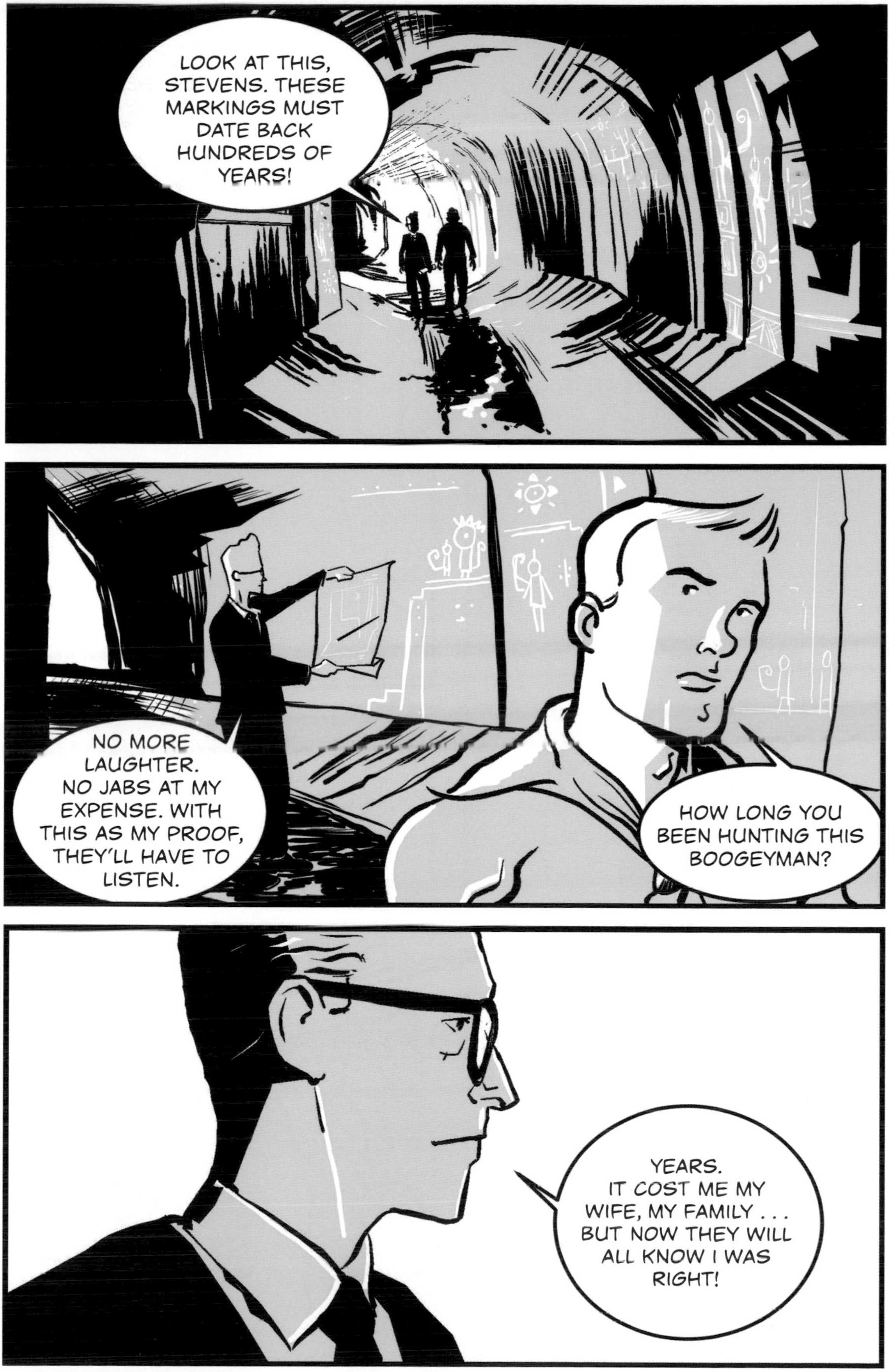
LOOK AT THIS, STEVENS. THESE MARKINGS MUST DATE BACK HUNDREDS OF YEARS!
NO MORE LAUGHTER. NO JABS AT MY EXPENSE. WITH THIS AS MY PROOF, THEY'LL HAVE TO LISTEN.
HOW LONG YOU BEEN HUNTING THIS BOOGEYMAN?
YEARS. IT COST ME MY WIFE, MY FAMILY . . . BUT NOW THEY WILL ALL KNOW I WAS RIGHT!

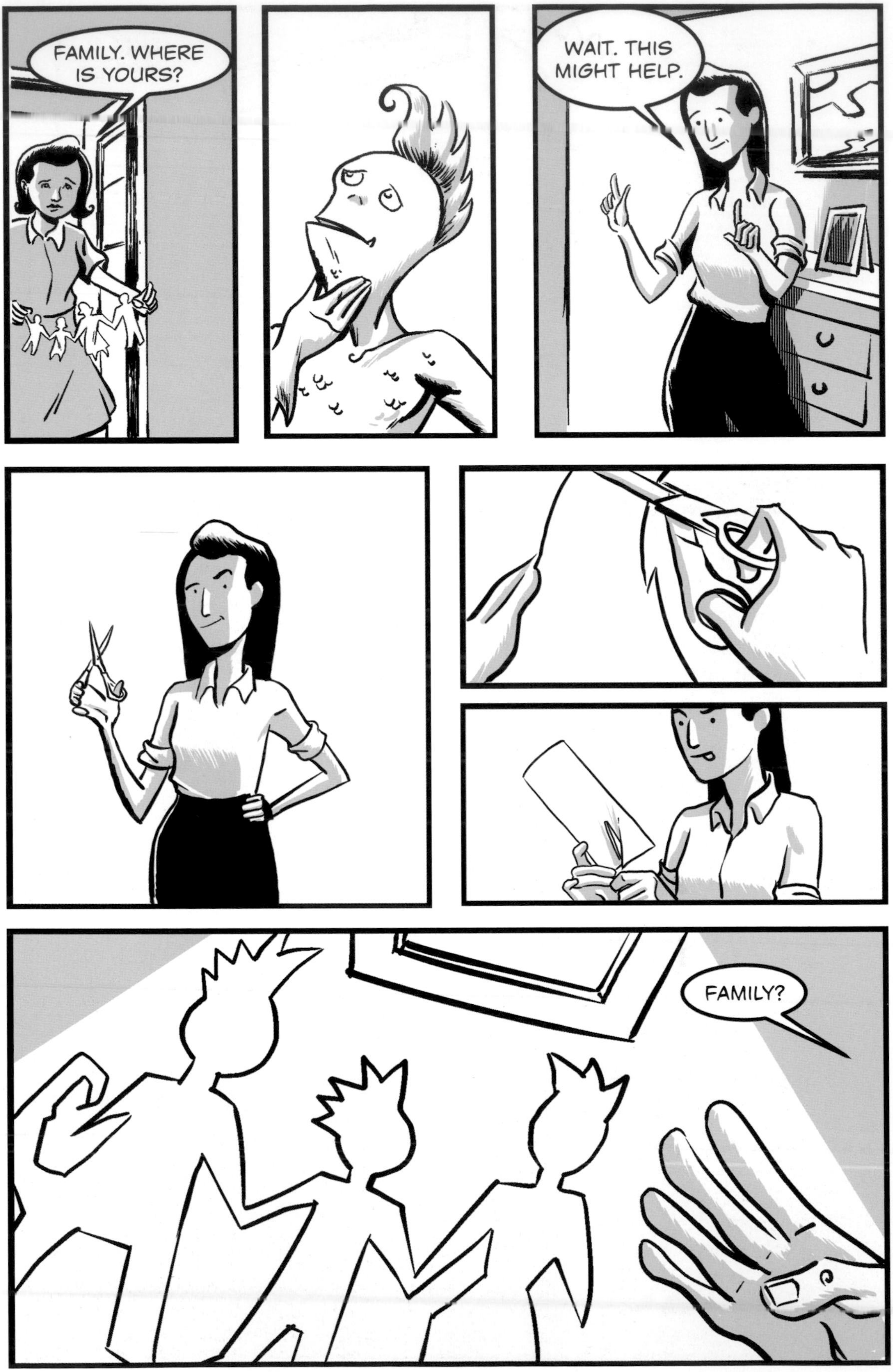
FAMILY. WHERE IS YOURS?
WAIT. THIS MIGHT HELP.
FAMILY?

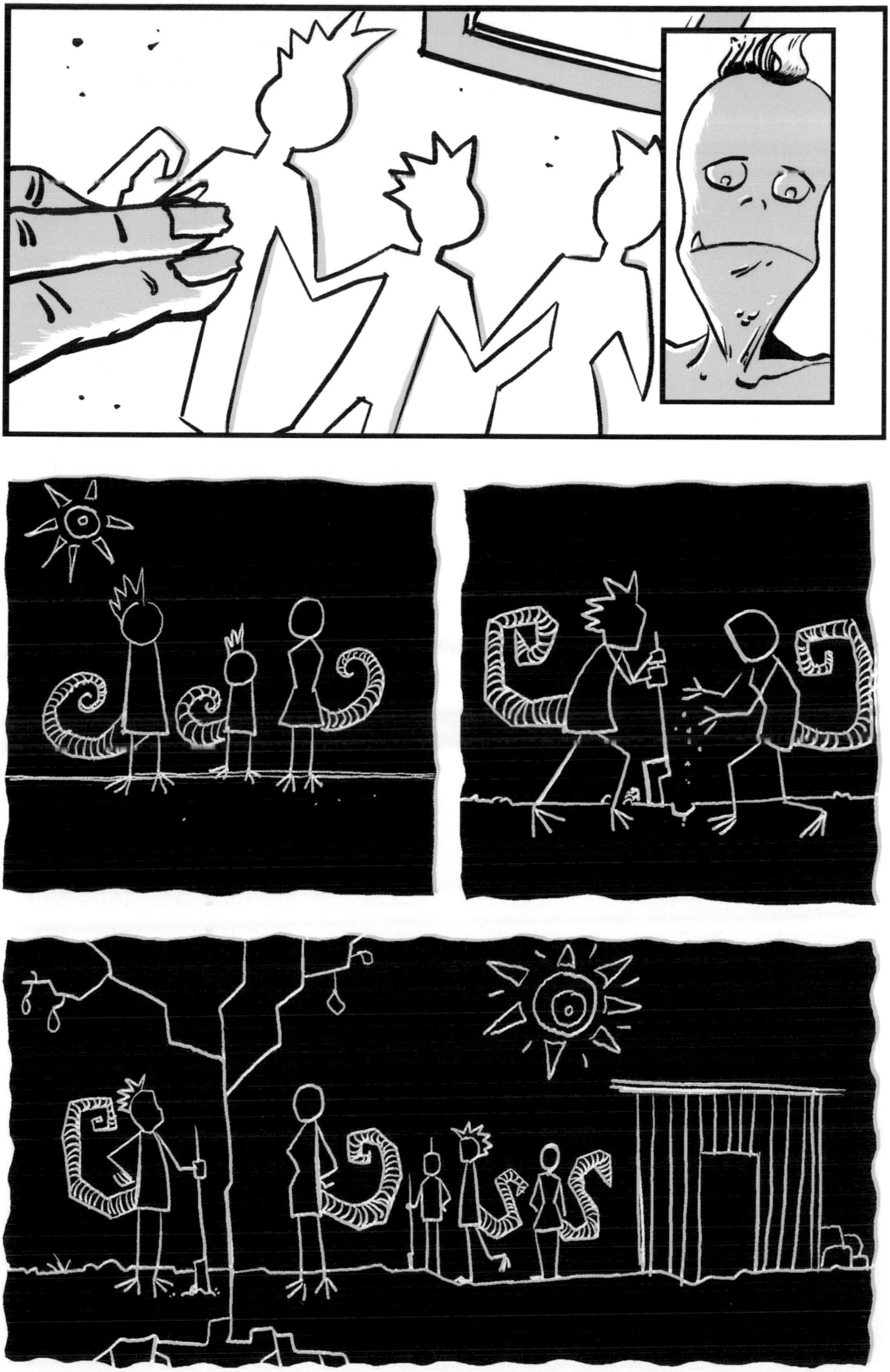

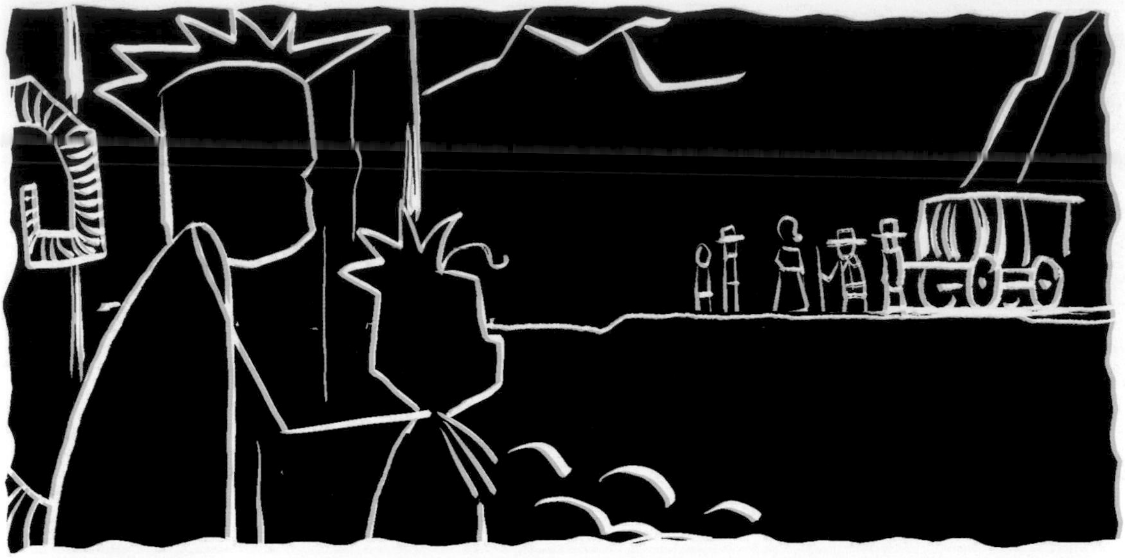

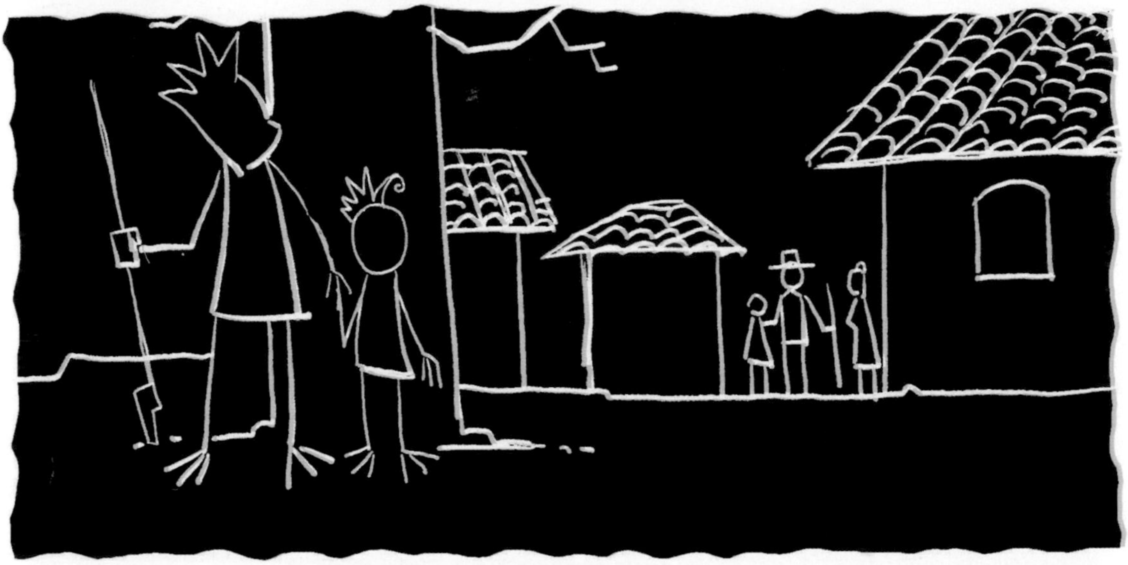

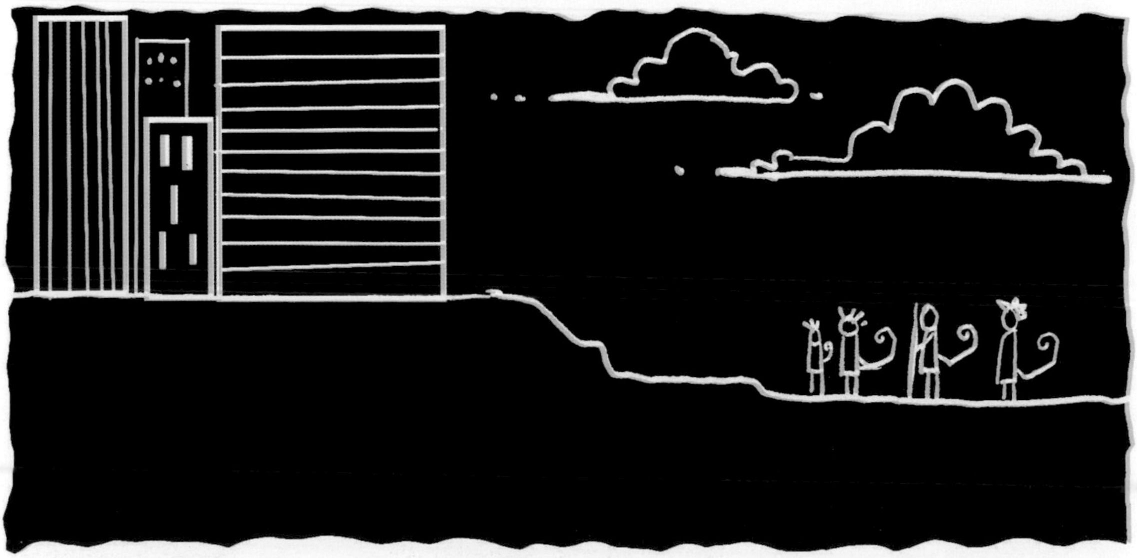

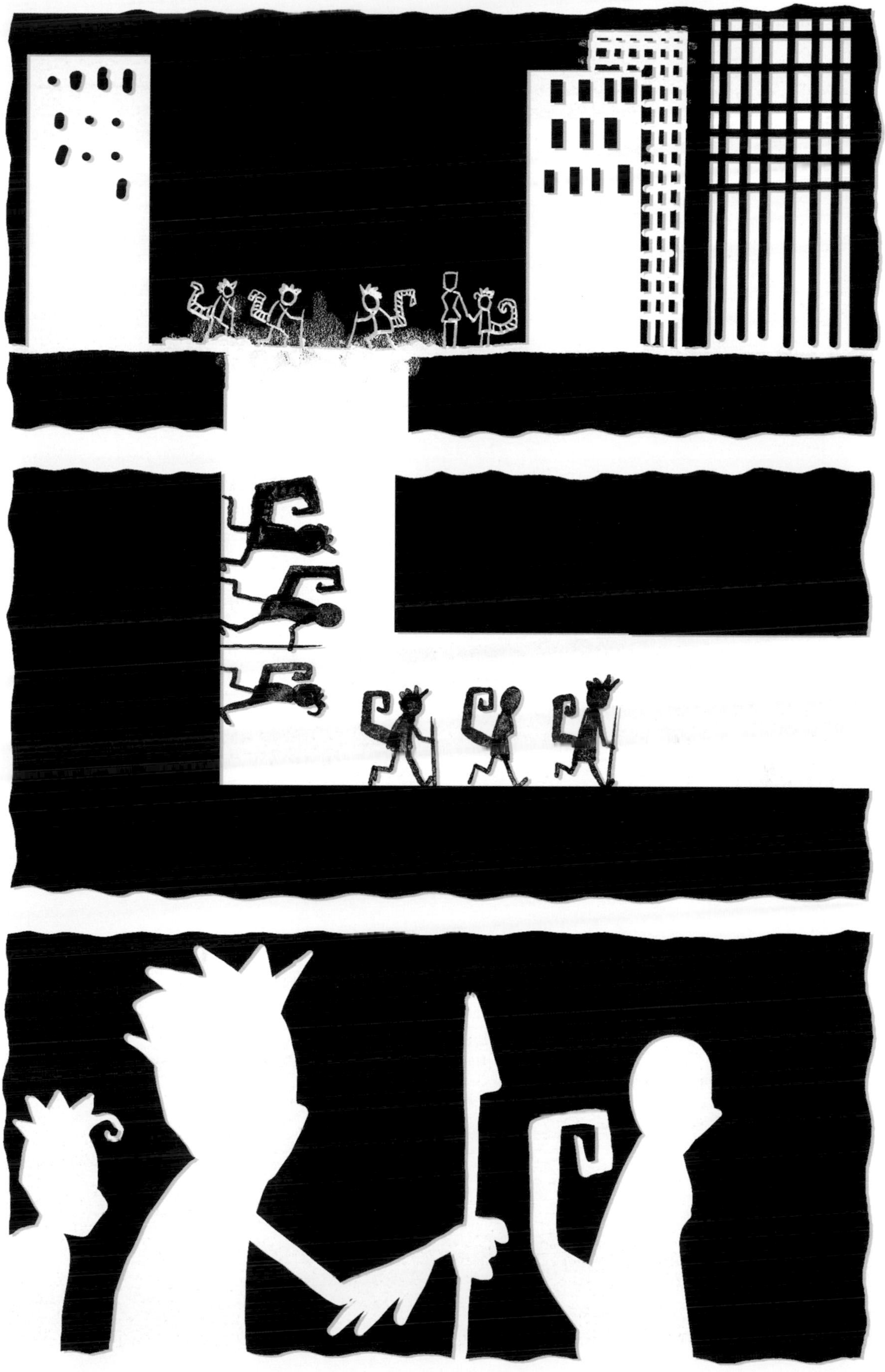

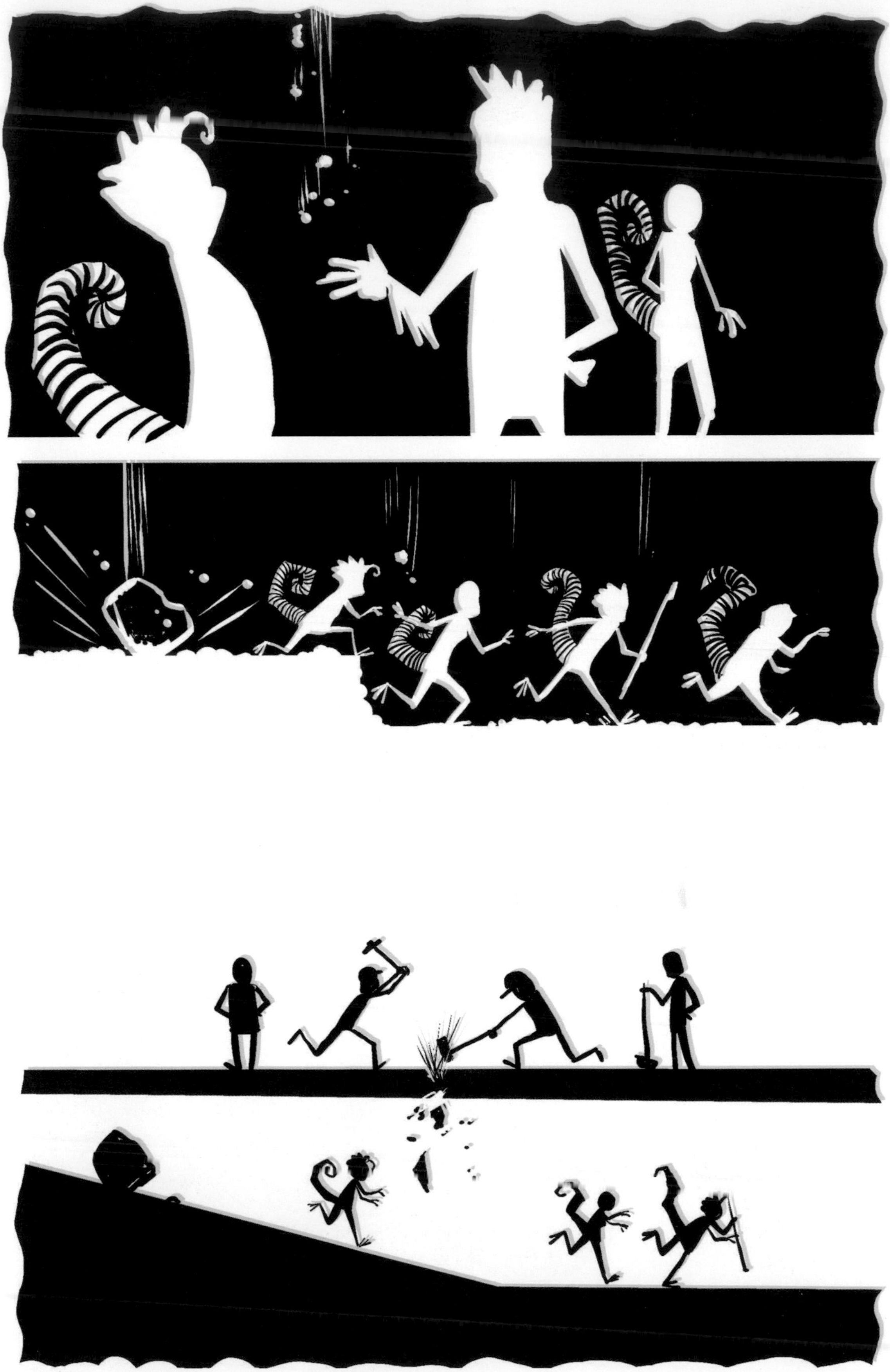

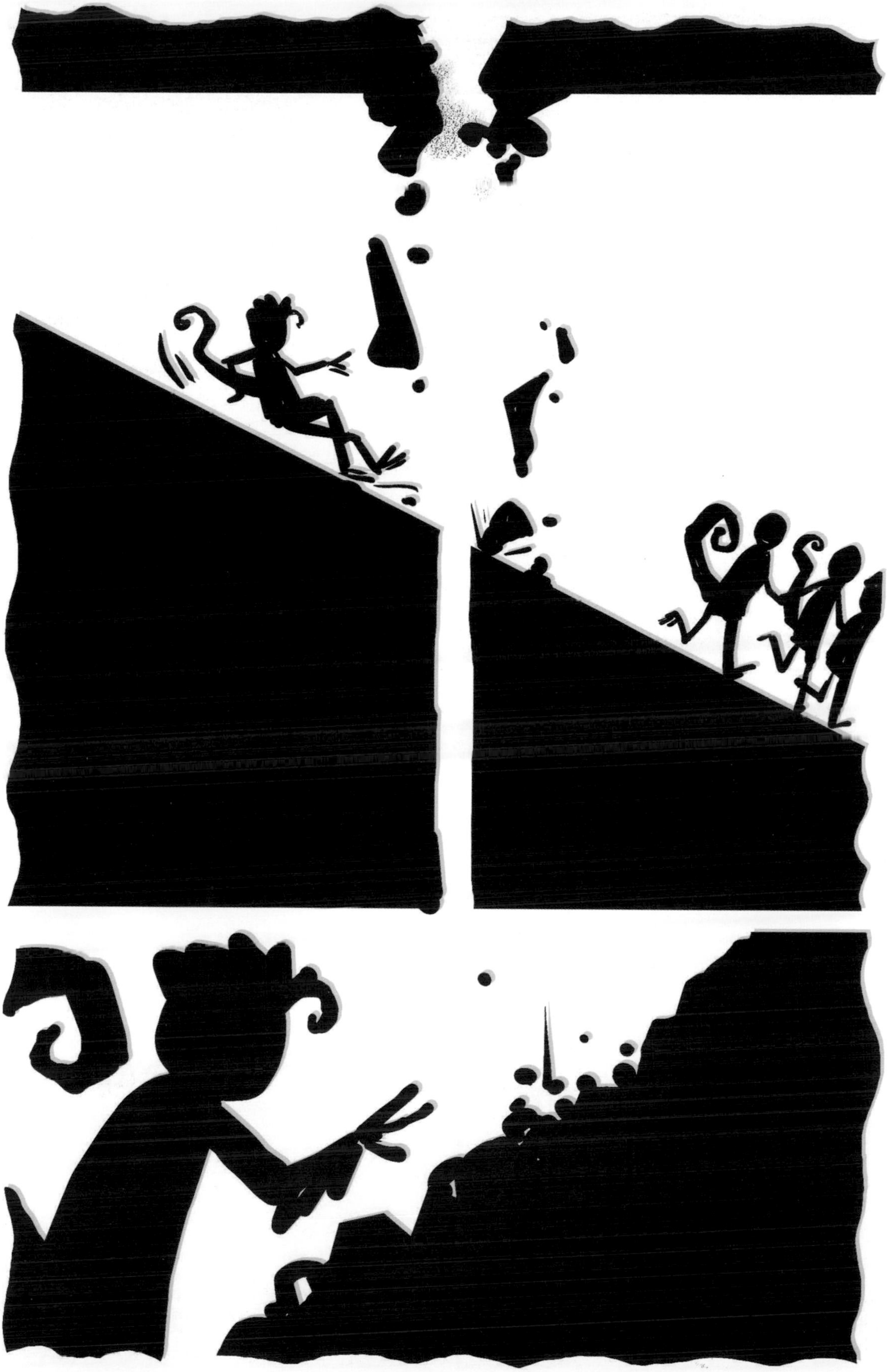

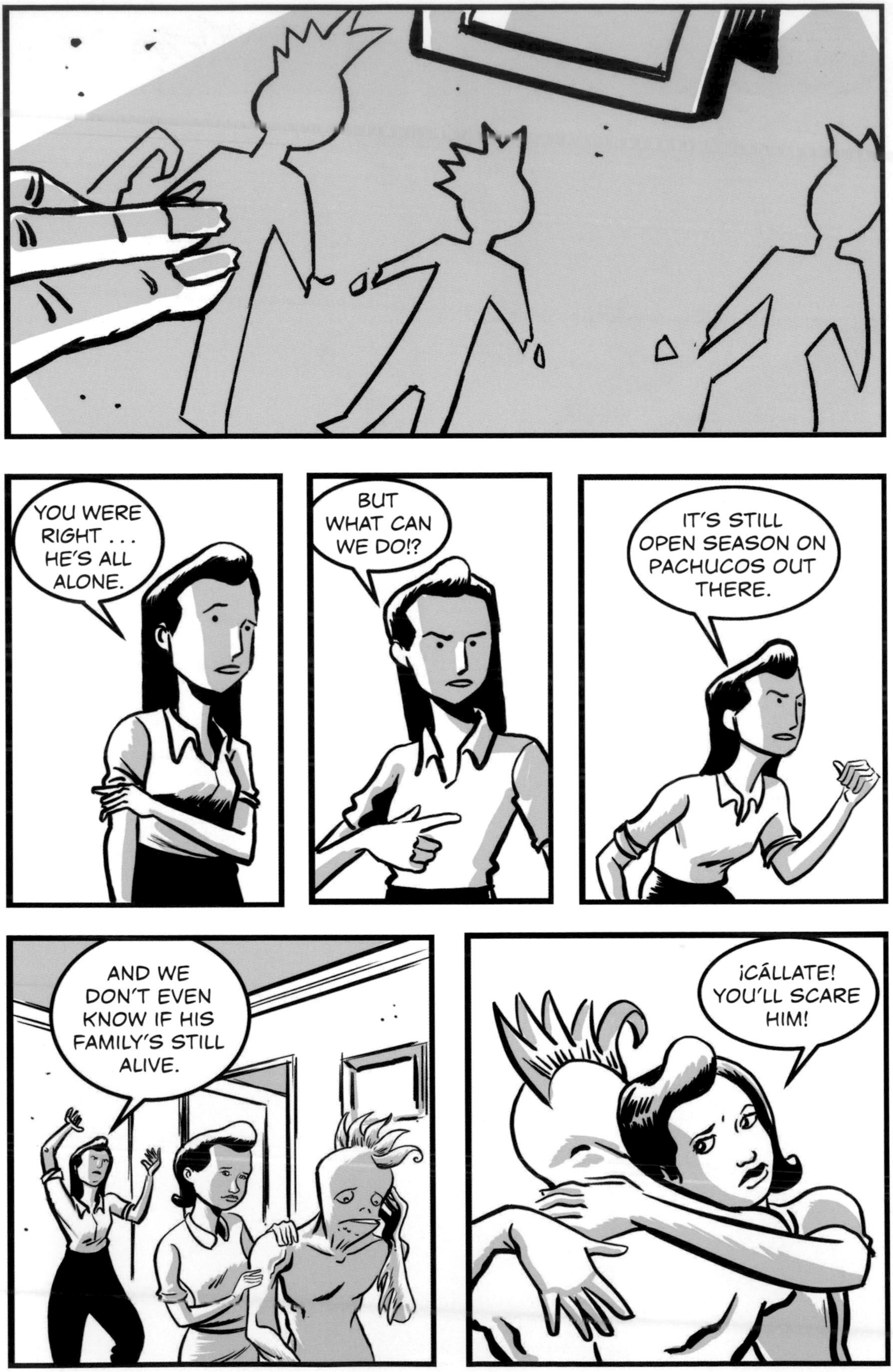
YOU WERE RIGHT . . . HE'S ALL ALONE.
BUT WHAT CAN WE DO!?
IT'S STILL OPEN SEASON ON PACHUCOS OUT THERE.
AND WE DON'T EVEN KNOW IF HIS FAMILY'S STILL ALIVE.
¡CÁLLATE! YOU'LL SCARE HIM!

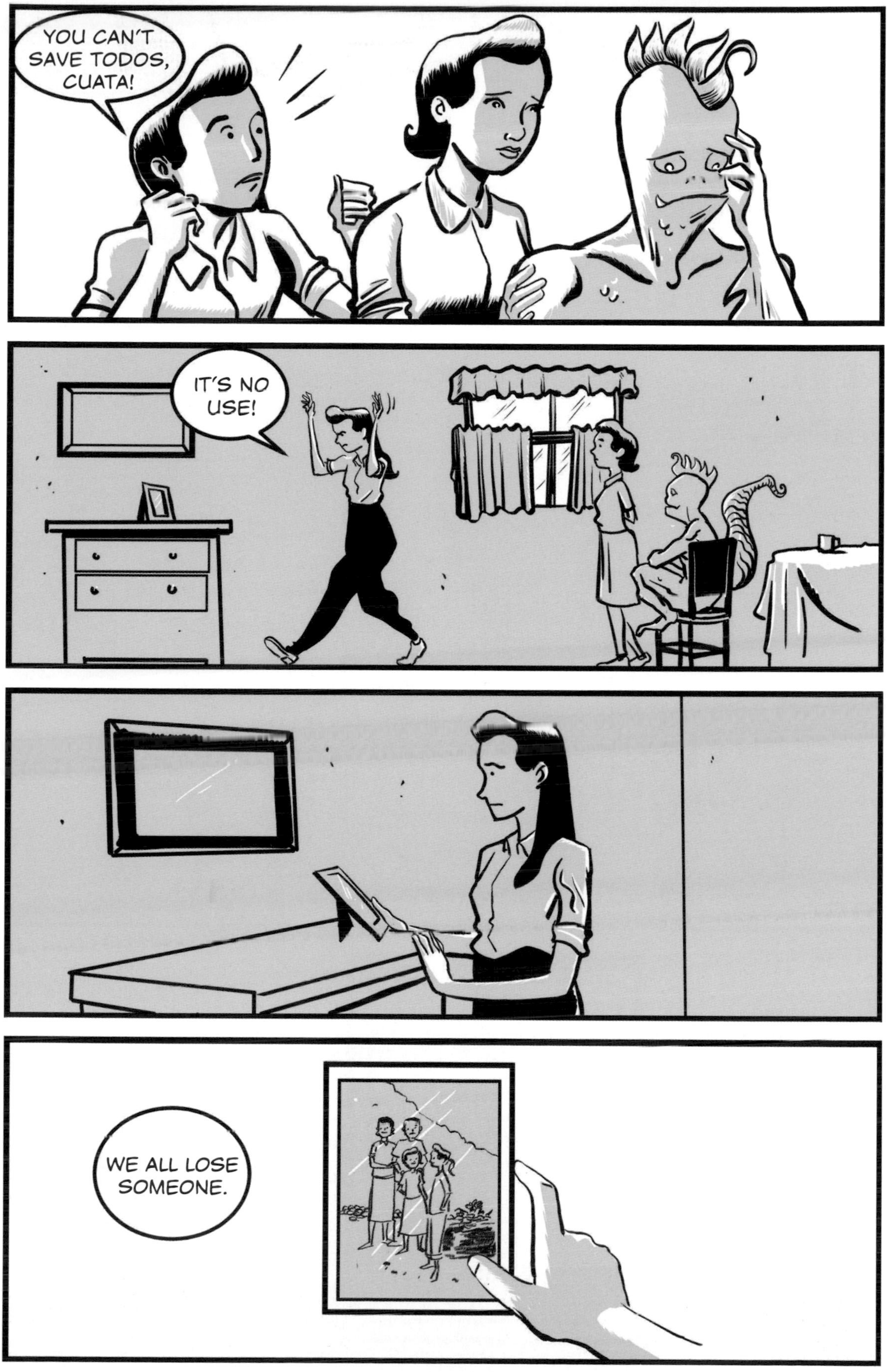
YOU CAN'T SAVE TODOS, CUATA!
IT'S NO USE!
WE ALL LOSE SOMEONE.

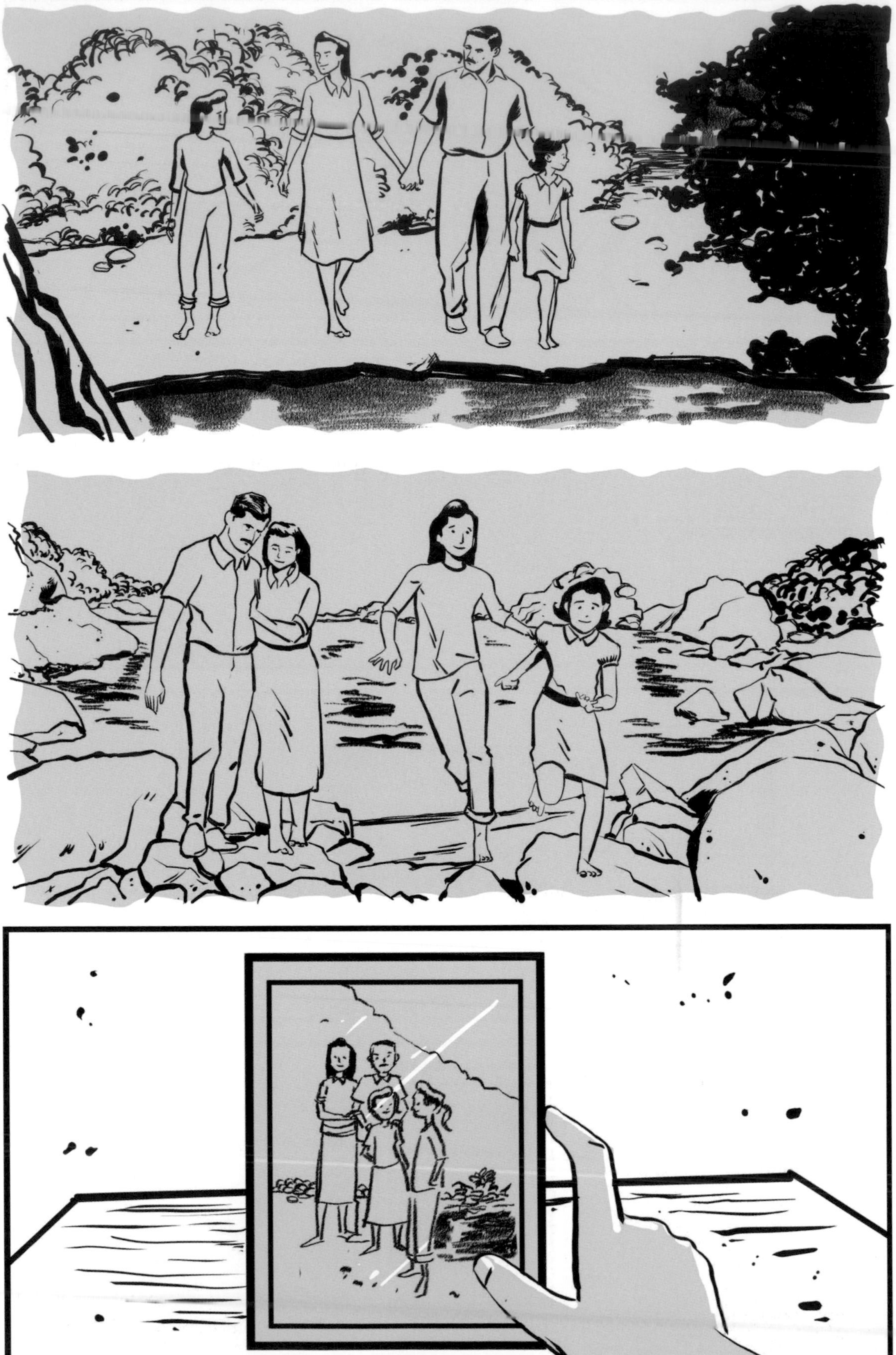

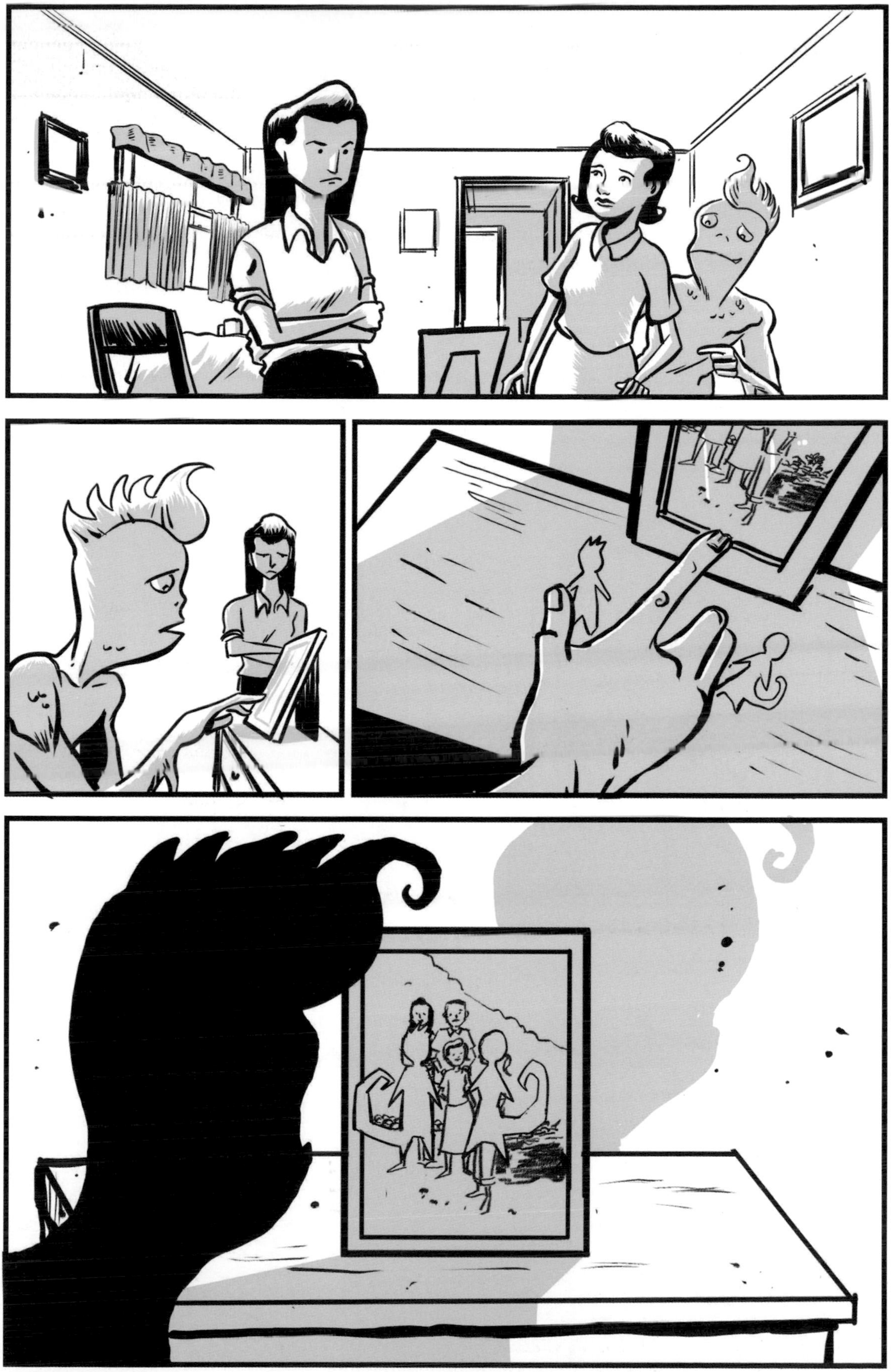

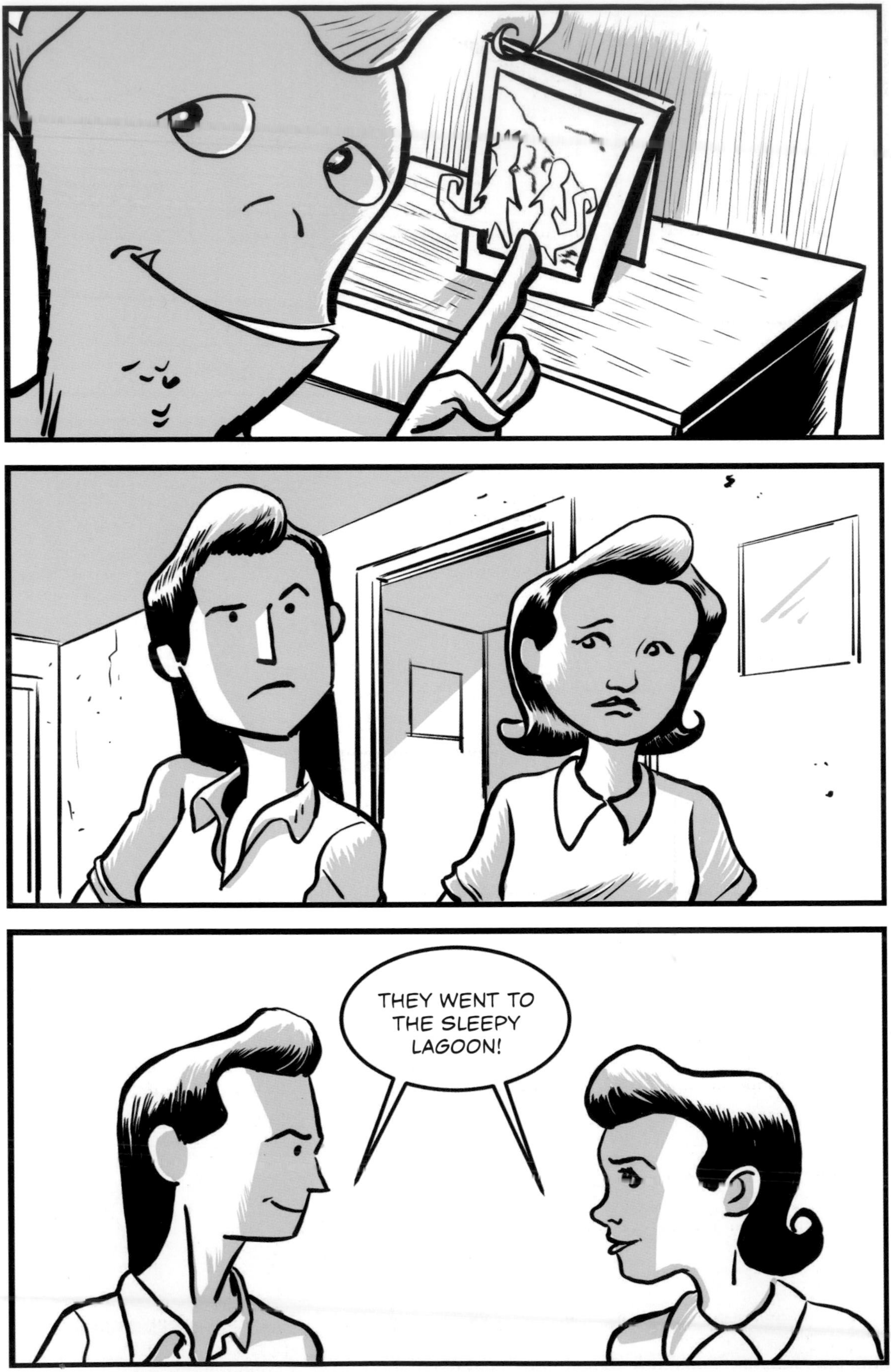
THEY WENT TO THE SLEEPY LAGOON!

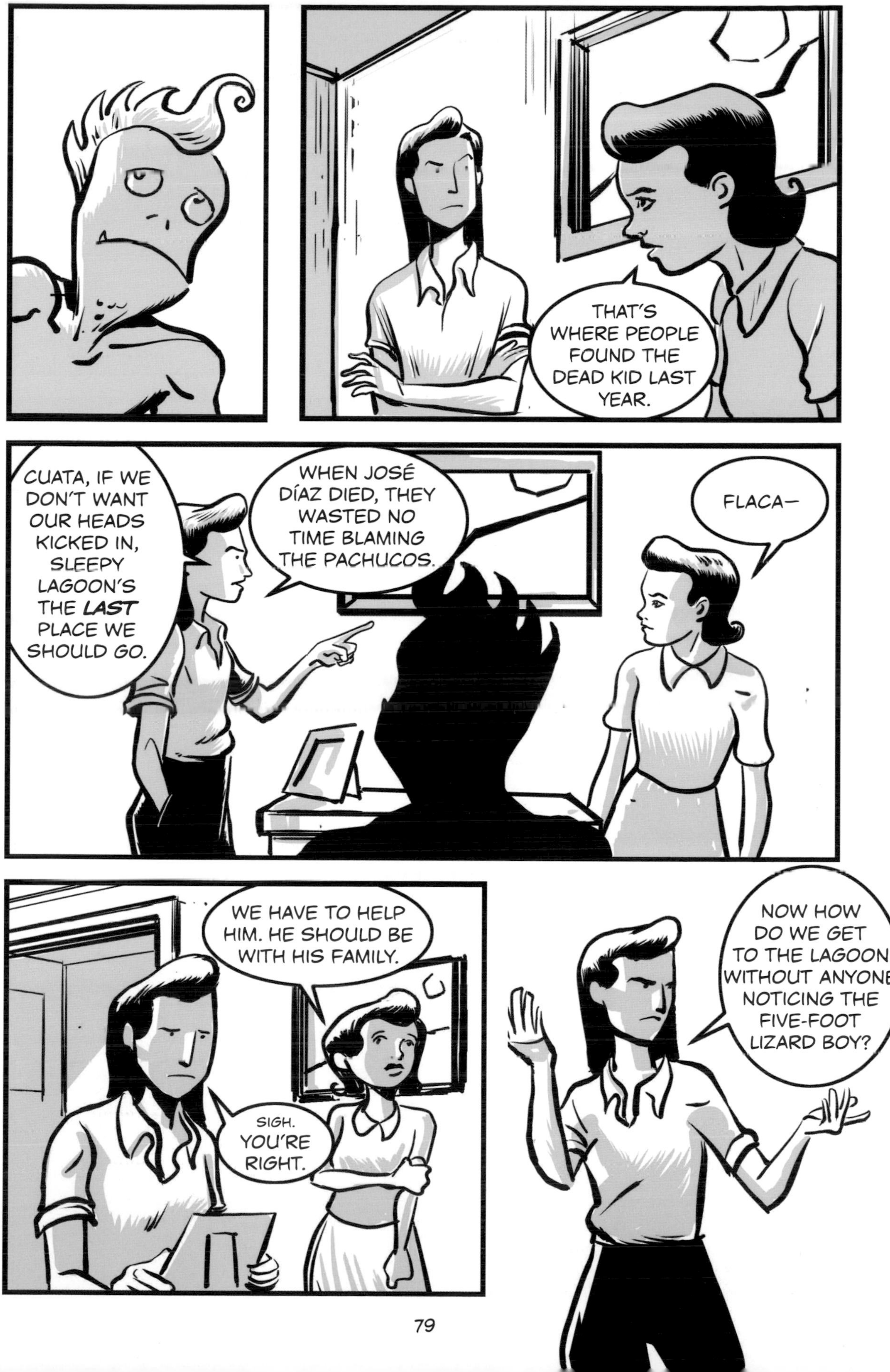
THAT'S WHERE PEOPLE FOUND THE DEAD KID LAST YEAR.
CUATA, IF WE DON'T WANT OUR HEADS KICKED IN, SLEEPY LAGOON'S THE *LAST* PLACE WE SHOULD GO.
WHEN JOSÉ DÍAZ DIED, THEY WASTED NO TIME BLAMING THE PACHUCOS.
FLACA—
WE HAVE TO HELP HIM. HE SHOULD BE WITH HIS FAMILY.
SIGH. YOU'RE RIGHT.
NOW HOW DO WE GET TO THE LAGOON WITHOUT ANYONE NOTICING THE FIVE-FOOT LIZARD BOY?

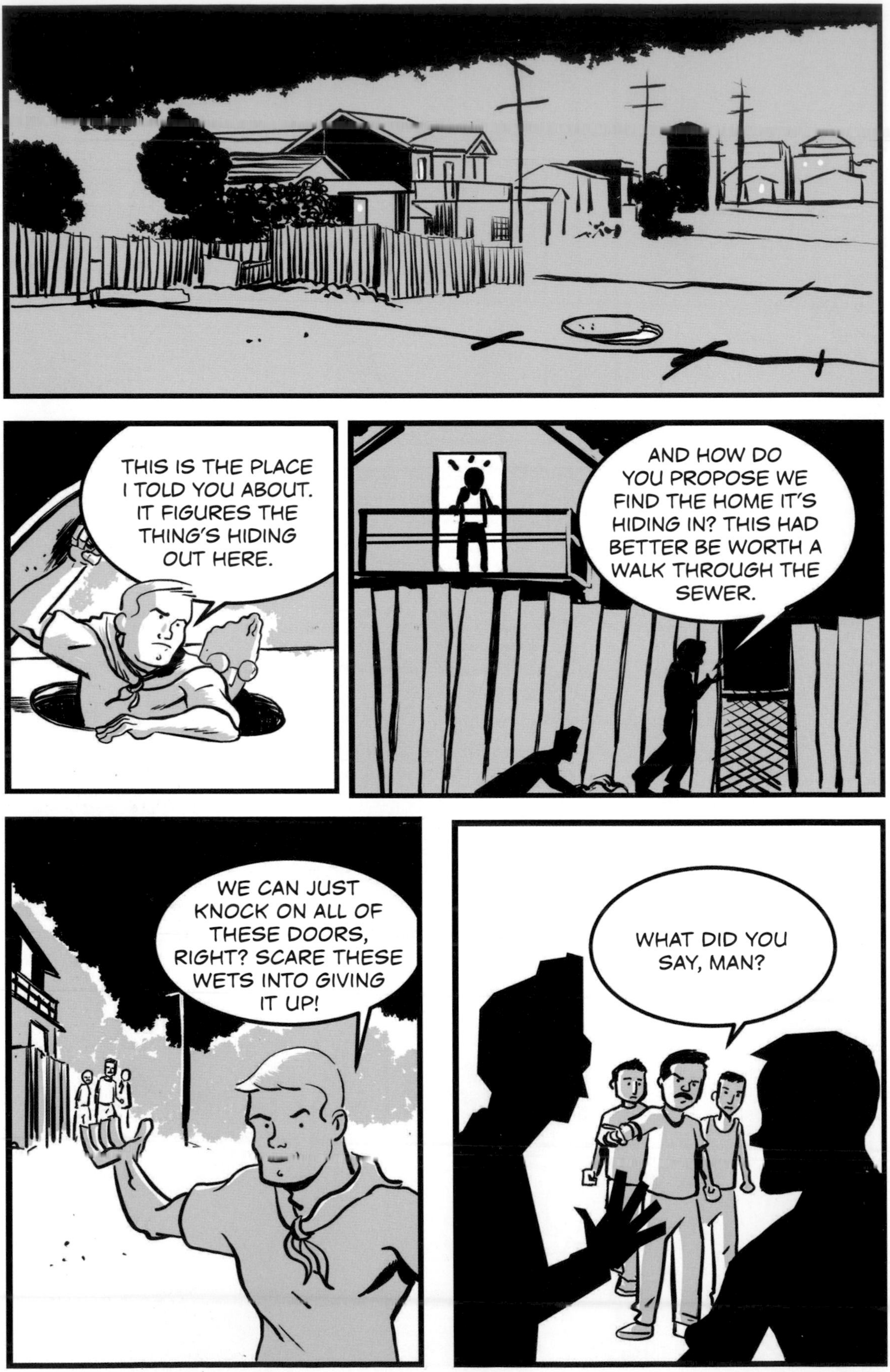
THIS IS THE PLACE I TOLD YOU ABOUT. IT FIGURES THE THING'S HIDING OUT HERE.
AND HOW DO YOU PROPOSE WE FIND THE HOME IT'S HIDING IN? THIS HAD BETTER BE WORTH A WALK THROUGH THE SEWER.
WE CAN JUST KNOCK ON ALL OF THESE DOORS, RIGHT? SCARE THESE WETS INTO GIVING IT UP!
WHAT DID YOU SAY, MAN?

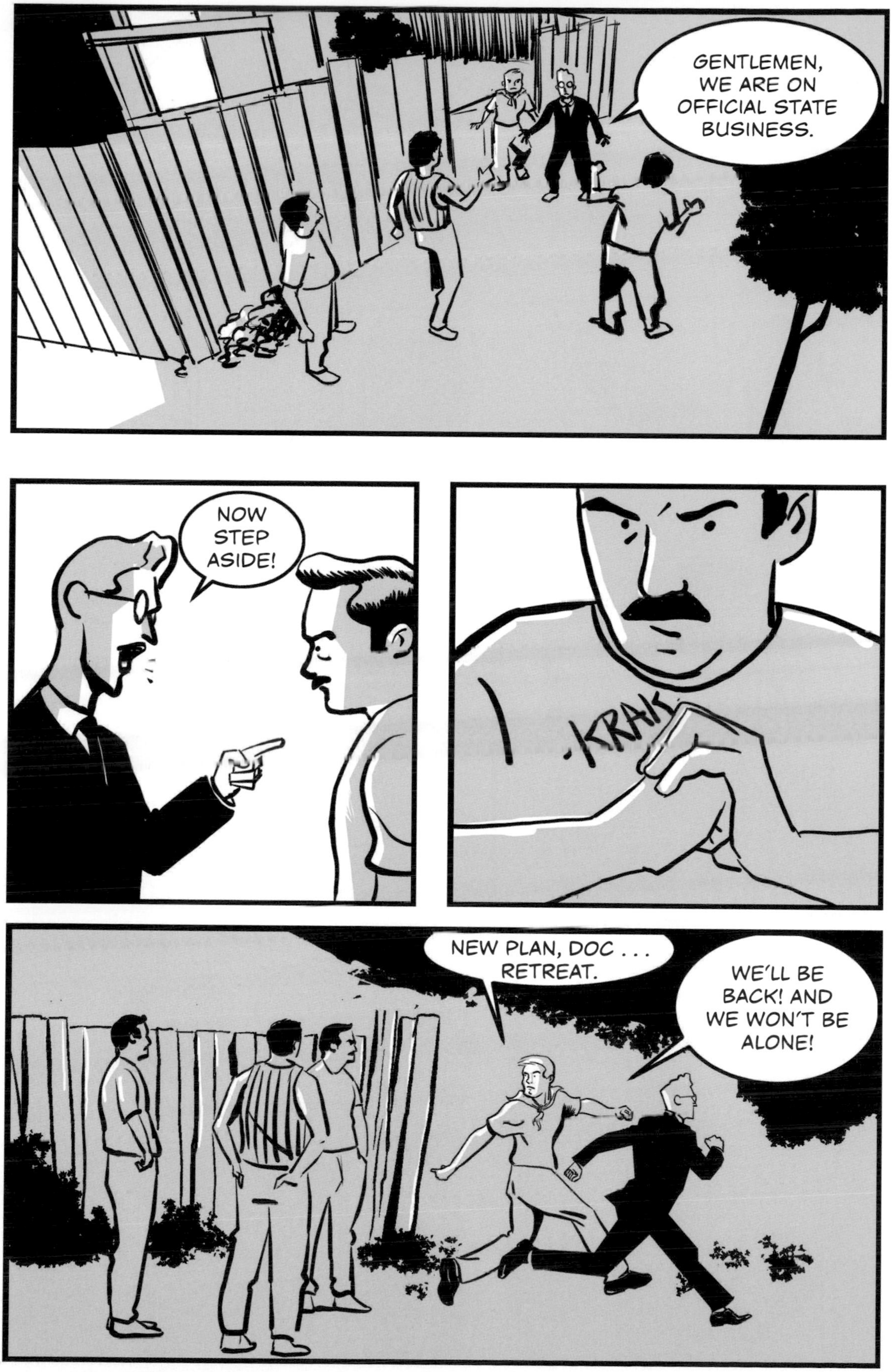
GENTLEMEN, WE ARE ON OFFICIAL STATE BUSINESS.
NOW STEP ASIDE!
KRAK
NEW PLAN, DOC . . . RETREAT.
WE'LL BE BACK! AND WE WON'T BE ALONE!

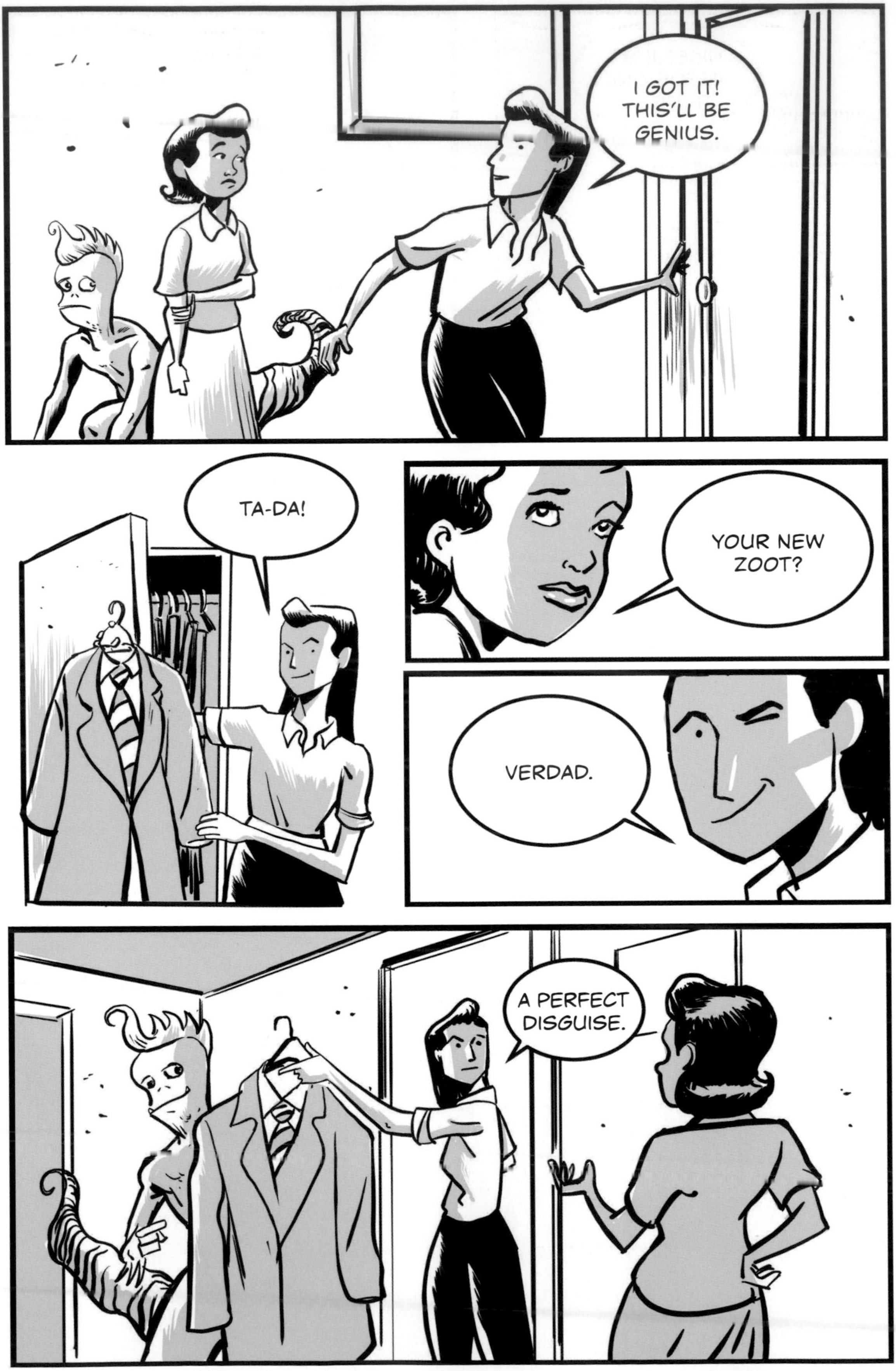
I GOT IT! THIS'LL BE GENIUS.
TA-DA!
YOUR NEW ZOOT?
VERDAD.
A PERFECT DISGUISE.

NICE! JUST NEEDS ONE THING . . .

ACCESSORIES!

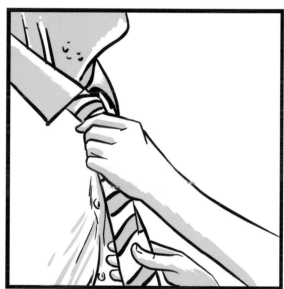

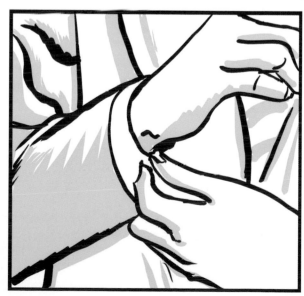

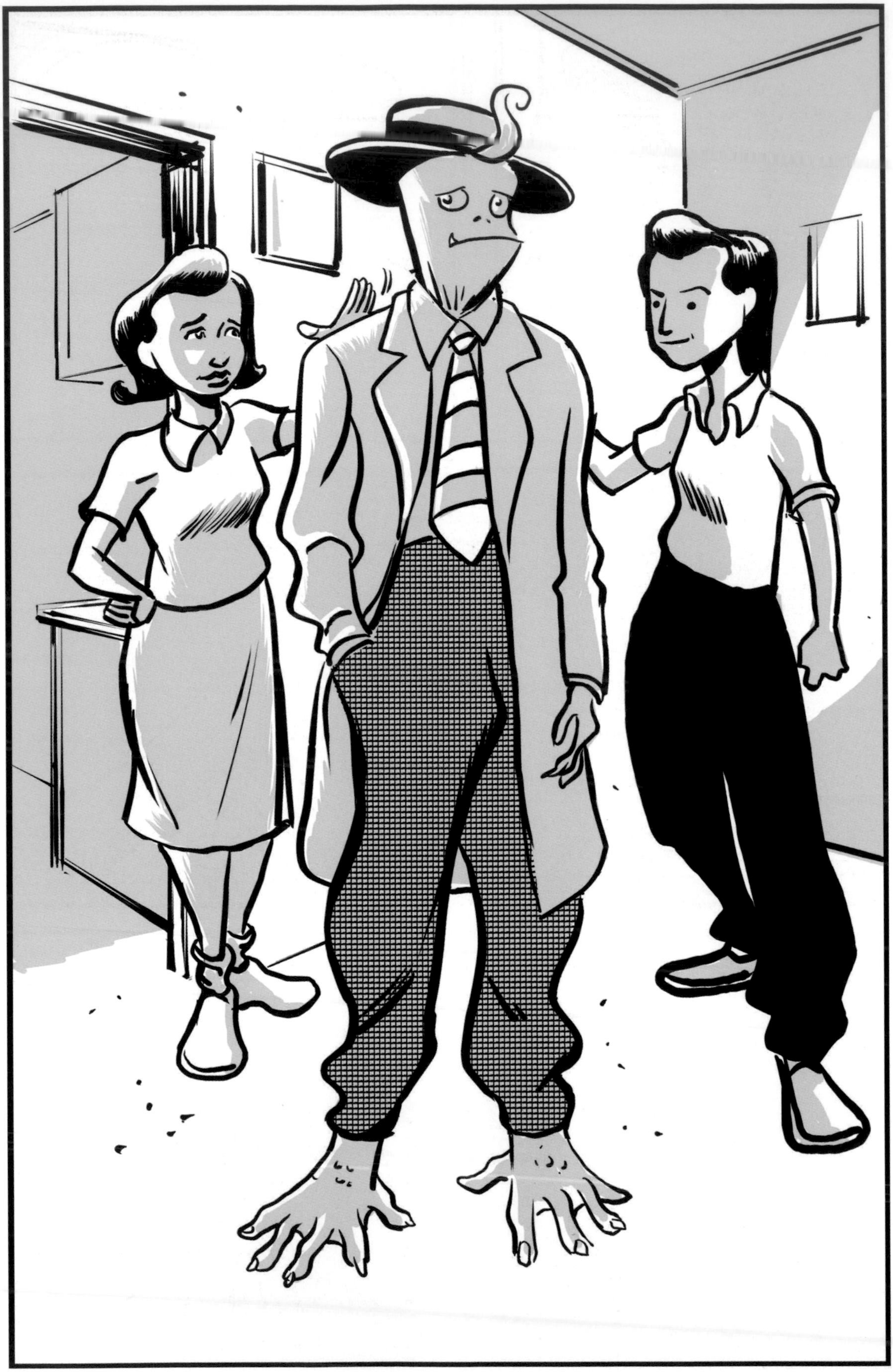

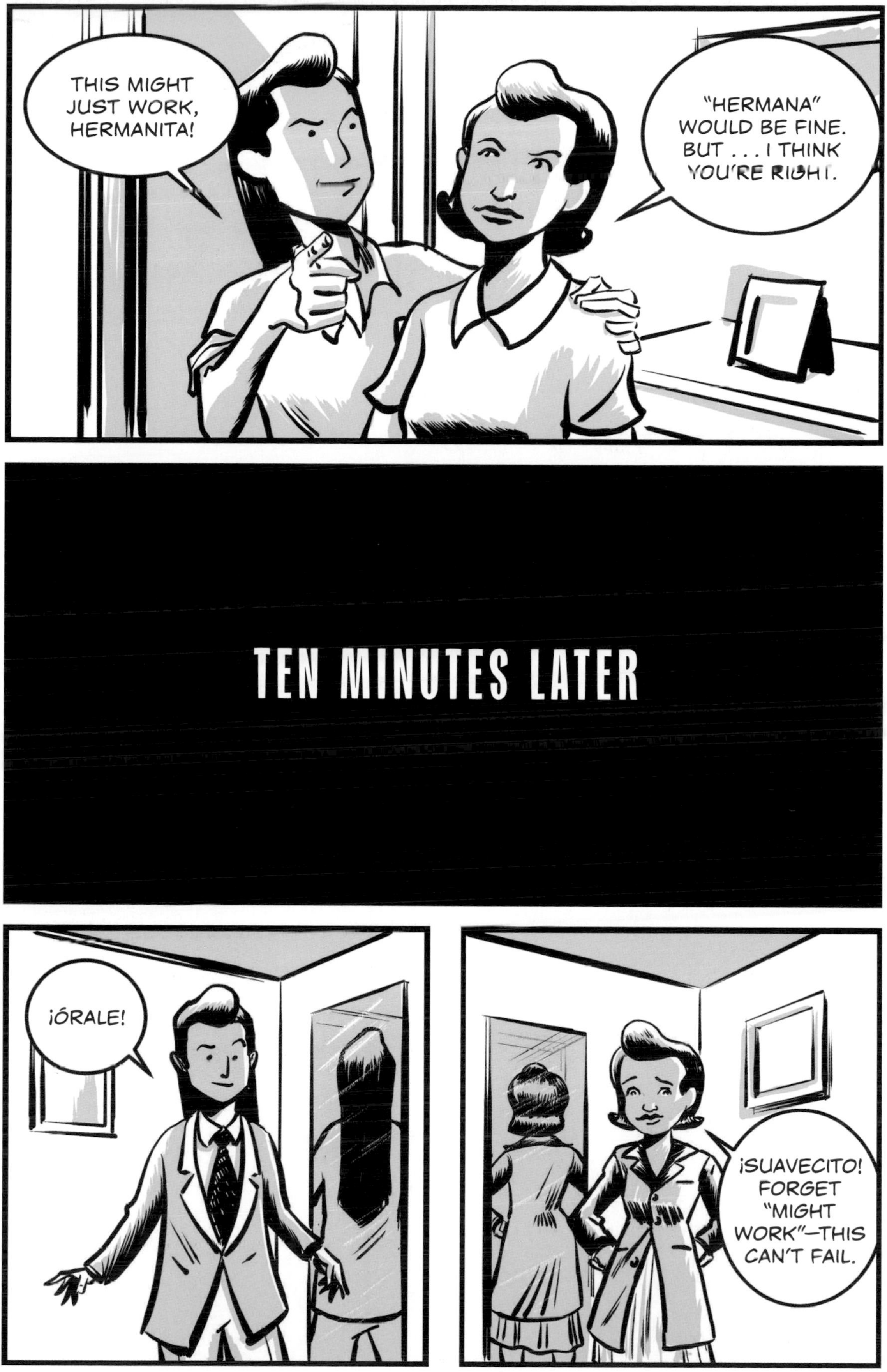
THIS MIGHT JUST WORK, HERMANITA!
"HERMANA" WOULD BE FINE. BUT . . . I THINK YOU'RE RIGHT.
TEN MINUTES LATER
¡ÓRALE!
¡SUAVECITO! FORGET "MIGHT WORK"—THIS CAN'T FAIL.

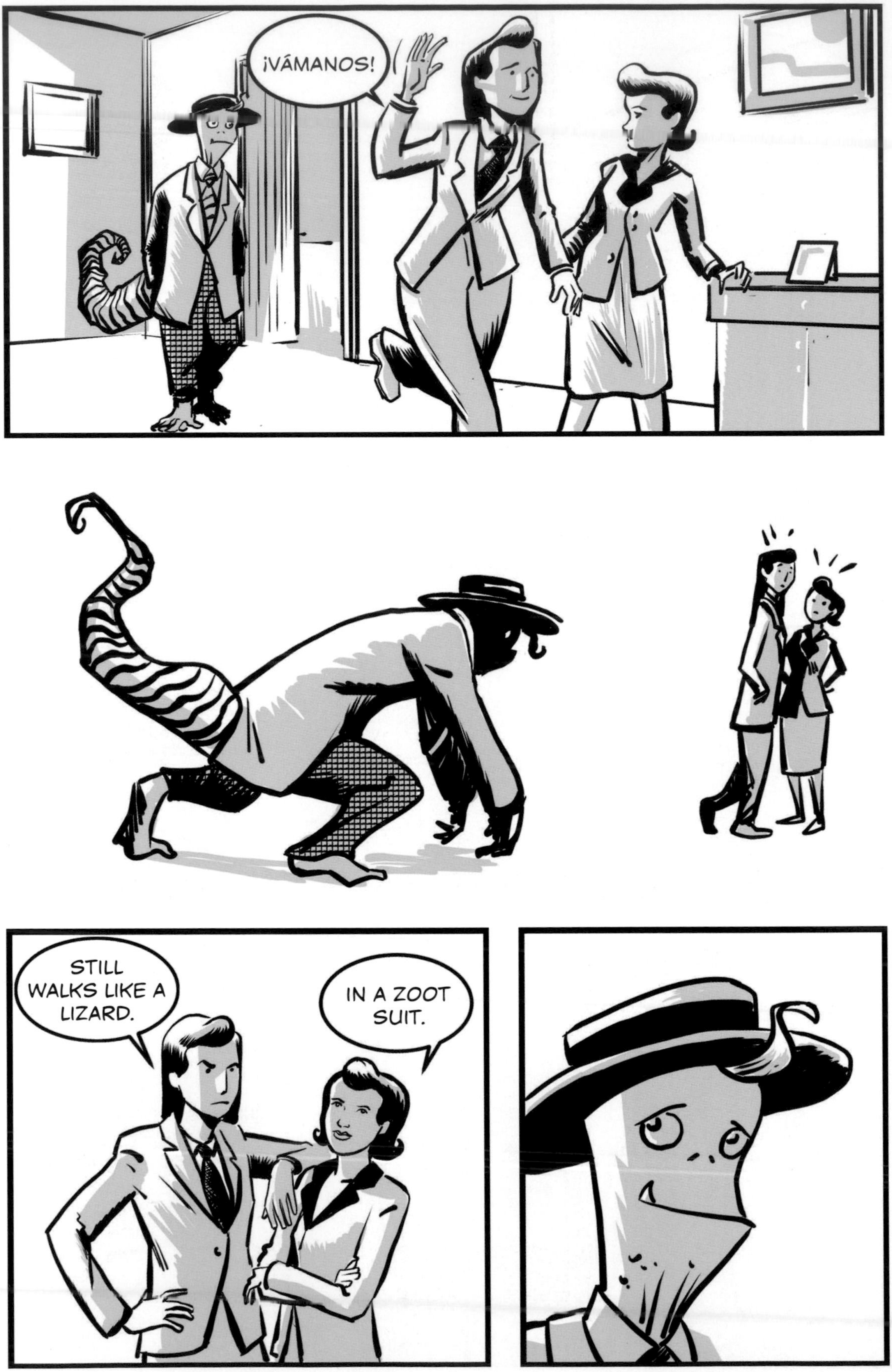
¡VÁMANOS!
STILL WALKS LIKE A LIZARD.
IN A ZOOT SUIT.

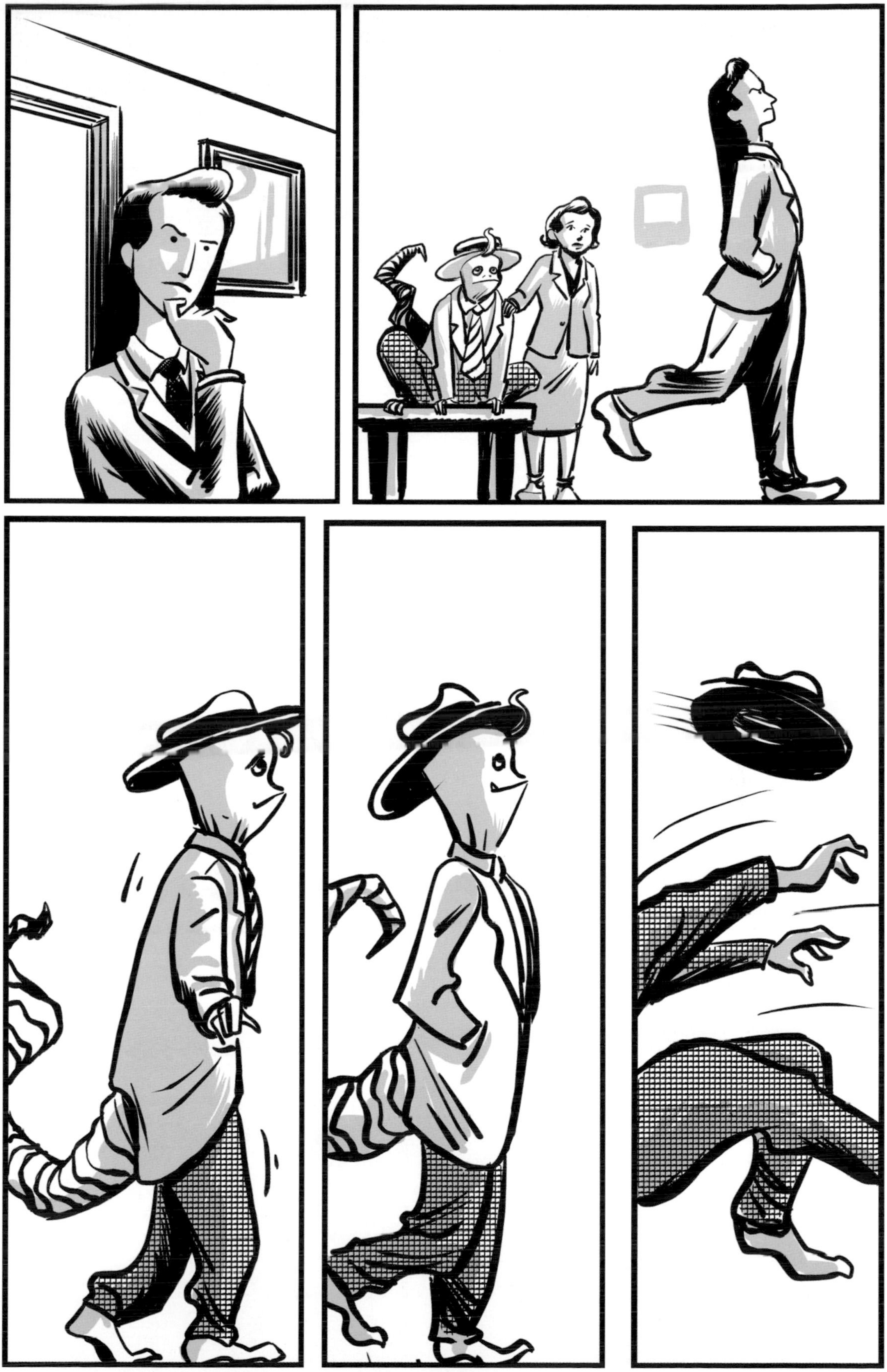

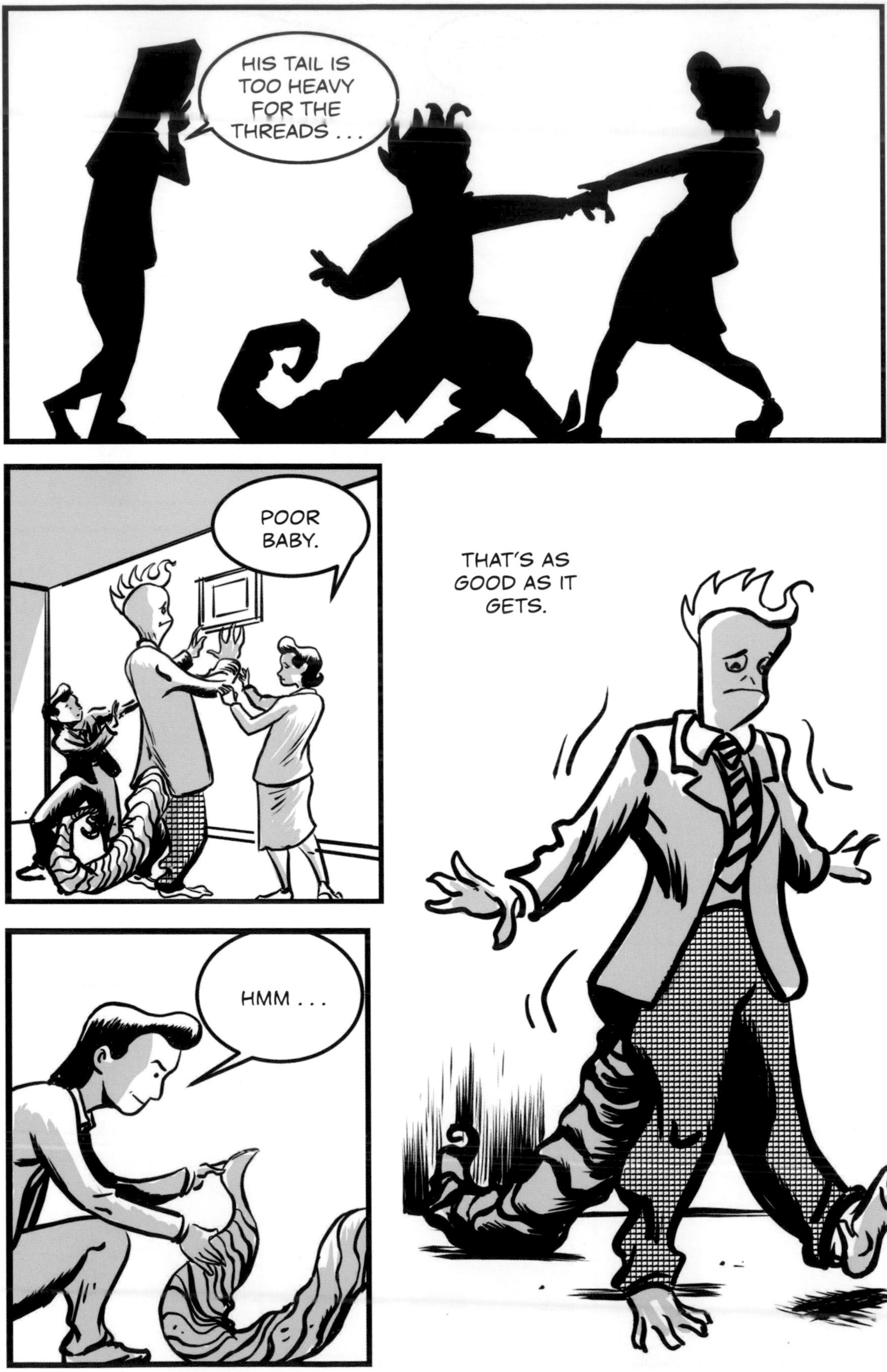
HIS TAIL IS TOO HEAVY FOR THE THREADS . . .
POOR BABY.
HMM . . .
THAT'S AS GOOD AS IT GETS.

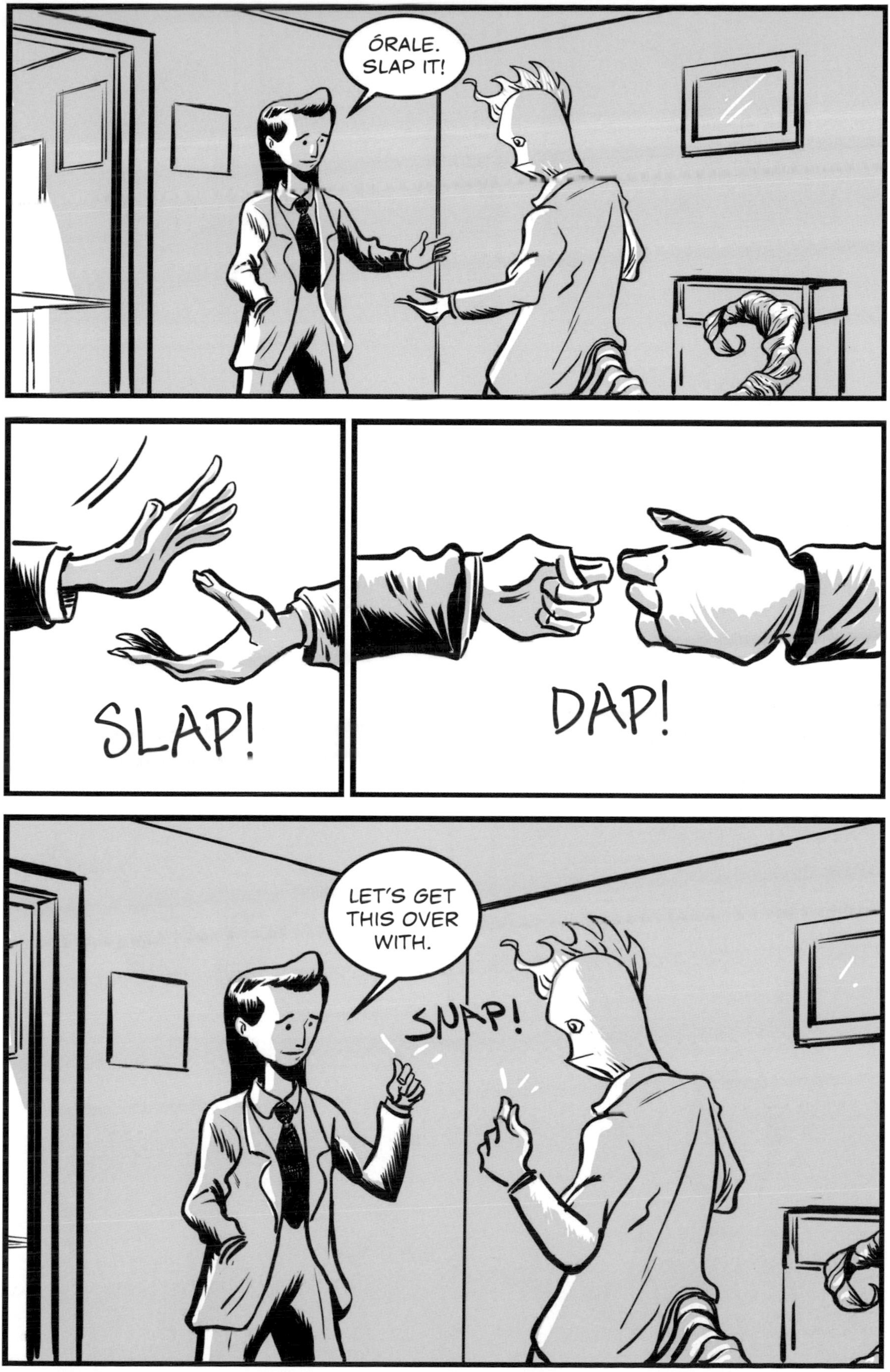
ÓRALE. SLAP IT!
SLAP!
DAP!
LET'S GET THIS OVER WITH.
SNAP!

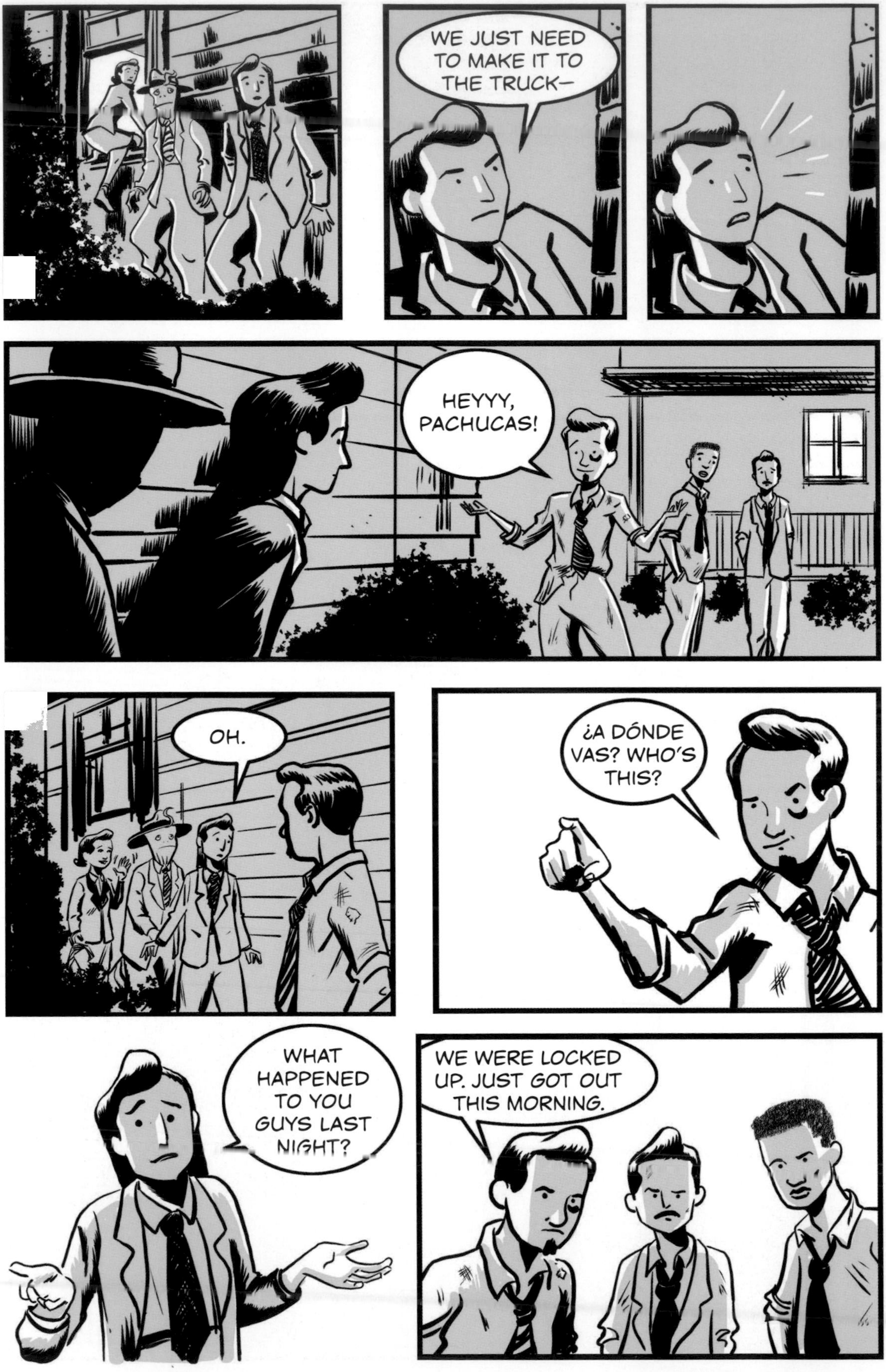
WE JUST NEED TO MAKE IT TO THE TRUCK—
HEYYY, PACHUCAS!
OH.
¿A DÓNDE VAS? WHO'S THIS?
WHAT HAPPENED TO YOU GUYS LAST NIGHT?
WE WERE LOCKED UP. JUST GOT OUT THIS MORNING.

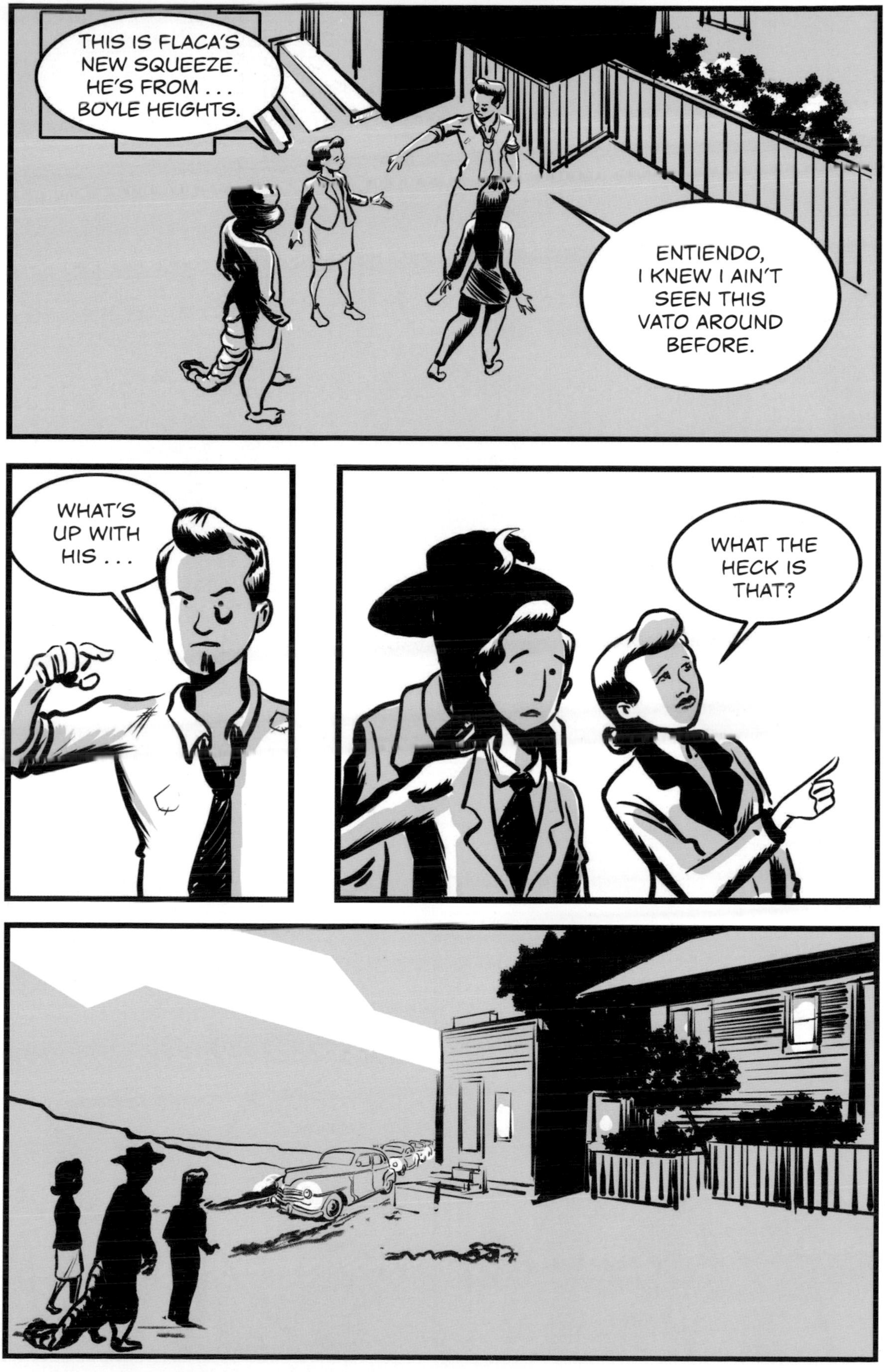
THIS IS FLACA'S NEW SQUEEZE. HE'S FROM . . . BOYLE HEIGHTS.
ENTIENDO, I KNEW I AIN'T SEEN THIS VATO AROUND BEFORE.
WHAT'S UP WITH HIS . . .
WHAT THE HECK IS THAT?

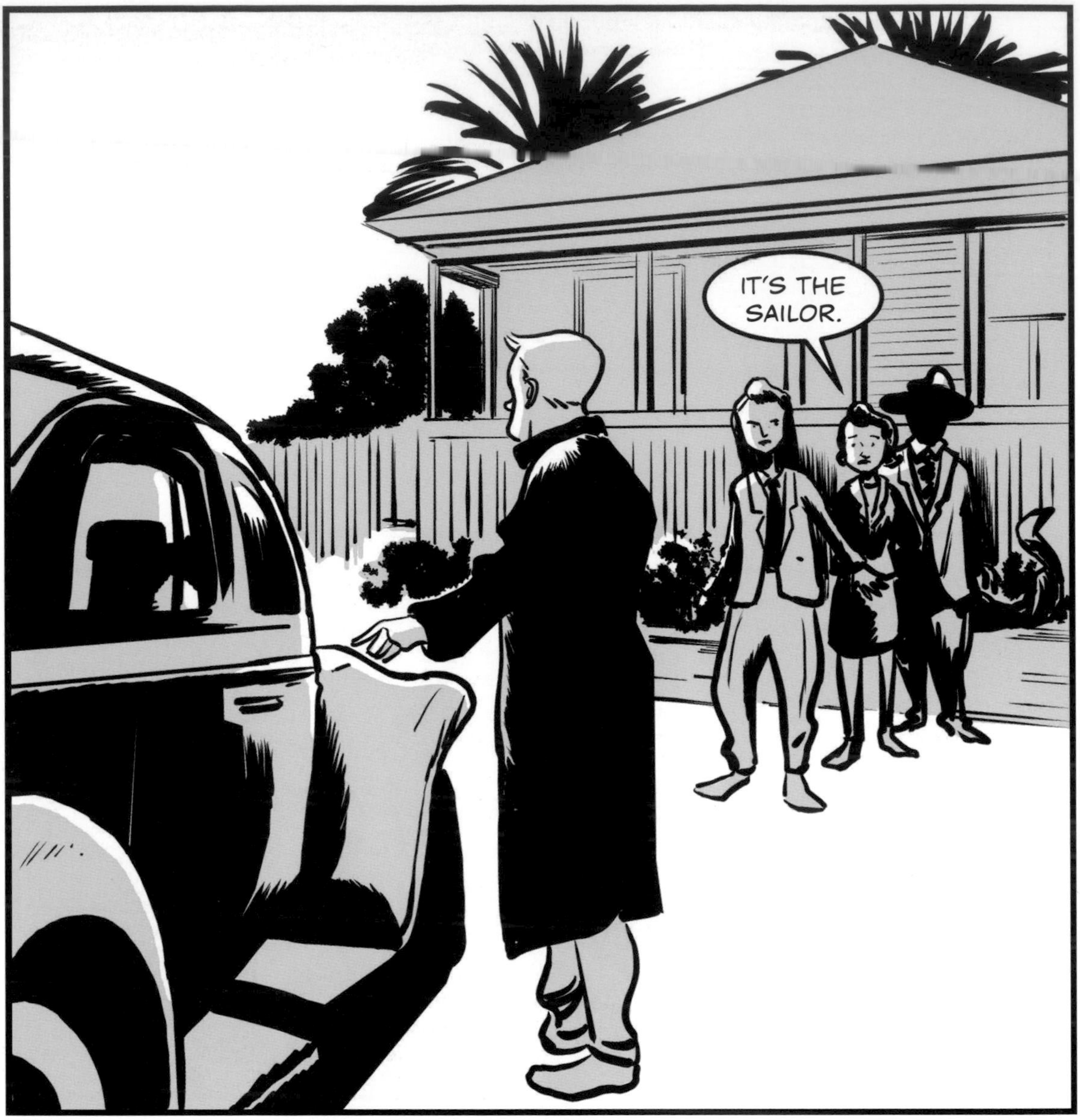
IT'S THE SAILOR.

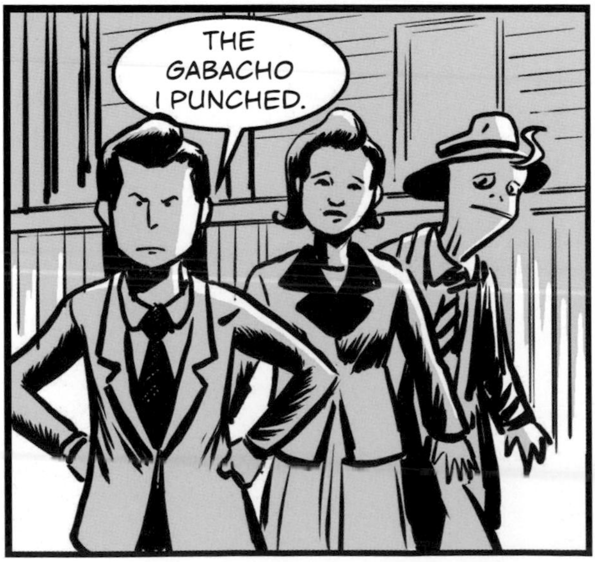
THE GABACHO I PUNCHED.

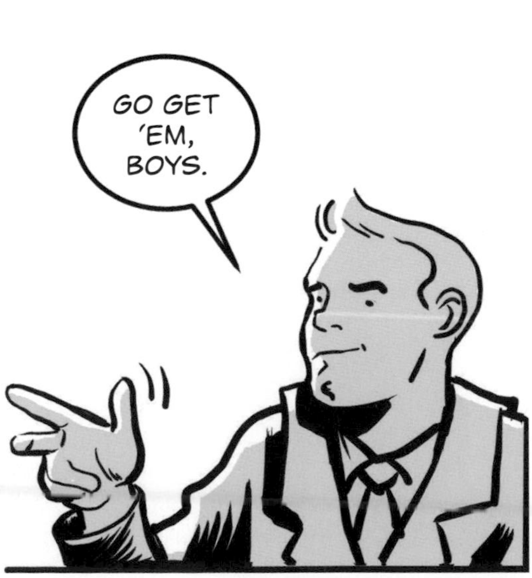
GO GET 'EM, BOYS.

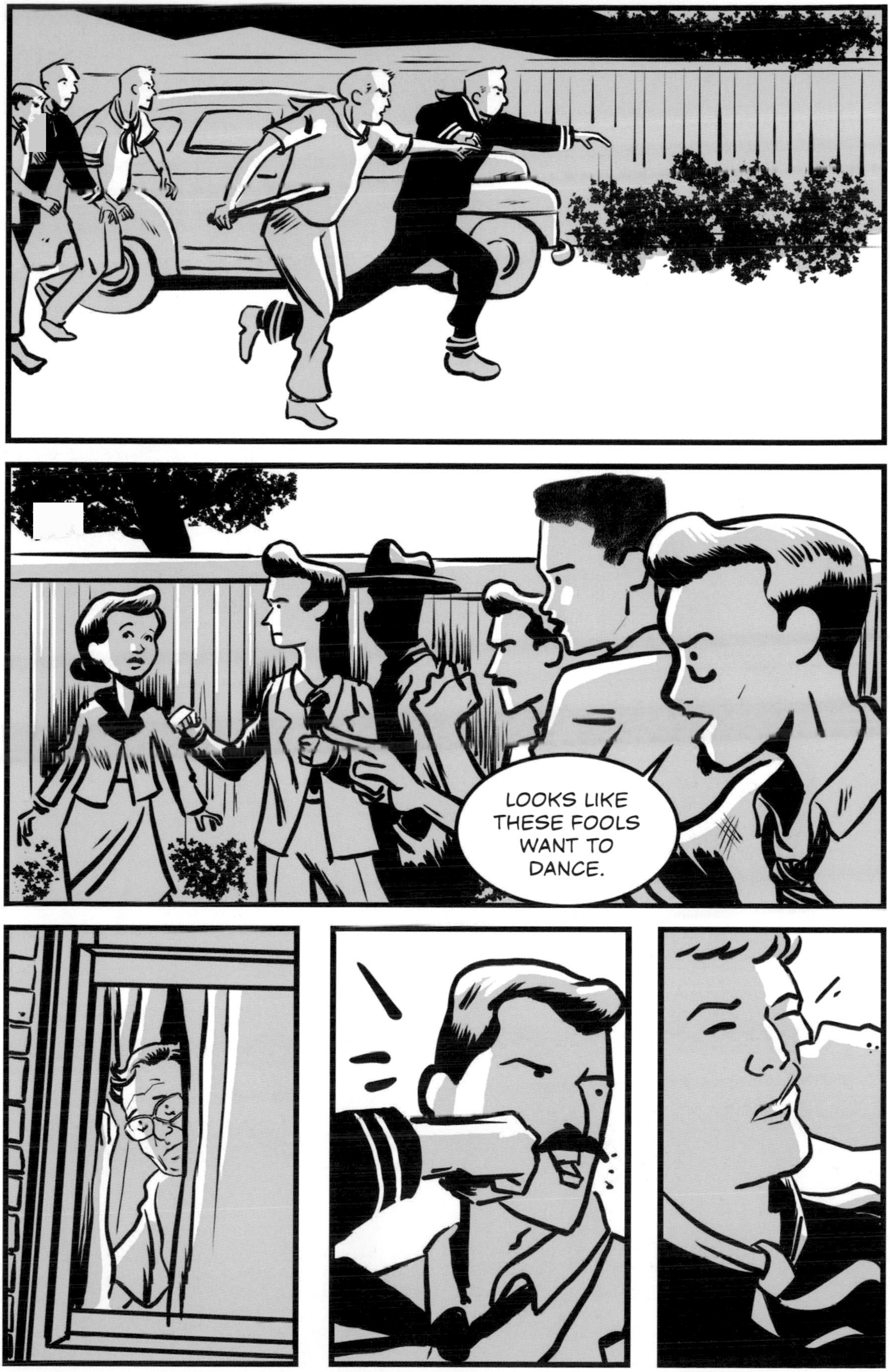
LOOKS LIKE THESE FOOLS WANT TO DANCE.

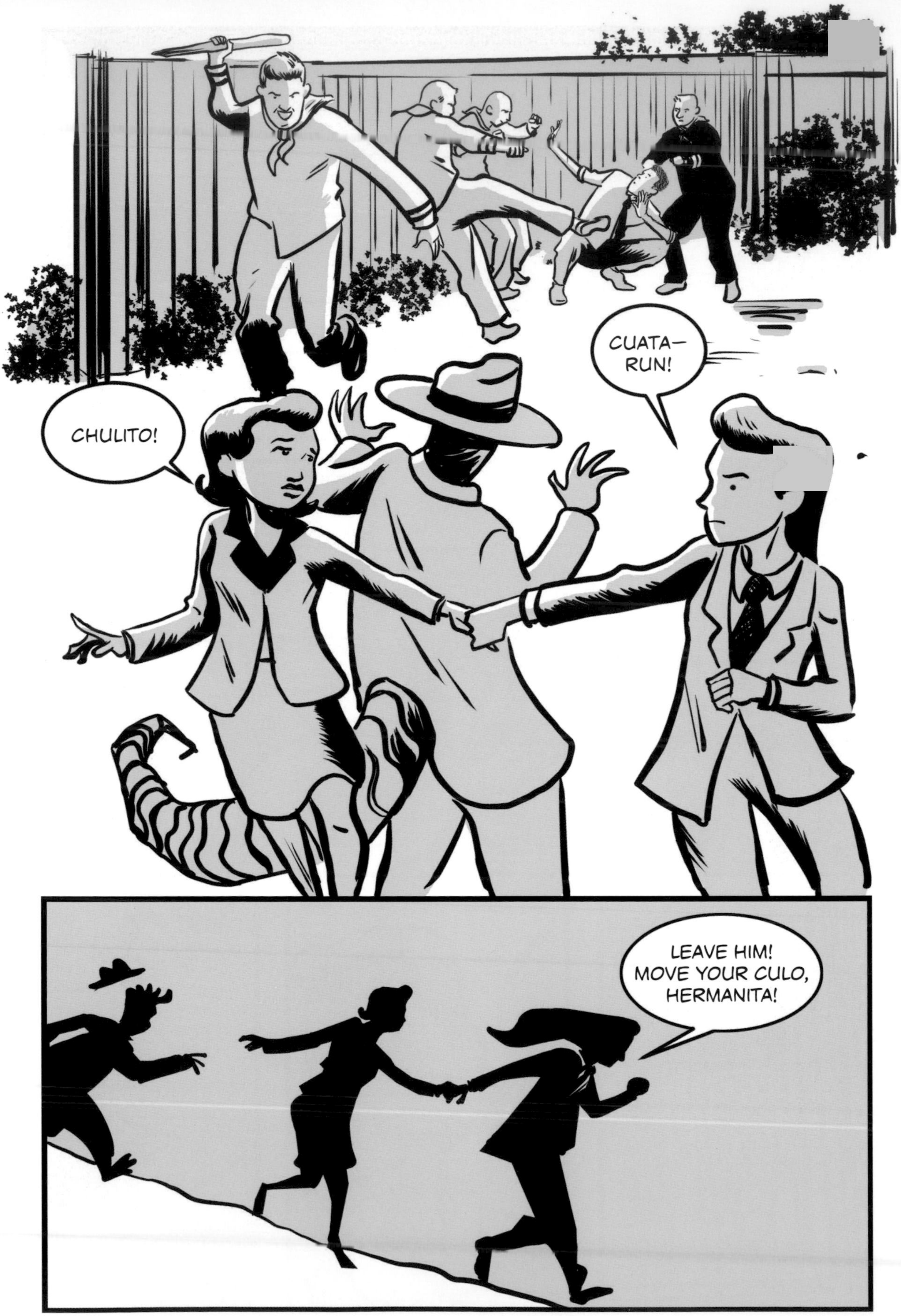
CUATA—
RUN!
CHULITO!
LEAVE HIM!
MOVE YOUR CULO,
HERMANITA!

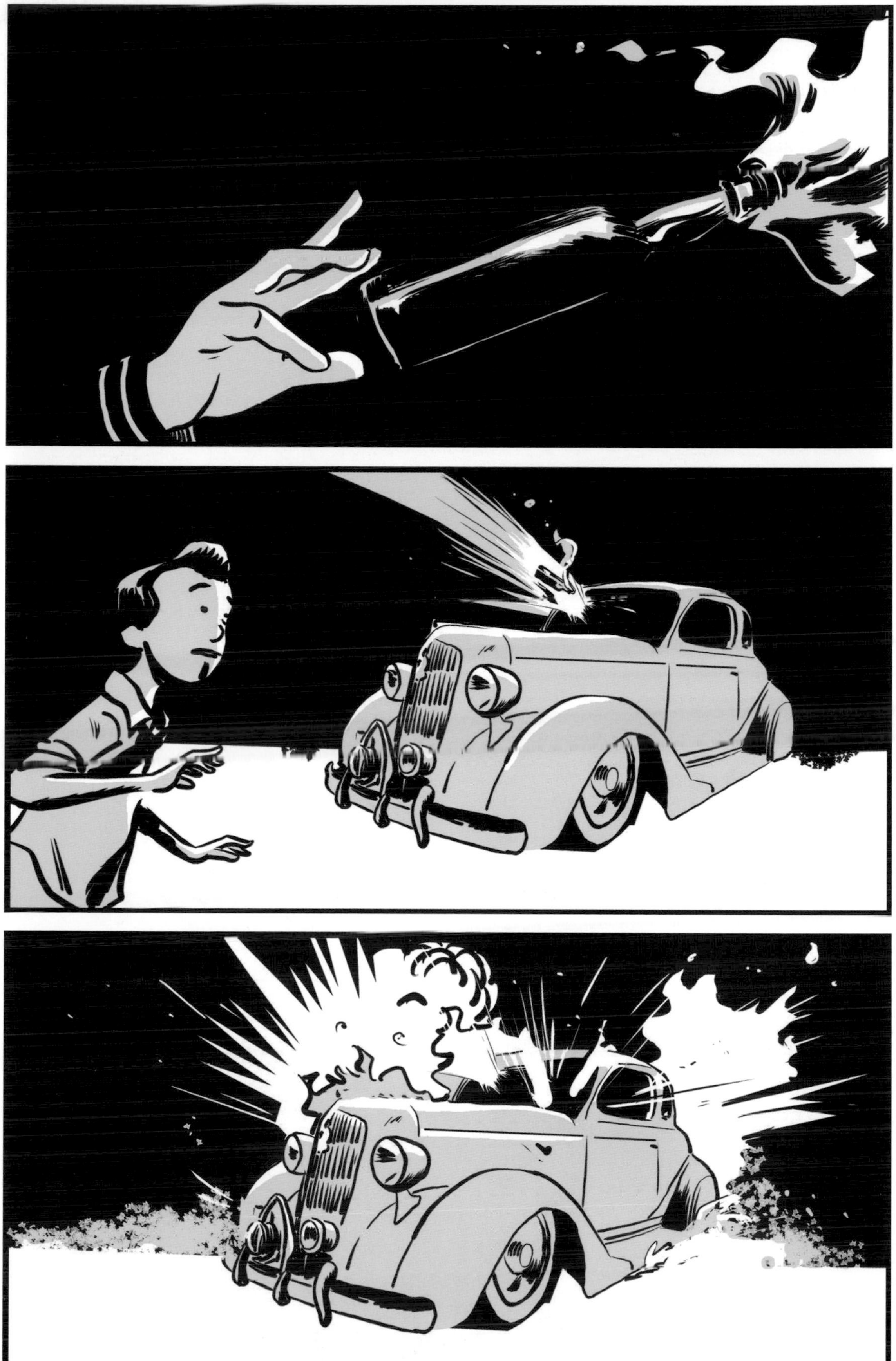

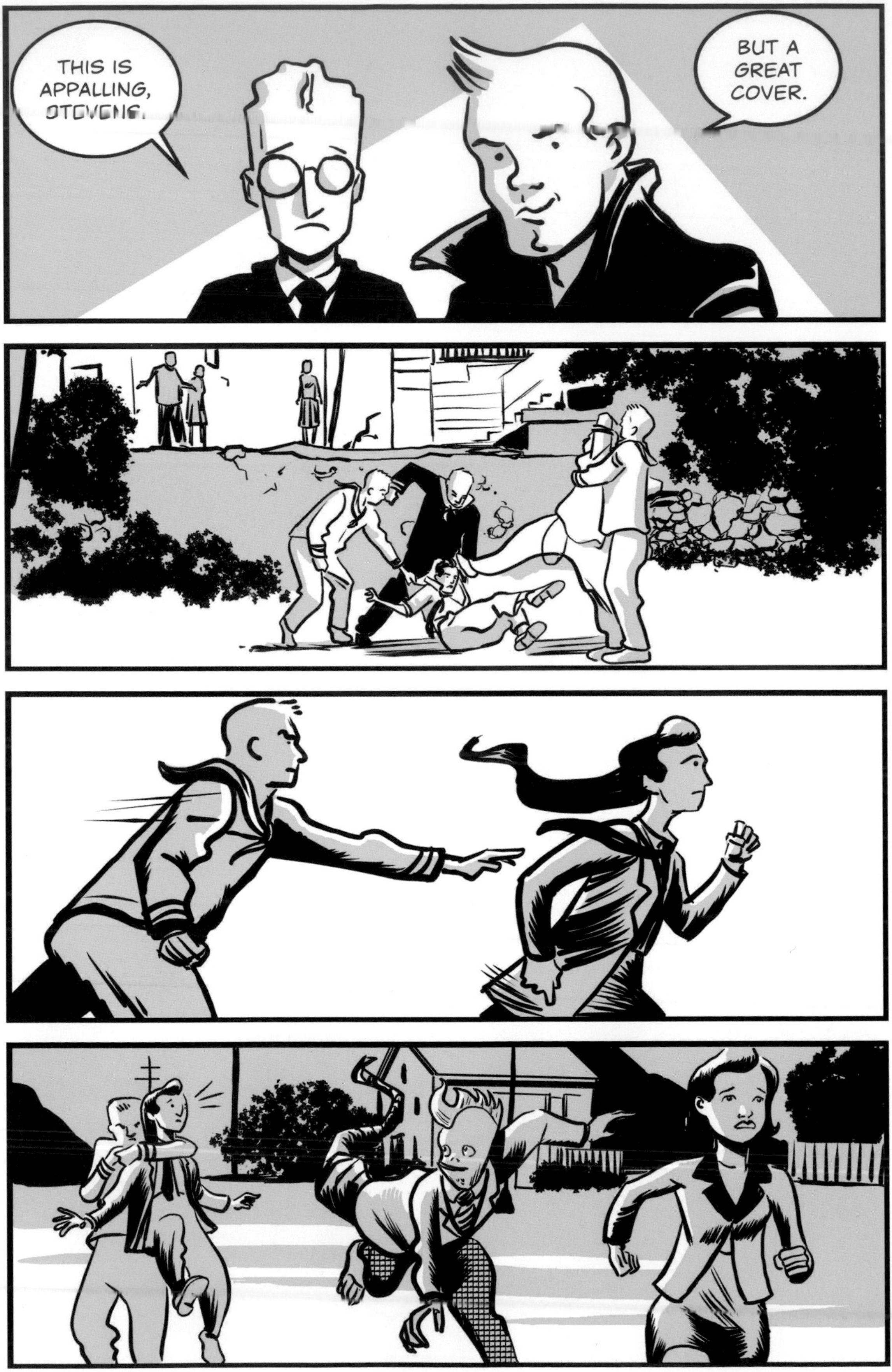
THIS IS APPALLING, STEVENS.
BUT A GREAT COVER.

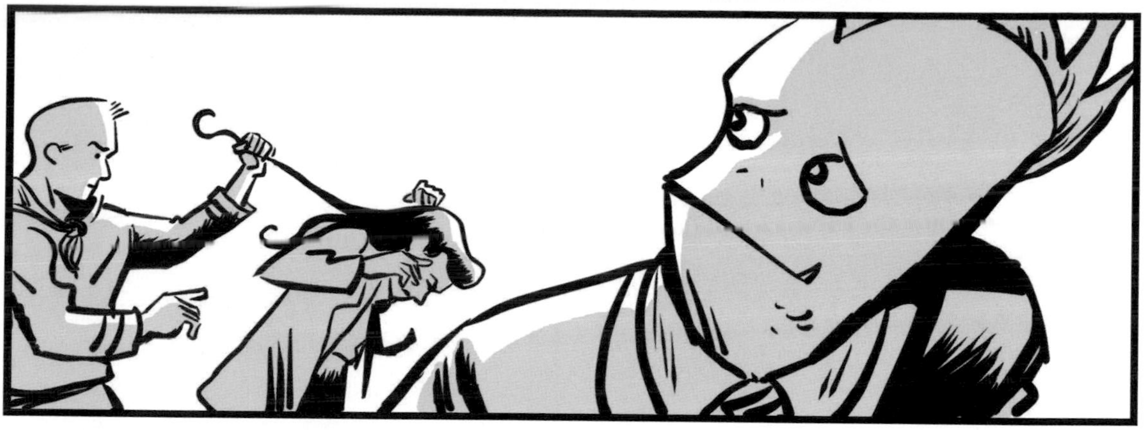

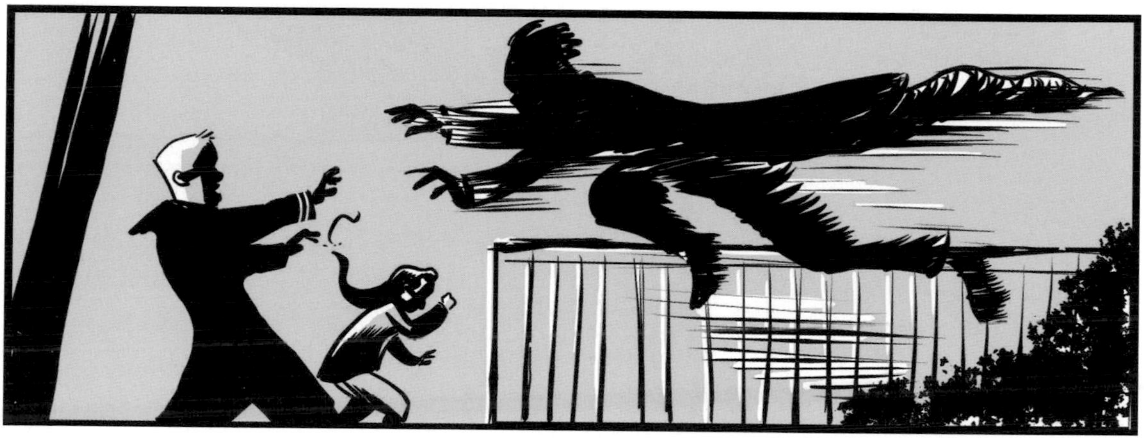

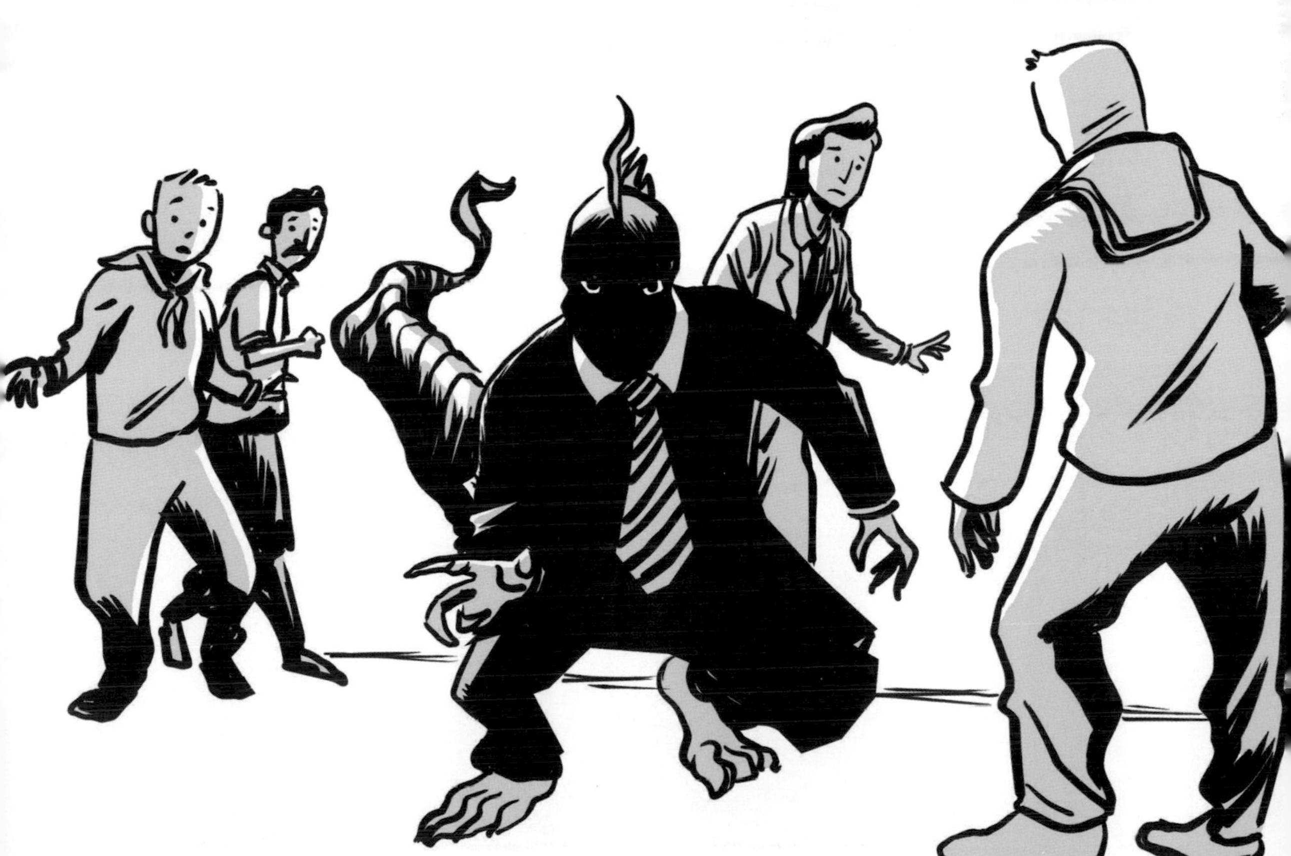

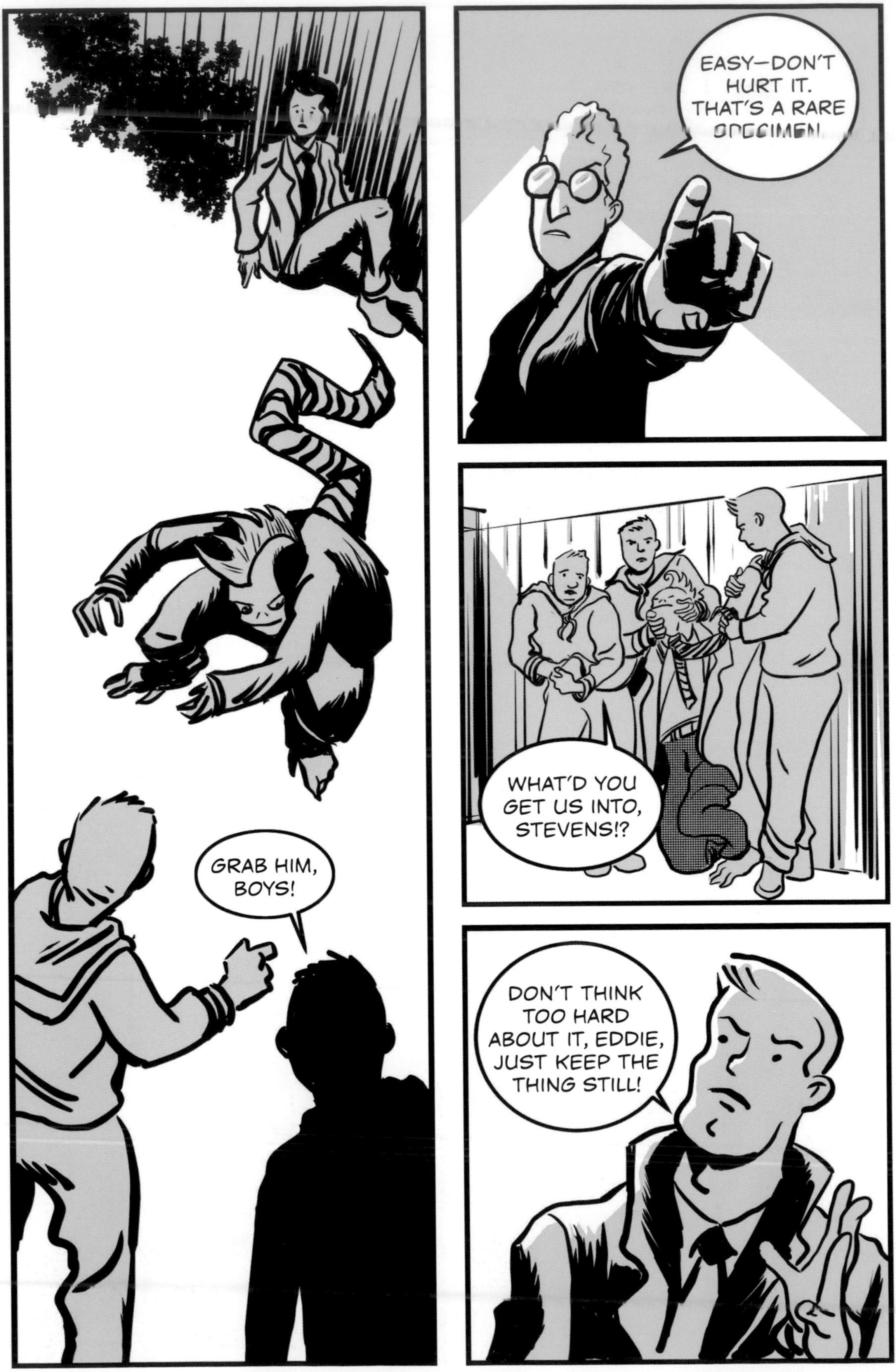
GRAB HIM, BOYS!
EASY—DON'T HURT IT. THAT'S A RARE SPECIMEN.
WHAT'D YOU GET US INTO, STEVENS!?
DON'T THINK TOO HARD ABOUT IT, EDDIE, JUST KEEP THE THING STILL!

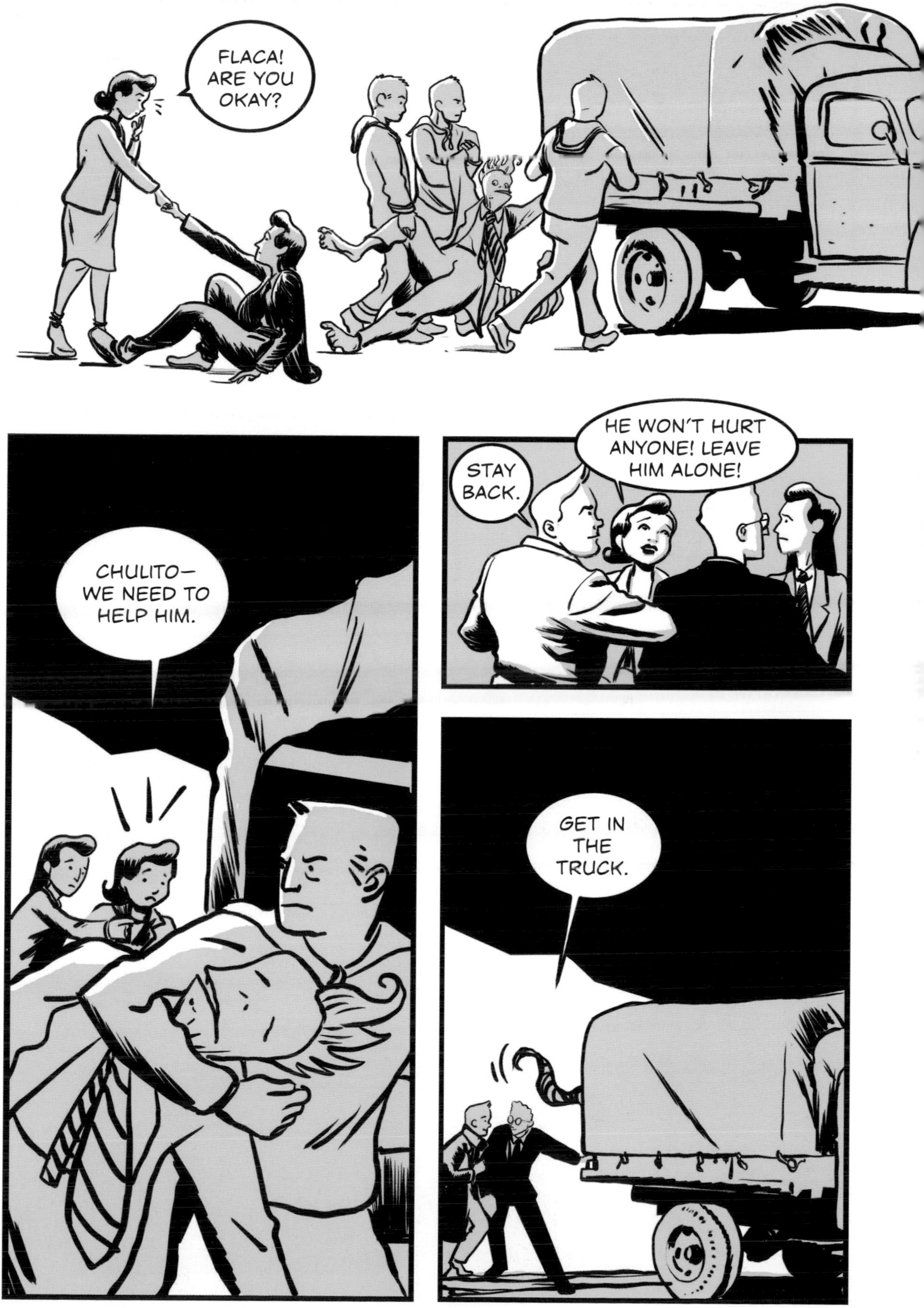

FLACA! ARE YOU OKAY?
CHULITO— WE NEED TO HELP HIM.
STAY BACK.
HE WON'T HURT ANYONE! LEAVE HIM ALONE!
GET IN THE TRUCK.

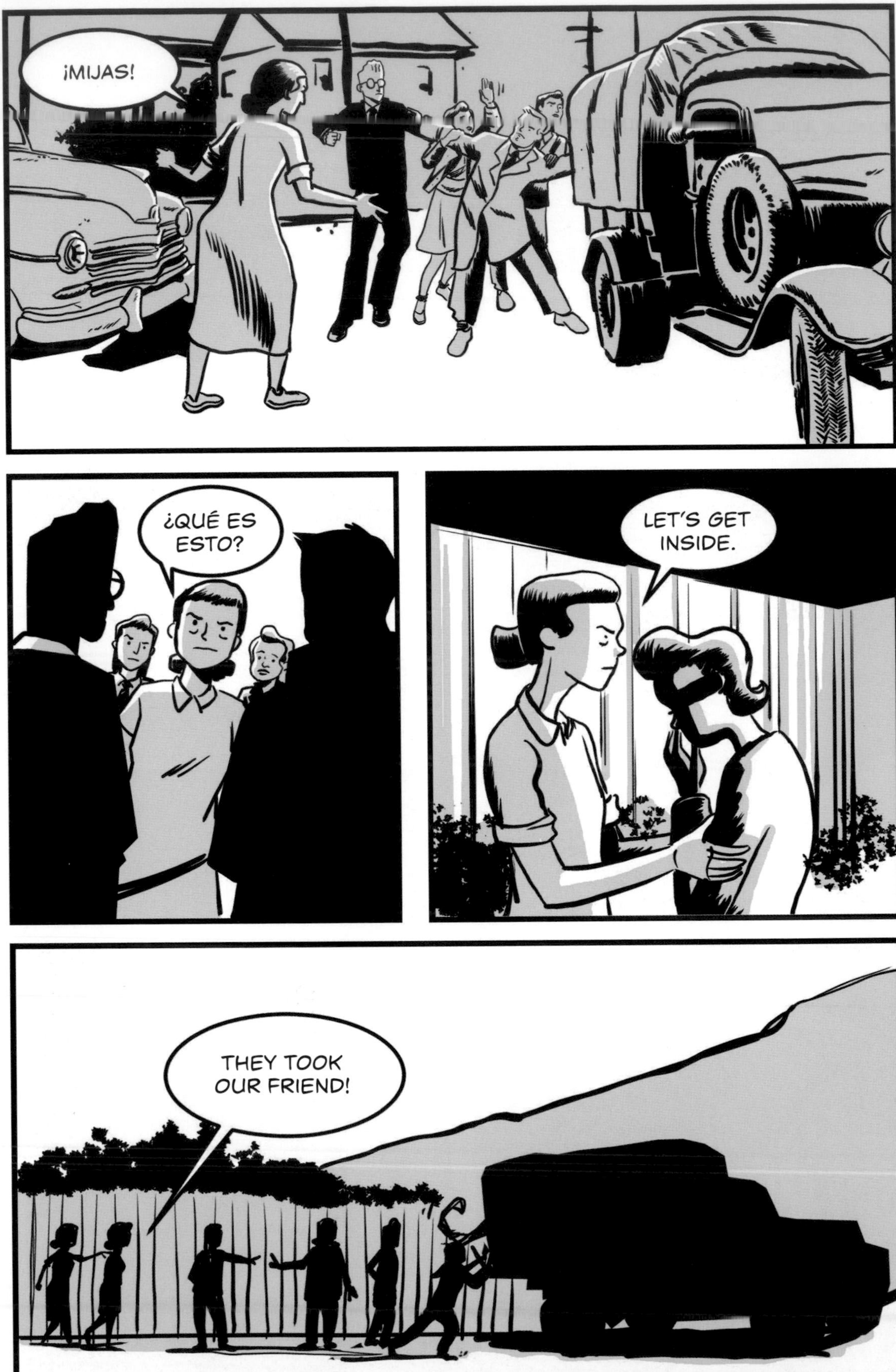
¡MIJAS!
¿QUÉ ES ESTO?
LET'S GET INSIDE.
THEY TOOK OUR FRIEND!

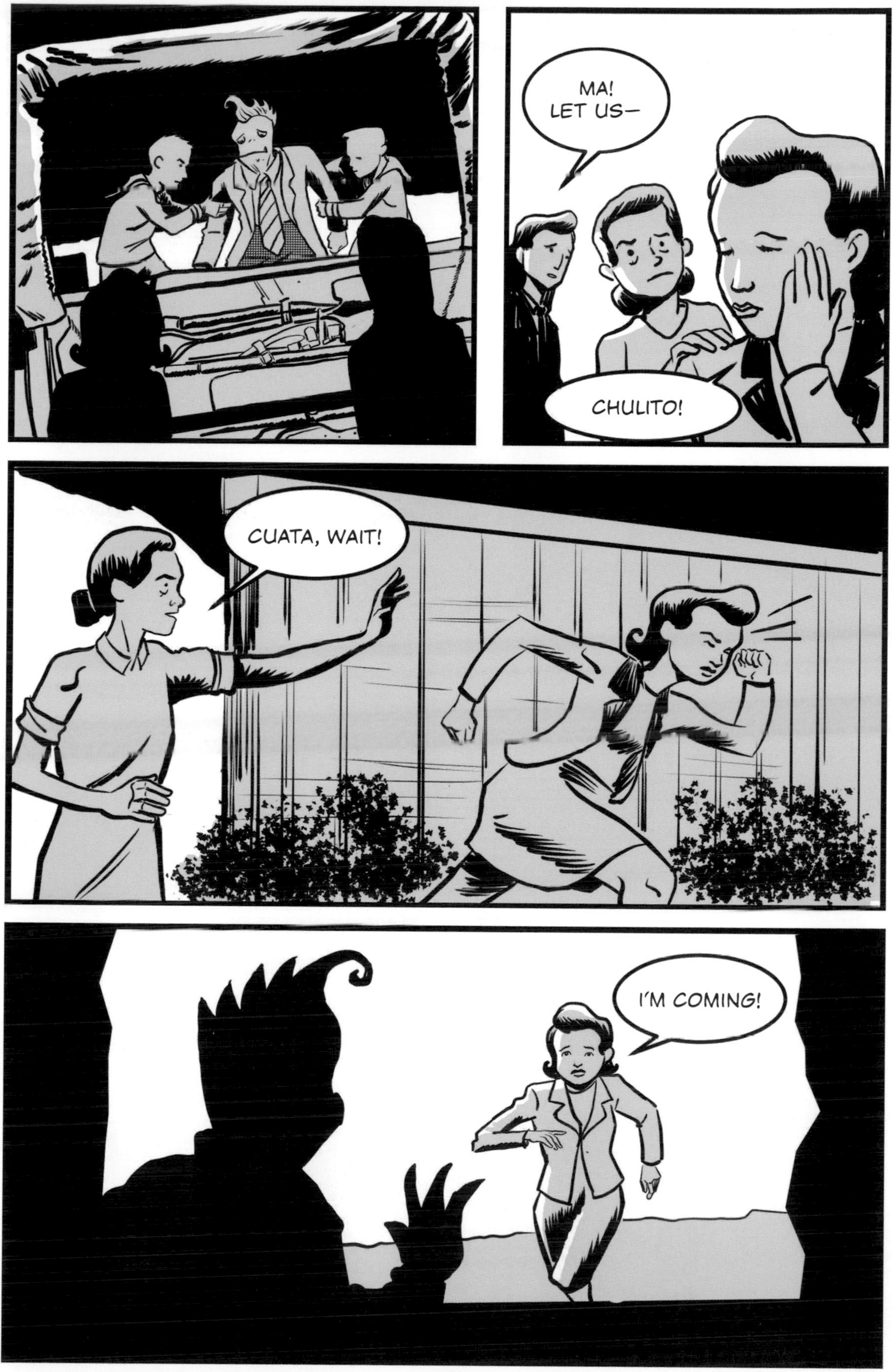
MA! LET US—
CHULITO!
CUATA, WAIT!
I'M COMING!

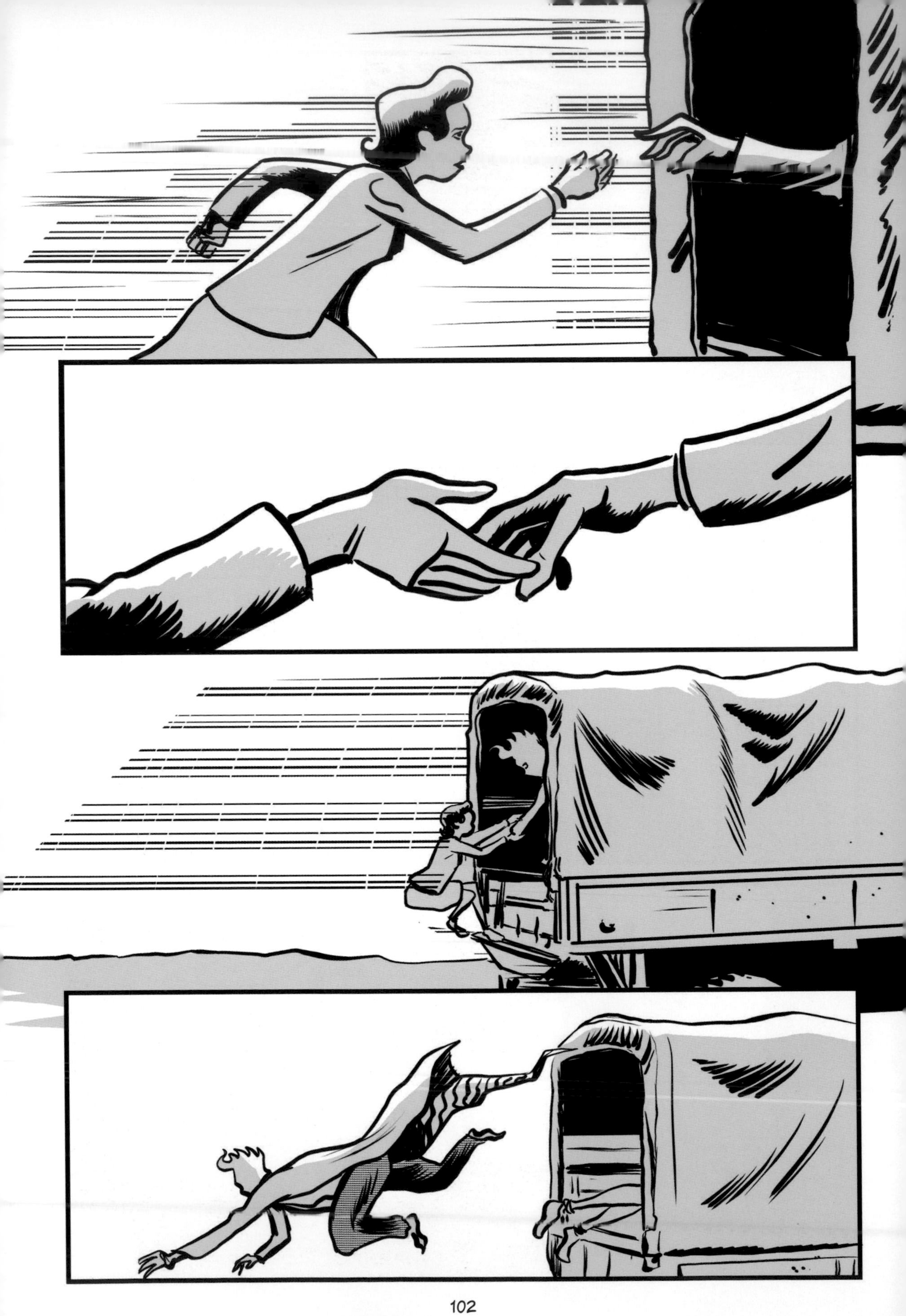

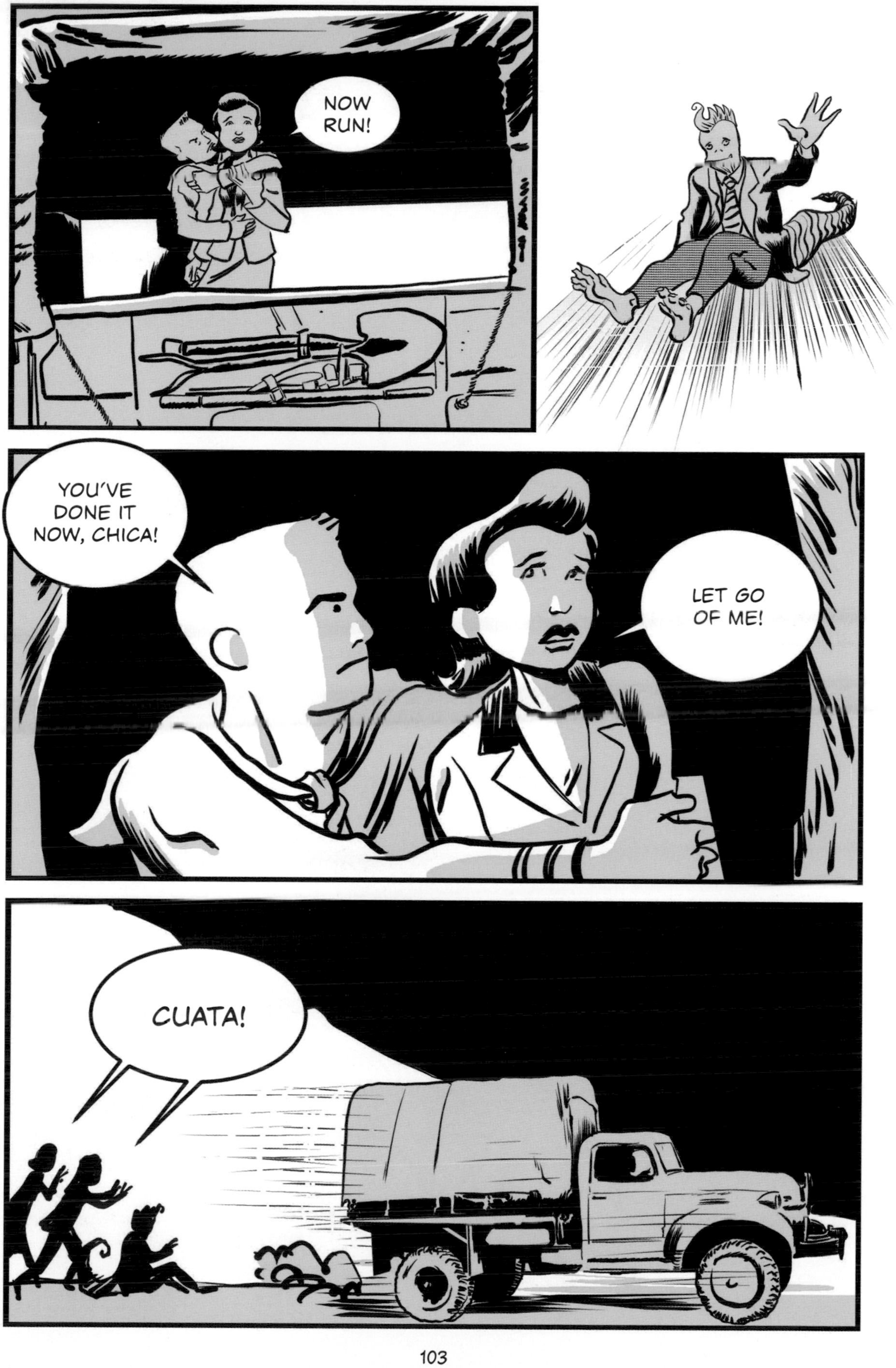
NOW RUN!
YOU'VE DONE IT NOW, CHICA!
LET GO OF ME!
CUATA!

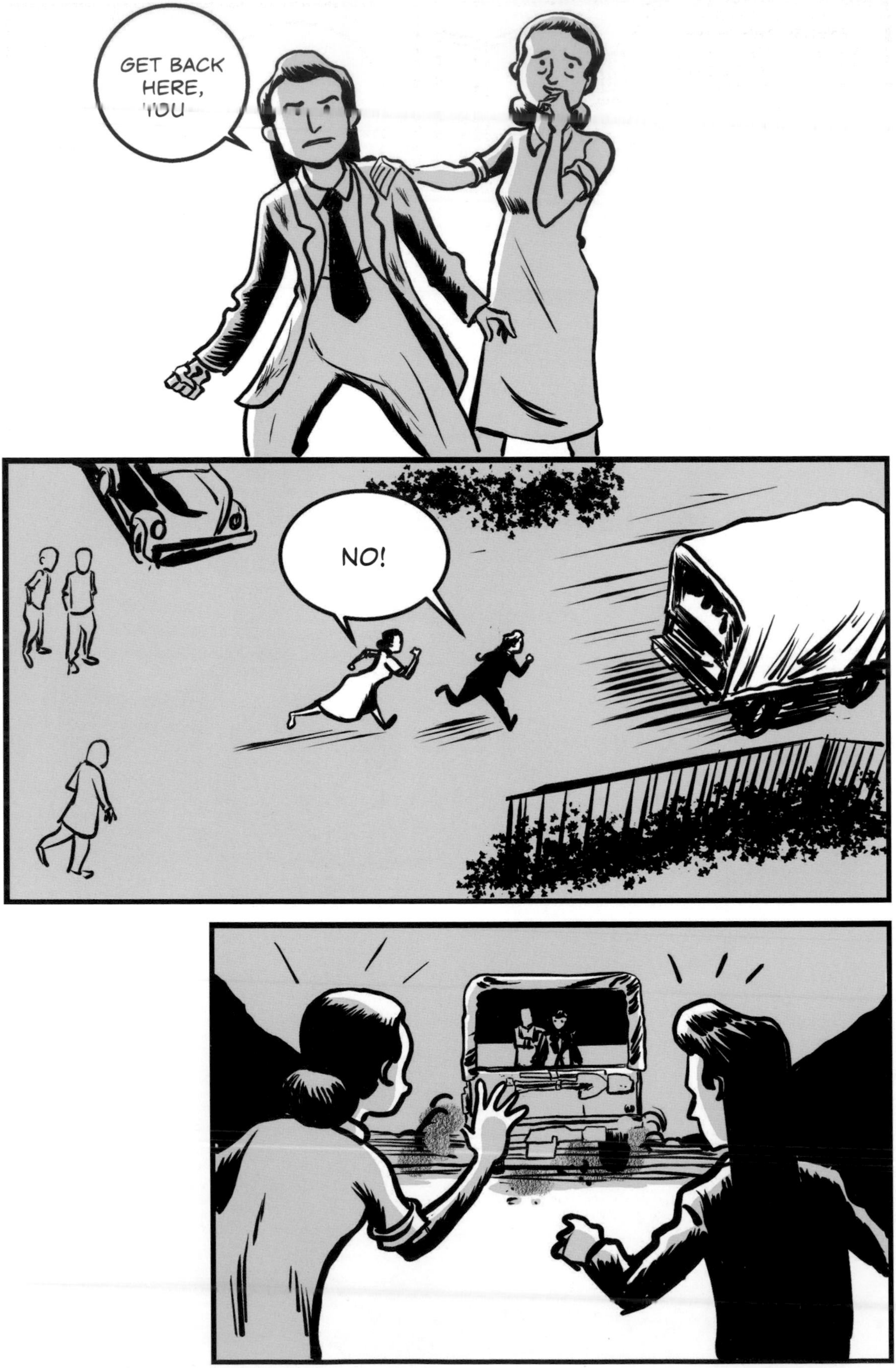
GET BACK HERE, YOU
NO!

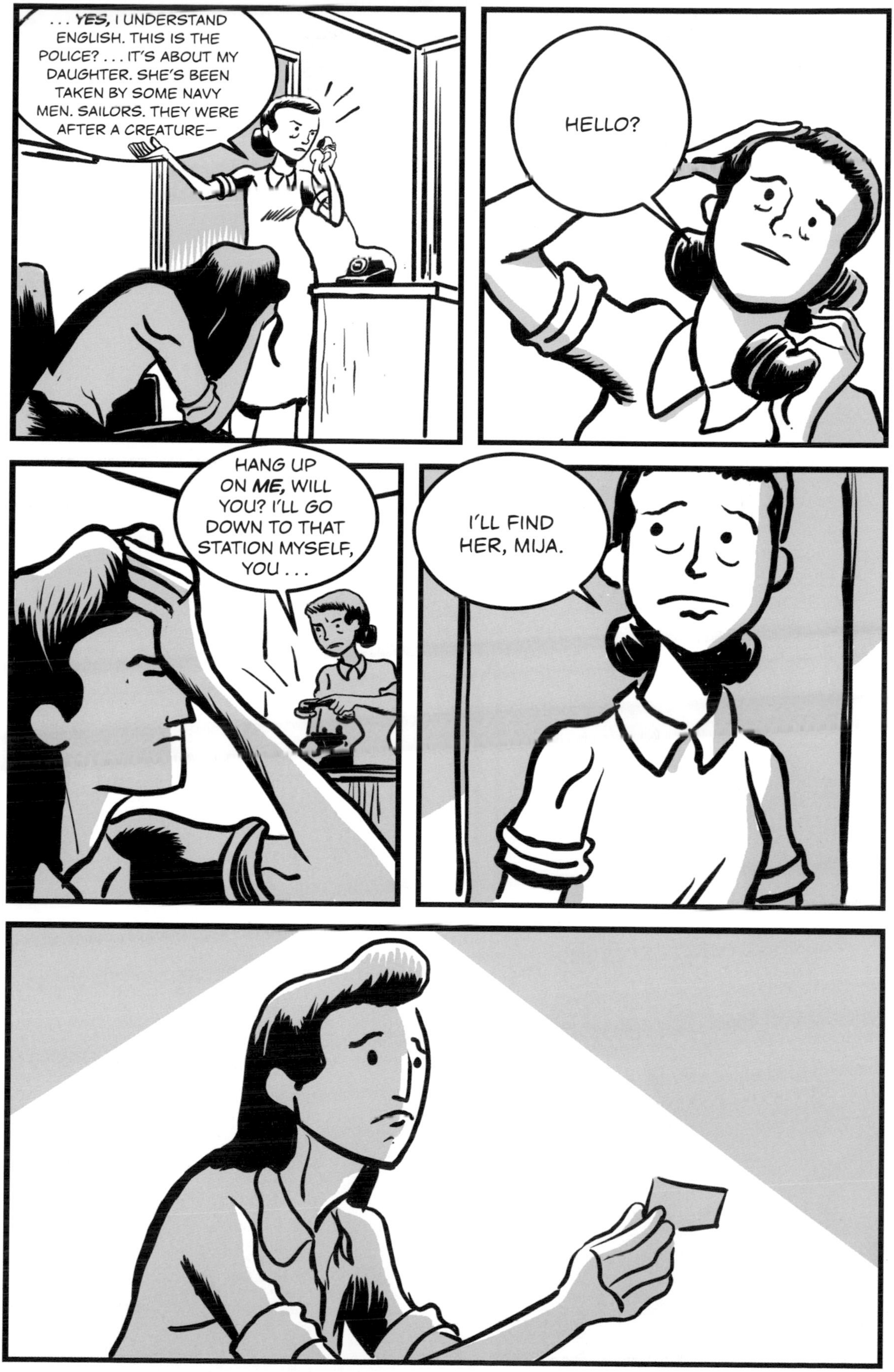
. . . YES, I UNDERSTAND ENGLISH. THIS IS THE POLICE? . . . IT'S ABOUT MY DAUGHTER. SHE'S BEEN TAKEN BY SOME NAVY MEN. SAILORS. THEY WERE AFTER A CREATURE—
HELLO?
HANG UP ON ME, WILL YOU? I'LL GO DOWN TO THAT STATION MYSELF, YOU . . .
I'LL FIND HER, MIJA.

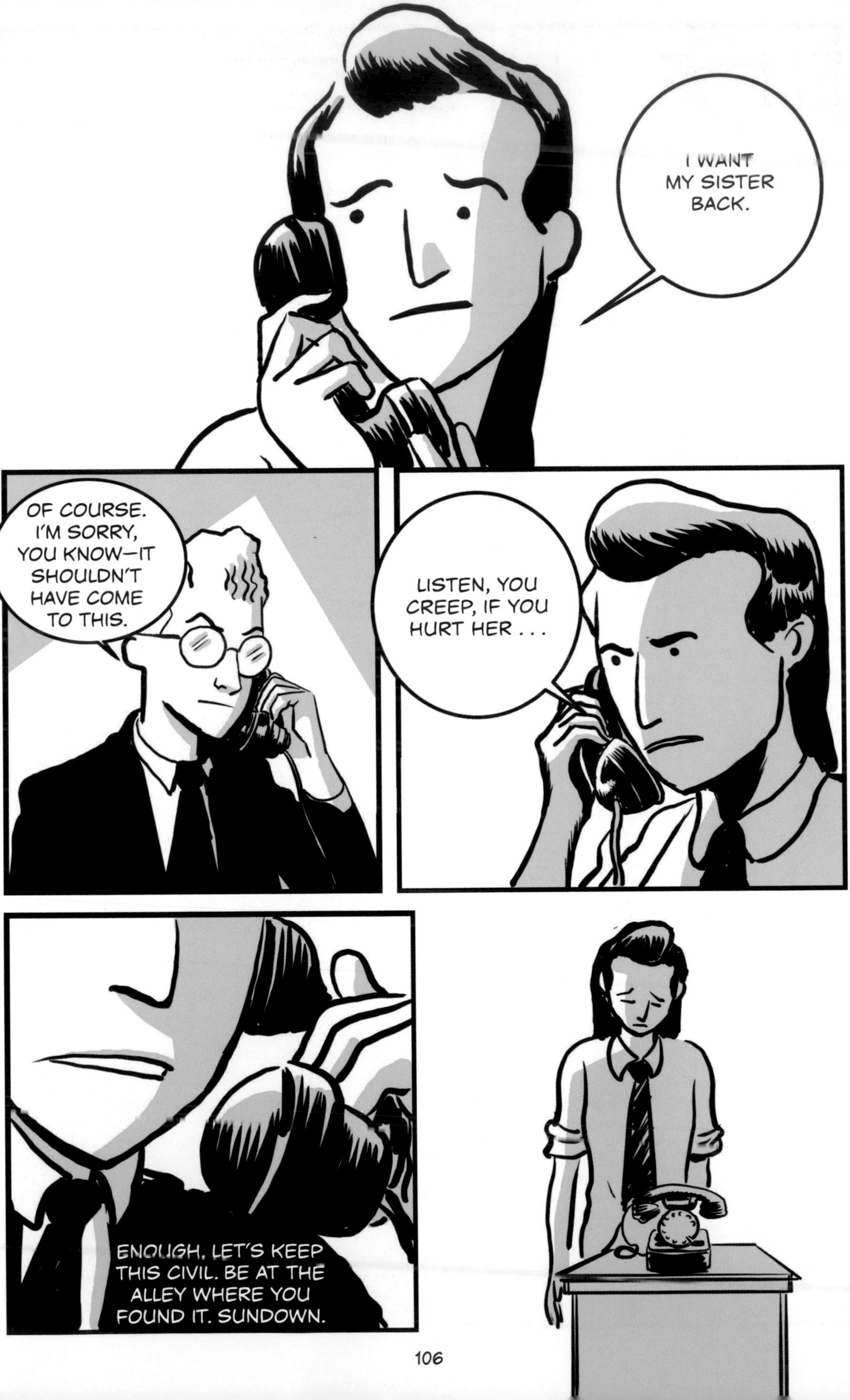
I WANT MY SISTER BACK.
OF COURSE. I'M SORRY, YOU KNOW—IT SHOULDN'T HAVE COME TO THIS.
LISTEN, YOU CREEP, IF YOU HURT HER . . .
ENOUGH. LET'S KEEP THIS CIVIL. BE AT THE ALLEY WHERE YOU FOUND IT. SUNDOWN.

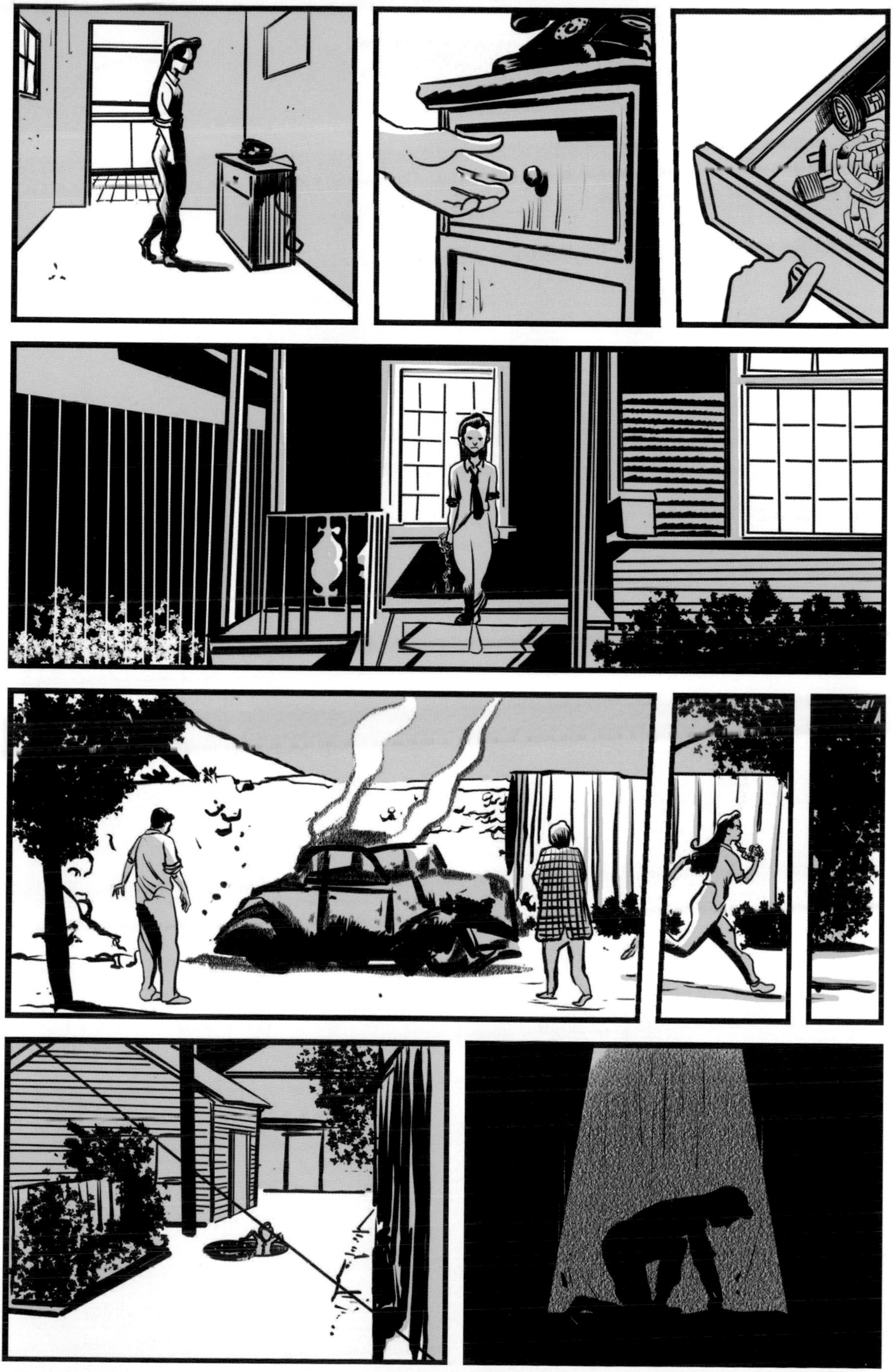

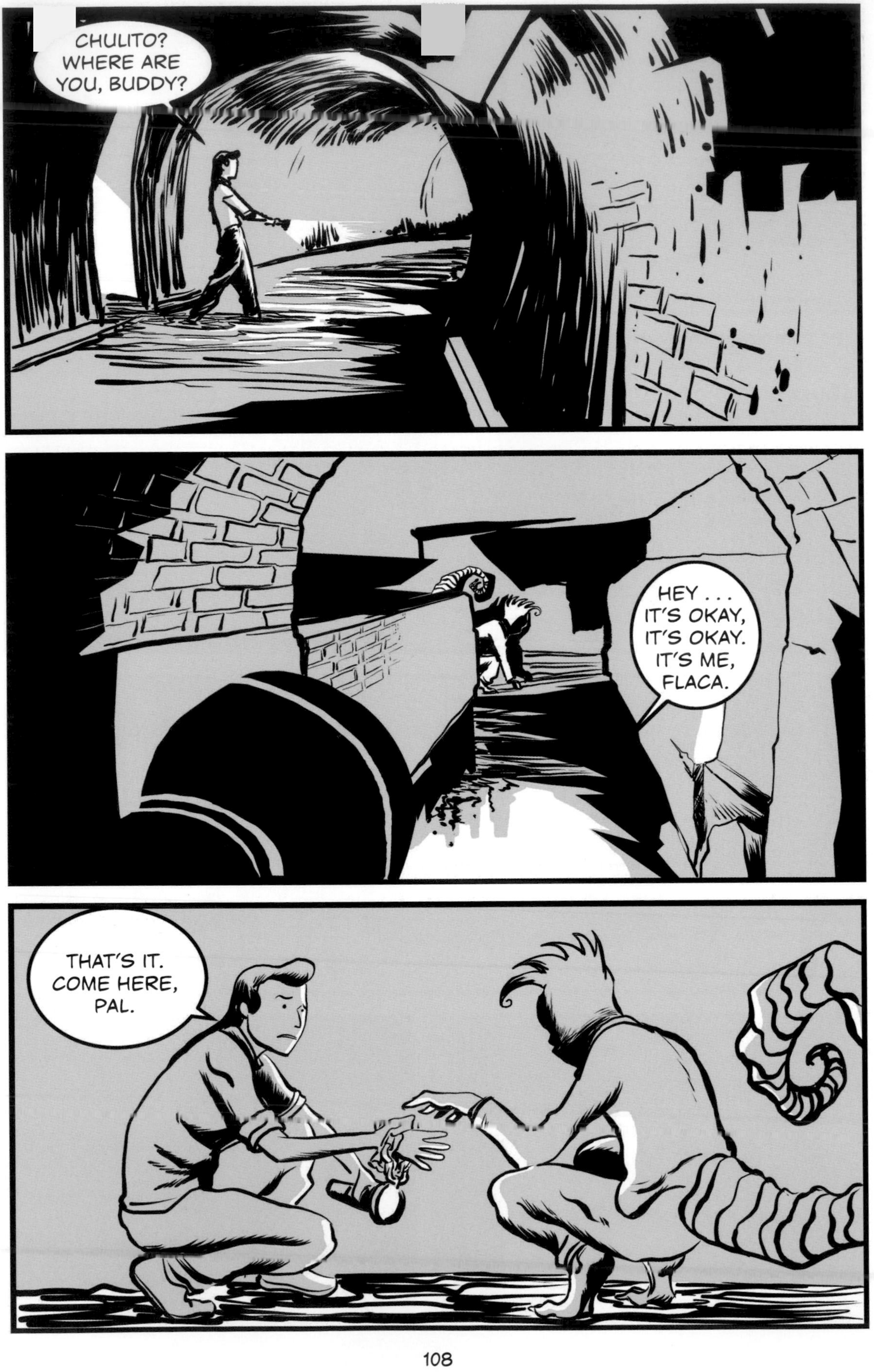
CHULITO? WHERE ARE YOU, BUDDY?
HEY . . . IT'S OKAY, IT'S OKAY. IT'S ME, FLACA.
THAT'S IT. COME HERE, PAL.

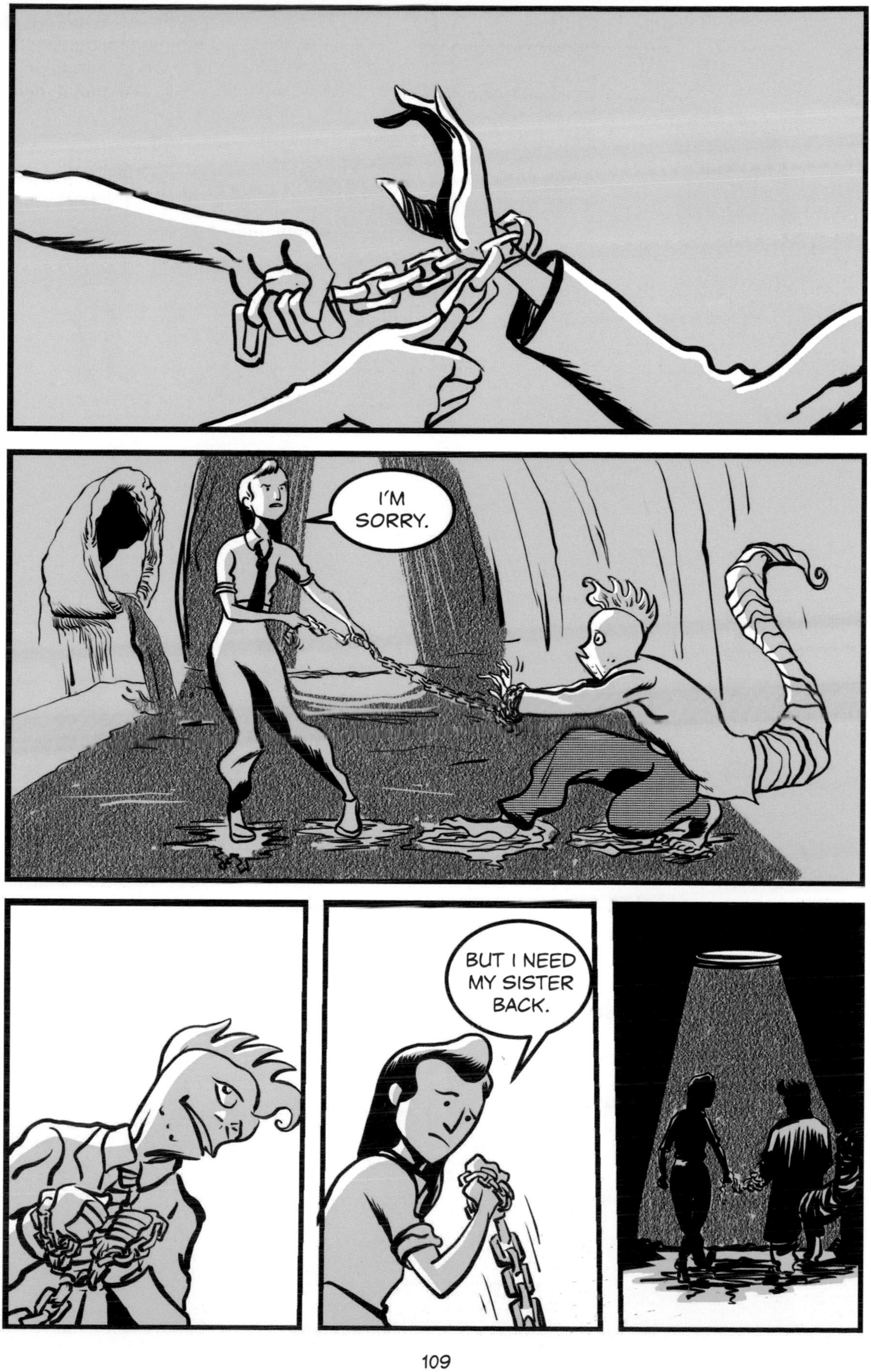
I'M SORRY.
BUT I NEED MY SISTER BACK.

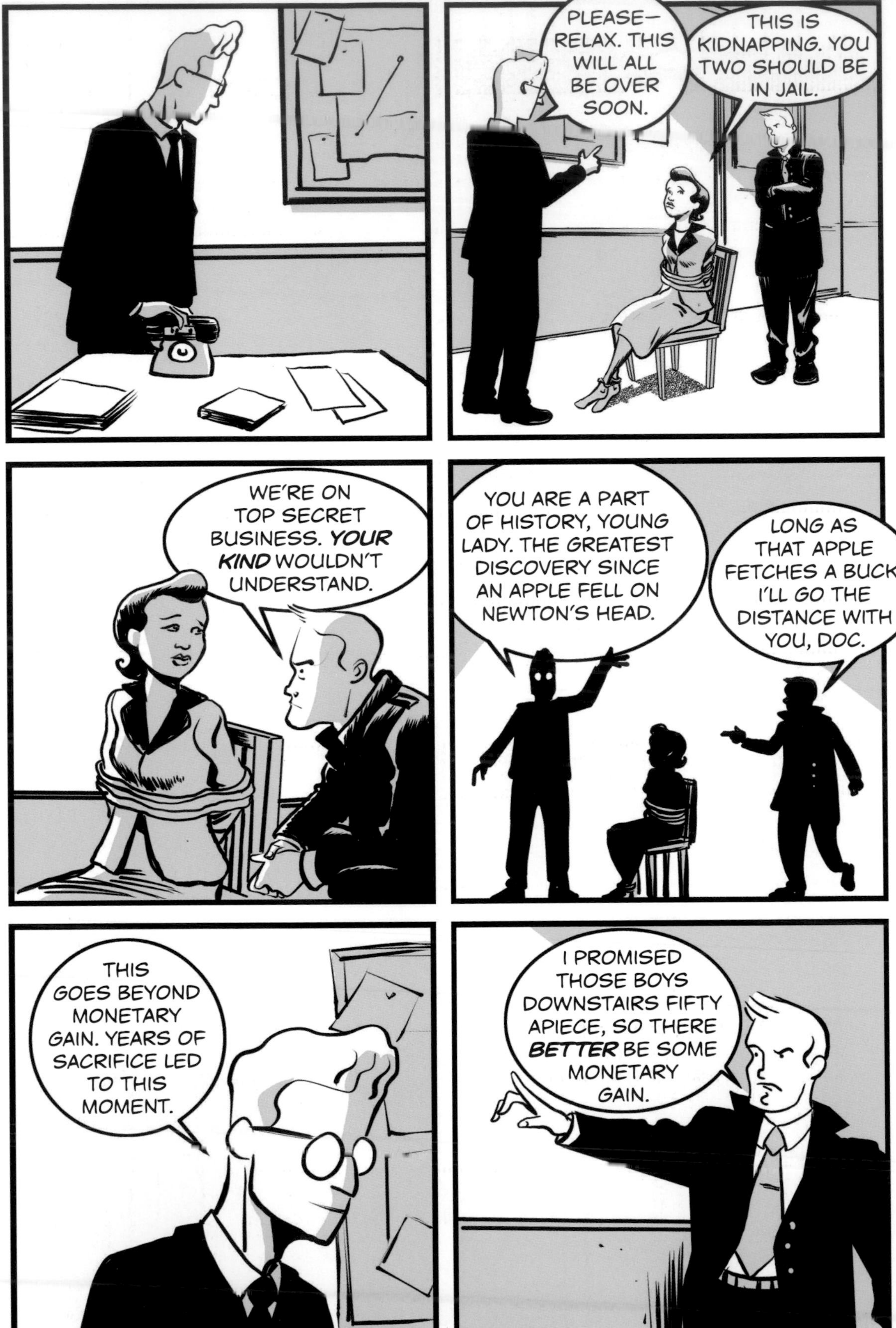
PLEASE—RELAX. THIS WILL ALL BE OVER SOON.
THIS IS KIDNAPPING. YOU TWO SHOULD BE IN JAIL.
WE'RE ON TOP SECRET BUSINESS. ***YOUR KIND*** WOULDN'T UNDERSTAND.
YOU ARE A PART OF HISTORY, YOUNG LADY. THE GREATEST DISCOVERY SINCE AN APPLE FELL ON NEWTON'S HEAD.
LONG AS THAT APPLE FETCHES A BUCK, I'LL GO THE DISTANCE WITH YOU, DOC.
THIS GOES BEYOND MONETARY GAIN. YEARS OF SACRIFICE LED TO THIS MOMENT.
I PROMISED THOSE BOYS DOWNSTAIRS FIFTY APIECE, SO THERE ***BETTER*** BE SOME MONETARY GAIN.

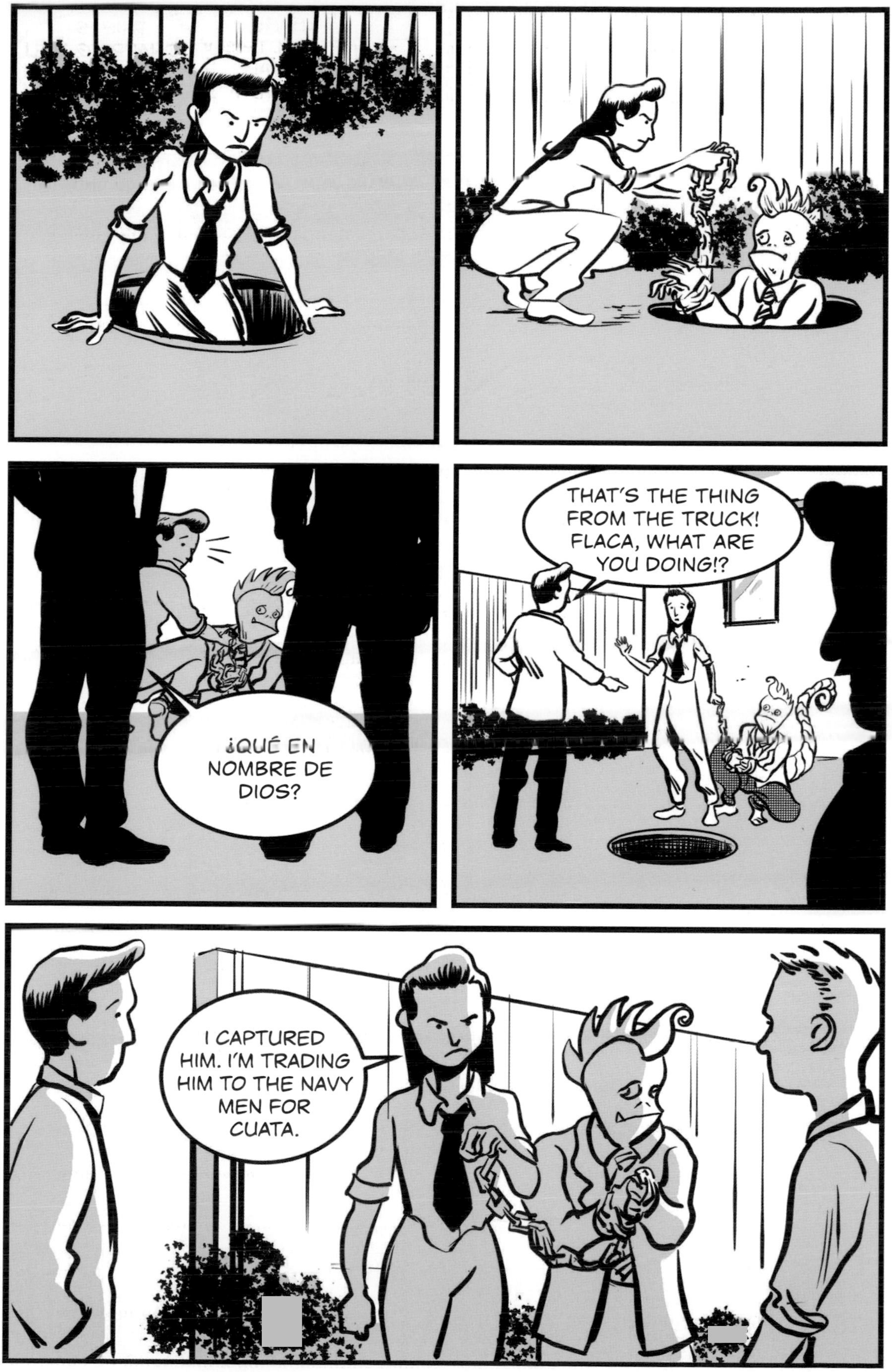
¿QUÉ EN NOMBRE DE DIOS?
THAT'S THE THING FROM THE TRUCK! FLACA, WHAT ARE YOU DOING!?
I CAPTURED HIM. I'M TRADING HIM TO THE NAVY MEN FOR CUATA.

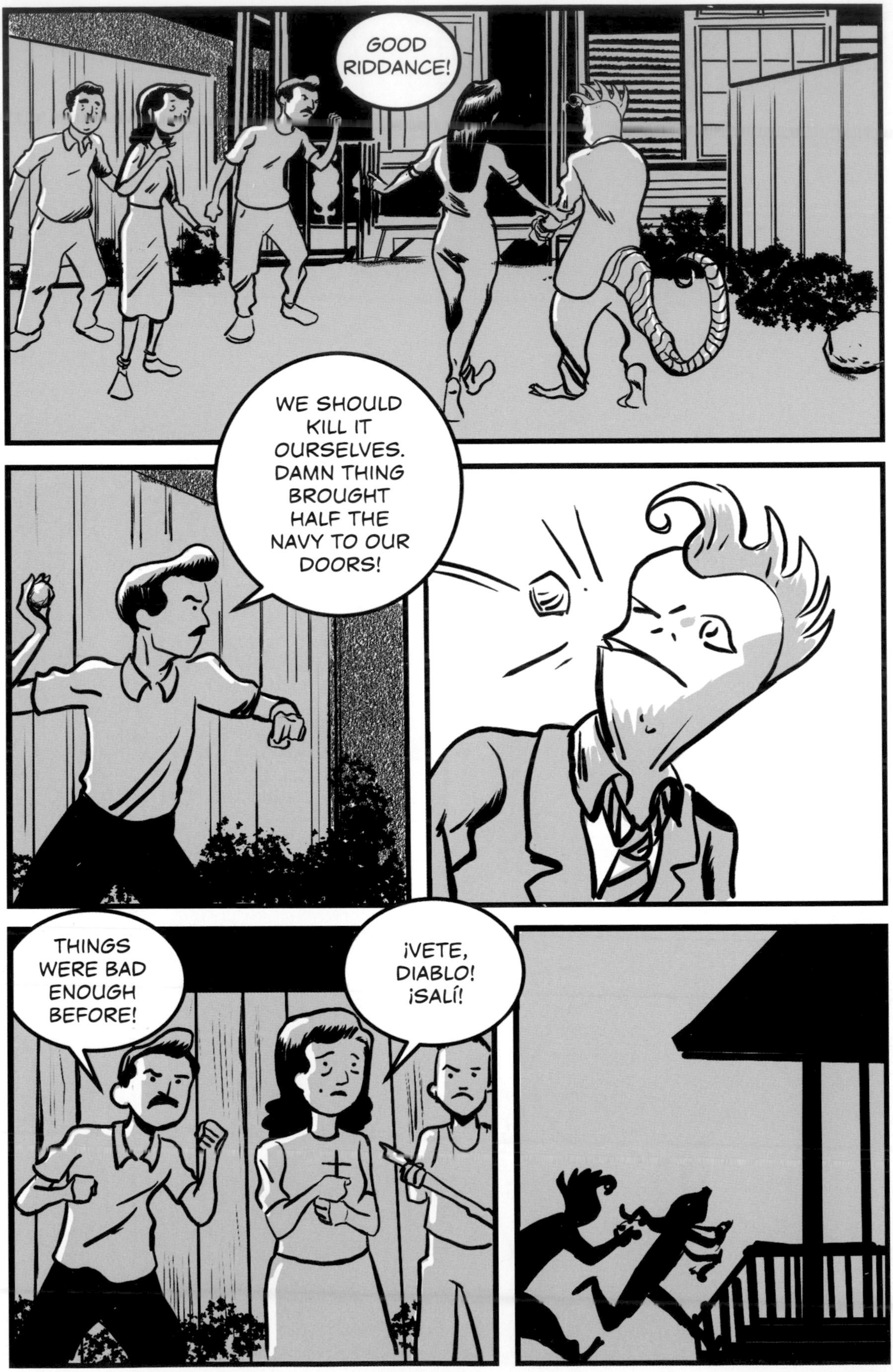
GOOD RIDDANCE!
WE SHOULD KILL IT OURSELVES. DAMN THING BROUGHT HALF THE NAVY TO OUR DOORS!
THINGS WERE BAD ENOUGH BEFORE!
¡VETE, DIABLO! ¡SALÍ!

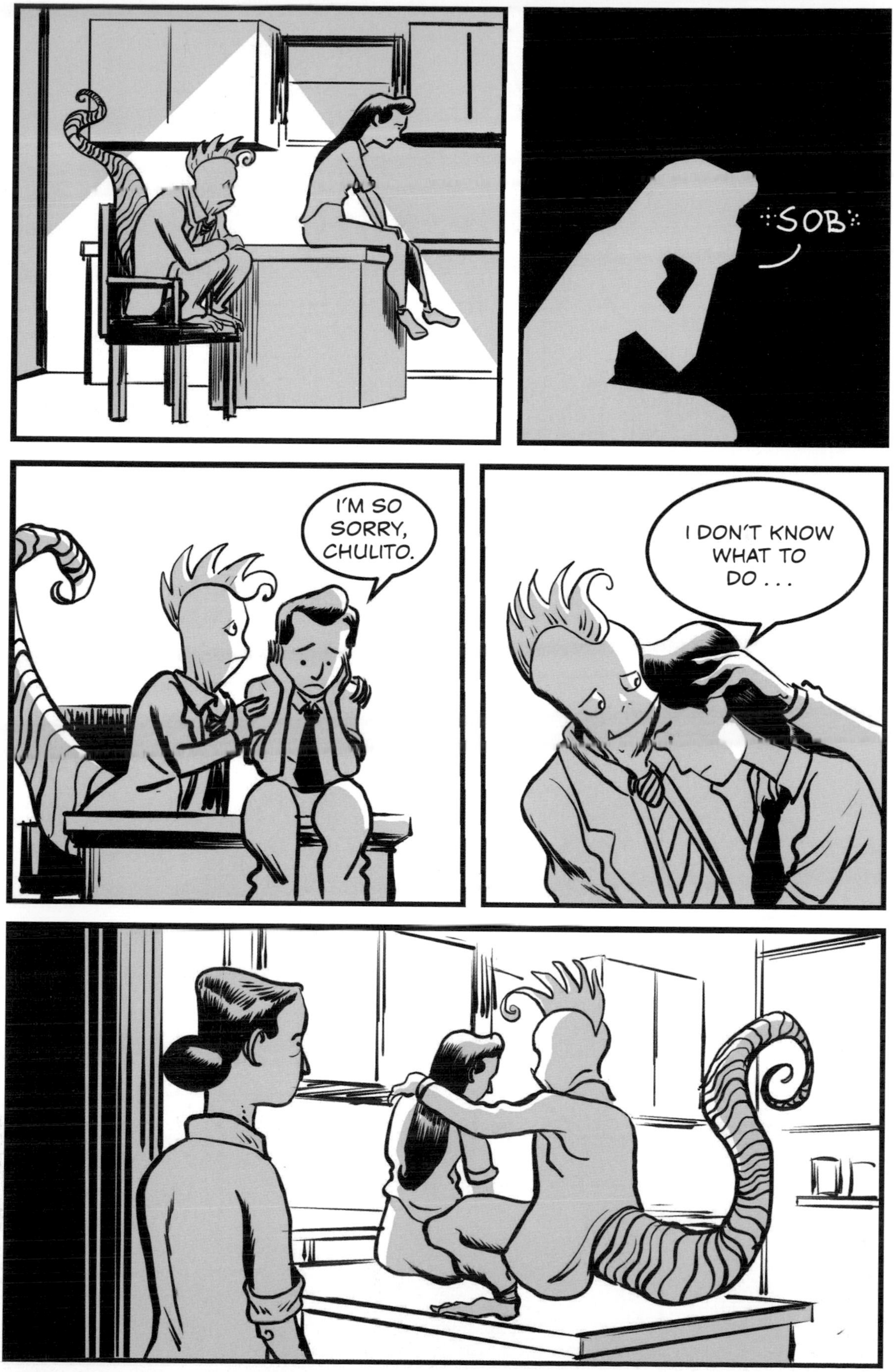
SOB
I'M SO SORRY, CHULITO.
I DON'T KNOW WHAT TO DO . . .

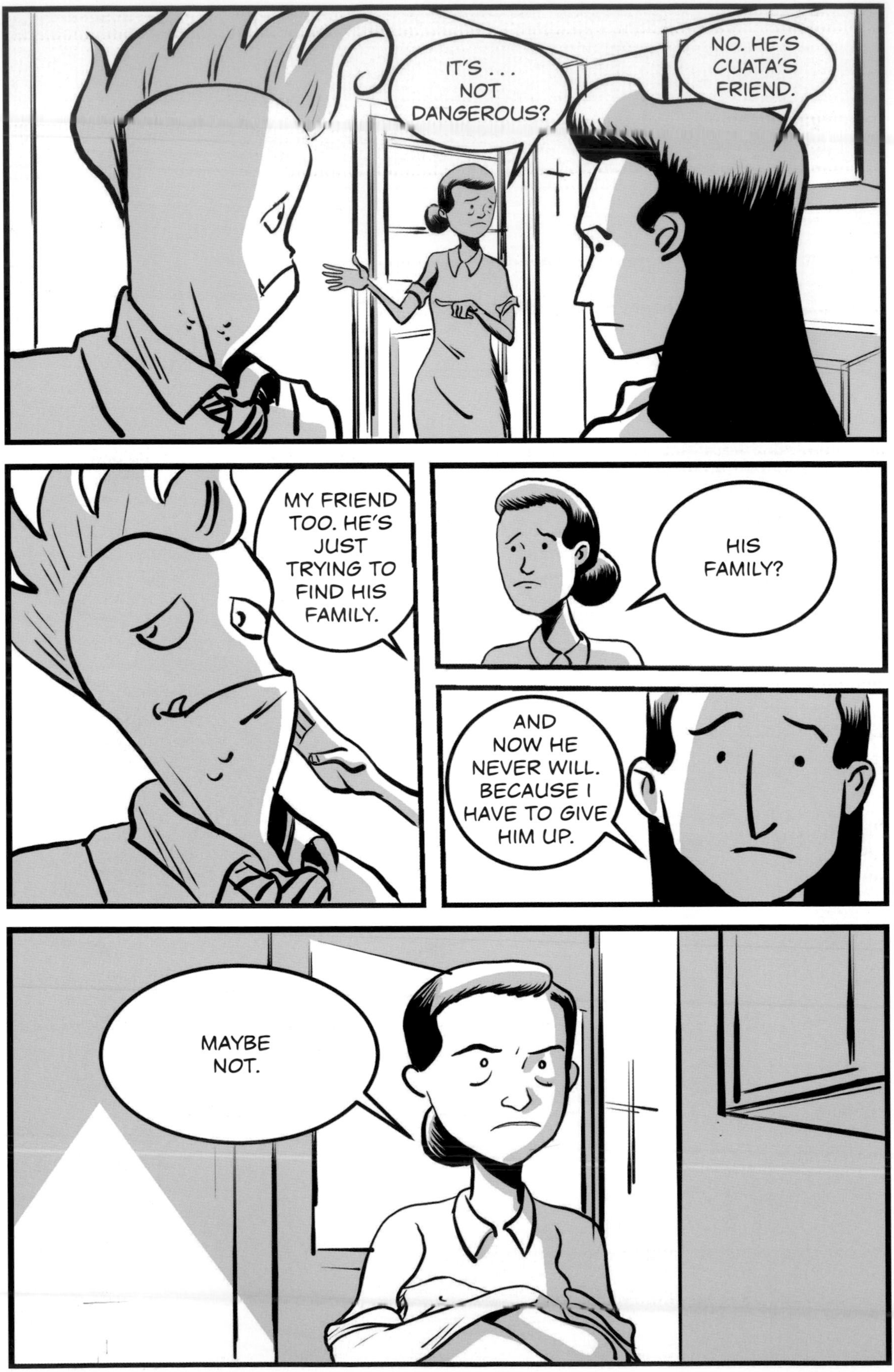
IT'S . . . NOT DANGEROUS?
NO. HE'S CUATA'S FRIEND.
MY FRIEND TOO. HE'S JUST TRYING TO FIND HIS FAMILY.
HIS FAMILY?
AND NOW HE NEVER WILL. BECAUSE I HAVE TO GIVE HIM UP.
MAYBE NOT.

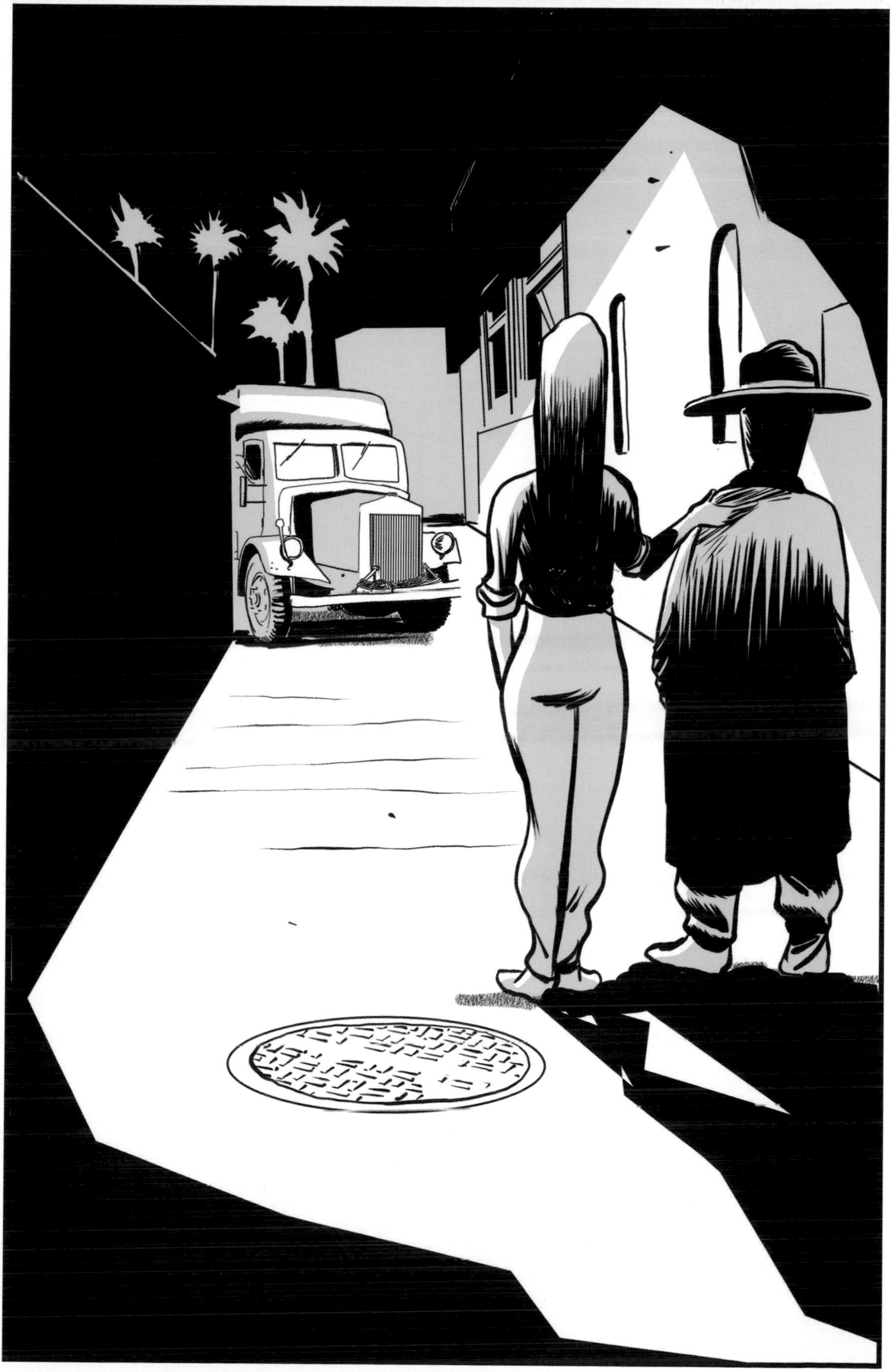

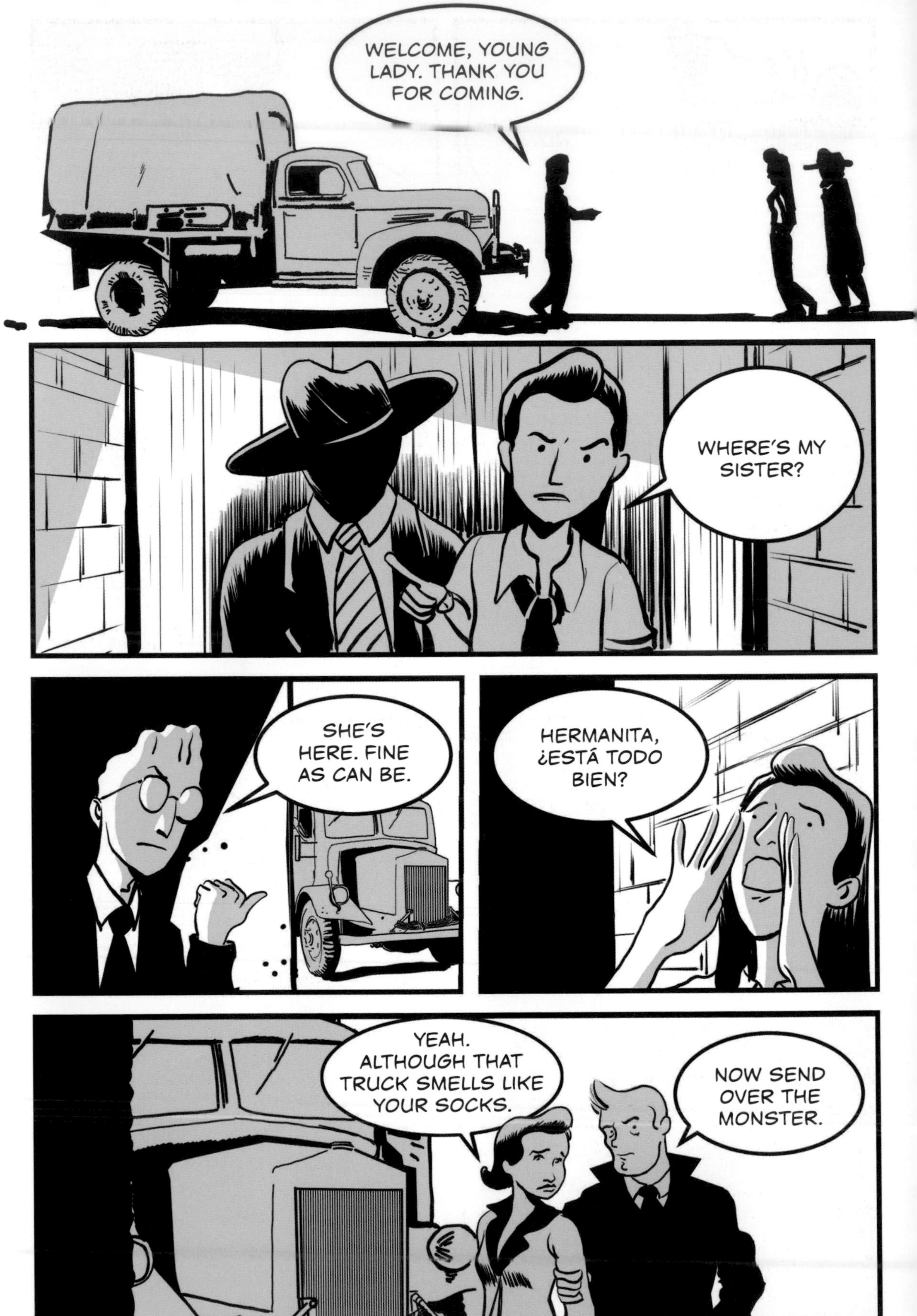
WELCOME, YOUNG LADY. THANK YOU FOR COMING.
WHERE'S MY SISTER?
SHE'S HERE. FINE AS CAN BE.
HERMANITA, ¿ESTÁ TODO BIEN?
YEAH. ALTHOUGH THAT TRUCK SMELLS LIKE YOUR SOCKS.
NOW SEND OVER THE MONSTER.

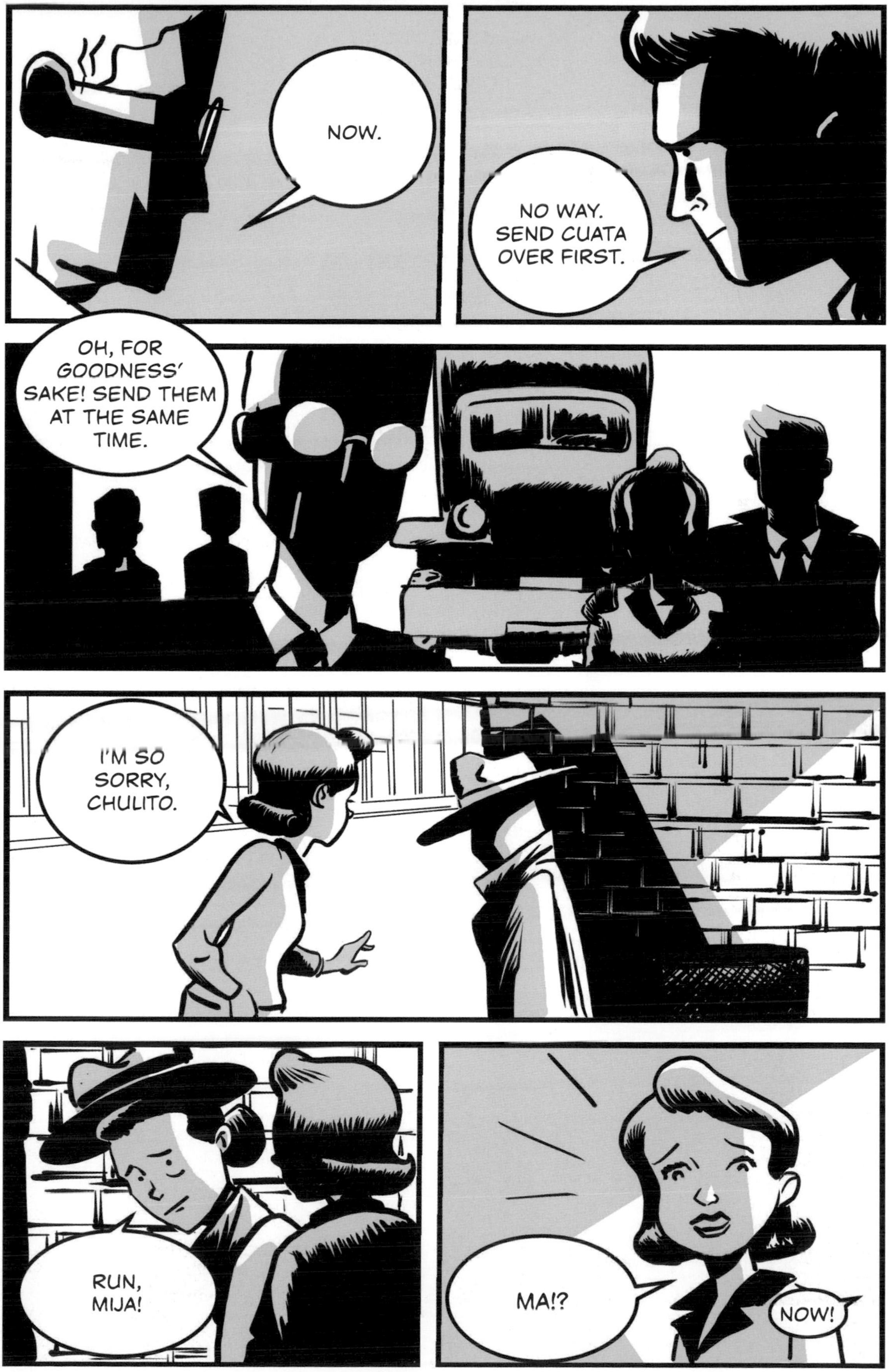
NOW.
NO WAY. SEND CUATA OVER FIRST.
OH, FOR GOODNESS' SAKE! SEND THEM AT THE SAME TIME.
I'M SO SORRY, CHULITO.
RUN, MIJA!
MA!?
NOW!

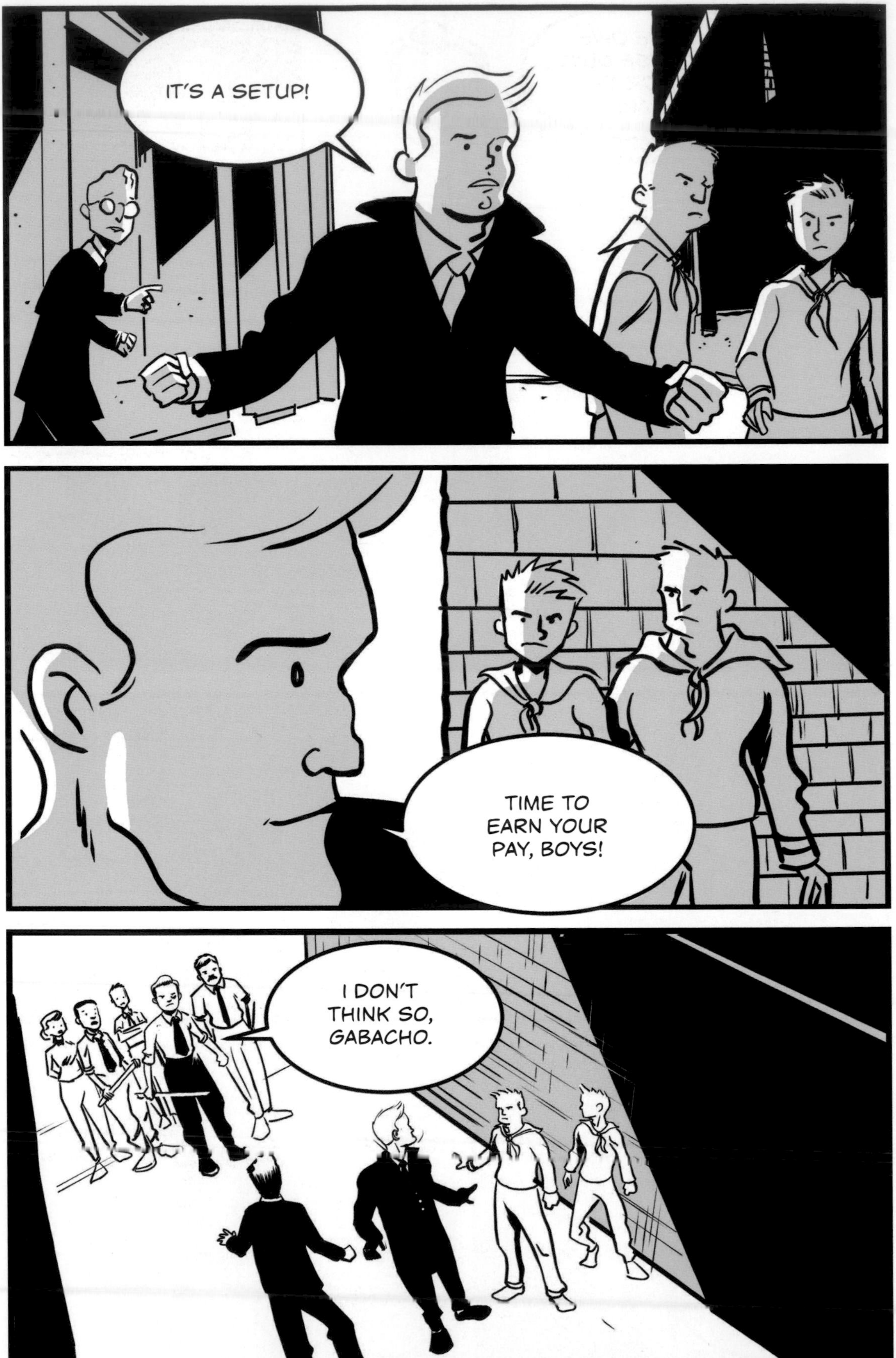
IT'S A SETUP!
TIME TO EARN YOUR PAY, BOYS!
I DON'T THINK SO, GABACHO.

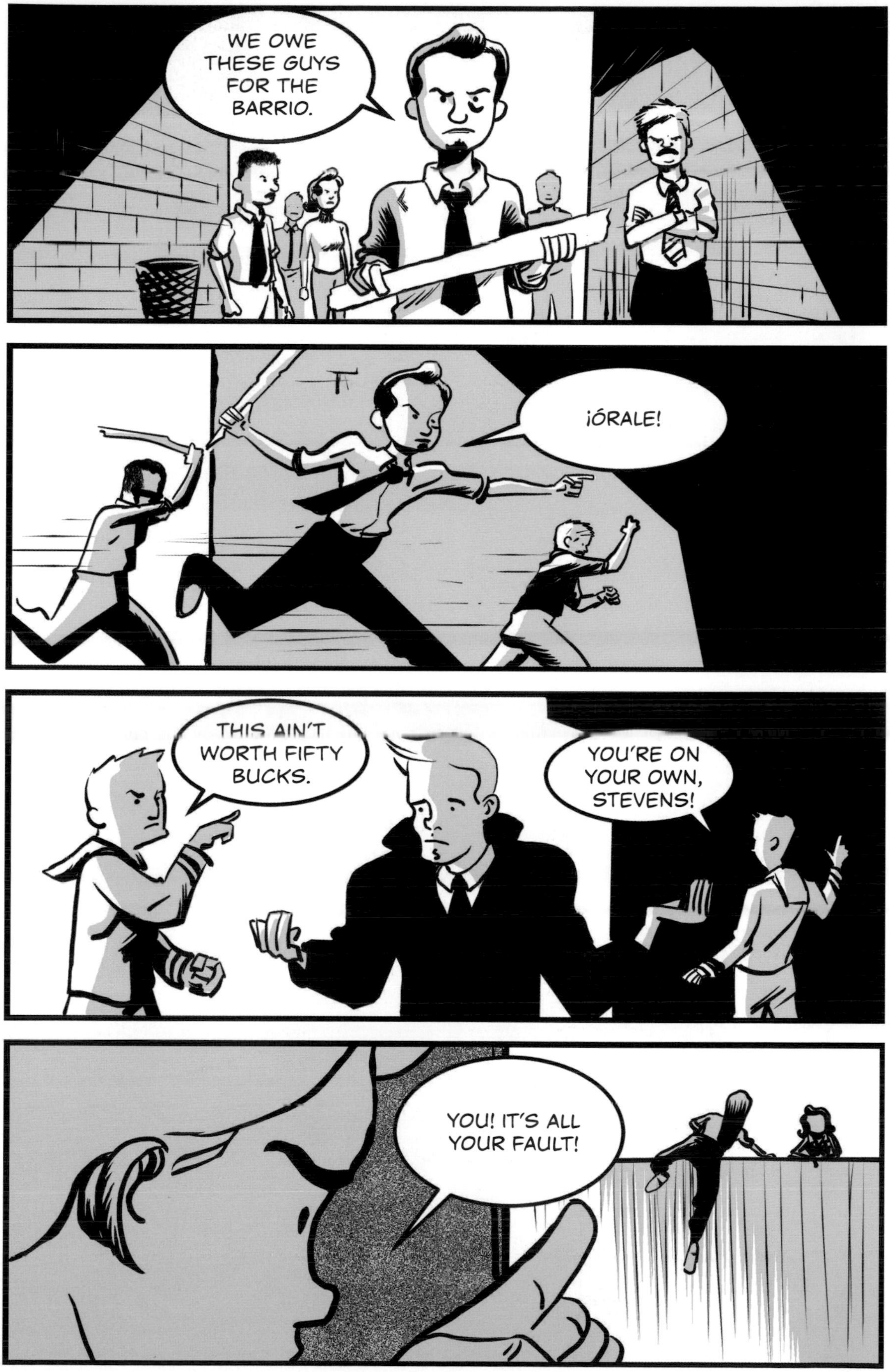
WE OWE THESE GUYS FOR THE BARRIO.
¡ÓRALE!
THIS AIN'T WORTH FIFTY BUCKS.
YOU'RE ON YOUR OWN, STEVENS!
YOU! IT'S ALL YOUR FAULT!

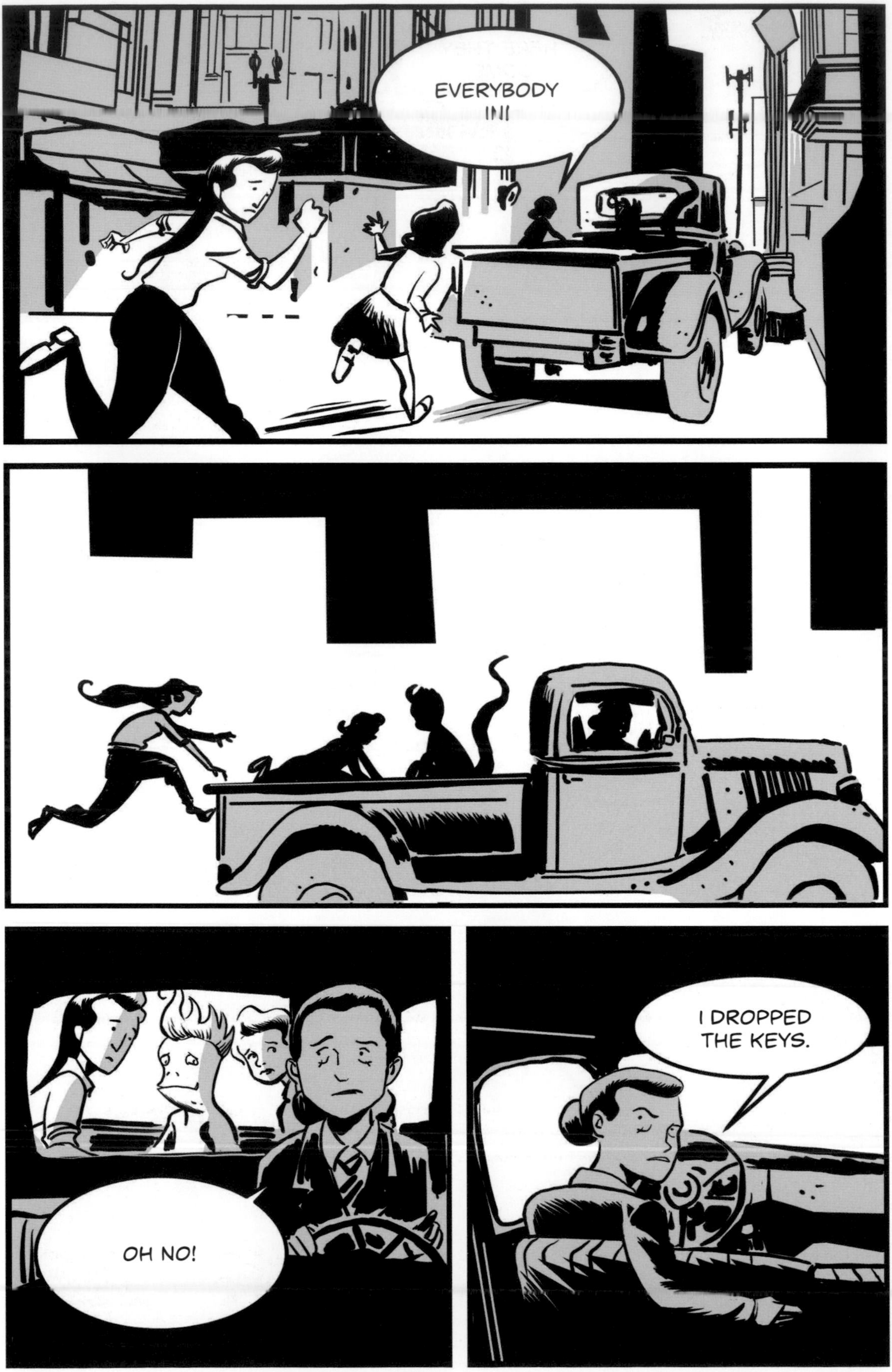
EVERYBODY IN!
OH NO!
I DROPPED THE KEYS.

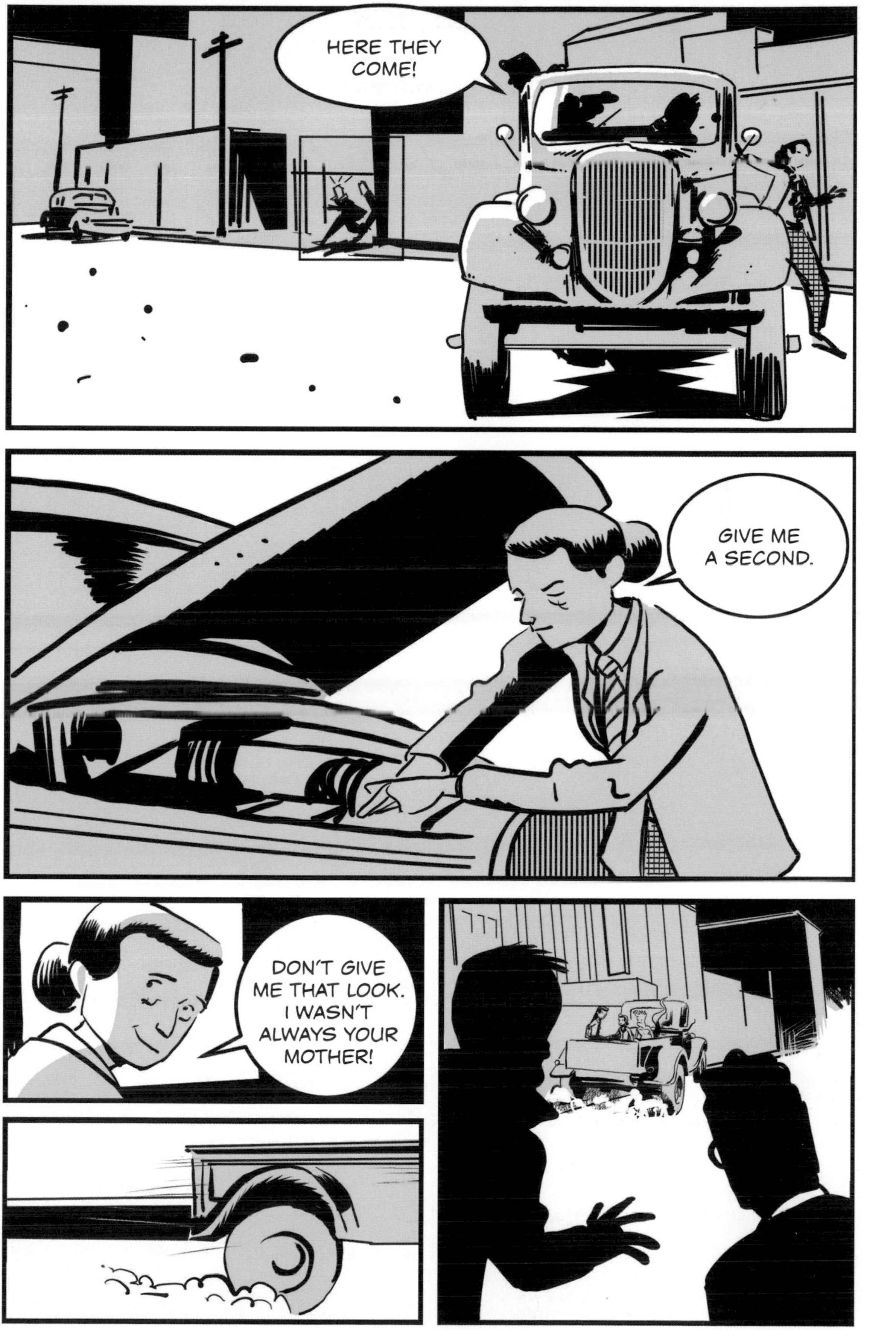
HERE THEY COME!
GIVE ME A SECOND.
DON'T GIVE ME THAT LOOK. I WASN'T ALWAYS YOUR MOTHER!

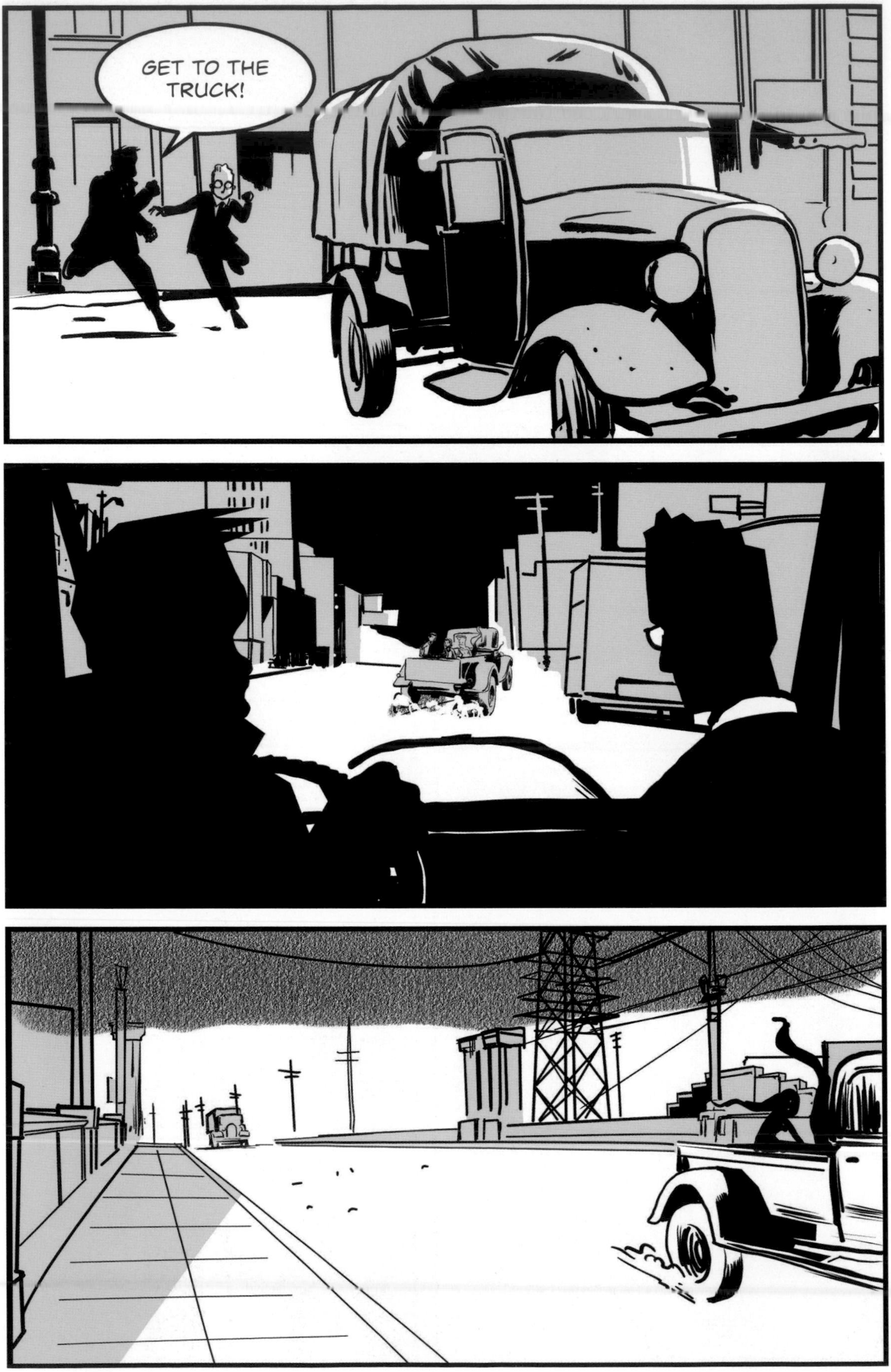
GET TO THE TRUCK!

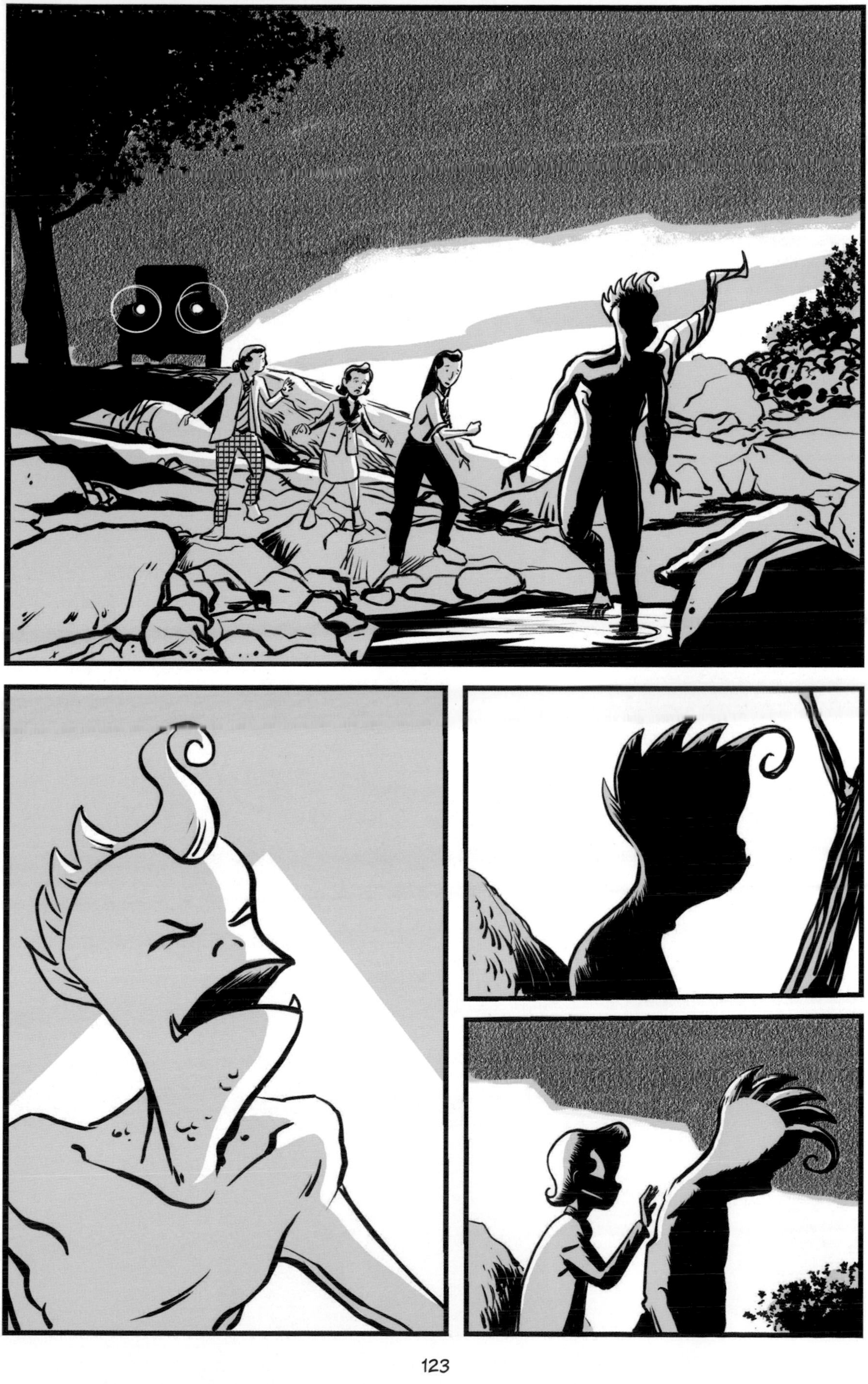

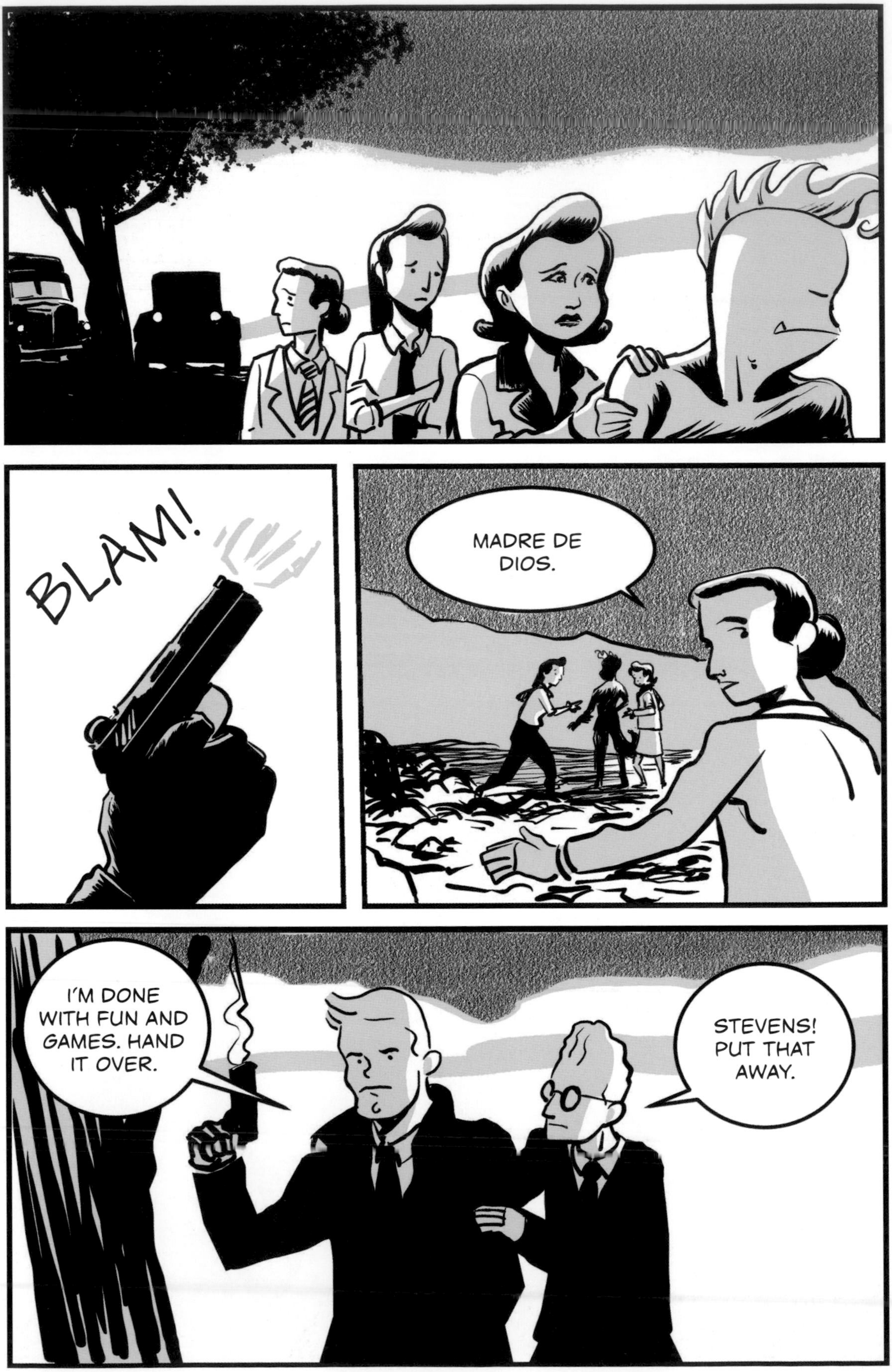
BLAM!
MADRE DE DIOS.
I'M DONE WITH FUN AND GAMES. HAND IT OVER.
STEVENS! PUT THAT AWAY.

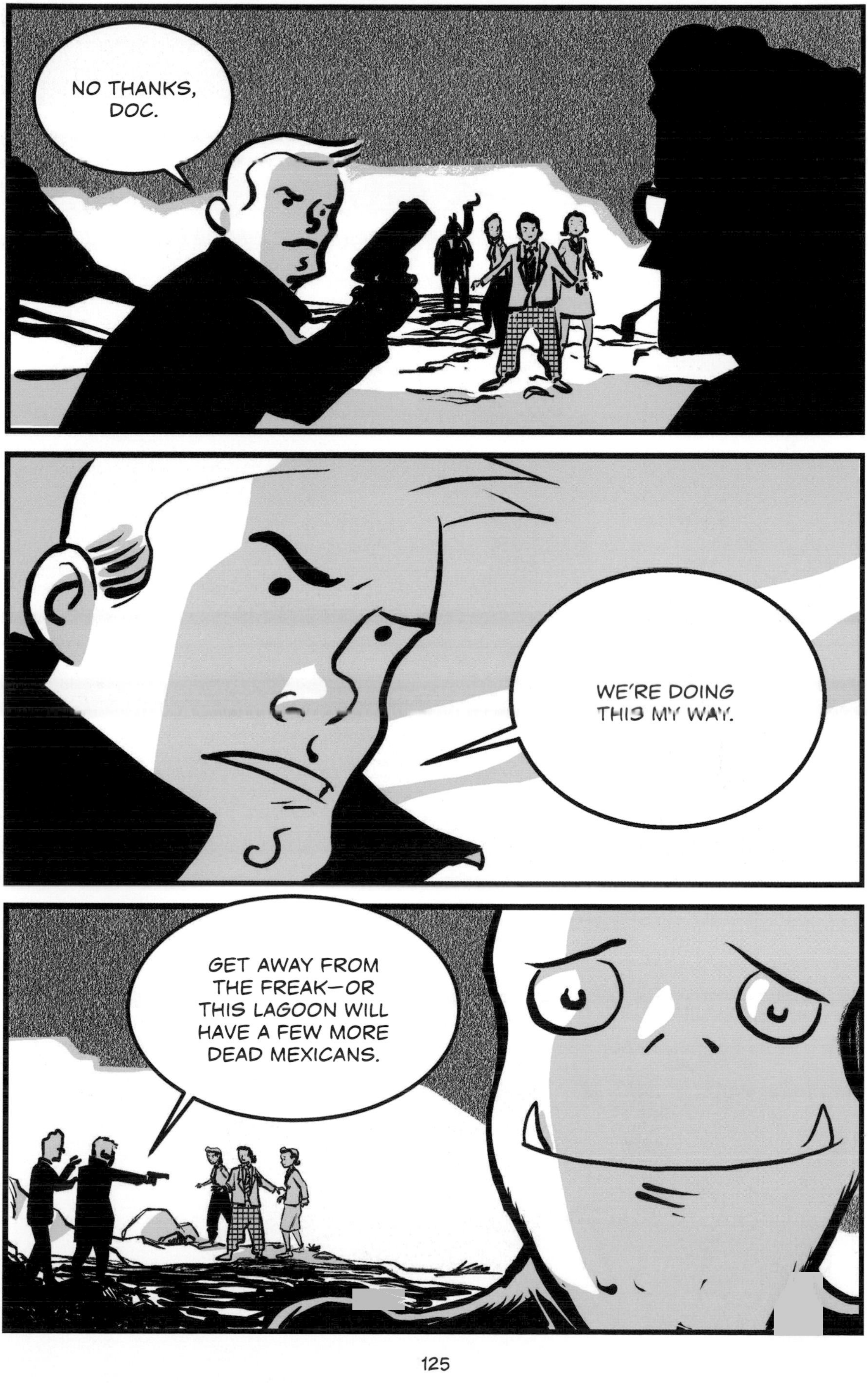
NO THANKS, DOC.
WE'RE DOING THIS MY WAY.
GET AWAY FROM THE FREAK—OR THIS LAGOON WILL HAVE A FEW MORE DEAD MEXICANS.

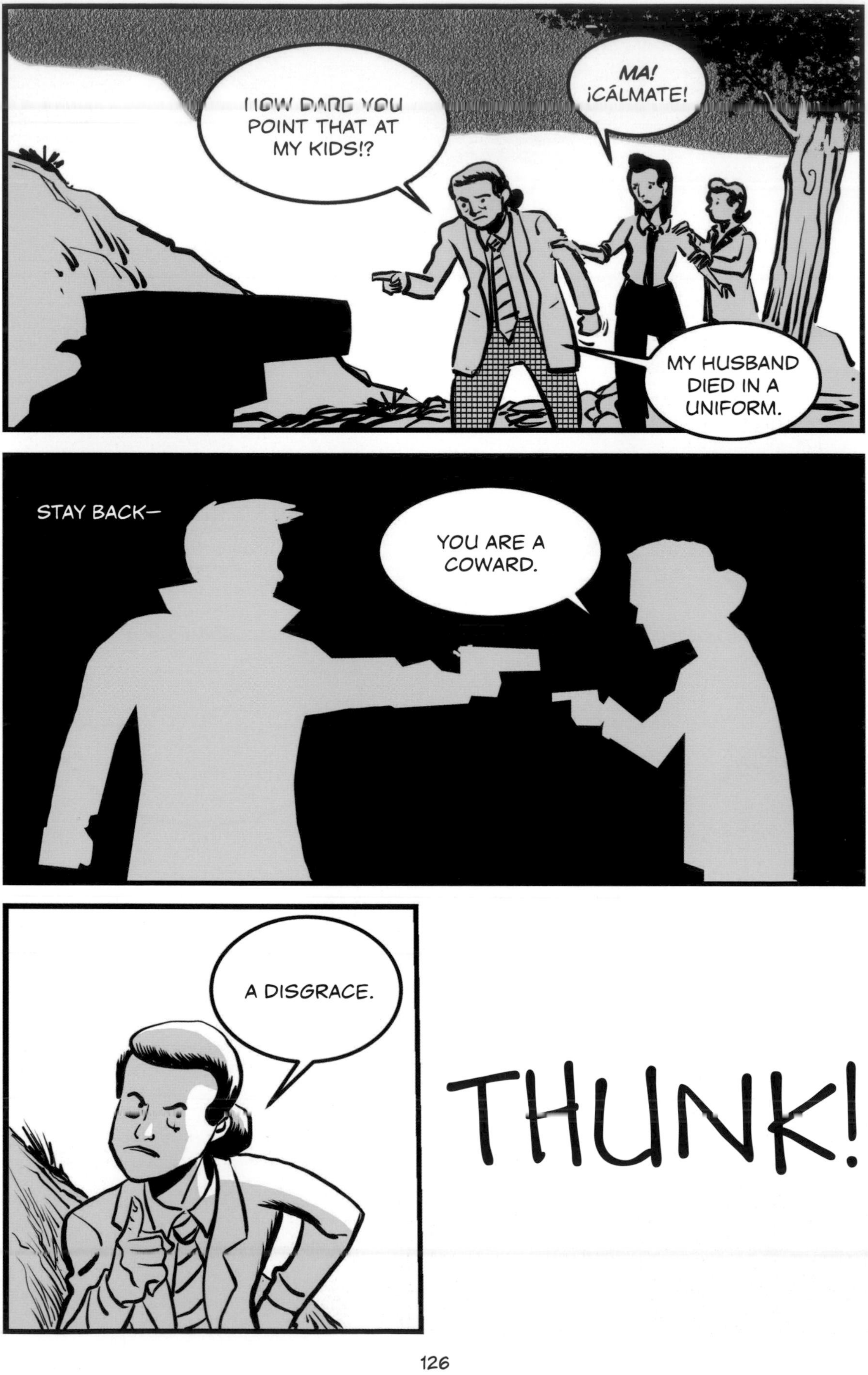
HOW DARE YOU POINT THAT AT MY KIDS!?
MA! ¡CÁLMATE!
MY HUSBAND DIED IN A UNIFORM.
STAY BACK—
YOU ARE A COWARD.
A DISGRACE.
THUNK!

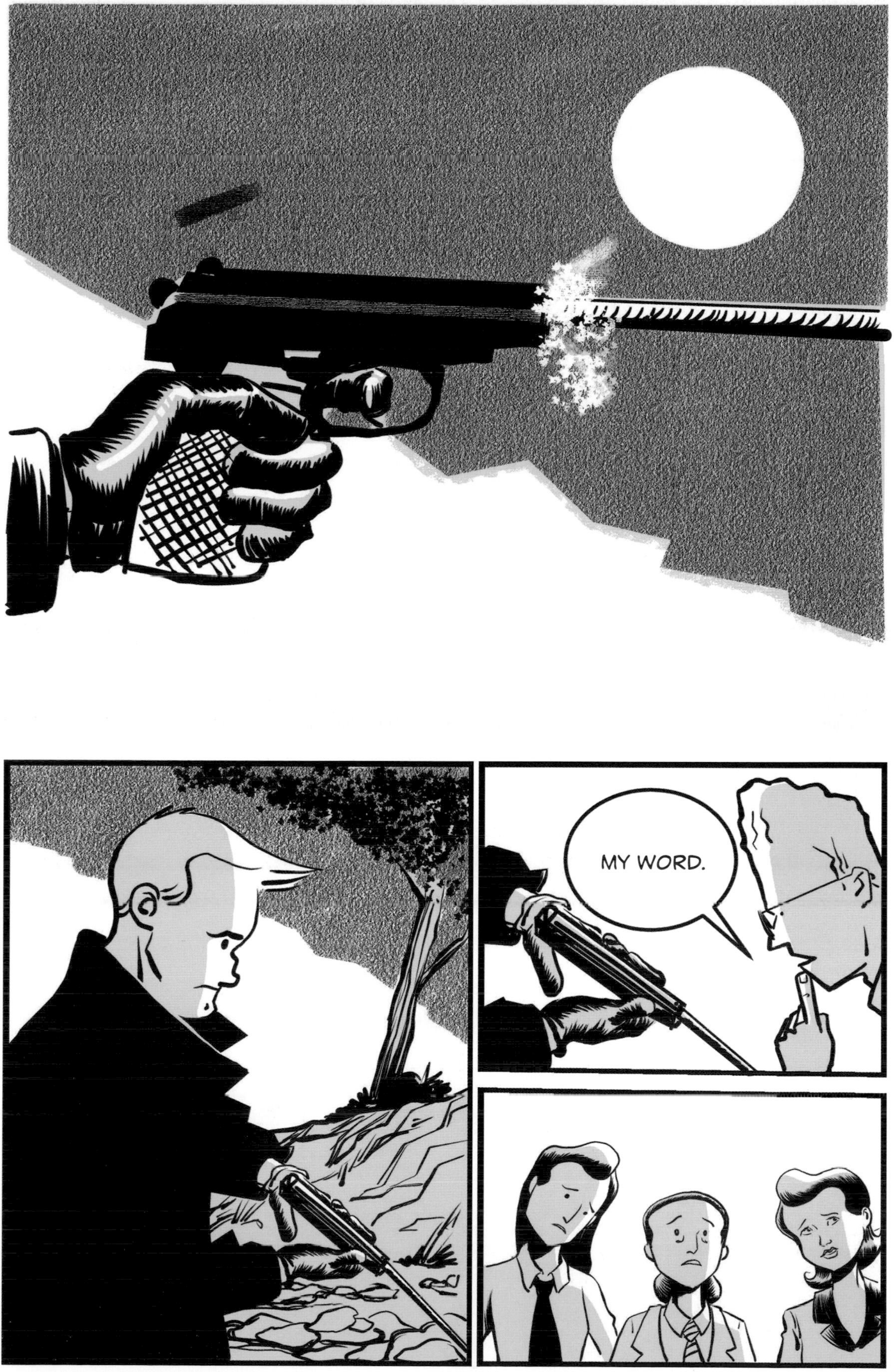
MY WORD.

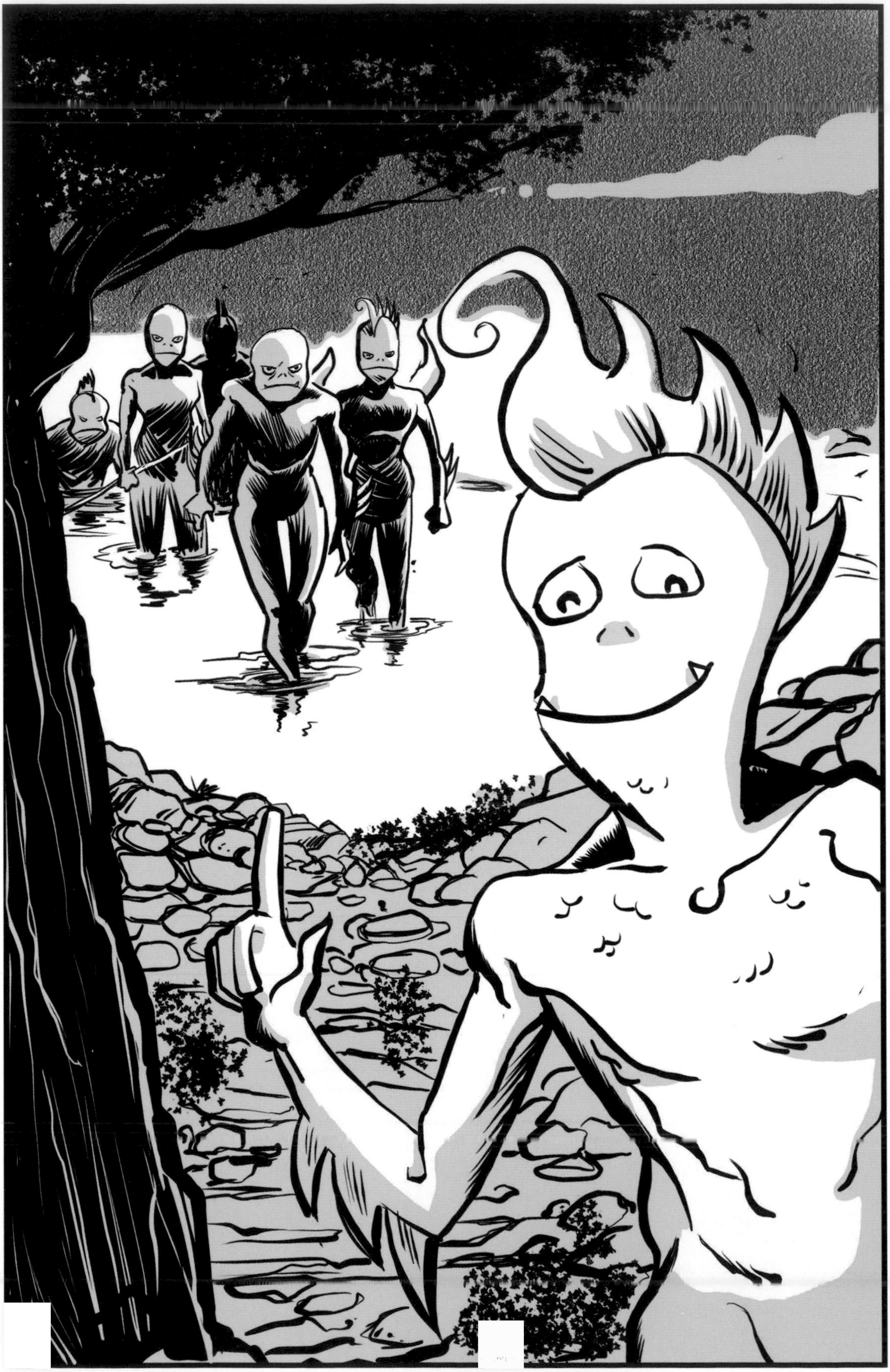

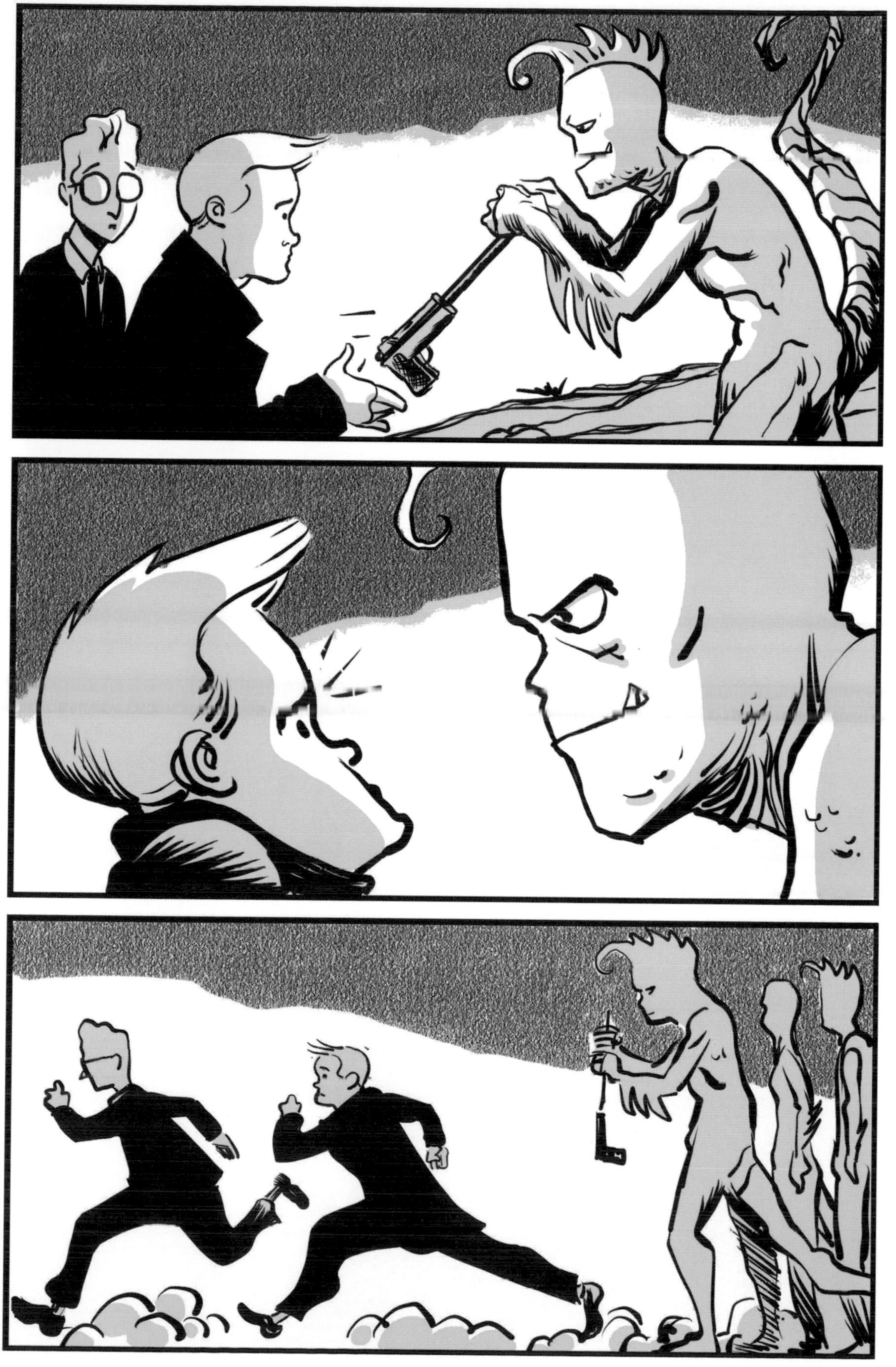

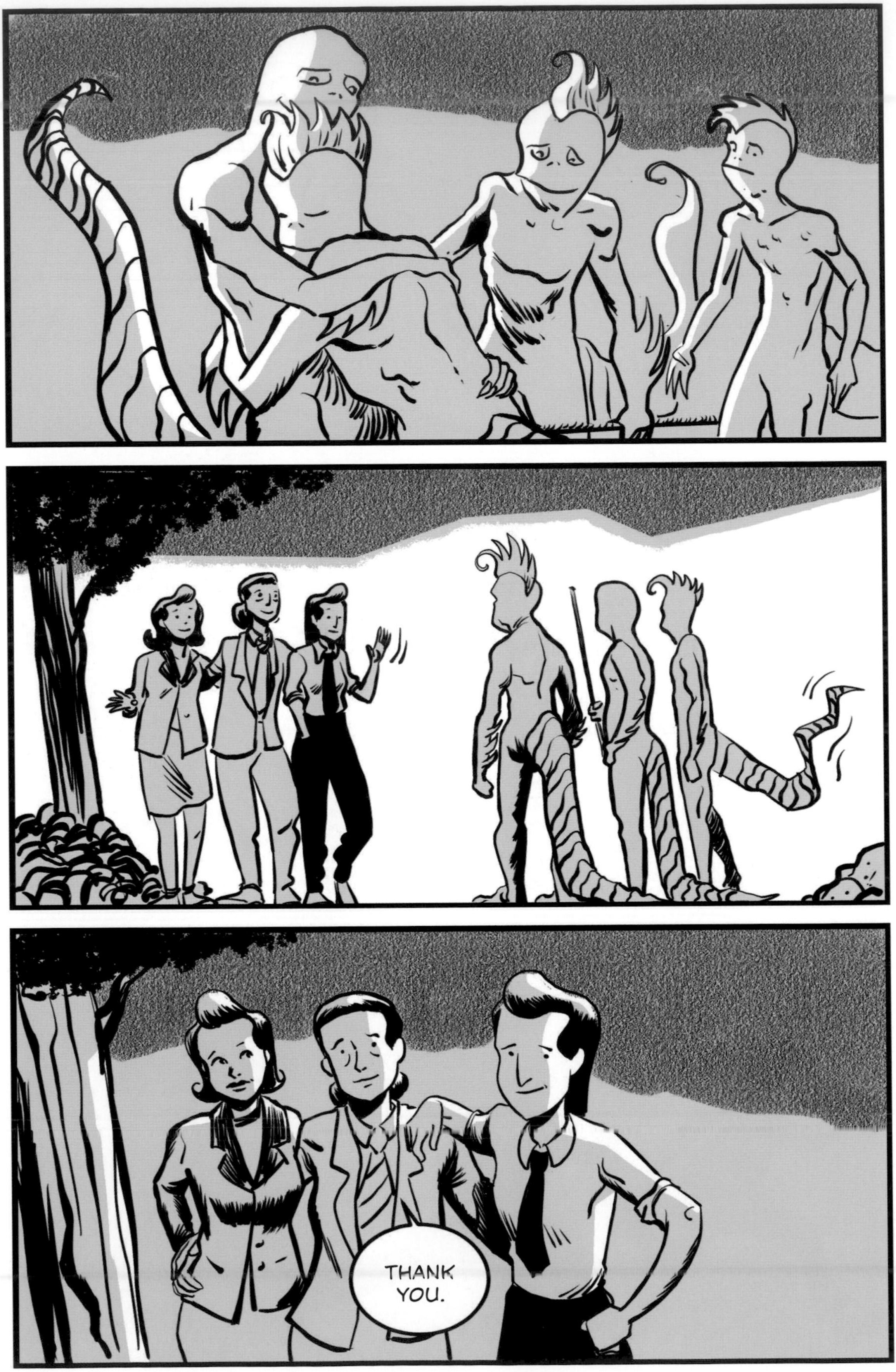
THANK YOU.

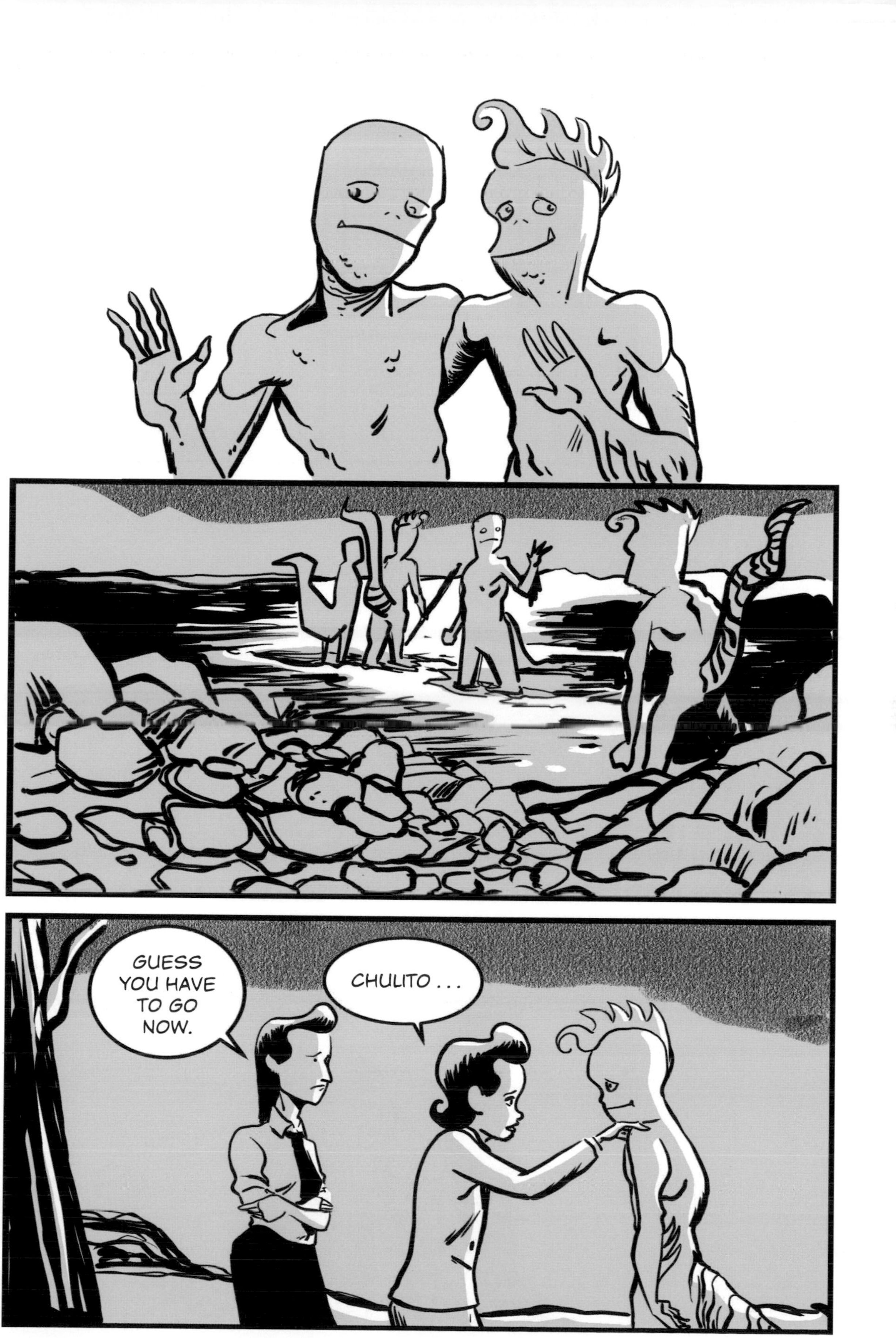
GUESS YOU HAVE TO GO NOW.
CHULITO . . .

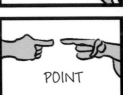

¡ÓRALE!

DAP

POUND

POINT

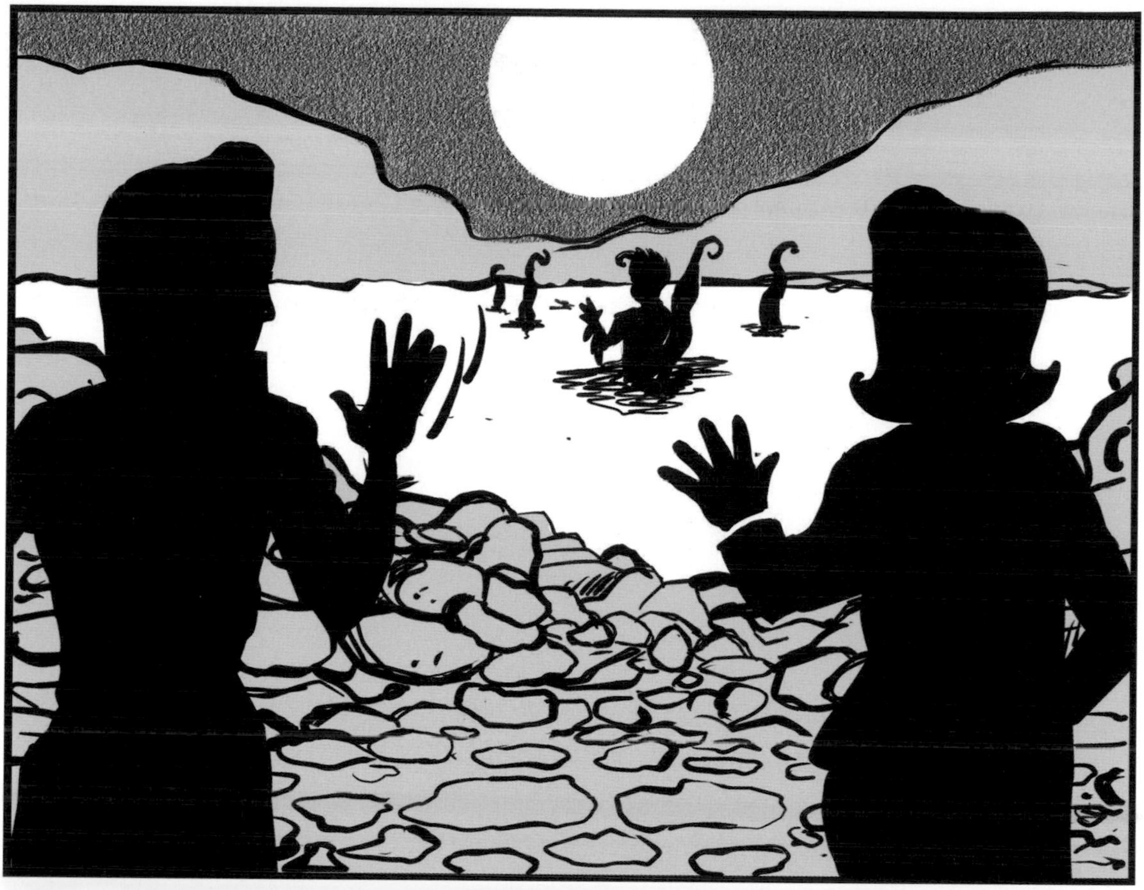

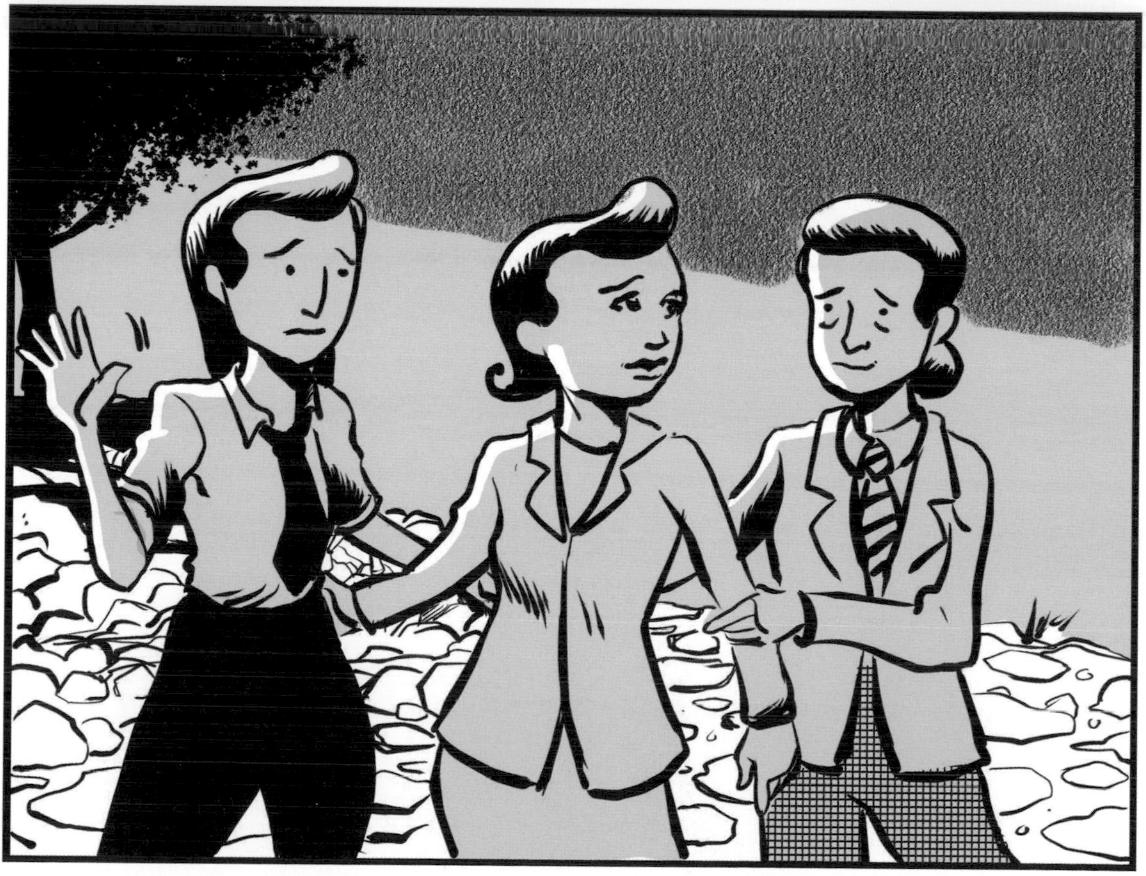

I GUESS WE GO HOME NOW TOO.
YEAH. HEY, I'M STARVING. ¿Y TU, HERMANITA?
HERMANA, POR FAVOR.
CUATA HOW SHORT IS THAT SKIRT?
THE END

WHAT WERE THE ZOOT SUIT RIOTS?

In the summer of 1943, the United States was embroiled in conflict. Abroad, soldiers fought in World War II. At home, changing cultural attitudes created clashes of their own. Los Angeles was one site of conflict. By 1943, poor city planning and new zoning laws had created a culture of segregation and animosity. The city was rapidly expanding, with white residents beginning to displace members of LA's large Mexican American population. New homes, schools, and businesses sprung up in historic Mexican American neighborhoods, and people who had lived there for generations began to see their home disappearing.

Adding to the tension, military planners placed the Navy and Marine Corps Reserve Armory, a whites-only training school, in the heart of a mostly Mexican American area. Here, hundreds of newly trained, mostly white military personnel waited to be shipped off to war, surrounded by a culture quite different from what many of them were used to. They soon found a new, violent way to spend time before deployment. The result became known as the Zoot Suit Riots.

Although the Zoot Suit Riots put a spotlight on Chicano zoot suit culture, the style emerged years before 1943. A decade earlier, dance halls were flourishing throughout New York City. In the predominantly Black neighborhood of Harlem, dancers escaped the stresses of the Great Depression through movement. The zoot suit's oversized trousers, carefully cuffed at the ankles, allowed men to move more easily on the dance floor. Over time, the zoot suit look came to include long, colorful jackets with oversized shoulder pads; lengthy, sparkling watch chains; and an assortment of lively hats. These outfits became a key part of Harlem jazz culture. They eventually inspired Mexican American young people all the way on the West Coast. Zoot suits embodied not only the unpredictable nature of jazz but also a larger stance of defiance. Among LA's young residents of color, their popularity soared.

World War II cut the fun short. After the United States entered the war, cloth was strictly rationed. Critics saw zoot suits, which used large amounts of fabric, as wasteful or even unpatriotic. Resentment toward brightly dressed "zoot-suiters" grew, a combination of patriotic zeal and prejudice against young people of color. Since wartime rationing effectively banned the production of the suits, bootleg tailors rushed to fill the need. This led to even more public outcry about the supposedly criminal nature of zoot suits and zoot-suiters.

While the dramatic flair of young men's zoot suits captured national attention, the role of women—particularly Chicana women—in the movement went mostly overlooked. But like their male counterparts, Chicana women embraced the rebellious swagger of zoot suits. They developed their own fashions, which often included flared skirts, wide-shouldered jackets, and tall bouffant hairstyles. These trendsetting young women pushed past acceptable standards of femininity and built their own vibrant Southern California subculture, a stylish blend of their Mexican heritage and American upbringings.

Animosity toward Mexican Americans grew following the Sleepy Lagoon case in January of 1943. After the death of a young Chicano man at the Sleepy Lagoon swimming hole outside Los Angeles, authorities arrested twenty-two Mexican American men on murder charges. The young men were tried as a collective in one of the largest, most widely covered cases in California history. At the end of a trial loaded with racist rhetoric, the court found twelve defendants guilty of murder (although the convictions would be reversed two years later). Reflecting the trial's rhetoric and the biased journalism that perpetuated it, many white people across the United States used the Sleepy Lagoon case as an example of the allegedly bloodthirsty mentality of Chicano boys and men. This belief would become justification for assaults on people of color daring to wear zoot suits later that summer.

Despite the tensions simmering between stationed military men and young locals, the exact beginning of the Zoot Suit Riots remains uncertain. Military personnel and residents of color gave conflicting reports of the events leading up to June 3, 1943. Newspaper articles that pointed blame at Mexican American youth further muddied the waters. It's likely that a few days before the full riots began, a violent clash between young Chicano men and servicemen took place, with servicemen using this incident as justification to search the streets for anyone they thought deserved a beating.

On June 3, 1943, a posse of fifty uniformed sailors left the Navy and Marine Corps Reserve Armory. Unable to smuggle weapons out of the armory, the sailors had loaded rolls of coins into their neckerchiefs. Riding in the taxis and cars of private citizens who had offered them free rides, they hunted for any young people wearing zoot suits. When the sailors found someone, they beat the person and stripped them of their clothes. Word spread about the attacks, and the next night, some two hundred more sailors, soldiers, and marines joined in. The servicemen recruited twenty taxis to drive them downtown to carry out vigilante justice.

Soon military men in full uniform were not just attacking Mexican American youths in zoot suits but any brown men they could find. Black and Filipino people were especially popular targets—despite the fact that most of them were not dressed in zoot-suiter styles. Rioters even invaded movie theaters, bars, and other gathering

Two young men recover on the sidewalk outside a Los Angeles movie theater on the evening of June 7, 1943. Earlier, a group of servicemen had assaulted the two youths, stripping one of them of his clothes.

spaces, taking young men out of their seats and dragging them into the streets. As the riots continued over the next few days, crowds of civilians joined in the raids. Servicemen from around the state traveled to Los Angeles by the hundreds. By June 7, thousands were marching across the city or cruising in taxis to find targets.

Despite prominent Mexican American professionals calling on city officials to end the riots, the mayor of Los Angeles and governor of California did not intervene. In fact, the police often watched attacks as they happened. Sometimes, after the crowd moved on, officers arrested the bruised and half-naked victims, supposedly for their own safety, and threw them in jail. Meanwhile, the press demonized the zoot-suiters, with the *Los Angeles Times* praising military men for giving them "a great moral lesson." During the height of the riots, the paper even published a how-to guide for stripping a zoot-suiter and destroying his outfit.

Finally, after five days of violence and chaos, the US military took steps to end the violence, forbidding military service members from leaving their barracks after June 8. The riots slowed thereafter and then stopped on June 10, 1943. The City of Los Angeles issued a ban on zoot suits, placing the blame squarely on the shoulders of its young residents of color. Incredibly, no one was killed during the riots, but at least 150 people were injured and approximately 500 Mexican American boys and men were arrested and put in Los Angeles jails.

At first, it looked as if no formal investigation would be made into the cause of the riots. Few military men were arrested, and most white Los Angeles residents went back to their lives as if nothing had happened. Only after the Mexican Embassy sent a complaint to California did Governor Earl Warren create a committee to investigate the violence. His committee found that racism had been the main motivator for the attacks. The committee also explained that the police's negligence and inflammatory press coverage made the situation far worse. Los Angeles mayor Fletcher Brown disputed the report, blaming the riots on local gangs of young Mexican American men.

CREATING *LIZARD IN A ZOOT SUIT*

Like many other kids, I first encountered zoot suit lore through Luis Valdez's play of the same name. I remember catching a filmed version on PBS and asking my ma about it. She told me about friends of hers who had grown up in those times. She also told me about the prejudice they faced because of the color of their skin and the clothes they wore.

One of my goals when I set out to write *Lizard in a Zoot Suit* was to cast some kids who readers may not have seen in an adventure story. Growing up in the 1980s, most of the adventures I saw starred kids from the suburbs who had big houses. I wanted my characters to have daily struggles in addition to their great adventure. Then, over the course of a few days, I reread Valdez's *Zoot Suit* and *Chavez Ravine (a play)* by the performance troupe Culture Clash. And it all came together.

Flaca was the easiest of the bunch to design. She came out pretty much fully formed in my early sketches. I wanted her to be the opposite of a typical 1940s female character. She's the toughest kid in the barrio.

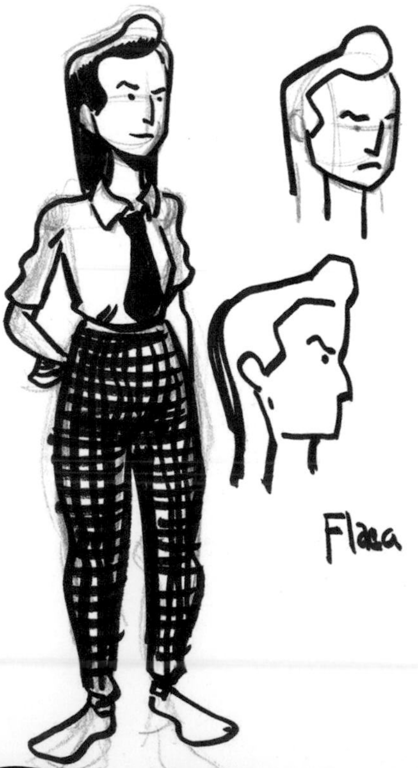
Flaca

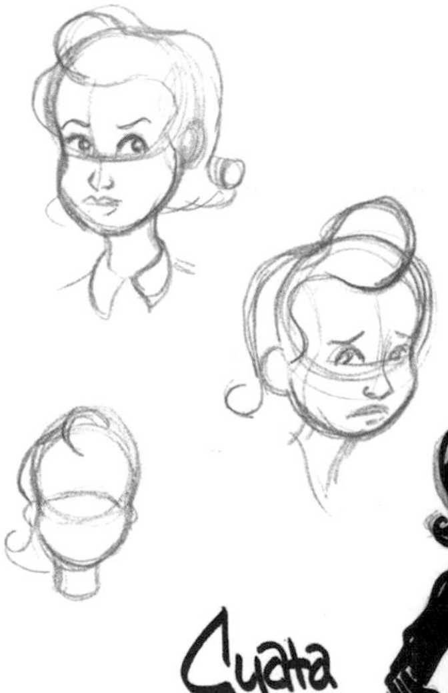
Cuata

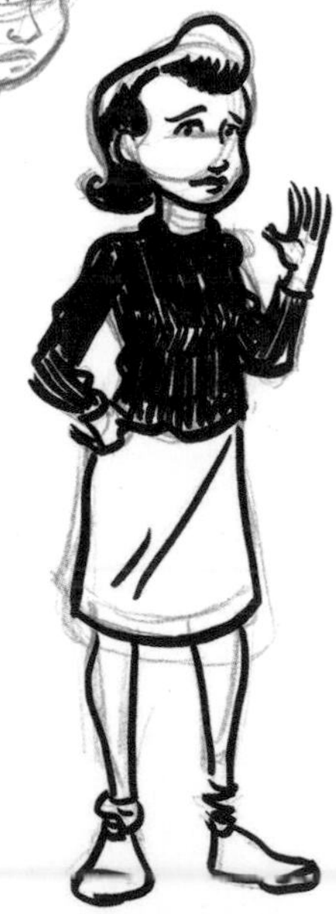

Cuata was the complete opposite of her sister and was the character I struggled with the most. She's interested in gossip and the latest trends, but she's also intuitive and empathetic. I feel that Chulito isn't the first creature she has rescued.

Chulito was tricky too but a blast to draw. I tried to keep the rubber-suit vibe of classic creature films but still put a unique twist on it.

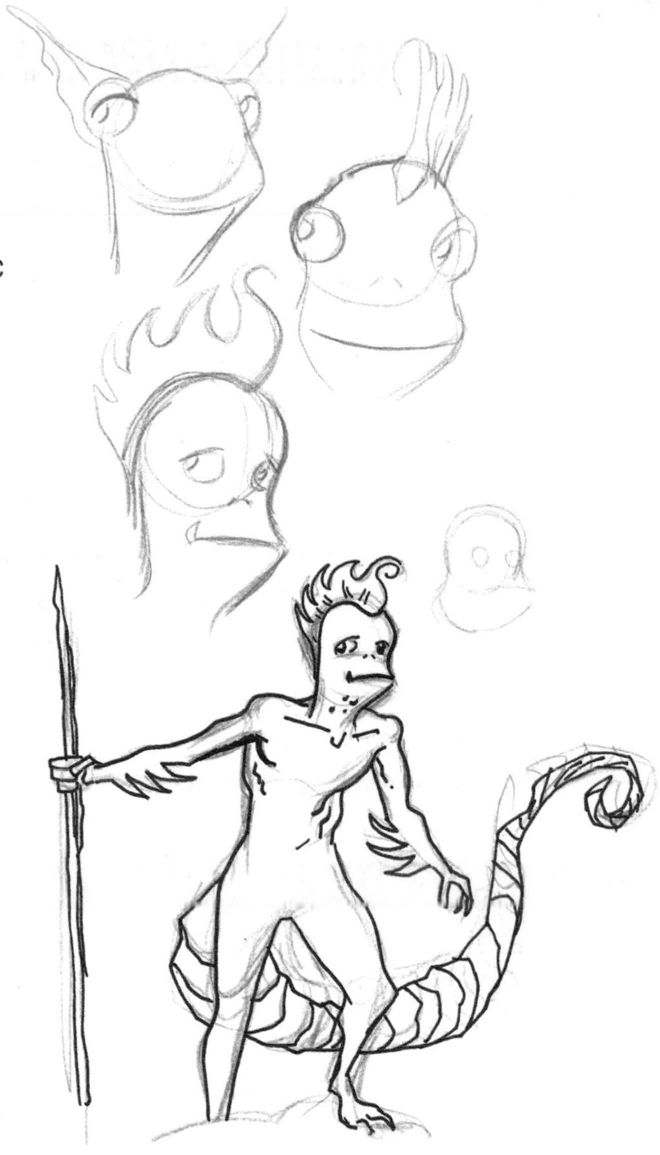

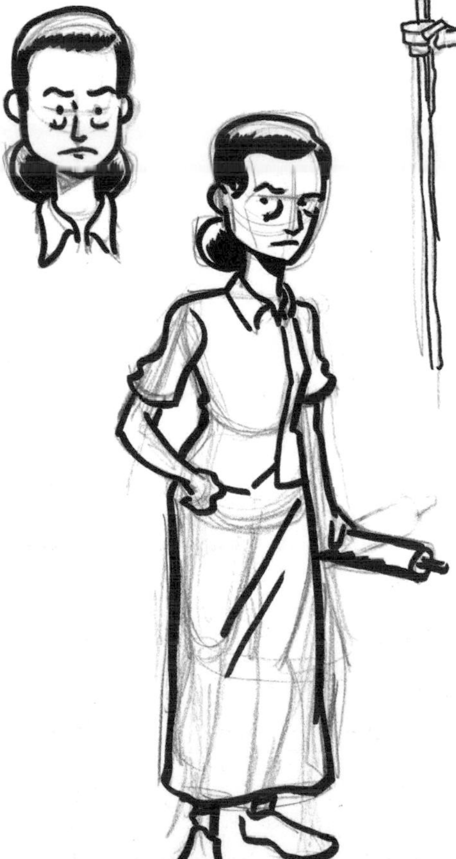

Ma turned out to be fun to write *and* draw. She definitely has my own ma's personality, and her working at a factory is a nod to my ma's days of working at a similar factory job in El Paso.

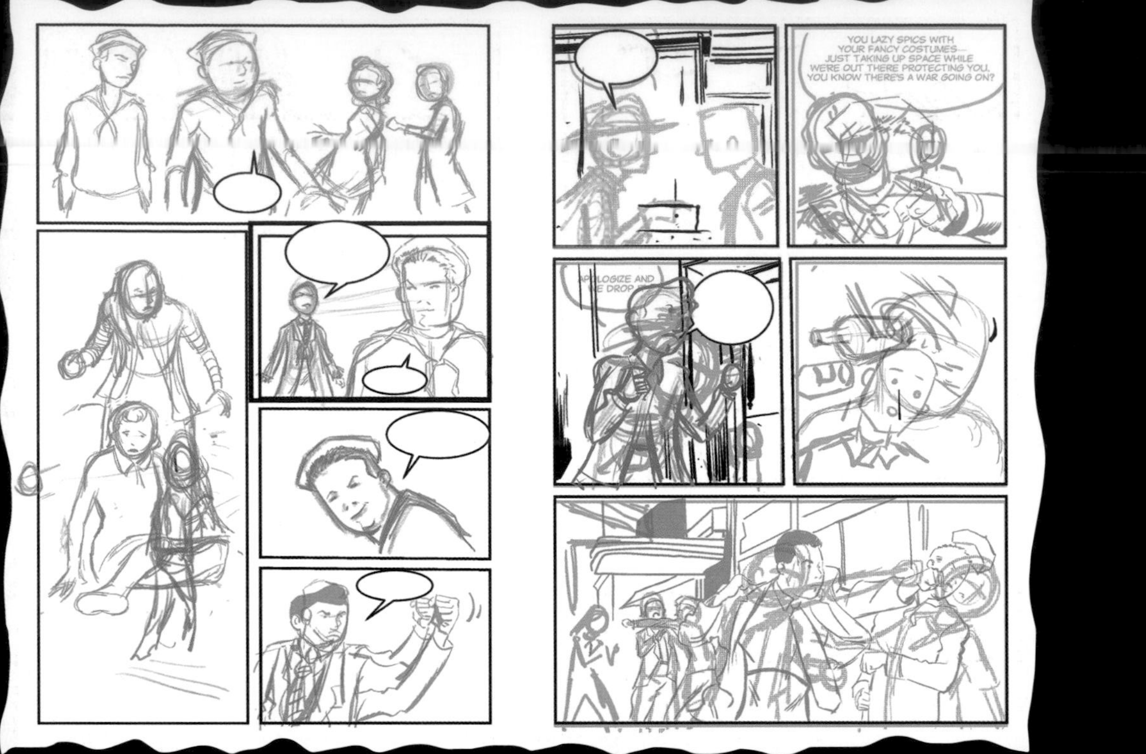
YOU LAZY SPICS WITH YOUR FANCY COSTUMES— JUST TAKING UP SPACE WHILE WE'RE OUT THERE PROTECTING YOU. YOU KNOW THERE'S A WAR GOING ON?

What always struck with me about my ma's descriptions of the zoot suit days was how people like her friends had been expected to give up the sidewalk when service members walked by. Of course, in this scene with the sisters and Puppet, that's not exactly what happens.

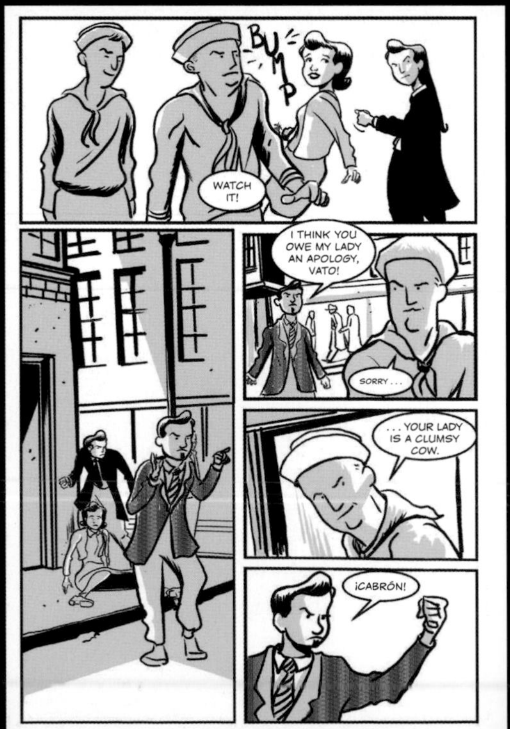
BUMP
WATCH IT!
I THINK YOU OWE MY LADY AN APOLOGY, VATO!
SORRY . . .
. . . YOUR LADY IS A CLUMSY COW.
¡CABRÓN!
30

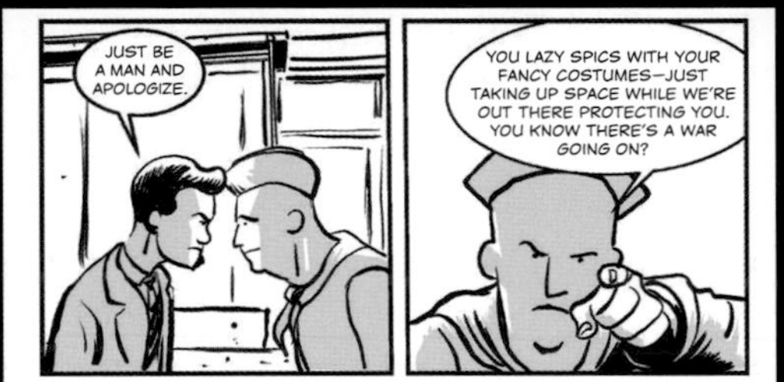
JUST BE A MAN AND APOLOGIZE.
YOU LAZY SPICS WITH YOUR FANCY COSTUMES—JUST TAKING UP SPACE WHILE WE'RE OUT THERE PROTECTING YOU. YOU KNOW THERE'S A WAR GOING ON?
APOLOGIZE AND WE DROP IT.
31

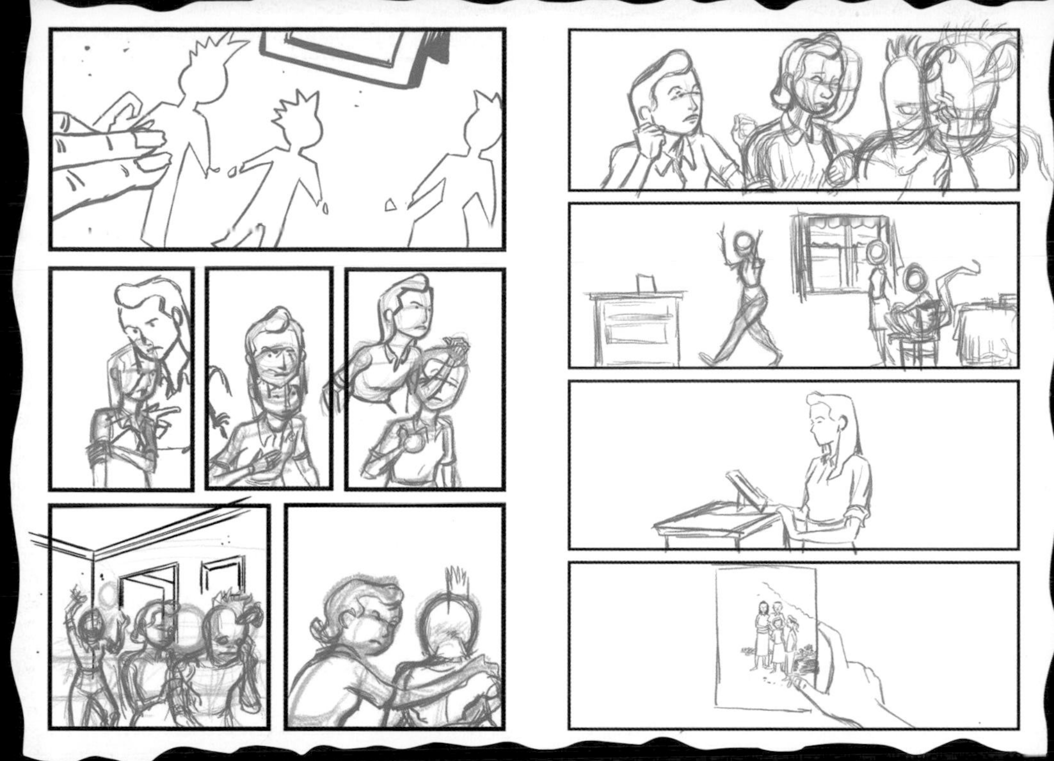

When Flaca says "It's still open season on pachucos out there," she's referring to herself, Cuata, and young men like Puppet and his friends. This term, common to Los Angeles youth culture of the time, originally referred to transplants from El Paso—or as the kids called it, "El Chuco." Hence, "pachucos" and "pachucas."

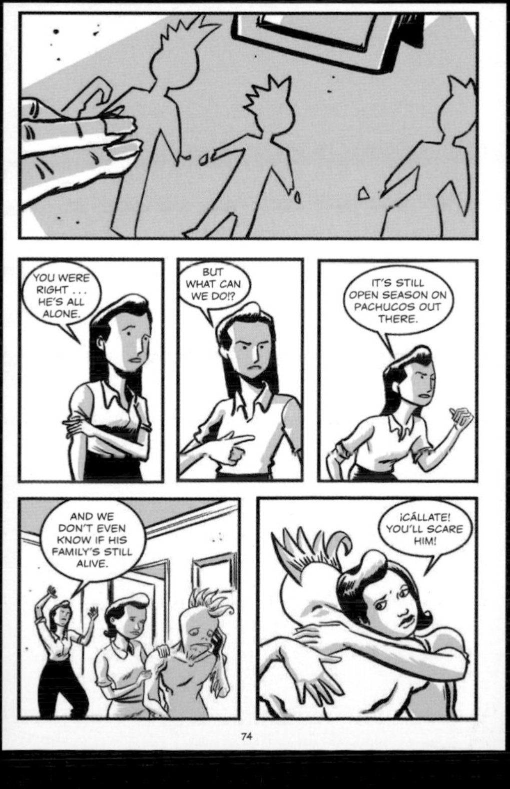
YOU WERE RIGHT . . . HE'S ALL ALONE.
BUT WHAT CAN WE DO!?
IT'S STILL OPEN SEASON ON PACHUCOS OUT THERE.
AND WE DON'T EVEN KNOW IF HIS FAMILY'S STILL ALIVE.
¡CÁLLATE! YOU'LL SCARE HIM!
74

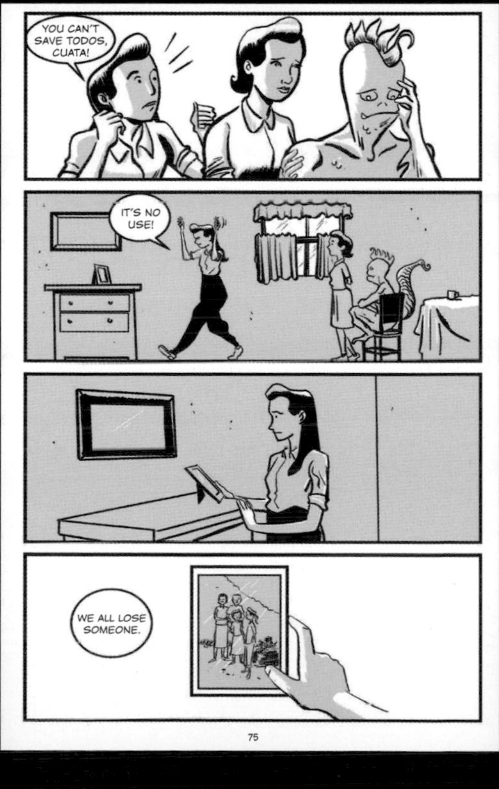
YOU CAN'T SAVE TODOS, CUATA!
IT'S NO USE!
WE ALL LOSE SOMEONE.
75

ABOUT THE AUTHOR

Marco Finnegan is a storyboard and comic book artist known for his work with 12-Gauge Comics, Image Comics, Vault Comics, and Lerner Publishing. He graduated with a BA in art from California State University, Fullerton, and teaches graphic novel and art classes for high school students. He lives in Southern California with his wife and children. You can find more of his work on Twitter at @marco949.